KU-297-928

Rock Chick Revolution

Discover other titles by Kristen Ashley at:
www.kristenashley.net

Copyright © 2013 Kristen Ashley
All rights reserved.

ISBN: 0615840841
ISBN-13: 9780615840840

Rock Chick Revolution

Kristen Ashley

Dedication

This book is dedicated to Kerrie Gisborne, a reader who turned into a friend. My first fan outside my posse—I'm pleased as punch she's now a member of that crew. And lucky for me, I'm a member of hers too. Miss you, Kerrie.

Acknowledgments & Author's Note

First, credit has to be given to Ebony Evans for the title of this book, *Rock Chick Revolution*. Ebony contacted me eons ago with the title suggestion and I loved it the minute I read it. I had other thoughts and other suggestions, but Ebony's suggestion wouldn't let me go. So thank you, darlin', for a *great* title that fits this book perfectly.

Second, I want to thank my best bud Kelly Brown who was the inspiration for Ally. Fearless. Intelligent. Funny. Loyal. Strong. Kelita, when we were in that cave in Venezuela and you rushed ahead to spot that old lady in her clickity-clack heels (in a cave!), leaving me behind to watch where every foot fell (and fear the bats hanging from the ceiling), I was in awe. I hope you feel Ally does you justice because I think you kick ass and I know you can do *anything* (mostly because you've already done it).

And last, I have to share with my readers that this book was the most difficult book I've ever written. This is the first series where I let my Rock Chick Flag fly and decided to write what I wanted, to hell with "the rules." I started this series because I was living in England and very homesick for Denver, pouring out these words as a love letter to that city, my country, and the people I left in them. I shared with my readers many characters who are loosely (and not-so-loosely) based on people I love, including Tex, Tod, Stevie, Ally, Annette, Nick, Reba, and Herb and Trish.

I also shared many good times (and bad) from my own life. For instance, Jet's response to seeing her mother after her stroke was my response to seeing my Momma after hers. And Indy and Roxie's dash through the Haunted House was near-on exact to a hilarious event that happened to my friend Cat and I.

So, in a way, these books *are* me, or many important parts of my life, both living and breathing and treasured memories.

Knowing in starting this book that I would be saying good-bye to the gang at Fortnum's was bittersweet. Maybe this is why I cried so hard in many scenes that my tears projected onto my glasses. Or laughed so hard I choked.

Or got up after writing a scene and danced around my office (no joke, and I've never done that before).

So I guess I loved writing this book, too.

And I truly hope you experience the same tears, laughter and jubilation.

But all good things must come to an end. And they must so we can open ourselves to other good things. However, my greatest fear with these novels was that this cast of characters would grow stale and tired. Seeing as I love them as if they were real, and these zany, wonderful, loving characters shouldn't feel stale and tired, I never, *ever* wanted that to happen.

So with this book—and a warning, this book is a true *revolution*—I bid farewell.

Of a sort.

Because with this book, I'm opening myself to other good things.

And seeing as this gang is worth my time, we haven't seen the end to them yet.

Just the start of new beginnings.

A massive thank you to my readers for loving these books as much as I do. For giving your hearts to my characters. For spending your time with me. And for championing a Rock Chick who breaks the rules.

And Chas, Rikki and now Gary, thank you for taking the ride with me.

Now, as ever and always, my Rock Chicks and Rock Gurus, strap in, put your hands straight up in the air, get ready for one helluva ride and never forget to **Rock On!**

Prologue
No More Anything

I woke up naked, in a motel, with a man behind me.

We were spooning.

Ren always spooned me.

No, that wasn't right. He didn't always spoon me. Sometimes he tucked me into his side when he was on his back. Sometimes he tucked me to his front when he was on his side and I was on my back. Sometimes I spooned him. But when I did, he held my hand to his chest, even in his sleep, so I couldn't escape.

He was a maximum contact sleeper.

I loved that.

Secretly.

The problem was, as far as I was concerned, he was just a fuck buddy.

Lorenzo "Ren" Zano didn't feel the same way.

We'd been dancing this dance for over a year now. Ren trying to convince me we had something. Me disagreeing.

Nope. Again that wasn't right. Ren wasn't trying to convince me we had something. He was simply convinced, and for the last eight months had been acting like he was my boyfriend. If boyfriends were bossy, annoying and in your face all the time, telling you what you could and couldn't do (in my case, it was mostly what I *couldn't*).

The months before that, Ren had been trying to convince me we should explore what we had.

I guessed he just gave up trying to convince me and decided to be my boyfriend even if I didn't agree.

The problem with me not agreeing was I tended to do a few things when Ren was around. One was argue with him like he was my boyfriend. Another was to have the occasional meal (or maybe not so occasional) with him and shoot the breeze, like he was my boyfriend. Another was sleep with him, and spend the night, like he was my boyfriend.

"I know you're awake."

I rolled my newly awakened eyes.

Ren always woke up before me in the mornings and always sensed when I was awake.

Except once.

Our first time together.

But what happened after I woke up that time nearly killed me, so I didn't think about that.

Always when he sensed I was awake, he commenced with The Talk (necessitating capital letters because Ren considered these Talks gravely serious and took them that way; again, I disagreed).

Usually these Talks centered around what we argued about before I jumped him. Or before he jumped me and we went on to have hours of mind-boggling, soul-enriching, life-changing sex, then passed out and Ren instigated Maximum Contact Sleep.

Today, I could tell by his tone, was not going to be different.

"I need coffee," I told him.

"I'll get you coffee after we talk."

See?

There it was.

The Talk.

And bossy.

I sighed and stated, "Zano, I don't wanna talk."

He put a hand in my belly, slid away and pressed me to my back so he could loom over me. Then he proceeded to press deep into me with most of his body, but some of it up on an elbow on the bed, and loom over me.

Exhibit A. Ren assumed dominant positions regularly and often in order to best be bossy, annoying and in my face; like, say, pressing me to my back in a bed and looming over me after I said I didn't want to talk.

I caught his eyes.

God, he had gorgeous eyes.

To block out those eyes, I closed mine.

Still, I saw him, *all* of him, in my mind's eye.

His eyes, his face, his hair and other parts of his anatomy (that would be all of it) usually were my undoing, and thus I would end up jumping him even in the midst of a fight. Or, alternately, I wouldn't struggle too much if he jumped me.

He was Italian, straight up, no other blood in him. He might be American—fourth generation American to be precise—but other than not speaking a different language, I was pretty certain his entire family thought they still lived in Sicily, even though most of them lived in Englewood, Colorado. With the exception of Ren and his cousin Dominic Vincetti. They both lived fifteen minutes to the north in Denver.

Ren was tall, very tall. Taller than me, and I was tall for a woman.

And he had a fabulous body. Lean hips that he knew how to use (big time). Broad shoulders, the power of which he also put to good use (in a variety of delicious ways). Sleek, defined muscles all over that I knew he put a lot of work into in a way he got off on (and I did too, but for a different reason).

But his way wasn't so he would look exceptionally hot (which he did). It was having time to be in his head and shut everything else out, be centered, get focused, be healthy. It was, like a lot of things about Ren, *righteous.*

And last, he had unbelievable abs and hip muscles, which I thought should be photographed and put in a museum. They were so perfect everybody should get the chance to see.

He also had thick dark hair that felt good just normally, but it felt *awesome* when your fingers were buried in it when his tongue was buried in your mouth (or elsewhere on your body).

All that was fabulous, but there were three things that *really* did it for me with Ren.

His eyes were this beautiful espresso color, so rich and deep, if you weren't careful, you could lose yourself in them in a way you never wanted to be found.

And he was confident. Not arrogant. It wasn't about swagger. *Confident.* He just knew what his body and mind could do, he knew what he liked, what he wanted and he was comfortable with all that. It oozed off him in the way cool oozed off people who were cool. And Ren was just that: *cool.* He was like a rock star without the guitar and in a suit. It was phenomenal.

And last, he dressed really well. For work, fabulous suits that were tailored for him. Outside of work, he could do jeans and even tees, and he wore them well, but usually he put on a shirt or a sweater (if it was cold) with his jeans and he wore those *way* better.

But with Ren it wasn't about the clothes. It was about the man.

And Ren Zano was all man.

Unfortunately, I liked men who were all man.

I also had a weakness for men in suits.

I just didn't like bossy, annoying and in my face.

And, of course, someone who would eventually break my heart, even though I figured he genuinely didn't know he was going to eventually do it.

But I knew he would.

His voice came at me, smooth and deep, but also soft and sweet.

"Ally, baby, last night proved we have to have this out, once and for all,"

Shit.

He was using his sweet voice. That always did a number on me. I knew this because, when he switched to it during a fight, this would be around the time I'd jump him.

I opened my eyes. "There's nothing to have out."

His eyebrows shot up (he had great eyebrows too, by the way).

"Have you lost your mind?"

Ren asked this a lot.

"No," I replied.

And this was always my answer.

His hand, still in my belly, pressed lightly as his face dipped closer. "Babe, straight up, last night you fucked up. You've fucked up before, but last night, you *totally* fucked up. It'll take me, Uncle Vito, your brothers, *both* of them, Marcus and pretty much every-fuckin'-body to cover your ass for the shit you pulled last night."

Thus commenced the me-getting-pissed portion of The Talk, which usually led to the me-yelling portion of The Talk, and that moved into the Ren-yelling portion of The Talk, which tended to culminate in the me-stomping-out-portion of our talk (or, alternately, us having a hot, great, fast quickie, *then* I'd get dressed and stomp out).

"I saved Faye's life last night," I reminded him curtly.

"You got on some serious as shit radar last night," he returned.

"I got them what they wanted." I kept sharing recent memories.

"You got on radar," he semi-repeated. "You do not want a single one of those men to know you exist. You *really* don't want them to know you got access and skills. You dabble in this shit, Ally. It isn't your life. It's a pastime. You do not have a solid network. You do not have back up. You do not have experience. So far, all you've got is a shitload of luck and persistence. The first eventually is gonna run out. The second is gonna make it run out and get you into trouble."

I didn't hear a lot of what he said since I was stuck on a word he used close to the beginning.

Dabble.

"Dabble?" I whispered warningly.

I knew he caught my warning because we'd managed, even as fuck buddies (according to me), to spend a lot of time together the last year, so he could read me.

I also knew he caught my warning because he threw one of his long, heavy, muscled legs over mine and he got even closer.

"Ally—"

"*Dabble?*" My voice had risen as my eyes had narrowed.

"Do you get paid for this shit?" he asked.

"Not in money," I answered.

"Then it's not a profession. It's a hobby. And it's dangerous, Ally. And this is the last time I'm gonna tell you, you gotta stop doing it."

My eyes narrowed further. My chest started burning and I opened my mouth to commence the yelling portion of The Talk.

Rock Chick Rewind

Backing up a bit, my name is Allyson Nightingale, but everyone calls me Ally. And I'm a Rock Chick, in name and deed.

That is to say, I worship at the shrine of Rock 'n' Roll and I live the rock star life, doing what I want when I want how I want. When I'm not working as a bartender or backup barista, of course, and with a lot less money.

Me and my best friend, India "Indy" Savage (now Nightingale since she married my brother, Lee) have a posse called the Rock Chicks. It's our posse mostly because we're the band leaders, as it were, and being rock chicks, *they'd* be Rock Chicks.

So they are.

Indy and I began the tradition. And some of the Rock Chicks might not be as crazy as me and Indy, but they're Rock Chicks to the core.

Definitely.

The Rock Chicks do not include my brothers (because they're dudes, and unless the dude is gay, he can't be a Rock Chick), Henry "Hank" Nightingale and Liam "Lee" Nightingale. They're both older than me.

Hank's a badass cop. As far as I can tell, Lee's just a professional badass.

My dad is also a cop. So was his dad. Gramps died in the line of duty.

So badass and brave runs in the family.

And as far as I'm concerned, I got those genes.

It's just that no one agrees with me.

⚔

See, about two years ago Indy caught a bit of trouble. She owns a used bookstore called Fortnum's, but it also serves coffee. In fact, if she didn't serve coffee, she'd be screwed because she doesn't sell very many books.

She also landed herself a barista named Tex (who is a bona fide nut, but a lovable one—mostly) who's a latte/cappuccino/espresso-making genius. He's the Yo-Yo Ma of coffee. In fact, Mr. Ma would put down his cello in the middle of a performance to take a sip of Tex's coffee, it's that good.

Seriously.

Anyway, Rosie, the barista before Indy recruited Tex, did something stupid. Indy got dragged in, and Indy's been my best friend since I could remember. Our parents were best friends. And, as I mentioned, she's now married to my brother. So naturally, I got dragged in right with her.

Or, if I'm honest, I waltzed in. Happily.

I'd never been one to shy away from trouble. Or make my own, as the case may be.

That started a lot of stuff. As in, *a lot*. Some of it bad. Some of it very bad.

But most of it was *awesome*.

As for me, when Indy was in trouble and I got involved, we'd been after Rosie because he'd disappeared. And when no one could find him, I did.

That's when I got bit by the bug. Like my dad and brothers, I was good at this badass investigation shit.

A natural.

So I kept doing it.

⚔

Don't think I'm stupid. I'm not.

Along the way, I learned a lot. At first, I only did it for friends in a jam, snooping around, doing things such as getting the goods on a cheating ex, shit like that.

But I always took care of the situation.

Then my friends told their friends and I got referrals.

Eventually, shit got serious.

But I'm a Nightingale. I don't shy away from serious. No freaking chance.

But Ren was wrong. I had a solid network. I had backup.

Because I got help.

~¤~

One of my partners is Darius Tucker. He's one of Lee's best friends (and one of mine, too). He's an awesome guy who I love and have loved since he started hanging with Lee way back when they were in school. He's an awesome guy I love more now because he's cool, he's kind, he takes my back and he believes in me.

He's also an ex-drug dealer and current private detective on staff at Lee's agency, Nightingale Investigations.

Even though Darius got out of the trade that doesn't mean he doesn't know everybody. And if he doesn't *know them* know them, he knows *of* them.

My other partner is Brody Dunne, another friend of mine for forever. Brody's a boy-man (with more boy than man, even though his age says more man than boy) who could work a computer like Yo-Yo Ma a cello, Stephen Hawking an equation and Tex an espresso machine.

As you can see, both good partners to have.

~¤~

Fast forward to last night, when I found out another friend of mine, Faye, was getting buried alive because her boyfriend's dad is a dick.

Don't ask, it's a huge-ass story.

Anyway, someone had to step in. And since I'd been monitoring the situation for some time, I was in a place to do that.

So I did.

And I saved her life.

⧖

However, it must be said that Ren was not wrong (though I was not going to admit that to him).

The men involved, including Faye's boyfriend's dad, were not good men. Not even close.

⧖

Fast Forward——Hit Play

"*This is the last time you're gonna tell me?*" I yelled at Ren.

"Baby——"

I shoved at his shoulders and succeeded in rocking him back enough I could roll across the bed.

This I did, snapping, "Don't you *baby* me."

I got a foot to the floor and nowhere fast because Ren hooked an arm around my belly and yanked me back into bed.

Then he covered me with his body.

This was an effective maneuver he utilized often during Our Talks because I could possibly land a knee to the 'nads, but I was loath to do that since I liked his 'nads as they were in those times we weren't fighting.

Other than that, he was bigger, heavier and stronger than me so I was totally screwed.

Exhibit B. Ren had no problem using his physical advantages to give him more opportunities to be bossy and in my face.

"Get off me," I demanded.

"Listen to me."

"Get *off* me," I ordered on a buck of my hips.

When my hips settled back on the bed, Ren was still on me.

Fuck!

Then his hands moved to frame either side of my face. He dipped his head so he was all I could see and his voice was a voice he'd never used. It was deep and it was sweet, but it was also weighty and thick and it kind of freaked me out (in a maybe good way) when he said, "Ally, baby, *listen to me.* I care about you, *you mean something to me,* and I don't want to see you in a box under three feet of dirt *without* the tank of oxygen to keep you safe until I find you. Are you understanding me?"

He cared about me.

I meant something to him.

Yeah.

Right.

I'd give it to him. That was a maybe.

He just cared about someone else a whole lot more.

"I'm understanding you're a bossy, annoying, in my face *jerk* who thinks he can tell me what to do when he *cannot,* no matter how often I tell you it's *my* damned life and I'll do with it as I please," I retorted.

Something flashed in his eyes so fast I couldn't catch what it was before he started, "Ally—"

"Now, get off me. I got shit to do. I have to get home to Denver."

His body pressed mine into the bed. "We're finishing this here."

"Fine by me," I agreed readily. "We're finished. Leave me alone, and we're *all* done." I drew out the "all" sarcastically.

His face changed to a face I'd never seen before, either. It wasn't sweet. It wasn't impatient.

It was infuriated.

He'd been mad before, even *really* angry (see aforementioned notes about us yelling at each other a lot).

And his anger had a physical presence. So much so, its weight could fill a room.

But this was different.

The room didn't feel its usual stifling.

It felt still.

And that freaked me.

"I just told you you mean something to me and you won't give me ten minutes to talk this shit through?" he asked with deceptive quiet.

"No, because the only outcome that's acceptable to you is unacceptable to me, so we have nothing to talk *about.*"

He shook his head, still looking very, *very* angry.

"Unh-unh. You rewound too far. You just ended things with me like it's all the same to you."

"Well it is," I clipped (lie!).

"Bullshit," he fired back (he knew I was lying).

"How many times do I have to tell you? We're fuck buddies, Zano."

He shook his head again, his thumb sweeping across my cheek and his face getting so close to mine, his lips nearly brushed my own.

"No, baby, we are not. I've had fuck buddies, Ally. And not one of them looked like you look when I slide inside you, *every fucking time* I slide inside you. Like a piece of you has been lost and now it's found."

Oh crap.

I probably looked just like that.

Because when he slid inside me, that was precisely what it felt like.

My eyes drifted away.

"Look at me," he ordered.

"Get off me," I returned.

He went silent.

I let him and waited, hoping this would be a morning where Ren would give up, roll off and wait to fight another day.

It wasn't going to be that kind of morning. I knew this when he kept talking.

"Your brothers by now are gonna know about this. And when you roll into Denver, they're gonna lose their minds."

"They'll get over it."

"If you think you're pullin' shit on them, Ally, you're wrong. Lee and Hank know everything that goes down in that town, and they know you've been doin' your thing and just how long. Make no mistake, they've been distant, but they've been in your business. Part of it was to keep an eye, part of it was to have your back. But you never got this deep or went this far."

I slid my eyes back to him.

"Newsflash, Zano. I'm not Nancy Drew, solving crimes as a hobby just out of high school. I'm a big girl. I know my brothers know and I don't care what my brothers think."

Something flickered in his beautiful eyes. His fury was long gone, and just then his voice went back to sweet. "Baby, I'm trying to impress on you, *this is different.* And I was worried before at the shit you were doin'. But now I'm fucking *alarmed.*"

It was then, something happened.

I didn't know what did it for me. The new tone to his voice. That look on his face. His warm, hard body pressing mine into the bed after a night of mind-boggling, soul-enriching, life-changing sex. Knowing he found out what was going on last night and drove for hours to get from Denver to the Colorado mountain town of Carnal where all the bad stuff was going down in order to get to me. Or the fact that he *really* sounded like he meant what he said.

Whatever it was, it did it for me and it led me to doing something I'd never done with Ren.

I agreed.

But I did it quietly.

"I get you."

He blinked. "You get me?"

I nodded, not about to say it again.

His eyes grew sharp but his face went guarded. "Maybe I should understand what exactly you get."

This was a weird thing for fuck buddies, and another way I had to admit we kind of broke that mold. It was also something Ren used repeatedly to press the fact that we weren't actually fuck buddies, but together *together*. We just didn't go out on dates or meet each other's parents… yet (the "yet" part was Ren's).

And what that weird thing was was that he knew me. I also knew him. He paid attention, when we were having sex and when we weren't. I did the same.

So it wasn't surprising he asked this question.

"Those dudes were bad dudes," I explained. "I know how bad, Ren. I'd been poking around them for months." I put my hand to his chest to press my point home since his face went unguarded and his eyes started to warm. "But they *buried Faye alive.* I knew the risks. I weighed them and my friend got pulled out of that box breathing. Barely, but she made it."

He moved one of his hands down to the side of my neck so he could stroke my throat with his thumb. This was another something new. Then again, I didn't give him many opportunities to show affection like that and I was thinking that was a good thing seeing as it felt *incredibly* nice.

Kristen Ashley

"There's gonna be a path you cross," he said gently. "A path that no matter what firepower you got taking your back, they're gonna try to take you down. I do not want you to get to that place, baby."

Unusually, I used a calm voice rather than an irate one when I explained, "I'm not exactly being stupid. I've got Brody and Darius. I'm careful."

That was only mostly true.

I slid my hand up his chest, exploring this unchartered territory of intimacy and sharing, and wrapped it around the side of his neck, putting pressure on. He gave me what I wanted and his face drew even closer.

"I like doing this, Ren. I *like* it. I've tried a lot of things in my life. I've got a bachelor's degree. I'm a certified radiology tech. I've done nails. And I'm thirty-two years old. Now I work part-time in a bookstore/coffee shop and full-time slinging drinks. I don't like doing any of that as much as I like what you don't like me doing. That's why I keep doing it, even though I know a lot of people, not just you, don't like me doing it. Because I *like* it. It feels right. It feels like I finally found what I wanna be. It's like I finally found *me*."

He studied me and for once said not a word.

Again unusually, I kept talking rationally.

"I know you're worried about those guys I got involved with last night. So are Darius and Brody. So am I. But I took a calculated risk to save my friend. I'll watch my back and I have good guys watching it, too. So I'll be all right."

He kept studying me, but I had nothing else to say.

Finally, he spoke.

"You know, just sayin', you said this shit to me like you just said it to me rather than yellin' at my ass until the only option I have to stop you from yellin' is to tap *your* ass, it might have penetrated about ten months ago."

Something about that made me laugh. Maybe because it was funny.

And there was something about this that I liked. And there was no maybe about the fact that it not only seemed he listened to me, but he heard me and he *got* me.

And I liked that.

When I quit laughing, Ren was smiling down at me.

My heart skipped a beat.

I didn't get many of those, seeing as we fought all the time and when we weren't his mouth was engaged with doing other things.

But just like now, when I did get a smile from Ren Zano, it hit straight to the heart of me.

His smile downgraded to a grin and his eyes moved over my face, something happening in them I didn't quite get. But whatever it was seemed to mean something. It looked like he was about to say something, but he thought better of it and kept quiet.

I didn't.

"I dig the mountains, but me and the boys shot up here without provisions and I've got shit to do at home, so it might be time to get a move on."

"Right," he replied. "There's a drugstore across the street. I'll go over, get toothbrushes and shit. There's also a coffee shop down the street. You wanna make coffee in that little pot on the dresser or you want me to pick you up a real coffee?"

I stared up at him.

We'd never done anything like this, acting semi-normal and not always crazy.

I was a little stunned he could be thoughtful.

No. That wasn't true. I knew he was the kind of guy who could to be that way. He often demonstrated thoughtful tendencies. Like when I'd show at his house in the wee hours after a bartending shift, he'd ask me if I'd eaten and I'd find he'd made a batch of spaghetti sauce or some cannelloni and he'd heat it up to feed me. And I knew he probably didn't make that just for himself, but also preparing to feed me later.

Shit like that.

But everybody had to eat, so going out of his way to be thoughtful? I'd never seen that. Mostly because I'd never given him the chance.

Except last Christmas, when he'd been *really* thoughtful.

So maybe I wasn't staring up at him stunned because he was being thoughtful.

Maybe I was doing it because this demonstration of further thoughtfulness moved me.

Shit.

"I, uh…" I started and stopped since it took me a bit to shake it off, how nice it felt to be this way with Ren. But I managed it and kept going. "We'll start with coffee here and get a real one for the trip home. But a toothbrush wouldn't go amiss."

"Gotcha," he muttered, dipping close to touch his lips to mine, and he did this *for no reason*. Something else he'd never done. Then he pulled away, rolled off me and exited the bed. He yanked the covers over me after he did (again, thoughtful) and proceeded dressing.

It was then I lost the ability to think about anything as I watched Ren move, going from naked to dressed, so I laid there and let myself enjoy the full-ness of that (as well as the heat it caused in me). The show was so good, I was rerunning certain parts of it in my head when it was over and this made me an unmoving target when Ren came back to the bed. He hooked a hand around the back of my neck, pulled me up and again touched his mouth to mine.

"Back in a few," he murmured. He gave me a small grin that warmed his eyes in a way that ratcheted up that heat in me, then he walked to and through the door.

I stared at the door for a good long while.

Then the name he'd murmured in the back of my hair over a year before… a name he murmured while we were in bed, naked, he was holding me and he was asleep… a name that wasn't mine… came back to me.

And it reminded me this wasn't real.

I truly believed Ren wanted it to be.

But I knew it was never going to be, not in the way I needed it to be.

So I shoved thoughts of his warmth and thoughtfulness aside, jumped from the bed and started coffee.

I was in the shower when he returned and I knew he returned when he joined me in the shower.

Me wet and soapy, Ren wet and naked meant things happened, and those things included me getting an against-the-tiles-in-the-bathroom-of-a-moder-ately-priced-motel-in-a-small-Colorado-mountain-town orgasm.

Like every orgasm Ren gave me (yes, I said "every", and that is no lie), it was freaking *righteous*.

I was in my bra and undies, Ren in his boxers. We were both at the small sink brushing our teeth while I braced myself against liking another heretofore unknown intimacy when Ren gave me the ammunition to forever put the "us" he wanted us to be to rest.

He did this by spitting out foam, rinsing and catching my eyes in the mir-ror after he wiped his mouth with a towel.

Then he said, "Got Ava and Stark's wedding invitation. I know you're in the wedding party but I'm gonna take you."

I still had my brush in my mouth, but my eyes locked to his as my insides froze stone-cold.

I forced myself out of the freeze, pulled the brush out of my mouth and asked through foam, "Are you shitting me?"

His brows shot together and he answered, "No."

I leaned forward, spit but did not rinse. I spoke again after I swiped the back of my hand across my mouth and my words came out biting.

"Tell me you're shitting me," I demanded.

He rocked back and crossed his arms on his chest, murmuring in a way I knew he was annoyed and didn't expect an answer, "Jesus, what's up your ass now?"

He was.

He was *totally fucking* shitting me.

And that burned through me. Not with anger.

With pain.

So much of it, my voice was actually weak—fuck me, *weak*—when I answered, "What's up my ass, Ren, is that you just asked me to go with you to the wedding of the woman you're in love with. *That*," my voice—goddamn it!—broke on that word, but I kept going, "is what's up my ass."

I registered the shock on his face. It would be hard to miss seeing as it suffused every feature and shot from his eyes.

"What the fuck?" he whispered.

"So no," I whispered back, the pain still affecting my voice, making it come out shaky. But I couldn't stop it. I also didn't have it in me to try. "I will *not* go to Ava and Luke's wedding with you. And also," I swallowed, "this shit, you and me, after you'd ask me something like that, is done. Over. No more fuck buddies. No more *anything*."

And on that, I didn't stomp out of the bathroom.

I ran.

Chapter 1
You're a Nightingale

Rock Chick Rewind

Thirteen months earlier...

I woke up in Ren Zano's four poster bed, with its wine colored sheets, that was in the bedroom of his awesome house in Cheesman Park, knowing I'd done it.

I wasn't certain it was going to happen to me. I didn't want to admit it, but I was beginning to think it wouldn't.

That happened to some women. They went their whole lives and didn't find *the one*.

The man who, just looking at him, made your blood warm.

The man who, when he smiled at you, made your heart skip a beat.

The man who was so attuned to your body, he could use his hands, his mouth, his words, his *everything,* and make it sing.

Even the first time.

Or, I should say, in Ren's and my case, the first *three* times.

And the man who was interesting, charming, maybe a wee bit edgy and mysterious (but that wee bit was *way* hot and something I liked a whole lot) and made no bones about the fact he was into you—into you in the sense that he wanted to get *in* you—and that way would last awhile.

That while maybe being forever.

Okay, so last night in the parking lot of Herman's Hideaway, Ren had fought with Luke, one of the Hot Bunch (in other words, one of my brother's guys) over my friend Ava.

But then Luke accidently elbowed Ava in the head. They took off in his Porsche and I'd stayed in the parking lot giving Ren what for for being a macho asshole and fighting in a freaking parking lot (I mean, *really?*). Then I'd noticed he was still pissed. He appeared to give more than a passing shit about Ava (and there was reason for this; she was in the middle of a shitstorm, not unusual with the Rock Chicks) so I decided to get a few drinks in him.

When I offered this suggestion, he stopped being pissed for a second, looked me up and down, and agreed.

This led us to going to My Brother's Bar where I worked as a bartender. We got a back corner booth and commenced in tying one on.

At first, I avoided the subject of the Luke/Ava/Ren triangle because he seemed to be getting his shit together and I didn't want it to slide back. Especially if he intended to get shitfaced. I didn't want to watch another hot guy go gonzo, even verbally, and especially drunkenly, over another one of the Rock Chicks.

That wasn't my idea of a fun night.

I'd had that when Indy got pursued by Lee.

And when Lee's best friend Eddie went after my friend Jet.

And when Hank decided, for him, it was Roxie.

And also when another one of Lee's boys, Vance, locked his sights on a woman we eventually recruited into the Rock Chicks, Jules.

And last, I was currently swimming through the crazy waters of Luke staking his claim with another one of my friends, Ava.

I couldn't say all this wasn't exciting—sometimes *way* exciting, sometimes hilarious, sometimes not a small amount of insane—but the end was always good. The guy got his girl, the girl got her guy, and everyone was happy.

As happy as I was for my friends—and make no mistake, I was happy, and the rides to get to the end of their kickass, modern-day fairytales were all sorts of sick, delicious fun—I was thinking it wasn't going to happen for me.

But until recently, I'd been going out for a while with Carl, who was a good guy. He was into me, the sex was great, the banter almost better, but something about him just didn't *do it* for me.

It didn't make me look the way Indy looked at Lee, Jet at Eddie, Roxie at Hank (I think you get me).

Like he was *it*. Like the search was over. Like I'd made the epic journey and found treasure beyond my wildest imaginings.

I didn't usually think shit like that.

I was a Rock Chick. I had a lot of friends. I had a lot of good times. The concept of "anything goes" was pretty literal for me. I didn't have issues speaking my mind. And I didn't have issues creating a drama if the situation deserved it. I also didn't give a shit if someone disagreed with the situation deserving it.

I was... *me*.

I wasn't girlie.

I wasn't romantic.

I didn't have fantasies (except those that came while wielding a vibrator).

Let's just say the knight in shining armor concept did nothing for me.

I also didn't want the picket fence, the two-point-five kids, the meatloaf in the oven and the snuggle during Letterman that would lead to missionary sex that lasted ten minutes and then dreamless sleep.

But that wasn't what my Rock Chicks were getting.

They were getting something else. Something big, bold, bountiful and amazing.

For one, I knew all about their sex lives, and missionary was on the menu but it was *far* from the only choice.

But that wasn't it. Not even close.

And I was beginning to want a little bit of that for me. So when Carl got accepted into the FBI not too long ago and went off to Virginia to train, he'd asked me to come.

I didn't go. Instead, I let *him* go.

It sucked but he wasn't *it* for me. I dug him, we had great times.

But I wanted *it*.

So listening to possibly *the* most handsome man I'd ever laid eyes on pining about a woman, who might be my friend, but who already had her own hot guy (she just hadn't accepted that...yet), was not something I was up for.

But Ren didn't do that.

As the beer and bourbon flowed, we both got talkative.

I noticed a few things right off.

He was not a lightweight. He could totally hold his liquor (like me). Which, you think it's right or wrong, I thought was hot. It was an indication he enjoyed life however he wanted, like me.

This didn't mean we weren't feeling easy, and getting to feel easier. But it wasn't leading to loaded, which led to sloppy, stupid and unattractive.

And once the event was put behind us, he didn't once bring up Ava or Luke.

He asked about me.

And he sounded interested.

And last, along with being hot, in a hot guy way that was totally cool, he was funny.

So in the end, it was almost like a date.

A good one.

Maybe even the best I'd ever had.

And it got better when we got to know each other, got more comfortable, and the questions became more meaningful. The banter became teasing. Then suggestive teasing. Then the physical distance evaporated when Ren slid closer to me in the booth seat, pinning me against the corner. Something I was wishing he'd do, and he did.

But it was more. In doing this, focusing his attention solely on me, he made the bar melt away and made me feel like I was the center of his universe.

I'd never felt that.

But I bet Indy, Jet, Roxie and Jules had.

And none of it was about booze and earlier emotional upheaval.

It was about connecting.

Ava and Luke and what happened that night drifted away, and it was about Ren getting to know me and me returning the favor.

And enjoying every *second* of it.

The end of it went like this:

"You have to give me a minute," I told him, "I'm having trouble fighting the urge to run shrieking from the bar."

He grinned. I watched it and I liked it.

"Babe, not a crime to be a Bears fan."

"Zano, totally a crime to be a native Denverite and be a Bears fan," I contradicted with the God's honest truth.

His arm was on the back of the booth and suddenly his fingers glided through my hair, sliding it off my shoulder, then moving away; a smooth there-and-gone-making-you-want-more move that worked on me *huge*.

"Lived in Chicago a long time after my dad died," he said after the smooth move, and at his words, I focused through my buzz closer on him. "Mom couldn't deal, moved us back to her hometown to be closer to her sister and cousins. I was there from three to thirteen. I was born here, Ally, but bred to be a Bears fan."

Well, if there was a reason to dis the Broncs, that was it.

But what he shared was deep. It felt good he trusted that little bit to me and so it couldn't be ignored.

"Sorry about your dad," I said softly.

Something I didn't get moved through his face before he said, "Long time ago."

I found that an interesting response.

"Indy lost her mom when she was five. I was five when we lost her, too. Auntie Katie was around all the time, so she was like a second mom to me." I reached out a hand and curled it around his thigh. "I know when people try to understand where you are, they can't understand because they're not you. But even so, even though I don't get you, I still kinda do."

It was then something moved into his eyes, stayed there, and I got that. It was a mixture of sweet and heat that I liked a whole lot.

His hand covered mine on his thigh and he murmured, "Thanks, honey."

"And, not to be flippant about the death of a parent," I started in order to move us to less deep, melancholy waters. "But I will say it does provide you with an acceptable pass on being a Bears fan in Broncos Country."

That got me another grin.

Then his eyes locked to mine and he asked, "Your brothers, your family, I'm thinkin' you know me."

Oh I knew him all right. I also knew what he was asking.

I'd lived in Denver all my life. I had a long string of friends that covered a wide spectrum of the population. And I had two cops and a private investigator in the family. Not to mention, I'd been doing my thing, nosing around, and sometimes that took me into the underbelly of Denver.

I knew all about the Zanos.

Particularly the fact that Ren's Uncle Vito was a crime boss. What he did, I steered clear of. You didn't make an enemy of the Zanos and you didn't get in their business, no matter how you might do that.

I also knew Ren worked for his uncle.

Word on the street, he was in charge of the legitimate side of the operation. The part that they used to hide the part that was far from clean.

But any part of that kind of thing still made you dirty.

Furthermore, it was known widely Vito was grooming Ren to take over the family business when he retired.

Which meant he'd be all kinds of dirty eventually.

At that moment, with not a small amount of bourbon and beer in me, his deep voice, his handsome face, his unbelievable body all close to me, I didn't care.

It was also no secret in certain sets of Denver that my brother Lee played shit fast and loose and wasn't above doing what he had to do to get the job done. And what he had to do also might not always be lawful.

I admired Lee. He was badass cool, didn't give a shit what anyone thought of him and forged his own path.

So who was I to judge?

But the bottom line of it was, I was me and if I wanted something, I got it or took it, whatever the case may be. And, like Lee, I didn't give a shit what anybody thought of it or how I went about getting it.

And right then, I wanted Ren Zano.

I'd always thought I was the white hat type of girl. I'd always gone for the good guy.

But maybe I didn't mind that hat being a little dusty.

"I know you," I confirmed.

"So, you know me. You got a problem with getting in a taxi with me, comin' to my place, letting me take your clothes off and then letting me do a shitload of other things to that beautiful body?"

His eyes traveled down my front as he asked this.

As for me, I felt my nipples get hard as he asked this.

I also knew the answer to his question.

I had absolutely no problem with that.

So I said, "Actually, I would have a problem if you *didn't* do any of that."

His eyes came back to mine.

They were beautiful normally. Hot with open anticipation, they were *amazing,* and they did amazing things to me. As in, for the first time in my life, just looking at a guy, I might have had a mini-orgasm.

He took out his wallet. Then he threw a bunch of bills on the table, grabbed my hand and yanked me out of the booth.

Then he put me in a taxi.

He gave me my first orgasm on the stairs in his house and he didn't take off all my clothes before he did it.

The next two were in his bed and we were both naked.

By the time the sex and booze wore us both down to the point of passing out, tangled together in his wine colored sheets, I knew I'd found it.

Something big, bold, bountiful and amazing.

Something that wasn't about meatloaf and missionary sex.

Something that was about looking forward to a life that was going to be a bumpy ride filled with jerks and quick turns and unexpected stops and hair-raising plummets... and loving every minute of it.

So lying on those wine colored sheets, I smiled just as Ren, his body and heat curved into my back, his arm around me, shifted closer. His hand drifted up and curled around my breast and I felt his face burrow into the back of my hair.

I smiled bigger.

Then he murmured sleepily, "Ava."

My mind blanked, my heart squeezed and my eyes blinked.

His hand dropped from my breast but his arm stayed around me, his body pressed into the back of mine.

I didn't move.

Then I did.

Carefully, I slid from under his arm and away from him. Silently, I got out of bed. Stealthily, I found my clothes and put them on.

All but my shoes.

I wanted to make no noise on his wood floors.

I looked at his sleeping beauty in the bed, his olive skin sheathing his defined muscles exposed from the waist up, his dark hair falling on his forehead, his handsome features relaxed to almost boyish (but still hot) in sleep, and the cut on his lip put there by Luke's fist.

Taking all that was him in, I felt something die in me.

As I mentioned, I was not girlie. I was not prone to romance or fantasy.

I'd only given myself that this one time.

No, Ren had given it to me.

In one night, he made me believe in the modern-day fairytale I watched all my girls get, and he made me believe life had that in store for me.

And he made me want it.

Ava. The memory of his deep, drowsy murmur assaulted my brain.

Hearing that, he took it all away.

So I got the fuck out of there.

Fifteen and a half hours later...

My eyes opened when I heard the banging on the door.

I stared at the clock on my nightstand.

Jeez, it was after midnight.

Well, one couldn't say this kind of thing didn't happen occasionally. I had a variety of feelers out on a variety of things and information trickled in in a variety of ways.

However, none of it had ever trickled in by banging on my door in the wee hours of the morning. Maybe in the not so wee hours of the morning, but everyone knew not to disturb my neighbors.

I threw back the covers, opened my nightstand, got my stun gun and flipped it on.

I stomped to the front door of my apartment and aimed an eye to my peephole.

Then I whispered, "Fuck."

Ren was standing out there, head turned to the side looking absently down the hall.

By the time I got to the door the banging had stopped, but as I kept looking out, wondering what to do, I saw him turn his attention from the hall to my door. I noted he looked a might angry, and I heard as I watched him start banging again.

It would appear he wasn't going to go away. And seeing as I kind of liked my apartment, but mostly liked that my neighbors were all pretty cool—either old as the hills, thus went to bed early and didn't have the energy to get in my business (outside of finding it diverting, should they bump into an informant in the hall), or young and hip and digging the life of living in the awesome environs of Washington Park (much like me)—I wanted to stay in that apartment. And some hot Italian dude banging on my door might wake my neighbors and make them tetchy.

So I turned off the stun gun and set it on table by my door. I threw back the chain, unlocked the locks and pulled open the door.

"God, Zano, are you trying to wake the dead?"

This was a pertinent question, seeing as some folks in my apartment building had one foot in the grave.

I didn't get the chance to share that info with Ren. His eyes pinned me to the spot and I was right earlier. He was angry.

"What the fuck?" he asked.

"What?" I asked back.

"What…" He took in a breath through his nose. "The." He went on and kept scowling at me. "*Fuck?*" he finished tersely.

I was confused, and I wasn't a big fan of being confused. Especially not late at night when a hot guy who had fucked me but who was in love with a good friend of mine was banging on my door and asking me bewildering, but clearly angry, questions

"What the fuck what?" I asked.

He kept scowling at me.

Then it became apparent he was done simply scowling at me. I knew this when he put a hand in my belly, shoved me back and followed me, walking right into my apartment.

He slammed the door.

I lost my mind.

"Zano, *hello?*" I snapped. "I didn't invite you in. And something to know about me, I'm not the kind of girl who gets off on some guy doing whatever the hell he wants to do, especially around me, and especially *especially* when it happens to be something I don't want him to do."

"You invited me in, Ally," he replied. "Around the time you came when my mouth was between your legs on my stairs. Then again when you came when my cock was driving into you in my bed. Then again when you wrapped your mouth around my cock, also in my bed. And a-fuckin'-gain when you found it while riding my cock, also in my bed. And last, when you wrapped your sweet, hot, naked body around me and passed out *in my bed.*"

Okay, I'd had a variety of Rock Chick chinwags where the girls let it all hang out about their guys and how they communicated in Asshole, but I'd never experienced it personally. And Ren had just demonstrated he was fluent in Asshole.

It must be said, I didn't like it much.

Therefore, I invited acidly, "Rewind and try that again."

He didn't accept my invitation.

Instead, he turned. I saw him locate the light switch and flinched when the overhead light came on.

When I quit flinching, I noted his angry attention was back to me and he asked, "Were you drunker than I thought last night?"

"No," I answered.

"So you remember what went down last night."

"Yes," I snapped, then tried to get him onto a subject I wanted to talk about, namely him leaving, but I didn't get the chance.

He kept talking.

"*All* that went down last night?"

"Yes!"

My voice was rising because I *did* remember all that went down last night. And how I felt when I woke up that morning. But mostly I remembered the name he called me when I was lying there, thinking he was my *one,* and he was lying there holding on to a substitute body that, since he had no shot with the real one, was just going to have to do.

"So tell me, honey, if you weren't hammered and you remember all that went down last night, why did I wake up to an empty bed this morning?" he asked.

"I had shit to do," I answered, and it wasn't totally a lie. I always had shit to do. I was a busy girl.

"You had shit to do," he said low, and his eyes were a tad bit scary.

But I didn't scare easily.

"Yep," I replied.

"And it was so pressing you couldn't wake me and tell me you had to go?"

"Yep, it was that pressing." Now, that was totally a lie.

"And it was so pressing you couldn't find a minute to jot down a note?"

Okay, suffice it to say, I was done with this bullshit. If he needed someone to give it to him regular while he waited for Ava, and to continue to give it to him regular when he realized that he'd never get Ava, he'd have to find someone else.

In order to communicate that to him, I stated, "Dude, we hooked up. That's it. Or that's all *I* remember. But maybe I *was* drunker than I thought. Did I miss the part where you slid a ring on my finger?"

This was the *wrong* thing to say, and I knew it when the room filled with something so oppressive, it was stifling. No joke. I literally couldn't breathe.

As I mentioned, I didn't scare easily.

But the truth of it was, I didn't get scared. There wasn't a situation that I remember ever being in where I didn't feel in control or think I could find a way to regain control. I also had the gene passed down through my family where I could sense when things were going bad in a way that I would lose control and not get it back, and I was smart enough to get the fuck out of Dodge when I found myself in those kinds of situations.

But right then, feeling suffocated by the sheer force of Lorenzo Zano's anger, I felt a hint of genuine fear.

Then his anger dissipated.

Vanished.

It did this instantly when he said, "I get it. You're a Nightingale."

My back snapped straight at his tone, which said it all about his implication. I just didn't know for certain what he was implying, just that it was no good.

So I asked, "What does that mean?"

"That means both your brothers laid waste to most of the talented pussy in Denver. Took what they wanted, walked away and never looked back. Not surprising, you a Nightingale, that's your thing. Except you collect cock."

And on that very effective parting shot, he turned, jerked open the door and slammed it behind him.

Standing in my apartment in the dead of night staring at the door, I didn't feel my heart squeeze.

I felt it shrivel up and die.

Not surprisingly, in the coming days as Ava's drama (that partly had to do with her courtship with Luke, but mostly had to do with the fact that the Rock Chicks were magnets for trouble) played out, I saw Ren again.

Both times he was up in Ava's business, giving her soft looks and taking her back.

However, he did look at me. Once. When Ava's drama reached its grand finale.

But the look he gave me was far from soft.

Unsurprisingly.

I acted like I didn't give a shit.

Deep down, though, I knew it didn't make any sense.

I also knew it killed.

Chapter 2
We Got a Deal

Three weeks later...

I was sitting at the bar in Club, a happening hotspot in Cherry Creek that posed as a posh eatery but was mostly a pickup spot. I had on a little black dress that did the best it could (and its best was far from bad; the dress was *scorching*) with what little cleavage I had. I had on killer strappy black sandals that I'd borrowed from Indy, who had borrowed them from our friend Tod, the premier drag queen in Denver, and she'd not returned them.

Tod wouldn't mind. He was generous with his shoes. I had three pairs of them in my closet already. He also had two pairs of mine.

I was there because I had my eye on Zach Gilligan, the guy a friend of mine, Helen, was dating. They'd been together for a while and she liked him a lot. But she suspected from some of the behavior he was exhibiting that he had a nasty habit that was the reason she had cash going missing from her wallet more than once. And last week, she'd "lost" the diamond pendant her grandmother gave her when she graduated from the University of Colorado ten years ago.

She feared her cash and the diamond she treasured was going up his nose.

I had no idea how I was going to prove this fact, outside of watching him with his buds, eating steak, drinking martinis, laughing, and him being the loudest and liveliest of the lot because he was so obviously coked to the gills. But I couldn't just tell Helen he looked high. She was into him and *really* didn't want to believe he was stealing from her.

It was going to have to be an eye witness account.

I was hoping that eye witness account wouldn't include me following him to a meet with a dealer. I tried to give dealers a wide berth. Jules got jacked up by a low level dealer and ended up killing him before he killed her because he'd already put a fair amount of effort into that (in other words, two bullets in her body). For obvious reasons I wanted to avoid situations like that.

I didn't even own a gun. I wasn't prepared for getting on dealer radar, nor did I ever think I would be. Though, since I planned to keep doing what I was doing, I knew it might happen.

I just wasn't prepared (yet).

So I was waiting for my shot to follow him to the bathroom. If guys were in there and they saw me when I entered, I'd pretend I was tipsy and went in the wrong door. But I was willing to do it in the hope I'd catch him in the act. If I caught him in the act, Helen would believe me. Totally. We were tight.

I was thinking this when I heard a familiar voice say from behind me, "Ally."

Chills slid over my skin and weight settled in my gut as I realized my mistake.

In order to watch Zach with his boys in a back booth, I'd put my back to the door.

Which meant I was ripe for attack.

Fuck.

I turned on my stool and looked up at Ren.

He was wearing a well-tailored suit that looked good on him.

As for the rest, everything that was him, top to toe, was the thing of dreams.

It was then something I always loved—the fact that Denver was huge, sprawling, dynamic, eclectic, diverse and energetic, but could still be a small town—became something I hated.

Living there my whole life, I never went out without knowing there was a very good chance I'd bump into someone I knew, liked, and would shoot the shit with them in a grocery aisle or arrange to go to a movie or end up in a bar sucking back Fat Tires until we had to order a taxi.

Then there were times, and there were few, when I ran into someone I most definitely did not want to see.

Like now.

"Hey," I greeted.

"Hey," he replied. He looked at the empty stool beside me and back at me. "Got a minute?"

I didn't. I had to keep an eye on Zach and time his bathroom break so it worked for me, and hopefully for my friend Helen.

But I didn't want to blow off Ren. That might give him the impression he'd shredded me. Or at the very least upset me.

He *had* shredded me. No doubt. It made no sense. Drinks, conversation, great sex and just one night. How that could lead to me feeling dead inside, I had no clue.

I just knew it did. And I wasn't one of those chicks who denied things. I was real with everybody. Including myself.

But not including Ren. No way *in hell* I was going to let on he'd done that to me.

Therefore, I said, "Sure," and turned my whole body his way.

He sat and caught the bartender's eye.

As we were waiting for the bartender to arrive, I looked for a hot babe hanging back and found none, so I asked, "You here alone?"

His eyes came to me. "Business dinner. Saw you, told them to start without me."

That was interesting. We hadn't really parted on good terms. If it were the other way around, I wouldn't make the approach.

Before I could dig deeper, or, the better option, find some way to blow him off without letting on I was doing it, the bartender came.

Ren ordered, "Vodka gimlet," and I felt my eyes widen slightly. "What?" he asked when he looked at me.

"You're a gimlet man?" I asked back.

"I like booze," he answered. "I'll drink anything but tonight I'm in the mood for sour."

I didn't know what to do with that.

His brows went up a couple of centimeters. "You got a problem with the gimlet?"

"I'm a bartender, Ren. A gimlet order is rare. But when it comes, it's women who order it."

His eyes narrowed slightly. "Know you're tight with men who drink blood and eat nails, babe, but just to say, what a man drinks does not make that man."

I didn't know what to make of that either, except I didn't like it all that much. Much like I didn't like his parting shot of weeks ago, also a slur on my family.

"Do you have a problem with my family that I don't know about?" I asked.

"No, and don't know how you got that from what I said. What I got a problem with is you giving me shit about what I drink."

"I wasn't giving you shit. I was just surprised," I corrected him.

"Ally, in case you don't know this already, a man is not gonna take kindly to anyone sayin' he drinks a woman's drink or does a womanly *anything*."

I had to admit, he had a point. And I had to admit, I'd done that. I also had to admit, that was a wee bit uncool.

Still, he didn't have to get so irritable about it. I mean, I was very well acquainted with his manhood *and* his ability to utilize it with exceptional proficiency. I'd communicated learning this knowledge by having orgasms the likes of which he could not mistake as fake. Therefore, I'd hardly question it.

Whatever.

Seriously time to move on. I shouldn't have said yes to his "minute." I shouldn't give a shit about what he thought about me. I didn't anyone else. Why him?

Instead of pondering that question now, I decided to do it later and asked, "I see you stopped by to spread cheer, but I'm in the middle of something. So maybe we can wrap this up so I can get back to it?"

His eyes looked to my untouched martini, my dress, my legs, my ass in the stool and around the restaurant before coming back to me. "What are you in the middle of?"

"Something," I replied. "Now is there something you needed?"

He studied me, again did his scanning thing of me and our surroundings, then he looked back at my face and stated straight out, "I fucked this up."

That was a surprise statement so my head cocked to the side. "What?"

His gimlet arrived, taking his attention again. He told the bartender to put it on his table's tab and turned again to me.

"I didn't come over here to be a dick. I came over here to apologize for being a dick."

Now that...

That threw me.

The men of my acquaintance didn't apologize. They admitted no wrong verbally and instead did things (maybe) to make amends physically.

Of course, most of that was the Hot Bunch dealing with their Rock Chicks so I had not experienced it personally. Still, I'd heard about it. *All* about it. And sometimes I'd witnessed it. But I'd never experienced it.

I said nothing.

Ren kept talking.

"I had a good time with you. You're funny. That whole thing you got goin' on." He flipped a hand out to me, my guess his flip indicating all that was me. "It's good. It works for you. It works in a big way for me. You're fuckin' gorgeous. You're a fantastic fucking lay. It was a good night. I got pissed you took off when I wanted more. Came to your house, acted like a dick and you didn't deserve that shit. No excuse for it. But you gotta know, I felt like an asshole because I *was* an asshole. I'm glad I had the chance to tell you I know I was an asshole."

On that, as I stared at him, lips parted, he grabbed his drink and slid off the stool.

Looking down at me, his gaze moving over my face and hair, he finally caught my eyes and said quietly, "And you look good tonight, honey. Beautiful."

Still staring at him, lips parted, he turned and walked away.

It took me a while to stop focusing on all that he said, and the vision of him burned into my eyeballs walking away (he seriously could rock a suit), in order to pull myself together.

But I was Ally Nightingale, so pull myself together I did.

I turned back to Zach, but grabbed my martini on the go. I wasn't a martini girl. More like tequila. Though I was like Ren, I enjoyed booze and could drink anything. But the martini was what I had and I needed to wash what just happened away, at least for now, so it would have to do.

Fifteen minutes later, Zach got up to go to the bathroom.

Thirty seconds after that, I followed him.

I didn't have to do the tipsy act when I hit the men's room because no one was visible when I walked in. But there were shoes under a stall, standing sideways so not using the facilities, just using the stall for privacy to hide a nasty habit.

Loser.

I opened the stall next to Zach's, stepped up on the toilet, balanced and looked over the divider.

He had a vial in his hand and a spoon to his nose.

"Hey, Zach," I greeted.

He jumped and his vial of cocaine fell into the toilet.

I swallowed a laugh.

His head snapped back to look up at me. "Ally, what the fuck?"

I answered his "what the fuck" with, "Kiss Helen good-bye, you thieving, asshole cokehead."

Then I stepped off the toilet, pushed out of the stall and moseyed out of the bathroom, ignoring Zach making desperate fumbling noises in his stall and calling my name.

I took the back exit.

It was closer, for one. Zach wouldn't expect it, for another.

And I wouldn't have to see Ren as I walked through the restaurant, for last.

⌐╦╤─

I sat in my Mustang outside Ren's place, staring at his door.

His house really was great. It looked like it could be in The South. It had that kind of grace with a veranda, big multi-paned windows, a brick paved walkway and lush landscaping. It had a welcoming settled feel like old houses did. I liked it.

You look good tonight, honey. Beautiful.

I sighed.

A simple compliment. And highly effective.

It works in a big way for me.

My thing worked for Ren.

Well, one could say Ren's thing worked for me, too.

Big time.

And he'd apologized for being a dick. Straight up. I'd been a bitch, stupidly spitting in the eye of the tiger by making an idiot remark about his drink after he'd approached to apologize. Then he didn't push the drink issue and apologized.

Class.

I got pissed you took off when I wanted more.

He wanted more.

Well, one could also say I wanted more, too. Hell, my Lelo Lily was constantly on her charger, she was used so much, me on my back in my bed, my Lelo between my legs, Ren in my head.

Fuck.

It was going on summer so the days were longer, but it was full-on dark so it was really late.

Still, I threw open my door, folded out of my car and clicked on my high-heeled sandals across the street (I hadn't changed, for a reason that would hopefully work for me), up Ren's brick paved front walk and to his ash green front door.

He had a doorbell so I didn't pound. And anyway, I wasn't pissed. I just rang the bell, and seeing as I could see light filtering around the drapes to my left, I figured he was up.

Ren didn't strike me as early to bed, early to rise.

He wasn't.

The door opened and there he stood wearing the trousers from his suit (dark blue with a hint of a shine, perfect freaking fit) and his tailored shirt (blue, gray and black stripes on white, open at the collar, rolled back at the cuffs; hot).

"Ally," he greeted, staring down at me, and strike that on the list of one of the many things that did it for me with Ren.

He was up a step, but I was in four inch heels. Being five nine that put me at *tall*. Still, he was way taller than me. So much taller, no matter what shoe apparel I was wearing, if he wanted to take my mouth, he'd have to work for it.

The thought made my inner thighs quiver.

Time to do what I came there to do.

"Zano, I know it's late, but I was out and I thought I'd come by to say it was totally cool what you——"

I spoke not another word since his arm flashed out, hooked me at the waist and I was flying through the air. I landed full-frontal against his body and a quarter of a second later his mouth landed on mine.

He dragged me in as I opened my lips and his tongue thrust inside.

He kicked the door closed behind me.

We made it to the bed this time before I had my first orgasm.

But when I had it, we were both still fully clothed.

The next three, he gave me naked.

❦

The next morning...

I woke up naked and mostly sprawled on Ren.

There was a heavenly throb between my legs that suggested strongly that the first time with Ren was not a fluke.

He really did *totally* know what he was doing.

"You awake, babe?"

I lifted my head from where it lay on his chest and looked at him.

God.

That hair, his face, his corded neck, the column of his throat, all sleepy or tousled and resting against a backdrop of wine colored sheets that I knew, because I could feel, were the softest sheets in history—definitely what dreams were made of.

"Hey," I said as my good morning.

His lips quirked. "Hey."

Yeah. A rough, drowsy, deep voice with all the rest.

Dream material.

Ren kept talking.

"Just in case you didn't get my message last night, pretty fuckin' pleased you came by to accept my apology."

I felt my lips tip up.

His eyes watched.

I felt my happy place pulse.

His eyes moved to mine; my happy place must have communicated its happiness on my face because his face got dark. His arm, already around me, tightened, and he dragged me up his chest, even as he rolled. His body pinned mine to the bed as his lips covered mine for a deep, wet morning kiss that was so damned good, it made my happy place pound.

Ren then pressed a knee between my legs. I opened them in invitation, and for my graciousness, I got a hard muscled thigh pressed tight against my happy place.

I moaned down his throat.

He pushed his hips against my thigh and groaned down mine.

His happy place was happy, too.

I decided I needed to do something about making it happier.

So I did.

As did he.

Thirty minutes later, we were both still breathing a little heavily. Ren's face was in my neck. He was buried deep inside me. Our skin was misted with damp. The fingers of one of my hands were in his hair. My other arm was curved tight around his back, and both my legs were wrapped around his thighs.

After a late night that included lots of mind-blowing sex, I had just discovered he was also good in the morning.

Why did I not find this surprising?

He lifted his head and his warm, sexy eyes caught mine. This had the result of making me catch my breath.

"You want me to make you breakfast?" he asked.

Jeez.

Seriously?

This guy could also cook?

I tested the waters.

"Are we talking instant oatmeal or eggs benedict?"

That got another lip quirk before he answered, "I was thinking croissants, eggs whatever way you want 'em, fresh strawberries, bacon and tater tots."

Did he say tater tots?

For breakfast?

"Did you say tater tots?" I asked in order to confirm.

"Baby." His hips pressed into mine. I bit my lip at how good that felt and his face dipped close. "Tater tots rock breakfast."

Ren Zano ate tater tots for breakfast and served them up to his fuck buddies.

He *was* a dream.

"I'm totally down for breakfast," I answered.

At that he smiled and my world ended.

Again.

Because I wanted that smile every morning right after mind-blowing sex and right before my tater tots.

And I wanted it for a lifetime.

Don't ask me how I knew this, I just did. Deep down, I knew it. Right to the very heart of me.

But I didn't let on.

Again.

Forty-five minutes later...

"You're right. Tater tots rock breakfast," I said to Ren, incidentally saying it around a mouth full of ketchup-covered tater tots.

He grinned at me.

I returned the favor (closed mouthed, because food grins were gross) and looked down to my plate of food.

We were standing in his kitchen. Or he was. He'd cooked for me while I made coffee and then watched him cook. His scrambled eggs were fluffy, cheesy and delicious. His bacon was crisped to perfection. His croissants were bought fresh from a local bakery and they were buttery and amazing.

But when he offered me my filled plate and told me to take it to the dining room, I hefted my ass up on the counter and commenced eating.

This might have been rude, but I didn't want to give him the wrong impression. I accepted his apology. I accepted his body. I gave him mine. That was as far as this was going to go.

You might think I was crazy, but a man doesn't fight over a woman, take her back, carry her from a crashed car that would eventually explode (told you the Rock Chicks were magnets for trouble—when I said trouble, I meant *trouble*), and speak her name in his sleep with another woman in his bed and not be hung up on her.

This was fact.

So I wasn't going to set myself up for that kind of heartbreak. I wasn't like Ava, blonde with lots of tits and ass. Okay, so I had some ass, but not lots of it. And I was a girl so I had tits, just not the kind of rack Ava had. I was also a brunette.

I wasn't his type.

I was just available.

And I'd continue to be available, especially if fantastic sex came with breakfast that included tater tots.

But I was drawing that line. No doing budding couple stuff like sitting at the dining room table, eating breakfast and sharing after a night of great sex.

No, it was going to be snarfing down your delicious fluffy eggs and tater tots in an I'm-a-girl-on-the-go kind of way, then being the girl on the go by *going*. Then, if the spirit moved him or me, coming back for more.

The weird part of me making this non-verbal statement was that Ren didn't push it. Instead, he watched me hop up on his counter. His eyes flashed with humor even as his lips quirked with it, and he settled his hips against the counter kitty corner from me.

But he kept his eyes on my ass on his counter in a way that told me he was currently—and would later—be thinking about my ass on his counter in a good way. This made me think about other ways my ass could be on his counter, and these were good, too.

My happy place, sated and content, started getting happy again.

I didn't need to get happy again. I *wanted* to get happy, but I didn't need it.

I needed to get to Fortnum's, hang with my friends and be in my normal. That was to say, see if one of Lee's other guys decided to wade into the troubled life of some sick gorgeous woman who had people wanting to kidnap her, stab her or steal her money, and wade into that.

I also needed to make some money. I might not be girlie, as it were, but I liked my rock concerts and LBDs, and neither of those came cheap.

Therefore, I declared, "Glad we did this, Zano. It's good we didn't leave it as it was. Where this is at right now is much better. But after I help you with the dishes, I gotta bounce. I have to get to work."

As I spoke, his gaze went from my ass to my eyes, and when I was done talking, he announced, "I'd like to take you to dinner tonight."

Shit.

I'd like that too, but that wasn't going to happen.

I shoved the last tater tot in my mouth, jumped off the counter and turned to the sink. I rinsed my plate, put it in the sink and turned to him.

Leaning a hip against the counter, I caught his eyes and gentled my voice when I told him, "Listen, this is good and I like it. But I just got out of a some-what long-term relationship and I gotta sort my shit before I move on from that."

This wasn't exactly a lie. Carl and I were close. I missed him. I wasn't pining for him; I knew I'd made the right decision. But it wasn't like we ended things six months ago. Our break was recent.

But it wasn't just that.

I went on.

"And you've got the Ava thing."

Now that was definitely not a lie.

His head cocked to the side, his eyes went guarded, and he asked, "The Ava thing?"

23

I wasn't going to go there, but also, I didn't want to take him there. Things were settled with Luke and Ava. They were all kinds of happy. Ren probably knew that and I shouldn't remind him of it. In fact, I shouldn't have said anything.

I moved us around that. "What I'm saying is, if you're cool with it, I'm cool with this being casual." I smiled at him. "In fact, I'd be way cool with that."

He studied me a moment before he moved into me, getting close. He leaned around me to put his plate in the sink, straightened, caught my eyes again and stayed close.

He was talking as gently as I did when he replied, "Had women say that to me, honey, but they didn't mean it."

"I'm not like other women."

His gaze moved over my face before locking on my lips and he murmured, "I'm sensing that."

I didn't know if that was good or bad, but I was taking it as good by the heat in his eyes.

"So if we continue to hook up, I'm down with casual. Yeah?" I pressed so I could get away from the heat of his eyes. And also, the heat of his body. Both were doing good things to my happy place, which would mean I might not get my take of the tip jar at Fortnum's because, if I jumped him, I had a feeling I wouldn't want to come up for air.

As answer, he said quietly, "I like you."

Oh fuck.

There it was. My happy place got happy. My stomach dipped. But my heart squeezed.

"I like you too," I stated in a defensive matter-of-fact way. "But I'm not ready—"

He cut me off. "No, Ally, what I'm sayin' is, I like you. And if all you got in you right now is casual, I want more of you so I'll give you that. But women say shit they don't mean. I get that they do it to protect themselves and mean it when they say it. Then they get trapped in a place they created. This guy you had, you need time to get over that, I get you gotta take it. I'll also give it to you. But if the casual we got shifts and you get stuck and don't communicate with me the shift you want, which means I hurt you when I have no intention of doing that…" He took in a breath. "I like you and I don't want that to happen. So I'll take casual, honey. Just as long as, along the way, you're straight with me. And in return, I'll be straight with you."

I could be straight.

Mostly.

I nodded and asked, "So, do we have a deal?"

He smiled.

My heart again squeezed.

Then he answered. "Yeah, baby. We got a deal."

Chapter 3
Fucked Up As Love

Rock Chick Rewind

Two months later...

I was sitting in another bar; not like Club. This one was seedy and I didn't like it.

But I was all over finding out what the fuck was going on. I'd had an informant tell me she worked that bar, although I didn't know what "worked that bar" meant and only got the response, "you'll see," so I was there.

Informants sometimes sucked. A lot of time they were full of shit, and a lot of other times they got paid even better than me. Fortunately, this wasn't my problem. My "clients" coughed that up.

But the case I was on was confounding me.

Usually, I loved a bit of confounding. Finding a piece, fitting it into the puzzle, making the picture become clearer.

But with this chick, things never came clear. They just got fuzzier. And it was annoying.

I didn't get it.

But I would.

See, a friend of a friend of mine came to me, needing my services. He'd talked to his girl and his girl told him everything was a-okay.

But, according to him, she was totally lying.

Since her family didn't have any money, he was saving up for the wedding of his girl's dreams, seeing as he was gone for her. So he couldn't go to someone like Lee because Lee was seriously pricey. But he was worried and he needed answers.

So my friend told him about me.

It was another boy/girl problem (most of them were; more indication you shouldn't get mired down in romance). This time the girl had the boy's diamond on her finger. She seemed into him; completely in love, over the moon at the prospect of being married, but dragging her heels in doing something about it.

Her behavior had also reportedly changed. She'd disappear, sometimes for long periods of time. Not weeks, but days and nights. She would also not return texts or pick up calls, and have weak excuses about where she was and why she was incommunicado.

They didn't live together; not yet. This was because she was religious and wanted to wait until after marriage (fishy, because who did that anymore?—especially when she was letting him bang her; God could see all, so it wasn't like she was pulling one over on the Big Guy).

But the dude had the keys to her place. He'd gone in when she wasn't there and rifled through her shit, even bills and bank statements. Nothing was amiss. There were no drugs. No empty bottles of booze piled up in the recycling bin. No stockpiles of firearms and explosives or blueprints of banks.

Nothing that he could see.

Enter me.

I didn't do this for a living. I didn't do it for much of any payment. I spent my days in Fortnum's, my nights at Brother's, and not too long ago, got caught up in the next Rock Chick drama. This was my friend Stella's big thing with another of Lee's guys, Mace (seriously? How were we all connected, most of us for years, and this shit was happening *now?*).

That one got serious ugly with all the Rock Chicks again on the line; drive-bys, couch mutilations, and Stella's apartment had exploded.

Yes.

Exploded.

Kaplowy.

Dust.

But now, as luck kept having it (thank God), all was good (outside of all Stella's belongings being blown sky high and her being underinsured; but luckily, she'd just signed a recording contract and landed her hot guy, so her future was bright) and as usual, we were moving on while waiting for the next one up.

My guess, it would be Lee's last unattached guy, Hector. But there were bets (yep, the posse bet on this shit) on me.

Not a chance.

I'd lived through six of these and had intimate details. No way that shit was happening with me. Some over-the-top macho guy forcing his way into my life, taking it over and bossing me around?

Unh-unh.

I didn't care if it came with regular orgasms. That shit was *not* for me.

But, the thing was; with Stella's situation, someone had leaked a lot of personal shit to the media about Lee, Indy and the entire crew. The paper had done exposés on all of their romances at the same time they followed Stella and Mace's gig.

No one knew who leaked it, not even Lee, who had ways of finding out everything.

I'd also used my growing network of contacts to find out who the source was, but no one was talking.

It was weird. It wasn't like it was a state secret. But all lips involved were sealed, as in with super glue.

So I worked, spent time on finding out who was talking about the Rock Chicks and did my other business. Not to mention, I often hooked up with Ren so I woke up in his bed, or alternately he woke up in mine, with more than a hint of frequency (in other words, nearly every morning).

Therefore, I didn't have time to spend all of it following this woman. That meant it was about putting out feelers. With limited time, I needed to pinpoint my activities. And information sometimes came in slowly, especially about a girl who was not on the underworld grid of Denver. She worked in admitting at St. Joe's, went to church on Sundays, had a Shih Tzu dog she doted on, a pastime of gardening (seriously, her backyard was the bomb—I'd jumped the fence and looked) and loved her fiancé.

Because I didn't have the time, and this case was so weird, I'd called in reinforcements.

With the promise of a six-pack of Red Bull, a bottle of vodka and an entire afternoon of me at his place playing some game on his PS3 (this, a sacrifice for me; I rocked Guitar Hero, the rest of it I could take it or leave it—usually leave it), I'd talked my computer genius friend Brody into digging into this chick. I wanted to see if there was some electronic trail the fiancé couldn't find rifling through her desk.

I also needed to learn how to pick a lock. I wanted inside her place to see for myself. I'd bought a couple of locks at the hardware store to examine them and try to figure them out, but I hadn't had time to do that.

Alternately, I hoped the chick showed tonight and gave me some insight into why a good Catholic girl who loved her dog, geraniums and worked at a children's hospital would be coming to this bar and giving lame excuses to her supposedly beloved fiancé about why she wouldn't pick a date for the blessed event.

This was on my mind when I felt movement beside me.

I turned my head and saw Darius sliding into my booth.

I didn't know whether to take this as a good or bad thing. Darius and I were tight so if he saw me out and about, he wouldn't hesitate to approach. He also worked for Lee, so he could be anywhere at any time doing anything.

Then again, if he saw me out and about, he'd never see me someplace like this unless a Rock Chick was on the line. But we were currently in Rock Chick/ Hot Bunch Downtime.

I led with, "Hey," to get the lay of the land.

He shook his head and grinned.

Darius was black, had twists in his hair, soulful eyes, and the lean he had been when he was a drug dealer, which had bordered on hungry-looking and mean, had filled out now that he left that life behind. He looked healthier; not content but not angry, and his lean was no longer mean. It was kickass edgy.

Then again, he'd always been hot. Even when he was a drug dealer.

"Since it's you, I've decided to find this amusing rather than drag your ass outta here and tell you to get your head out of it," he declared.

I blinked.

Then I asked, "What?"

"Woman, you are not flying under radar."

I looked around the bar to see if eyes were on me, particularly if the woman I was hoping to see there was there and had, for some bizarre reason (since she couldn't know I was looking for her), made me.

"Not the bitch you're after," Darius said, and I looked back at him. "Lee."

Oh. That.

I didn't care about that.

"I'm not doing anything illegal," I pointed out.

He ignored me and said, "And Hank."

"So?"

He again ignored me and continued, "And Eddie. And your dad. And Indy's dad—"

I cut him off. "I get your point, Darius. I just don't know why you're making it."

"They're letting you do your thing. But you gotta know they're beginning to get antsy about it."

Uh-oh.

Letting me do my thing?

Letting?

I decided to let that slide since I loved Darius and figured he didn't mean anything by it (or I was giving him the benefit of the doubt) and focused on something else.

"Why on earth would they be getting antsy?"

"Because you aren't stopping."

Uh-oh again.

"Okay. Now tell me why they'd want me to stop? Or maybe the better question is why they're in my business at all?"

He turned and leaned closer to me before answering, "I don't know, Ally. Maybe it's 'cause you're their sister. Or as good as a sister, or a daughter, and they're worried. Maybe it's 'cause you're untrained, which is why they're worried. Maybe it's 'cause you're out at places like this and unarmed, which, if they knew you were here, they'd be all kinds of fuckin' worried."

"I have a stun gun," I shared.

"The last three years, this bar has had four hits carried out in it," he told me. "Bullets are flying, stun guns aren't worth shit."

Fuck.

Four?

That was a lot.

Hell, *one* was one too many.

I knew this place was seedy.

Maybe I should have asked Brody to do an electronic look-see into the location I was casing. I'd remember to do that next time.

"Ally," Darius called my attention back to him. When he got it, he said, "I can tell by your face you aren't listening to me."

"I am," I returned. "I just think you need to be straight up about what you're saying."

He leaned in closer and replied quietly, "You have no business being here."

"I have a friend who has a friend he cares about who has a fiancée who, I've heard, is tied up in some business here. He's in knots about it. He loves her. And he can't afford Lee. He can't even afford Dick Anderson."

Dick Anderson was another local PI, less expensive than Lee and his boys, also less talented. Though, a nice guy.

"So enter me," I finished.

"Whatever shit she's wound up in here is shit you don't want swirlin' around you."

I had a feeling he was not wrong.

"I'll exit this situation shit free. Promise," I assured him blithely.

"You do not have the skills to do that," he contradicted me.

My back went up, but my attention sharpened.

"Do you know the job I'm on?"

"Yeah," he didn't surprise me by answering. He'd already mentioned "the bitch" I was after. "Brody spilled," he went on. "You pulled him in, gave him the name. He talked to me. When he did, I decided it was time to stop delaying *our* talk."

That Red Bull, vodka and gaming session was exchanged for information *and* confidentiality.

If Brody got me good shit, he'd get his Red Bull and vodka. But for this crap, I was so totally not spending the afternoon with a joystick in my hand when I could spend it with Ren and a better kind of joystick in my hand. Or in other parts of me.

Brody. God, such a big mouth.

"Ally," Darius called again, and my attention returned to him. "Focus, woman. What I'm saying is important."

"What you're saying *would* be important if you had info on the woman I'm checking out."

Darius stared at me.

This lasted a while.

I let him. I could be patient.

Or I could be patient for a while.

Luckily, I was able to be patient for the while it took Darius to break his silence and mutter, "Stubborn."

Told you Darius had known me a long time.

"So, *do* you have info on this chick?" I pushed.

"No. Don't know who the fuck she is. What I know is that two kinds of women walk in those doors." He jerked his head to the door to the bar. "First kind is looking to score, and by that I don't mean get laid. I mean tweaker bitches too stupid and too desperate for their fix to stay away. The second kind is looking to get laid, but if that happens, they also get paid."

I knew both. I hadn't seen one woman there, outside me, who was not one or the other.

Therefore, this gave me nothing.

"You don't care," Darius declared, and I focused on him again.

"Care about what? I mean, you aren't telling me something I don't know."

"Care about your brothers, your dad, your friends worried about you."

I felt something unpleasant slither through me. Something that forced me to ask, "Has Lee shared with Indy?"

"No," he said firmly.

I liked the firm, but I needed more.

"Eddie with Jet?"

"No, Ally. No fuckin' way. They tell their women what you're doin', those crazy bitches will be all over gettin' in on the act. You think those men want their women involved in this brand of shit? That is, when this brand of shit doesn't hit them when they're actually *not* doing anything to buy it, rather than doing what you're doing, which means doing something that might buy it."

No. I didn't think that.

So good.

That secret was safe.

And it was a secret for precisely that reason.

I could sense danger, and stay away from it, but that didn't mean I didn't court it. And the Rock Chicks had had enough of that. With their track record, there would probably be more. I didn't need to be the one to bring that down on them.

Not to mention, if I did, Lee, Hank, Eddie, Vance, Luke and Mace would lose their badass minds, and I *really* didn't need that shit. Badasses were a pain in the ass to deal with. The Rock Chicks didn't agree, but then again, they were getting orgasms regularly given to them *by* said badasses, and it was my experience that colored a woman's thinking.

But it was more. I liked doing this. It was mine. And the Rock Chicks would be all over getting involved.

Doing this wasn't a fun diversion for me.

It was something else.

I just didn't get what it was, so I was riding the wave until the cosmos shared that intel with me.

And I was getting off on it.

"Fuck me," Darius murmured.

I'd lost focus on him again, but when I went back to him, I saw him eyeing me but shaking his head.

"What?" I asked.

He stopped shaking his head and locked eyes with me.

"The what is you're you. You're gonna do what you're gonna do. What you're not gonna do is do this shit not knowin' what the fuck you're doin'."

I opened my mouth to speak, but Darius shook his head again and kept talking.

"I get that you need this to fly under Rock Chick radar. And I *really* need this to fly under Rock Chick radar. Those motherfucking men will flip right the fuck out if their women get a hint of what you're doin', get involved and that somehow blows back on me. So we're keepin' this under radar."

I was down with that.

I just didn't know exactly what he was talking about until he told me.

"I'm talkin' to Zip. On the down low, we're takin' you in, gettin' you a weapon."

Oh shit.

Zip owned Zip's Gun Emporium. I'd been there. Zip was old. Zip was cantankerous. Zip was also a hoot. And his shop had all any badass needed to kit out his badassness and make it *lethally* badass. I loved his shop. I had a stun gun, Taser and a variety of mace delivery systems I'd bought in his shop.

Zip's place also had a firing range.

I wasn't sure about carrying a weapon, though. I could stun gun with the best of them, but a real gun?

"Darius, I—"

He lifted a hand. "No, woman. No fuckin' way. You're in a bar like this, you come in carryin'. But you come in carryin' and knowin' what you're doin'. I know your dad taught you how to handle guns. But before you go out packin', you're gonna shoot at Zip's and you're gonna do it a lot. We'll talk him into openin' the range after hours so you don't get seen there. And you work with your weapon so you're so comfortable enough with it that it feels like an extension of your arm. You understand it. You respect it. You know what it can do. And you know how to use it."

That sounded kind of exciting, but I didn't get to tell him that because Darius was not done.

And it got better.

"Lee uses this dude's place down in Colorado Springs. The guy's got three set ups. One's a warehouse you gotta clear, good and bad guys. One's a house you gotta clear. You walk through with your weapon shooting pop-ups. You fail if you take down one innocent, and that means you do it again. And again. And again. Until you pass. You don't go through it memorizing the scheme. He switches the pop-ups and you never know what you're going to get. You don't pass until you can get through it completely clean."

I *so* wanted to do that.

In fact, I couldn't fucking wait.

"He's also got a driving course," Darius informed me. "Learn to drive defensive, learn to drive a chase. You're doin' that, too."

I so fucking was!

"You're tall but you're slight," he continued. "That means you don't learn how to fight. You learn some defensive moves and you learn how to get away. I'll teach you that. But, starting tomorrow, and every day after that, you run. You got trouble, there's a high probability you're not gonna be able to beat it down. You do not shoot at it unless you absolutely have to. Stun guns and pepper spray can get commandeered if you don't got the moves to stop it, and then be turned on you. So you get your ass in trouble, you run away. But you're not in shape, that trouble'll catch you."

This did not sound all that fun. I wasn't an exercise sort of person, unless you counted walking in a mall. However, I didn't share that with Darius, in case me poo-pooing any part of the righteous deal he was offering would mean he'd take the deal off the table.

And anyway, if I ran regularly, that meant I could drink more Fat Tire and eat more LaMar's donuts.

So I decided to focus on that.

"You got it," I agreed.

He nodded once and kept going.

"From here on out, you start anything, you gotta be invisible."

"I already do that," I told him, but he shook his head.

"Not what you're thinkin'. I mean you go to Brody. He makes a mint off that game he programmed, but he gets off on this sleuth stuff. Lee pays him a whack, but that guy would come to work every day for free, he's so into this shit. You give him more, he'll be all over it. You can solve your problem with an electronic investigation that doesn't put your ass on the line, you do that." He paused. "First."

This made sense and would likely only cost me energy drinks, Costco boxes of king-size candy bars and Apple app gift cards all of which I could make my "clients" procure for Brody. Since all that was doable, I nodded my agreement.

Darius kept talking.

"And from here on in, I'm briefed in full about everything you do. I know all your cases. I know what you uncover. And you do not," he leaned in, "*ever* walk your ass into a place like this without me as your wingman. This last is the most important, Ally, and if you're not down with that, you lose all the rest. You also buy me goin' to Lee and lighting a fire under his ass to take you off Denver's game board in a way no one will ever contact you again for this shit."

Lee could do that.

And Darius *would* do that. He cared a lot about me.

And if either of them did that, it would piss me off.

But I didn't need to expend that energy, seeing as I had absolutely no problem with him being my wingman.

In fact, I had absolutely no problem with any of it (save the running, but I figured I could rock a track suit and I could get some of those kickass double hair band thingies to pull my hair away from my face while I ran and be totally stylin').

In order to communicate this to Darius, it was my turn to lean into him.

And when I did, I whispered, "You know, I totally love you."

Something moved over his face. Something I'd seen before when he didn't know I was watching.

Uncertainty mixed with melancholy. I didn't totally get it. What I did get was that Darius Tucker had had a beautiful life a long time ago. A big loving family, good friends, a bright future. And all that went to shit. He made desperate—and it had to be said, angry—decisions, and his life spiraled down the toilet. In that time, I suspected he did a lot of things that seared marks onto his soul.

I just didn't know if he was on a path to redemption or thought his future only held damnation.

That was his to know and share if he felt like it.

As for me, I'd learned over and over again, since Rosie dragged Indy into his mess (thus starting the Rock Chick Rollercoaster), good people did bad things and bad people did good things.

I just trusted God would sort it out as it needed to be.

When Darius said nothing, I assured him, "You don't have to say it back. I know where you are. And if I didn't, you coming here tonight and doing what you've done would have told me."

To this, Darius said, "You're a pain in the ass."

He so totally loved me.

"Good," I replied on a smile. "That's what I strive to be."

"Woman, trust me. You're succeeding beyond your wildest dreams."

My smile got bigger.

He took it in, shook his head, then looked back in my eyes.

"Tonight, you're done. You wait until we look over what Brody gets. He gives you what you need, you got no reason to come back. He doesn't, we'll assess and plan. You down with that?"

"Totally."

"Right," he muttered, sliding out of the booth. "Get your ass outta here. We'll go somewhere else and get a drink. You brief me, then I can end this day and get home."

I followed him out, asking, "Would it be a hit to your street cred if I held your hand?"

"Pain in the ass," he muttered as answer.

"Or hugged you?" I threw out an alternate suggestion.

"Total pain in the ass."

I grinned.

We hit the door.

Darius pushed it open for me.

I moseyed through.

⇥⇤

Two days later...

I hauled my ass up into Darius's black Silverado and slammed the door. I didn't put on my seatbelt. I leaned forward, put my elbows to the dash and drove my hands into my hair, yanking it away from my face and scrunching it at the back of my head.

Brody had found nothing.

But we'd just had a conversation with one of Darius's informants, and he knew everything.

The vehicle rocked when Darius folded into the driver's seat and closed his door. He didn't hit the ignition and the cab stayed silent.

It was the dead of night and we'd just cracked Garden Girl's case.

And what we learned *sucked*.

After some time, Darius broke the silence.

"Tomorrow," he said gently, "you report this to her man and walk away."

I sat back with a jerk, pulling my hands out of my hair and twisting to him.

"We have to do something," I snapped.

"We don't gotta do shit," he returned, his words harsh but his tone still gentle.

"Darius—"

He leaned into me and hooked his hand behind my head, pulling me close.

"This guy works at an electronic store and is payin' you by givin' you a discount on a new flat screen TV. You do not wade into a mess like that for twenty-five percent off a flat screen TV, Ally."

"That's a good discount," I shot back.

His lips curved up, but the humor didn't reach his eyes. "You give him what he asked for and let him deal."

"His woman is turning tricks to pay off her brother's drug debt," I told him something he already knew since he was the one who found the informant and he stood right by me when we both learned what had befallen Garden Girl.

"That is not your problem."

"Someone has to tell her it's not hers."

"That'd be her man's job."

"You think her man's gonna stick by her side, knowing she's giving fifty dollar blowjobs?" I asked.

Darius said nothing.

That meant no.

I kept going. "Someone has to kick her brother's ass straight into rehab"

"That'd be her job."

"Darius—"

His hand on my head tightened. "Ally, I know his dealer. I already told you, he's taken two digits, and he's threatening next up is this guy's dick. And this dealer will do that. He won't blink. And he'll keep sellin' to him 'cause he doesn't give that first fuck this guy's breakin' into cars to steal stereos to feed his habit or that his sister is spreadin' her legs to keep him trippin'. She should have *never* swung that deal. That's on her. Her man's worried about it. You found his problem; it's on him to solve it. You give him what he needs and walk away."

He waited for that to penetrate, and when I just sat there grinding my teeth, he kept going.

"And his dealer is all over havin' her sweet pussy out there bringin' in coin. You take that away, I take that away, we insert ourselves into a situation that is not ours to deal with, and we make a dangerous guy unhappy. That is not our mission. Our mission was to find out why that bitch was bein' hinky. We found out. You report it. We're done.

"This is fucked up," I hissed.

"Learn now," Darius returned. "You keep doin' this shit, you'll see a lot that's fucked up. Then you'll learn a whole new definition of fucked up, and that definition will keep changing. What you always gotta remember is that it's not *your* fuck up. It's someone else's. You never take that shit on. You do the job and walk away."

I clenched my teeth and slid my eyes away.

Then I looked back and asked, "Why would she do that for her brother?"

"What would you do, body parts from Lee or Hank came to you through the mail?"

I again clenched my teeth and slid my eyes away.

This was my answer, but Darius already knew it.

Kristen Ashley

I'd do anything.

"There is nothing stronger and there is nothing that'll get you as fucked up as love," Darius finished sagely, and I looked back at him.

There was a wisdom borne of experience behind that and I wanted to know what it was.

But, again, that was his to share.

The Rock Chicks, hell, anything (and this evening's activities proved it), I'd stick my nose in and not give up until I had it all.

Darius... I loved him enough not to go there until (hopefully) he gave it to me.

"You gonna be able to walk away?" he asked.

"Yeah," I answered.

He studied me before pressing, "Is that yeah firm?"

He so totally knew me.

My eyes moved to the side for a second before going back to him.

"Yeah," I whispered.

He held my gaze.

Then he nodded.

After that, he let me go and turned toward the wheel. Then he started up his truck and drove me home.

Chapter 4
Wash Him Away

Rock Chick Rewind

Two hours later...

There was a banging on my door.

My eyes fluttered open and I focused on the clock.

It was twelve seventeen.

I smiled to myself. I'd left my Lelo in the nightstand before going to sleep. This was not because, after that night, I didn't need some form of relaxation.

It was that I was hoping Ren would be the source of that relaxation, as these days he always was. He'd texted me earlier saying he had a late meet, but was hoping, if it didn't go *too* late, that he'd come to my house and spend the night.

It was late, but as ever with Ren and me (and we both knew it), no late was too late.

I threw the covers off, got out of bed and moved out of my bedroom.

I was wearing a sexy sapphire blue nightie with deep edges of black lace.

Everyone now knew Indy's former secret (a secret that was leaked by Indy herself during a Girls Night Out; it wasn't me who shared, swear) and that was that she always wore sexy underwear. This was because her grandma bought her some on her sixteenth birthday and told her every woman should have that particular secret. Indy took this to heart and lived it from that day forward.

Unfortunately, seeing as he's my brother, I also knew that Lee very much appreciated this now-not-so-secret.

As in *a lot*.

I couldn't say I very much appreciated knowing this about my brother. I could say it wasn't much of a surprise. I'd been underwear shopping with Indy, and often. She had good taste. And Lee was all man (of the Ren variety) so it wasn't a big leap that he'd get off on something like that.

What everyone *didn't* know was that because I'd known Indy since I was born (which meant I knew Grandma Ellen since I was born, and Grandma Ellen was like a grandma to me too), she gave me the same life lesson.

I just took it further. I wore sexy underwear, no exceptions, no holds barred. I had never owned a pair of granny panties from age sixteen onward.

And I never would.

I also never slept in anything unsexy unless I didn't sleep in anything (and that was the sexiest of all).

I'd learned that Ren was turned on not only by the tactile but also the visual. He liked watching me go down on him. He liked watching me ride him. He liked watching my face as he rode me. He also liked my nighties. The look *and* feel.

And I knew he'd learned if he showed late at my place he was in for a treat, because over the last couple of months I'd given him a lingerie cornucopia of delights that he showed his appreciation for in a variety of righteous ways.

And tonight's nightie was actually new. I bought it just for him.

Though I'd never tell him that.

I checked the peephole just to be certain and saw Ren again gazing down the hall. Since there was nothing there but carpeted hall and doors, I wondered what fascinated him about that.

Then wondering got in the way of opening the door and getting to Ren so I quit doing that, and I unlocked and opened the door.

He heard the locks so he was looking at me when I did.

I was lamenting the fact that when we had the chance to hook up, he usually had time to get home and change. That meant I didn't get him in suits very often. Like now, he was wearing a lightweight white shirt, sleeves rolled up, and faded jeans.

It wasn't a suit I could peel off him, but those everyday items of apparel looked better on him than any other man could pull off, so I wasn't quibbling.

I tipped my head back, smiled at him, leaned in and fisted a hand in his shirt. Then I pulled him in my apartment.

He kicked the door closed as I moved into him, my hand sliding up, my mouth aiming for his.

But he surprised me by putting a hand to my waist and holding on there even as he set me slightly back. He twisted and flipped the light switch.

I blinked at the sudden brightness and caught his eyes.

Then I smiled.

Yeah. Ren was visual. Whatever he had planned, he wanted to watch. And to be able to watch, he had to see.

It was always good, but I was thinking tonight was going to be better.

I leaned in and got up on my toes.

When my mouth was almost on his, Ren's head moved back an inch and his other hand curled firm at the side of my neck, holding me warm but steadily away from him.

What the fuck?

"Zano—"

"That night," he said, his eyes looking into mine in a weird way that felt intense and probing. "What were you doin' at Club?"

My head gave a little confused shake and I asked, "What?"

"That night I apologized," he gave me more info and I, unusually belatedly, sensed the danger and my body stiffened. His hand at my waist wrapped around it to hold me to him as his fingers at my neck dug in as he kept talking. "What were you doin' at Club?"

"Why are you asking this?" I queried.

"Why aren't you answering?" he returned.

My brows drew together. "Because it's none of your business."

He ignored that and tried a different tactic.

"Were you with a man?"

"No."

"A friend?"

"No, Zano," I snapped. "Why does it matter?"

"'Cause you weren't with anybody. You stayed a few minutes after I left you, took off to the bathrooms and never came back. I know. I watched for you."

He watched for me.

Nice.

"But you disappeared," he finished.

"So?"

"The exit's at the front," he informed me.

"So?"

"That means you exited out back."

"Jeez, Zano!" I clipped, pulling out of his hold, taking a step back and putting my hands on my hips. "What's with the interrogation? Who cares how I exited Club *two months ago?*"

He ignored my question—and my outburst—and kept at me.

"A few minutes after you took off toward the bathroom, some guy shot outta that hall lookin' freaked, as well as clearly so stoked on blow it's a wonder his heart didn't explode. You know that guy?"

"I know I'm not a big fan of being woken up in the middle of the night and getting treated to random twenty questions about a night that happened months ago."

"Just sayin', babe, you'll get a very *not* random twenty questions if Benito Valenzuela decides to make a meal outta you."

I clamped my mouth shut.

Oh shit.

That was the dealer who had his hooks into Garden Girl's brother.

"Yeah," he whispered, examining my face carefully. "Though, if Valenzuela gets more interested in you, you might not be available for twenty questions."

Okay, somehow Ren had cottoned on to my activities, and I knew this was definitely not good. He might not be a member of the Hot Bunch, but he was a full-blooded Italian hot guy member of a crime family. So I was thinking his rabid alpha behavior either equaled or rivaled any member of the Hot Bunch, including Luke, who, in my opinion, was totally OTT.

And the Hot Bunch guys had a definite aversion to the women in their lives being around danger.

"How do you know this shit?" I asked quietly.

"Dom gets around," Ren answered immediately. "Had a meeting with him tonight. He doesn't know about us, but we share an acquaintance with your brothers. Both of them. I think you get why, without me explaining, we tend to keep our eye on their activities. And tonight, in passing, Dom says that he's heard *you're* getting around."

Fuck.

Not good.

Ren kept talking.

"He thinks you're doin' shit for Lee. He heard a coupla nights ago you were with Darius Tucker in one of the bars Valenzuela's girls work. Says he also heard Tucker was makin' some enquiries about some new talent Valenzuela has for sale. Sweet piece. Catholic schoolgirl type."

Crap.

Again not good.

Ren didn't know a little. He knew a lot.

He leaned slightly into me, his eyes no less intent *or* probing. "The *real* kind of Catholic schoolgirl type. In other words, somehow her shit got fucked, and this is not an unusual situation for Lee Nightingale to sink his teeth into. Problem is, even Valenzuela thinks Lee swung you out there, and this guy is a lunatic. Anyone else, even a whiff Lee's involved, they steer clear. This guy, he's likin' that your piece is on the chess board. Thinks it's interesting. Wants to keep his eye on that shit, which means he wants to keep an eye *on you.*"

I kept my mouth shut, but mentally added a phone call to Darius to discuss this unpleasant news first thing in the morning.

Ren kept going.

"Dom told me and Vito. Vito is not about swingin' women's asses out there. He knows you, likes you, and if he gets in the mood to blow, he blows. So it's late and he still doesn't hesitate pickin' up the phone and tearin' your brother a new asshole. Problem is, Lee has no clue what the fuck he's talkin' about."

This also wasn't good.

"Figure, though," Ren went on. "He intends to find out."

That was a definite.

"I—" I began.

"What were you doin' at Club, Ally?"

"I was—"

"And what the fuck were you doin' in a bar that Valenzuela works with Darius fuckin' Tucker?"

I felt my back snap straight. "Darius is a friend."

"Darius was a friend, he wouldn't be sittin' with you in that bar havin' a chat. He'd be haulin' your ass *out* of that bar and laying into it to get your head sorted for bein' in that bar in the first fuckin' place."

Oh no.

He didn't say that.

"What the fuck are you into?" he bit out.

"None of your business," I snapped.

"Right." He leaned back. "Was gonna have this discussion with you when I wasn't pissed at you, but it needs to be said, and now's a fuckin' brilliant time to say it," he started in a way that I didn't find very promising.

Then he kept going.

"I'm thinkin' the nature of our relationship is movin' beyond casual. I'm thinkin' it's gettin' into the non-casual zone, seein' as we spend practically every night together, even if you roll into my house at three thirty in the morning after a shift at Brother's. This suggests to me that we can't get enough of each other, and since you haul your ass to my place most of the time, you can't deny that."

This was true. I couldn't deny it.

He wasn't done.

"So I'm thinkin' we're in the zone where we actually go out and eat a meal and get to know each other better. Not wolfing down breakfast, you go your way and I go mine. Or I make you spaghetti because you've been behind a bar all night and haven't eaten, then the minute you're done, we fuck each other's brains out. So, to end, if we're not casual, it *is* my business."

"I'm not feeling the love for not casual right about now, Zano," I shared.

He lifted a hand, palm out my way, and shook his head.

"Sorry, my mistake," he began and dropped his hand. "That came out like you had a choice. Which you don't. Tomorrow, you're in a nice dress. My pick is the one you wore to Club, unless you've got another one that makes my dick harder faster, which, babe, just sayin', will be a feat. Then I'm takin' you out to a nice dinner, and you're gonna share with me all your hopes and dreams. But right now you're gonna tell me what the fuck you're into."

Although one could not say I didn't like that he liked my dress—and why—I still crossed my arms on my chest and declared, "We're not going out on a date."

"You wanna get laid tonight?" he asked, and I felt my brows shoot up.

"Are you using sex as a way to get me to go out with you?" I clipped.

Suddenly he threw his arms out in exasperation.

"Jesus!" he exploded. "Ally, usually a guy's gotta take a girl out as a way to *get* sex."

"I told you, I'm not like other girls."

"Well, you've proved that statement correct a dozen fuckin' times since it came out of your mouth."

"What does that mean?" I asked.

"You over that guy?" he asked back instead of answering and my head twitched.

"What guy?"

Ren's chin jerked back, and his heavy angry vibe that was weighing in the air became stifling.

"What guy?" he whispered.

Uh-oh.

He was referring to Carl, probably because I used Carl as an excuse to keep our relationship casual. And since he wished to discuss us going out of the casual, he would naturally bring up Carl.

Shit.

"I, uh, I'm still working through that," I replied lamely.

"A second ago, you didn't even remember he existed," Ren fired back.

Damn it!

I threw out an arm and went on the defense. "I'm kind of not on my game, what with the late night grilling."

"I had my mouth between your legs, you'd be focused," he returned, and there it was.

I'd had many briefings about Asshole Speak, and that was proof Ren could equal even Luke.

"That's not cool," I whispered.

"But it's true."

It was true, damn it all to hell, so I decided not to reply.

"Was there even a guy?" he asked.

"Yes," I answered snippily. "His name is Carl and he's currently undertaking FBI training in Virginia and likely won't be stationed in Denver when they're done with him. So, since I don't intend to live anywhere but Denver, *I* had to make the decision to be done with him."

Some of his anger slid out of the room and his voice was less terse (though not gentle by a long shot) when he pointed out, "Do you know that that's the most personal thing you've shared with me since beer at Brother's?"

"Fuck buddies don't share their hopes and dreams, Zano. They fuck," I educated him.

It was his turn to clamp his mouth shut.

He did it better than me, and this was because a muscle jumped in his jaw which I found, unfortunately at that moment, all kinds of hot.

Crap.

I let him have his moment and didn't fill the silence.

He got over his moment and his voice was even less terse (but still not gentle) when he told me, "I'm pissed, and I don't know what's goin' on with you out there, which means I'm pissed because I'm worried. But that doesn't negate the fact that I like what we got and I want more."

Oh God.

He wanted more.

And he was worried about me.

Fuck.

I opened my mouth to speak, but he quickly closed the short distance between us, wrapped a hand around the side of my neck and dipped his face close so I closed my mouth.

"You're pissed too," he told me something I knew, but this time his voice was not terse at all. It was gentle and sweet. "So don't answer now. Not when we're both pissed. Give it some time and think about it. And think about sharin' with me whatever you're up to. You got some mission with one of your posse, I might be able to help. It's somethin' you and Tucker gotta keep close to your vests, I get it. But think about sharing, honey. If I can help, I will."

Okay, how did this happen? How was it that one minute we were having not very nice words and the next minute he was not only gentle and sweet, but also *nice*.

When someone was being nice, you couldn't be not nice back. It was a rule.

Shit.

"Just laying down the law now, Zano. When we're pissed at each other, you can't switch to nice. I can't do anything with nice. You know it, so that's not fighting fair."

His lips quirked. His hand at my neck slid up into the back of my hair and his other arm curved around me, pulling me close to his hard heat as he totally ignored me laying down the law, and replied, "You know what I like?" He didn't wait for me to answer. He kept going. "I like it when you act all badass, calling me Zano when I don't have my hands and mouth on you or my dick inside you. But when I do, all I get is sweet breathy Rens."

I lifted my hands to his chest and was pressing, at the same time ignoring my inner thighs quivering as I pointed out, "It's also not fair to be sexy."

He bent his neck, and with lips to mine, he murmured, "I don't fight fair, baby. I fight to win."

I made certain to make note of that.

He made certain I had no retort and did this by kissing me. Then he did it by keeping my mouth engaged as he picked me up like a groom carries his bride and walked me to my bedroom.

By the time we got there, I wasn't thinking about making a retort.

All I was thinking about was Ren.

Two weeks later. . .

Ren was moving inside me and I was loving it when his lips at my ear whispered, "This feel casual to you?"

It *so* didn't.

It felt beautiful.

Perfect.

My limbs tightened around him and I closed my eyes hard.

Then I turned my head, and, my lips at his ear, I whispered back, "I need more time."

His body stilled, unfortunately on an outward glide, and my limbs again tensed around him.

Then he started stroking, sweet, slow, gentle, and replied, "I'll give you that, baby."

I slid a hand up his spine and into his thick, soft hair, thinking, *thank God.*

Three weeks later. . .

I was sucking back coffee as Ren strode into the kitchen wearing a suit.

I stopped, giving myself a moment to appreciate the view. I grinned at him, moved into him and leaned up to kiss his jaw.

I pulled back and mumbled, "Gotta go, babe. See you tonight."

49

Before I could make a move to do that, his arm hooked around my waist and he pulled me into his side. His head turned, mine stayed tipped back, and he caught my eyes.

"Been keepin' an eye on things, and Valenzuela's lost interest in you," he announced.

I knew this. Darius was also keeping an eye on things.

I'd had my phone call with Darius the morning after the night of Ren's and my fight. He had already been made aware of this situation and assured me he was keeping an eye on things and running interference with Lee. Since neither of my brothers approached to tear into me, and Darius had reported Valenzuela was focusing on other things, I knew Darius was successful in these endeavors. So I moved on.

"I know," I told Ren.

He nodded, then said, "Even so, I also know your piece hasn't exited the chess board."

This was true. Darius, Brody and I had another case.

I decided against speaking.

Ren held my eyes, then thankfully changed the subject.

"You workin' Brother's tonight?"

I shook my head.

"Good, then I can take you out to dinner."

My heart squeezed, but luckily I had an excuse and it was not made up.

"I can't. Girl's Night In at Tod and Stevie's. Jet's wedding planning is heating up and things are getting out of hand. Her mother and soon-to-be mother-in-law are horning in, and Jet's freaking. One word: bunting. You may not get that because you're a dude. I'm a chick and I don't even get it, but according to Tod, it's a bride's worst nightmare. Roxie's also deep into the planning stages of her wedding, so Tod's decreed there are a lot of decisions to make and tonight's the night."

To that, he immediately asked, "You workin' tomorrow?"

I nodded.

He sighed.

Then he bent his neck and took my mouth in a kiss that was a whole lot better than the one I gave his jaw.

When he lifted his head, he murmured, "We'll sort out another night."

50

I again decided against speaking. Instead, I gave his arm a squeeze and threw another grin his way.

I broke free and executed a forced casual escape, calling, "Later!" as I did. Ren didn't reply.

⚛

One week later...

It was after a shift at Brother's. I was in my Mustang with my phone in my hand.

I texted Ren with, *On my way,* then I tossed my cell on the seat beside me.

I was about to set my car purring, which would mean my radio would start blaring. This meant it was unfortunate timing because I could hear my phone ringing when, if it had happened two seconds later, I would not. Alternately, this could be considered fortunate timing, depending on how you looked at it, considering what would happen during that call.

Personally, I looked at it both ways. But mostly the second. What went down was way better on the phone than face to face.

Seriously.

See, I saw my screen said "Zano Calling" so I tagged my phone and put it to my ear.

"Hey," I greeted.

"Hey," he replied, then didn't delay with laying it out. "Tonight doesn't work for me. Tomorrow, you can get away, we're havin' lunch."

Here we go again.

Him pressing for more. Me finding an excuse not to give it to him.

"I'm working Fortnum's tomorrow."

"You can get away to go shoppin' with Daisy, you can get away to have lunch with me."

Shit. I needed to learn not to share. The more he knew, the more he could use.

And he used it.

Daisy, by the way, was another Rock Chick. She wasn't hooked up with a Hot Bunch guy. She was married to Marcus Sloan, a colleague of Ren's (as it were). That was to say legitimate at the same time dirty.

I also stayed out of Marcus's business. This was because I liked him, regardless of the dirty part of what he did. And I liked him not only because he was a nice guy, but mostly because he loved Daisy to distraction.

Daisy, as it tended to be with the Rock Chicks, was a little nuts. She looked like Dolly Parton, talked like her, dressed like Dolly would if she was on speed, and Daisy's heart was made of pure gold.

So I loved her, and that meant Marcus loving her and knocking himself out to give her a good life (after one that was *really* not so good) worked for me.

"Zano—" I started.

His voice was gentle and sweet when he stated, "We have to talk, baby."

"About what?" I asked, but I knew, and this was beginning to get hard.

I was real. I said it like it was. I wasn't into duplicity and avoidance (okay, maybe *a little* into duplicity, if the situation warranted it). But definitely not with someone who meant something to me. And regardless of the boundaries I was working to keep around our relationship, Ren meant something to me.

It took a moment to realize he didn't answer.

"Zano?" I called.

"You know about what," he stated, and as I mentioned, I did.

He said nothing.

I didn't either.

Then he came to a decision.

No, that wasn't strictly true.

It was then he came to a decision because I'd forced his hand.

"Don't like this shit, would never do it, but you give me no choice, Ally," he said and my heart lurched.

"What are you talking about?" I asked, thankful my voice sounded strong rather than pained, which was what my insides felt like.

"Ending things with a woman on the phone."

Oh God.

Shit.

Fuck!

"Ren—" I whispered.

"You're not willing to go there with me. You've made it clear, baby," he said, still gentle and sweet. "Why you need that, I don't know. I just know you do. I also know what I want for the future, and that includes wife and kids. So as much as I like what we got, it's important you know where I'm at. If you're not into exploring that kind of future with me, Ally, we gotta cut each other loose."

I had to give it to him, he sounded like he didn't like saying those words, and it was very clear he was trying to handle me with care. And I appreciated that.

Still, it hurt.

But he was right. We weren't going there.

So we had to cut each other loose.

"I... I have..." I stammered, shook myself mentally and physically and got my shit together. "I'm not ready for that Ren."

"Right," he whispered, and didn't hide his disappointment.

I closed my eyes tight and felt my throat constrict.

"Be safe," he said quietly. "And be happy, baby."

Oh God.

Shit.

Fuck!

"You too, Ren," I forced out through my tight throat.

"Yeah," he murmured. "Bye, Ally."

"Bye, Ren."

He disconnected.

I let my hand drop and stared at my steering wheel.

It took a while, a very long while, before I got myself together enough to turn the ignition and drive myself home.

That night and the nights after, I didn't sleep in my bed. I slept on my couch.

And I did this because the sheets smelled of Ren and I didn't have it in me to endure the memory of what we had.

But I also didn't have it in me to strip them and wash him away.

Chapter 5
Backbone

Rock Chick Rewind

One week later ...

I sat in my Mustang outside the Balducci brothers' pool hall.

I had my gun in my purse.

As Darius promised, he'd taken me to Zip's Gun Emporium. I'd picked out a little .22 I could fit in most of my bags and Darius arranged for Zip to open late so I could go to his range with no one around, thus no one to see me, and practice.

I also ran once a day (mostly, and I was right—I rocked running gear *and* those awesome headbands, though I was only beginning to rock running; that shit was not easy). I went to Zip's one or two nights a week (depending on my shifts at Brother's). And last week, to get my mind off Ren (though Darius didn't know why I was fired up to go), Darius had taken me down to C. Springs to run the warehouse maze.

This was also not easy, and I knew this because I went through the drill six times and shot at least one innocent each time. I felt like a moron until Darius told me he'd taken that trip down to C. Springs three times before he ran the drill and passed.

We were going back next week, but not for me to go back to the warehouse. For me to run the defensive/evasive driving course before the weather turned iffy seeing as it was September (or, as it went in Denver, since the weather was always iffy, *iffier*).

But I was there, outside the Balducci's pool hall, with my gun because last night, Ricky Balducci raped Sadie.

No, that wasn't right. He'd beat the shit out of her and then he raped her.

And I'd been mean to her.

I didn't know she was Hector's. I thought they'd be sworn enemies seeing as Hector was the undercover DEA agent who brought down Sadie's drug lord

Kristen Ashley

father (suffice to say, trouble—this time crazy, serious, heartbreaking trouble—had hit a Rock Chick).

I learned that morning she was not only his, but also that the reason I'd been mean to her—that she'd done something nasty to Daisy at a society party—did not happen.

Daisy was beside herself with fury and sadness. The first, because Marcus knew Sadie never talked trash about Daisy and he didn't tell her, for reasons I got but were now very distressing. The second because Daisy had liked Sadie before she thought she talked trash about her. They were friends. Daisy cut her out and now her friend had gotten raped.

And I'd been a bitch. A bitch to a petite, scared woman who looked like a fairy princess and came to my brother yesterday to get his protection.

I'd been a bitch.

God.

I closed my eyes tight. My hand fisting, everything in me beating back the desire to grab my purse with my gun, waltz into that pool hall and pistol whip Ricky Balducci, an asshole who'd beat the shit out of a fairy princess and violated her, to within an inch of his life

I fought back that urge and when I opened my eyes, automatically, I scanned my mirrors.

That was when I saw the hips in suit trousers approaching my car.

My body stilled.

I knew those hips.

I loved those hips.

I *missed* those hips.

I swallowed.

Those hips approached the passenger side and Ren's handsome face appeared in the window.

His eyes locked on mine and I stopped breathing.

He lifted his hand and tapped a knuckle on the window.

I sucked in needed breath, hit the locks then reached out and grabbed my purse, clearing it from the seat seconds before Ren's fine ass settled in it.

He slammed his door and turned to me.

"Hey," he said softly.

"Hey," I replied, but my voice sounded croaky so I cleared my throat.

"How you doin'?" he asked, still gentle.

"Good," I lied in answer. I was not good, not with him in my car looking beautiful and being sweet. Not with me being a bitch to a girl who'd been raped. Not simply knowing someone who'd been raped. "You?" I asked.

He looked at me, his eyes traveling down my torso before his head turned to look at the pool hall.

He came back to me. "Been better."

He knew Sadie. He also knew what happened to Sadie.

This was not a surprise. Marcus, Vito, and Sadie's now incarcerated dad, Seth Townsend, all occupied the upper echelons of Denver's criminal underworld. It would make sense they and their families would hobnob.

"Can I ask what you're doin' here, honey?" Ren requested.

I held his eyes and whispered, "You know."

He studied me a moment before nodding. He knew.

Then he said, "Let me deal with it."

On one hand, I liked this idea. I'd seen Ren in action against Luke. On the badass scale, Luke blew the lid off, totally redefining the scale. And Ren not only held his own against Luke, he matched him. It was a fair fight that didn't go long enough to declare a clear winner. Seeing this, I knew Ren could undoubtedly fuck Ricky Balducci up big time. Because if he could go *mano a mano* against Luke, he could kick anyone's ass.

And if he did, I wanted to watch.

On the other hand, I'd been a bitch to Sadie, a girl who was Hector's, which meant she was a Rock Chick (though she didn't know it yet), which meant she was going to be family. And I'd done it the day of the night she got raped.

I needed to make amends.

"Zano, I—"

"Let me deal with it, Ally."

"What are you gonna do?" I asked, and his anger hit the car, stifling me, just as his eyes flashed with a light that even *I* found scary.

Right.

There you go.

Ren was going to deal with it.

"Don't hesitate to make a mess," I invited, giving in, and I actually *felt* him relax as the heavy air shifted out of my Mustang.

"Dry cleaning blood out of suits costs a fuckin' whack," he replied.

Yikes!

57

I was absolutely not going to go there.

"Take care of yourself, honey," he said quietly, ending our conversation, ending our time together, reminding me he'd ended us and that I was the reason there was no us.

In other words, major *ouch*.

I powered through the hurt and nodded. "You too, Ren."

He continued to hold my eyes, and long moments passed. Those moments feeling like he was waiting for me to say something, do something.

I did neither.

Then he turned, opened the door and angled out.

I watched him saunter to the pool hall and kept watching, even after he disappeared through the door.

I did this with a knot in my stomach, something stuck in my throat.

Then I pulled my shit together. Something I'd had to do a lot since Ren entered my life, and more after he exited it.

I decided I'd find another way to make amends to Sadie, though I didn't know how I'd do that.

I just knew I would.

I turned the ignition, put my car into gear and drove away.

⇌

One month, one and a half weeks later...

I was at Sadie's art opening at her gallery, but a more apt way to put it was that I was in hell.

This was because Ren was there and he was with another woman.

This was also because he was avoiding me.

This was not surprising. We were done and he was with another woman. I got a look, a chin lift and that was it.

It was the classy thing to do, not ignoring me, not getting in my space and being sweet or cool, and thus reminding me we were over and all I was missing.

Still, it hurt.

But this was mostly because, even avoiding him, that didn't mean my eyes, against my strong directive, kept moving to him.

Therefore I'd caught him watching Ava.

Worse, he did it with a soft look on his face I'd never seen. I was too far away to be certain it was longing. I just knew it was *something*.

He was still hung up on her.

The only thing I had going for me was that I looked hot. My dress was awesome, showed enough skin and was tight enough to be slinky, but not enough of either to be slutty. And my high-heeled sandals were my own, and they were even better.

That was all I had.

Sadie and Hector were, I was hoping, heading toward the Rock Chick Reward. That was, everything got sorted and they moved into their version of happily ever after. There were still issues, all the Rock Chicks knew, and it wasn't only because of the Balducci brothers (all of them were giving Sadie problems), we just couldn't put our finger on what.

"You okay?" I heard from my side, and I turned my head and saw Indy there.

My best friend had lots of fabulous red hair and a lush body of the Ava variety. In other words, old-fashioned Hollywood bombshell: great rack, lots of ass, long legs and the ability to work them all in a huge way, as her current dress and strappy heels, which were (almost) as awesome as mine laid testimony to.

"Yeah," I told her.

She studied me closely. "You sure?"

"Sure I'm sure," I answered casually.

Indy didn't take her eyes off me.

She'd been my BFF for so long, we were so tight, we knew each other's deepest secrets (well, in Indy's case, only most of mine). We'd been through pretty much everything, so even with the additions of the Rock Chicks, I would never have a BFF who was more of the "B" than Indy. I loved her. I would lay down my life for her and that was no joke. I knew she would do the same for me.

I also knew her just as well as she knew me.

And right now, she knew I was full of shit.

She leaned in, her eyes never leaving mine, and started, "Honey, you haven't been——"

She didn't finish. This was because a brouhaha was commencing. That was to say, Sadie's loud voice was coming at us and she was being sarcastic and bitchy.

Not good.

Indy and I looked that way to see Sadie was into it with some woman who Sadie clearly did not like.

"Here we go," Indy murmured and looked at me.

I threw her a grin and did what we Rock Chicks always did.

Got close to a Rock-Chick-in-need in order to take her back.

And I was right. As the events unfolded, one after the other, it became clear something was still very wrong with Sadie. It wasn't that she wanted that outed. It was just that what happened gave her no choice. Being recently raped and consistently traumatized by four criminally insane brothers (literally, to *all* of that), it was time for the lid to be blown off.

And blow off it did.

It happened after Hector lost his mind when we all learned Sadie was secretly planning to move to Greece (Greece! What the fuck?) and he dragged her to her office.

No, that wasn't right. It happened after what happened in her office leaked out into the hall when Sadie came rushing out.

"*I'm protecting you!*" Sadie screamed at Hector, "Don't you get it? I'm protecting you!"

My head whipped around to the hall, and at her tone, my body went tight.

She went on screeching.

"You deserve better than me, Hector Chavez! You're a good man from a good family surrounded by good people. My father was a Drug King. He kills people! It's what I am, he *made* me. And Ricky Balducci raped and brutalized me. You know it. You saw it. *You were even there!* You saw me! You told me you'd never forget. You saw me! You're better than that and I know it. You deserve more than that. You don't think you do but you've got a tattoo on you that reminds you to think with your head, not your body. I don't want to be the next tattoo you get when you learn your lesson one day and realize what you've done. That you could have had better. That you could have had more. That you could have someone good and clean and right. Someone who belongs at your side. Not someone vile and ugly and tawdry and used that you should have never, ever, *ever* settled for!"

I watched, my heart bleeding at her words, as she yanked free of Hector and started running.

"Don't follow me," she shouted over her shoulder. She stopped and turned. "*Don't!*" she shrieked in a voice so shrill, it lacerated me.

My throat closed and I was weirdly paralyzed as others sprung into action when Sadie made a desperate dash through the gallery, grabbed something from a drawer and took off.

God, I fucking *hated* it when the Rock Chick Drama entered this stage. When the raw thing the Rock Chick was hiding was exposed in all its hideousness and we got to see inside to what we were actually battling.

Not that something like that happened every time. Not that I was there to witness it every time it happened. But I still hated it, whether I saw it or heard about it.

I was good at giving one-liners, making people laugh, giving support in my way. I could be gentle with the honesty. And I was always there, no matter what, no matter when, if they needed me.

But I had no healing hand, like Jules did (because she was a cool chick, but also a social worker). Or like Jet did (because she was shy, quiet and sweet and had a way about her). Or like Daisy did (because she had so much love, it leaked out of her pores and you couldn't help but feel better if it leaked on you).

So I had not only not made amends for being a bitch to Sadie, I had nothing to give to her right now. I didn't have the skills to get in there and make her see she was not even *close* to the things she saw in herself.

And that killed me.

"Ally."

My head jerked at that familiar, deep, sweet voice and I looked up at Ren.

He was staring down at me looking gorgeous and worried.

"You okay?" he asked.

"No," I whispered.

He lifted a hand, and it seemed like he was going to touch me but I moved before he could.

Fast.

As quick as my four inch stiletto heels could take me, I dashed to the counter where Sadie had her cash register.

I grabbed my bag.

And I got the fuck out of there.

Three hours later...

I sat in the dark on my ass in my living room. My back was to the wall, my knees up. I was still in my killer dress, but I'd taken off my heels.

The Rock Chick phone tree had been engaged so I'd learned that Sadie was okay. She had her thing, let it out, and then Duke had done his thing.

Duke worked at Fortnum's with us. In fact, Duke had been working at Fortnum's way before Indy inherited it from Grandma Ellen, so he was the veteran.

He was a Harley guy with a gray beard, long gray hair and a rough voice that somehow felt smooth on your soul whenever he used it (even if he was tearing you a new one while using it; I know it sounds crazy but it's true, trust me). He wore Harley tees (always), leather vests (occasionally) and rolled bandanas around his forehead (without fail).

And he was wise. Very much so.

Therefore, when the Rock Chicks came to the point in their drama where it was clear everyone needed to quit fucking around because they needed their shit sorted—tough love or gentle and sweet (as the case may be)—Duke stepped in.

So it was Duke who stepped in with Sadie and sorted her shit.

Duke could do that.

But not me.

I closed my eyes, shook my head to get my mind off that path, and opened my eyes, pointing my thoughts in a new direction.

I stared into the dark at the shadowy shapes in my apartment and commenced trying to figure out what the fuck was up with me.

And not why Sadie's outburst that night so deeply affected me.

I sensed I wasn't ready to face that.

No, I thought about where my life was leading me.

I gazed at the shadows.

I liked my apartment. That said, it wasn't much to write home about, but since I wasn't there often, it didn't need to be.

The building was two-story and built in the fifties. The rooms were not spacious and there was no personality. Though, the last couple of years, the landlord had pulled out all the dull, uninspired bathrooms and kitchens and put in new dull, uninspired bathrooms and kitchens.

Not much, but it was something.

He'd also jacked up the rent.

Annoying but not surprising.

Recently, though, my unit had been getting a facelift that came all from me.

I had new cushiony, awesome furniture that invited you to sink in and stay forever (major discount from a person who used my services who knew a person who owned a furniture store). I had a new flat screen TV (ditto on the discount, as you know). Due to gift certificates from other "clients", I had new kitchen implements (not that I cooked much, seeing as I was never home; still, gadgets were gadgets, and everyone needed as many gadgets as they could get), new bathroom towels and sheets (total lush—I should so totally have gone the way of expensive towels and sheets *ages* ago; alas, a bartender/barista couldn't usually afford luxury).

Also due to my activities, I had more shoes and clothes in my closet and a collection of gift cards of a variety of denominations to restaurants, bars and movie theaters.

All payments for my services.

All making life that little bit sweeter.

I'd done the defensive/evasive driving course and kicked its ass. I was all *over* defensive/evasive maneuvers in a vehicle and could not wait to do the chase program. And with more practice at Zip's and wisdom from Darius, I'd also cleared the house in C. Springs without killing one innocent.

This shit was it for me.

I loved doing it and I was good at it.

And it made life better in a variety of ways.

So I didn't understand what was holding me back from going whole hog, getting licensed and putting out a shingle.

And maybe more importantly, with all that going so well, why did I think I was missing something?

That you could have someone good and clean and right.

Sadie's words haunted me, yanking me back to the path I was avoiding, and I closed my eyes.

I had to get on making amends. I had to be certain, in my way, to make sure Sadie knew she was part of the family.

She seemed to be getting there.

But I'd sensed she wasn't there entirely.

And tonight proved I was right.

On that thought, a knock came at my door.

I looked to the door. I didn't want to get it. I had no cases brewing. I'd cleared the slate when Sadie's shit hit so I could focus on that.

However, since I'd gotten home that night, my phone had been ringing. All the calls were from the Rock Chicks to natter about what happened and what we were going to do next about Sadie. So once I got the "all's good" with Sadie, I'd turned off my ringer.

Now someone was at my door.

I knew one thing. Behind that door was not a Rock Chick. They all had their Hot Bunch boys at home and it was past bedtime. They would be nowhere near my door.

So it was probably someone who needed me.

I wished I had an office with a hotline. This hitting my pad business, interrupting me while I was sitting on my ass in a sexy dress in a dark apartment evaluating my life was not working for me. Not that that happened all the time, but once was enough.

The knock came again, and when I gave it time and there was more knocking, I knew they weren't going to let up. So it would seem I had to haul my ass off the floor and tell them to take a hike.

This, I did.

Except when I got to the peephole, I saw Ren out there.

He wasn't looking down the hall this time. He was looking at the door-knob as if he expected to hear the locks turning.

Fuck.

I pulled away from the peephole and rested my forehead against the door.

He knocked again.

Fuck!

Okay, I was Ally Nightingale. I figured whatever this was wasn't going to be a lot of fun, but I didn't shy away from anything.

Sucking in breath, I unlocked the door and opened it.

Ren stood there in all his glory.

I swallowed the lump that suddenly clogged my throat and asked, "What are you doing here?"

"You didn't look good after Sadie's thing, honey," he answered.

I didn't look good because I wasn't good.

And he'd noticed and done something about it.

Why couldn't he be a dick?

I mean, seriously.

I didn't ask that.

I asked, "Where's your date?"

"I was worried about you. You weren't pickin' up your phone. Dropped her and came to you."

Again.

Why couldn't he be a dick?

Seriously.

"You still don't look good, baby," he whispered, and it happened.

What happened was something that never happened. Not to me. I was a Nightingale. I was a cop's daughter. I was the daughter of a cop's wife. I was tough. It was born in me *and* bred in me.

So it took serious shit, like Indy marrying my brother—something she and I both wanted since *forever*—to make me lose it.

But right then, I lost it.

I felt it happen and had no hope of stopping it. The wet forming in my eyes, making my vision bright. Then the tear breaking loose and gliding down my cheek. Then one on the other side.

"Ally," Ren murmured, eyes to my cheeks.

"I was mean to her," I whispered.

His eyes came to mine.

"Baby," Ren whispered back.

Another tear.

"I was mean to her, and that night, she was raped."

"Honey."

Another tear. "She looks like a fairy princess and she was *raped.*"

Then I totally lost it, taking two steps back to escape at the same time I stupidly lifted my hands to cover my face and hide my emotion (which would make escaping difficult, seeing as I couldn't *see*).

But I got no further.

The light from the hall was extinguished because Ren was inside, and I knew this because I was being held tight in his arms.

As I felt the strength of his arms surrounding me, the heat from his body penetrating, one of those hiccoughing sobs burned up my throat and made my body buck in his embrace.

God!

I so totally hated crying!

His arms separated, one going low and again tight around my waist. The other one moved so his hand could stroke my back and I heard him encourage into the top of my hair, "Talk to me."

I didn't know why I did it. I just knew I needed to do it and he was the only one around.

So I did it.

I pressed my hands and face into his chest and let it all hang out.

"I thought she'd been mean to Daisy. I thought she hated Hector. And I came to Lee's office the day she came to Lee's office to ask for his protection." My head shot back and I cried, "And I was mean!"

His hand soothingly stroking my back (and I had to admit, I'd lost it, but it still was soothing) moved to cup my jaw and he replied, "I know what went down with Daisy and Sadie, and also Sadie and Hector, and Sadie's not the kind of girl who lets people in. So at the time, honey, you couldn't think anything different."

"She got raped that night, Ren!" I stated loudly.

"I know, baby," he said comfortingly.

"Now she's a Rock Chick and you heard her tonight!" I kept talking loudly, tears sliding from my eyes. "And I haven't figured out how to make amends."

"You and your posse taking her in and having her back is doing that, Ally," he pointed out.

"Obviously not fast enough!" I returned. "But none of my posse was ugly to her. Except me and Shirleen, but Shirleen got her chance to make amends. Sadie even *asked* for her."

And this was true. Shirleen was Darius's aunt, Lee's receptionist, and also a Rock Chick of the Daisy variety (which meant she wasn't attached to a Hot Bunch boy, but she was a Rock Chick all the same).

She'd been snippy with Sadie that day. But when Sadie finally reported her rape, she'd asked for Shirleen to be there.

"Ally, baby, what happened with Sadie tonight didn't have anything to do with you."

"I know that," I snapped, yanking out of his arms and taking a step away. "But she..." I shook my head. "God, that monster broke her wrist. Gashed her face. Made her feel tawdry."

"Come back to me, honey," Ren urged.

I shook my head again. "No. I can't." I stopped talking, started pacing then kept babbling. "I have to sort this out in my head."

I continued pacing and Ren didn't say anything.

This didn't last very long before he said something.

"Jesus, you *really* can't deal with being mean," Ren murmured incredulously.

I stopped pacing and whipped around to face him. It was dark but I still could feel he was watching me.

"Not to someone who doesn't deserve it!" I yelled. "I'm all for a smackdown if a bitch is a bitch. But Sadie is no bitch."

"No, she's not," Ren agreed cautiously.

"So that means I kicked a sister when that sister was low. I don't do that shit, Zano."

"Fuck, you're back to Zano," he muttered.

"What?" I asked sharply.

"Nothing, honey. Just come here, will you?"

I shook my head again. "No. I..." my eyes narrowed on him and I re-asked an earlier question. "What are you doing here?"

He gave me the same answer. "I was worried about you."

"You ditched your date because you were worried about me?"

"Yes," he answered immediately.

Shit.

What did I do with that?

"Ally, look at me," he ordered.

I was looking at him, or at least I was looking at his shadow. But he sensed I wasn't focused, and how he could sense that, I had no clue. It weirded me out and made me feel all warm inside at the same time.

Still, I focused on him and he sensed when I did that, too.

Yikes.

When I did, hesitantly and gently, he asked, "Did something like what happened to Sadie happen to you?"

Oh God.

He thought I'd been raped.

That was why he was worried.

I couldn't let him think that so I replied softly, "No, Ren."

"Back to Ren," he whispered.

Oh shit.

He was trying to figure me out.

I couldn't let that happen.

Okay, time to end this.

"I—" I started to do that, but that was as far as I got.

"Shut up and listen to me."

I clamped my mouth shut, and I did this with a bit of surprise and not a bit of temper since he'd suddenly turned macho alpha on me.

Before I could start yelling, he started talking.

"I don't know what's up with you, but tonight, watching you at the gallery in a dress that succeeded in making me fight my dick getting hard faster than that other one, and your response to what went down with Sadie, I don't give a fuck."

He'd been watching me?

When?

And how did I miss that?

Ren kept talking.

"You take the backs of that crew of yours like your blood flows through their veins. Indy may be their foundation, Daisy and Shirleen the emotional support. But you're the backbone."

Jeez.

How did he know so much about the Rock Chicks?

And why did what he said make me feel even *warmer* inside?

And last, why the hell was he saying this shit at all?

He didn't make me wait for an answer to the last.

"You don't need to make amends to Sadie. You're set on giving her a lifetime of sisterhood the like she's never had before and never even dreamed of having. That'll do it, so you can let that go."

That was all nice, and true, and made me feel better, but unfortunately he wasn't done.

"You've got your way, the way you are and the way you are with the ones you care about. And that tells me, a man gets in there, you give that to him, the children you give him, that man will be all kinds of lucky. And I've decided we're gonna see if that man is me."

Oh my God!

Was he crazy?

He'd just been gazing softly at Ava (well, not "just", but not three months ago either!) and now he was saying this shit to me.

"Zano, we're done," I reminded him.

"You can be done, but I'm not. So we're gonna explore this and see where it leads until we both make a decision we agree on about where it's heading."

Oh crap.

Now he was giving me the macho alpha bossy shit.

"Zano, I—"

"Shut it."

My back snapped straight. "Don't you tell me to shut it, Ren Zano."

I watched his shadowy head shake before he stated, "Baby, you're gorgeous. The way you wear a dress is goddamned foreplay. The way you give me everything and nothing, making you a challenge only a real man would accept, is all kinds of hot. The way you give as good as you get in bed, totally unselfish at the same time phenomenally greedy... *fuck,*" he growled, and I felt that growl straight in my happy place. "You're the best I've ever had, Ally. Bar none. And the way you love, stubborn, tough, unshakable, is unbelievably fuckin' beautiful. And still you're a serious pain in my ass. But I found, not havin' you, I got off on the pain. I missed it. So I'm takin' it back and we'll see how it goes."

"I know how it'll go," I returned. "Nowhere. We're done, Zano."

"Tell me you haven't missed what we had," he demanded.

I clamped my mouth shut, because even for self-preservation's sake, I couldn't utter that colossal of a lie and I was totally down with lying if the situation warranted it (or when it didn't and I just needed to save my own hide).

He knew it, damn it all to hell, and I knew he did when he whispered, "Come here, Ally."

I put my hands on my hips and stated, "If you want to rewind and start up again, I'll consider it. But, pointing out, we're rewinding, not rewriting. We're fuck buddies, Zano. We enjoy each other. You go your way. I go mine."

"We were never fuck buddies, Ally."

I wished.

I also rolled my eyes.

"Now come here," he went on.

I rolled my eyes back to hm.

"Tell me, exactly, why it is *I* have to walk the three feet that separates us?" I asked.

He was on me in a flash, which meant I was in his arms, plastered to his body. He had one hand in my hair cupping the back of my head, holding it steady for whatever he wanted to do to me.

Great.

That was on me. I'd challenged the alpha and there I was.

I knew better.

One could say I was seriously off my game tonight.

God!

And he felt good. So freaking good. Hard with his heat burning into me.

He was also in a suit.

I was screwed.

"Do you agree to fuck buddies?" I pressed, even as my hands lifted to his biceps and felt the rich material of his suit jacket.

Nice.

"Absolutely not," he replied, right before he dropped his head and I felt his lips on my neck.

Very nice.

"Zano, we should get this straight before we start this up again," I told him, even as my hands slid up his arms to his shoulders then around his neck.

His lips slid to my lips and he invited, "You make your plays, Ally. I'll make mine. And we'll see where this is gonna lead."

Unfortunately, that sounded all kinds of fun.

And dangerous.

Both things I liked.

Too much.

Crap.

"I know where it's gonna lead," I retorted.

Suddenly I felt my stomach drop, my lungs evacuate all oxygen and my heart skip a beat.

This was because I also felt his lips smile against mine right before he said, with great authority, "So do I."

My inner thighs quivered and my happy place got really happy.

Then Ren quit messing around and kissed me.

After that, he *really* quit messing around and did a lot of other things to me.

And I was right.

It was all kinds of fun.

It was also dangerous.

And I loved every fucking second.

Chapter 6

Fuck Buddies Give Christmas Presents?

Rock Chick Rewind

Christmas Eve ...

Ren's voice came in my ear me. "Jesus, you're shitfaced at your brother's wedding."

I turned my eyes to see him close. So close, as I turned, he had to pull slightly away.

But he pulled away only slightly.

We were at Roxie and Hank's wedding. Do *not* ask me why Roxie invited Ren to her wedding. Though, truth be told, even though it seemed to go against all the laws of the universe (or at least *my* universe, save, of course, being fuck buddies with Ren), somehow along the way the Rock Chick tribe had gotten tight with all the Zanos. But I didn't think they were *that* tight.

All I knew was that Tod said any wedding needed all the hot guys it could get because love was in the air during a wedding and the girl who caught the bouquet needed something to dream about. And Ren was undeniably a hot guy you could dream about.

By the way, when Roxie tossed her bouquet, I was doing tequila shooters at the bar.

Therefore I was feeling very happy and this didn't only have to do with the tequila shooters. It had to do with the fact that my big brother and my good friend were all kinds of happy.

What I was not was shitfaced.

And I decided to inform Ren of this fact.

"I'm far from shitfaced, Zano."

"You're hammered," he returned

Hammered was not shitfaced. I was a bartender and lived the life of a rock star, I would know. I had studied the levels of insobriety both practically and observationally. Hammered was three steps down from shitfaced. There was smashed, blotto, and wasted to get through. I had at least six tequila shooters to go before I got even close to shitfaced.

I did not take the time to educate Ren about this.

Instead, I decided to get annoyed (as was my wont around Ren) and narrowed my eyes at him.

As was his wont, that was to say totally oblivious to my dangerous eye narrowing, he stated, "We have to talk."

We "had to talk" a lot. Ren's Talks were becoming part of our everyday repertoire. Though it should be noted that talking with Ren and *talking* with Ren were two different things.

We talked when we ate together at his place, or takeout at mine, before we fucked each other's brains out. We also talked while I ate the breakfasts Ren cooked for me (his place) or he ate the toast I toasted for him (my place) before we both tackled our days.

We *talked* when Ren got whiff of some case I was on and didn't like it. These Talks occurred after a fight about the same thing which led to no-holds-barred sex, sleeping tangled up in each other and after we woke up and were in bed.

But I could tell by the tone of his voice this was not a talk but a *Talk*.

I knew from details received from the Rock Chicks that they, too, had Talks with their badasses. Jet called them Eddie Chats. Roxie called the ones she had with Hank Conversations.

These talks always centered around the respective badass wanting his Rock Chick to bend to his will in some way. And they were usually successful in getting what they wanted though it wasn't always the talking that got them what they wanted. They tended to shift tactics and the way they did got them what they wanted. It also gave the Rock Chick what she wanted so although she bitched, she didn't quibble.

Ren's Talks were different. He shifted tactics during the preceding fight to end it by initiating mind-blowing sex and could shift tactics during the Talk but only when the Talk degenerated into a Fight. And although Ren's Talks happened frequently, they always happened at the same time in the same place and he never got what he wanted.

Partly because I was stubborn.

Okay, that was mostly why.

I was lucky Ren's Talks were different. Jet's Chats and Roxie's Conversations could happen any time, willy-nilly, so they could be unprepared.

I always knew when it was coming.

So this suggested Talk was outside the norm and at my brother's wedding. Therefore, in my opinion, I considered it a highly inappropriate sneak attack.

"We're not talking now," I denied.

He, as usual, ignored me.

"You've been hanging with Kevin James."

This was true. I had.

Kevin "The Kevster" James was a pothead. He was hilarious. He was clueless. His favorite movie was *The Big Lebowski* which said it all about him and all that said was good. And he was a friend.

However, lately I had not been hanging with The Kevster as a friend, sitting around with bowls of munchies while The Kevster smoked a doobie and we watched Jeff Bridges floating over Los Angeles.

We were hanging with a purpose.

"The Kevster's a friend," I shared with Ren.

At my words, Ren's brows shot together and he asked, "*The Kevster?*"

"His preferred handle," I explained.

Ren looked to the ceiling. I figured he did this because Ren might be a member of a crime family but he reeked class. He likely had no friends with "handles." Or that smoked doobies. And I didn't ask because I was scared of the answer, but there was a high probability Ren would not like *The Big Lebowski* and that might mean I'd have to question his taste. Since he very much liked the taste of me, I didn't want to do that.

"We've been friends ages," I went on and Ren looked back to me, now with brows raised.

"So he's not helping you find the grow house that friend of your other friend's sister thinks her son has set up in Littleton?"

Jeez, how did he find out all this crap?

I decided I didn't want to know and I also decided not to answer.

He got closer and reminded me, "Ally, we had a deal. You do this shit for people, you stay away from the drug trade."

We did have that deal, kind of. The "kind of" part was that during a Talk, I'd agreed to that, but I was also lying when I agreed.

"Pot isn't drugs," I pointed out. "It's flora. It's natural. And it's now legal."

"This grow house you're lookin' for isn't legal," he shot back.

This was true.

I again didn't reply.

He got even closer and ordered, "Baby, drop this case."

Uh-oh.

He was getting bossy.

I wasn't a big fan of bossy.

"Zano, I made a deal," I returned. "I'm not dropping this case. Especially since we're close to ending it."

"Drop it," he semi-repeated.

"I'm not dropping it," I snapped.

"This kid you're lookin' for, he just sat down with some serious players to supply their demand. Takes him out of having to deal with dealing. He just gets to grow and rake in the cash. This is an escalation for him that at his age with his inexperience is all kinds of dangerous. You do not wanna get involved in that shit."

That was not good news.

But as Darius told me (more than once), that was also not my problem

"You're right. I don't," I agreed (to that part). "But getting involved in that is not part of the deal I made. He's nineteen years old and his mother wants to know if he's growing weed. I find out, get the proof, hand it over to her, she does with it what she will and I'm out."

"And you think, she blows the whistle on her kid to teach him a lesson, his deal goes south, those players aren't gonna look your way for being the instrument of that loss of income?"

"Shit happens in crime, Zano, and if they're experienced players, they know to roll with the punches."

His face set and his jaw got hard. "I'm sure they do. It's just that I'd rather it wasn't *you* who took those punches."

I lost more of my patience.

"I'll be fine," I said for the ten gazillionth time.

"Yeah, because your brothers and their boys have labeled you untouchable. But there's gonna be a time where you piss someone off who won't give a shit what firepower you have at your back."

This, I knew, was true. Darius told me.

It didn't piss me off that Lee and the Hot Bunch made it clear on the streets I had their protection. This was mostly because they were staying distant and not getting in my business. It was also because it was sweet.

But I wasn't stupid and this constant refrain from Ren was inference I was.

"Tell me, Zano, if Lee was nosing into this for a client, would you think it was reckless for him to do so?"

"I think you're convinced you're bulletproof like your brother and his boys but they're not, Stark getting a gut shot proved that. You're *definitely* not because I don't care how often you're target shooting at Zip's, you got no play in the field."

I knew this was going nowhere and it was making me beyond annoyed so I also knew it was time to shut it down.

"We're not talking about this, Zano," I declared.

"Ally, we're talkin' about it until you see reason."

"I'm not being unreasonable." My voice was getting higher and tighter. "It's *my* life and what *I* like to do. And it's none of *your* business."

His eyes quickly skimmed my green velvet strapless dress-clad frame (Roxie, totally stylin' with her bridesmaid dresses; they were *the shit*) then came back to my face and he started the shift into Asshole Speak.

"That body's mine and I don't want it filled with bullets and tossed in the Platte. So, for the hundredth fuckin' time, babe, it *is* my business."

"My body isn't yours," I snapped.

"You could have fooled me, the way you went wild for me last night and let me do *all* I wanted to do to you, I got creative and the number of breathy Rens I got meant you seriously got off on it."

Total Asshole Speak.

Nothing flipped my switch like Asshole Speak.

And having not a small amount of tequila in my system, even in my bridesmaid dress, at my brother's wedding, I was not down with Asshole Speak and I was Ally Nightingale. So I was going to do something about it.

Therefore, I took a step back, cocked my arm and let 'er rip, shouting, "Go to hell, Ren Zano!"

Unfortunately, Ren caught my fist, kept tight hold and twisted it behind my back. This had the further unfortunate result of my body slamming into his and Ren being close enough to put his mouth to my ear.

"Challenge accepted," he whispered there.

Oh shit.

I struggled against his hold.

Seriously. When was I going to remember he was a macho alpha Italian hothead and I needed to be cunning, not reactive? Though, this would likely necessitate me laying off the tequila and I liked my tequila.

He moved to my side, keeping his and my arm behind my back and marched me out of the ballroom at the Denver Performing Arts Complex where Hank and Roxie's reception was taking place.

"Let go of me, Zano," I hissed, partly humiliated (with only myself to blame; still, I blamed Ren), mostly infuriated.

"Not a chance."

I yanked at my arm to no avail as he pushed us outside into the cold air.

Once there and with no one around and therefore not able to make a (further) scene, I wrenched my arm to get free, shouting, "Let go!" and found myself shuffled down the wide walkway, pressed into the side of the building with Ren's mouth on mine, his tongue in my mouth and both his hands at my ass.

Hell.

This meant Ren was done fighting and ready for other things.

And this also meant Ren could nonverbally talk me into being ready for those other things.

This, in the cold Colorado December air, he did with mouth, tongue and hands.

He spent some time doing this. I spent that time enjoying it. And when his mouth finally lifted from mine, I was enjoying it so much I went after it to keep it.

When I didn't get it back, my eyes slowly opened and I found my hands were under his suit jacket. One was pressed tight to the muscle of his back. The other was pressed tight to his hard ass.

Nice.

I also found his lips were quirking.

Annoying.

"That body isn't mine?" he whispered.

I made no response and not just because I was breathing too heavily to speak.

"Least that mouth is." Ren kept whispering.

I found my voice then.

"Kiss my ass, Zano," I whispered back.

That got me a smile which meant Ren got a squeeze.

His smile got bigger.

My heart lurched.

"I can do that," he stated.

I rolled my eyes even as my happy place quivered because he could, he had and I liked it when he did.

Still smiling, he bent his head and kissed my neck. Sliding his lips up to my ear, he murmured, "Let's go home."

Before I could say anything, he grabbed my hand and walked me quickly to his Jaguar (seriously, he was a bossy jerk, but his ride was sah-*weet*).

You will note, I didn't protest.

Because I might have been guarding my heart.

But I was absolutely not guarding my body.

⋈

Christmas Morning…

I woke, naked, tangled up with Ren in his bed.

I had my face stuffed in the side of Ren's neck, an arm thrown over his stomach and a leg thrown over his thigh.

He had an arm around me and the instant I woke, it tightened and his deep voice rumbled, "Merry Christmas, baby."

I closed my eyes hard.

What the hell was I doing?

Just as quickly as my mind asked it, I decided Christmas day was not the time to explore that question.

I opened my eyes, and being a holiday person, a family person, and a person who found every reason possible to party and/or celebrate, I didn't have it in me to lay down the boundaries during the most joyous day of the year.

Kristen Ashley

Not with Ren close and his voice warm and rumbly on Christmas morning.

Therefore, I lifted my head, looked into his beautiful eyes and replied quietly, "Merry Christmas, Ren."

His eyes dropped to my mouth as his arm got even tighter and dragged me up his chest.

But once we were face to face, it was me that went in for the Christmas kiss. And it was a kiss that I wasn't sure Jesus would approve of, but to me, it was heavenly.

When we broke the kiss, Ren lifted a hand to my jaw and said, "Let's get this part over with, honey."

Oh shit.

Before I could intervene in order to stop him from starting a joyous day in a non-joyous way, he went on.

"Before I give you your present and you take off to be with your family, promise me right now, and mean it, that you'll stay away from dealers, growers, manufacturers, suppliers and transporters."

Oh my God!

He got me a present?

"Ally," he called and I focused on him.

I took in a breath, holding the Christmas spirit close.

In other words, I replied calmly, "Ren, when I promise to help, I have to do whatever it takes to do the job."

He studied me. I waited for him to commence the Talk or go straight into the Fight.

Apparently Ren was feeling the Christmas spirit too as he didn't do either.

Instead, he held me to him as he mumbled, "Not gonna get into this shit on Christmas," and he twisted toward his nightstand.

He opened the drawer. I held my breath. Then he pulled out a small, jewelry-sized, exquisitely wrapped present, complete with bow.

Jewelry.

I was a Rock Chick. I accepted gifts of all forms.

I also gave them the same way.

But I never thought I'd be a girl who felt like I felt right then when a man was about to give her jewelry. And I didn't even care what was in that wrapped package.

It was indeed the thought that mattered.

And jewelry from a man, that man being Ren, said a lot about what he thought of me.

I pressed my lips together.

Ren settled on his back and offered me the present.

"Open it, honey."

I swallowed, looked into his eyes and took it.

As best I could still leaning into him, I pulled off the bow and wrap and unearthed a familiar blue box with a white ribbon.

Oh crap.

My throat got scratchy when I untied the ribbon and flipped open the box.

In it was a silver pendant on a chain.

The pendant was in the shape of a guitar.

Holy crap.

Tiffany's didn't only do elegant. It did *cool*.

Totally righteous.

"Ren," I whispered.

"I'll take that as you likin' it."

I didn't like it.

I *loved* it. It was *perfect* for me.

My eyes moved from the pendant to him. "Thank you."

His eyes were soft and sweet on me. "You're welcome, baby."

I pressed my lips together again then leaned in and pressed them to his mouth. Before I pulled away, he touched his tongue to my lower lip which made me shiver both internally and externally.

It was the kind of shiver Ren usually felt and did something about. But before he could, I pulled away, leaned into him to put the pendant on his nightstand then pushed further over him so my hips were at his gut and I was hanging over the side of the bed.

I reached under it to where I hid my present days ago (don't get excited— I hadn't since learned how to pick a lock—Ren had given me his key and his security code).

I pulled it out, pushed up and sat on the side of my hip as I set his present on his stomach.

"Fuck," he murmured, eyes on his present.

"Well, that wasn't the response expected," I remarked.

Kristen Ashley

He pushed up to rest against the headboard but did so looking at me, eyes warm but lips quirking, all the while asking, "So, fuck buddies give Christmas presents?"

It was Christmas. I was *not* going to get annoyed.

I told myself this, smiled and said, "Shut up.'"

He smiled back. My heart squeezed and he opened his present.

Then he burst out laughing when he shook out what was inside.

"Do not take this as me supporting your Bears habit," I warned and his warm dancing eyes came to me. "But Sweetness is Sweetness and everyone is allowed to worship at the shrine of Walter Payton."

This I'd proved by giving him a number 34 Bears jersey.

Ren's hand shot out, hooked around my neck, and he pulled me to him for a hard, closed-mouth kiss.

When he let me back an inch, he said softly, "Thank you, honey."

The way he said that hit me someplace deep, where he lived in me, where I kept him and what I wished we could be.

I kept it there. I locked it there. And part of me hoped I'd have those slices of our times together for eternity.

"You're welcome," I mumbled.

Then the jersey was crushed between us because Ren was on me, his hands were all over me, and I was on my back in his bed.

"Christmas quickie," he murmured into my neck.

Excellent.

My hands started moving on his skin.

His head came up and his eyes, lit with humor, caught mine.

"And, just sayin', babe, you lock my pendant away 'cause you don't want the questions the Rock Chicks will fire at you when they see my present around your neck, that's cool. I'll wait 'til you let me in for you to wear it."

He *so* knew me.

Everything.

That was a bit scary.

What was scarier was that he knew me in all my stubborn crazy, and it seemed he found it amusing.

I reminded myself it was Christmas and I was not going to get annoyed.

But even if it was Christmas, I couldn't allow myself to hope.

82

So I just rolled my eyes.

On the downward roll, he was kissing me. While doing that, an extremely proficient multi-tasker in bed, he commenced doing other things with me.

It was the best beginning of a Christmas ever.

Like a dream.

⇥⇤

The rest of the day wouldn't go so well as the Rock Chicks, Hot Bunch, Tex, Duke and a variety of other people witnessed my scene with Ren at Roxie and Hank's wedding and they were in my business about it.

I'd had some experience staving off such enquiries so it wasn't tough to keep the wolves at bay.

The problem was, after that scene, the Rock Chicks were on the scent. And this was not good.

But I couldn't concentrate on that. So I put it off (and put it off and then more putting it off) and decided to face that particular music if and when the time came.

I had enough on my hands dealing with Ren and me being fuck buddies.

Or, as Ren saw it, Ren and me being a *Ren and me*.

A game where I made my plays, Ren made his.

A game where our plays were the same even when I tried to convince myself they were different.

A game that would end on a morning in May in a moderately priced motel in a small Colorado Mountain town.

And it ended decisively.

Fast Forward—Hit Play

Chapter 7

Unconscious

May in a moderately priced motel in a small Colorado Mountain town...

I got into the bedroom, my hands on my jeans and was about to shove a foot through when they were yanked clean away.

I reared up and made a grab for them as Ren clipped, "Ally, what the fuck?"

"Give me my jeans!" I snapped loudly but he held them away.

Thus began a stand up tussle that included some slapping and grabbing (me), defensive maneuvers (Ren); my part desperate, his part possibly confused. Finally, he tossed the jeans behind him and since he was a tall, powerfully-built Italian hothead standing between me and my jeans, an obstruction I was not likely to breach, I grunted in frustration and shoved his chest (also in frustration).

He took two steps back and lifted both his hands, palms out my way.

"Right. Enough. Calm down and tell me what the fuck you're talkin' about," he demanded.

I locked my eyes with his.

"You fought over her that night."

His head jerked and he asked, "What?"

"That night!" I shouted. "That night we hooked up. You fought with Luke over Ava."

Suddenly, his body went completely still, as did the air in the room, and his eyes didn't leave me but they'd gone funny as he whispered, "Seriously?"

"Seriously," I hissed.

He shook his head, not in the negative, like he was trying to clear it.

Then he asked disbelievingly, "You're tellin' me we've been in each other's space for over a year and you're throwin' this shit in my face *now?*"

"Well, if that's not enough..." I shot back instantly, slamming my hands on my hips, something Ren's eyes watched before they came back to mine and I saw they were heating.

This was a warning signal I'd made a habit of not heeding. And at that point, I did the same and kept right on talking.

"There was the night at the art gallery where you said you had eyes on me but I never caught your eyes on me. But I *did* see you *gazing* at Ava!"

I sounded like a jealous bitch. I knew it. And I didn't care.

Because the big bossy jerk asked me to Ava's wedding!

Those eyes I was talking about narrowed and he returned, "I might have looked at Ava, Ally, but fuck, only because she was there."

"You didn't *look*, Zano, you *gazed*."

He blinked then asked, "Jesus, have you lost your mind?"

"No." I answered. "I'm a woman and I *know*."

"You know," he replied.

"Yep," I bit out. "I know."

"You know, for a year I've been bangin' you, busting my ass to find a way in with you, you gave me every sign I was succeeding… and before you open your mouth to deny it, I'll remind you about Christmas morning," he warned me.

Since I'd opened my mouth to deny it, at his reminder, I snapped it shut.

He kept going.

"And that entire fuckin' year you've been thinkin' I'm in love with another woman and you didn't say anything?"

God.

Was he serious?

"What do I say, Zano?" I retorted. "What questions do I ask when I don't want the fucking answers?"

"If you'd asked, you might have found you wanted the answers," he fired back.

Then, all Italian hothead badass, he lost it.

Lifting a hand, he tapped the tips of his fingers to his temple and jerked his hand out at the same time leaning into me and shouting, "You've totally lost your goddamned mind!"

"You know I haven't," I snapped.

"No," he clipped as he turned. His movements rough with suppressed anger, he stalked to my jeans, still talking. "What I know is, I wasted a goddamn year on a lunatic. Jesus. Fuck me," he bit out, bending and tagging my jeans. He turned and tossed them to me, continuing, "You hide it well, Ally. All that fucking crazy under all that hot. You had me snowed, thinkin', you allowed me to dig deep, I'd get the warm and sweet with the hot, not a hot fuckin' *mess*."

86

I'd caught my jeans and I had nothing to say to that remark but no chance to say it before he prowled by me, his anger now at such an extreme that his movements were fluid as his adrenaline flowed.

And he kept talking.

"You wanna go. Go. Be my guest, honey." He bent and grabbed his own jeans, tugging them on and not looking at me. "You want this over, you get it, 'cause now, with this, I see I've wasted a year on your bullshit, and honest to Christ, I never wanna lay eyes on your jacked ass again."

Ouch.

That hurt.

No, that wasn't right. It killed.

But I took his invitation.

And not only because it was the only option open to me.

Also because it was the smartest.

As fast as I could, I dressed and made sure I had my phone and all my belongings (not that I came with many, Ren dragged my ass there in another Italian hotheaded tizzy).

But I knew Darius and Brody were staying in the same hotel, I just didn't know their room numbers and I needed to get from here, to one of their rooms, then home, and fast (my pick, Darius).

But at the door, because he didn't get me, I decided before we were *over,* he was going to fucking *get me.*

Hand on the knob, I turned to him, dredging up what had been haunting me for over a year. Something that had killed the hope I had for my own kickass Rock Chick fairytale. Something that taught me the death of hope was the worst thing you could experience.

I saw he was pulling his shirt over his head and started, "That night, beer and bourbon and you liking the Bears?"

He yanked his shirt down and twisted only his neck so his burning eyes locked on me but he didn't turn to face me.

I sucked in breath as his gaze boiled away my flesh.

Then I did what I always did. I pulled it together, straightened my spine and held his eyes.

"The next morning, I woke up happy. So happy I was fucking *smiling.* It was the best date I ever had and it wasn't even a date."

That muscle in his jaw jumped but he didn't say anything.

I didn't need him to.

My voice quieter but no less emotional, I laid it out.

"Naked with you in your bed, smiling to myself and happy, you pressed into me, curled your hand around my breast and said Ava's name in my hair."

I watched his face blank even as his chin jerked back.

"So think what you want but I know I'm not jacked," I whispered. "That, Ren, when a woman lies naked, thus exposed, in a man's arms, when all she's thinking about his him, and he calls her another woman's name, *that's* how she knows."

And with that, I was done.

I turned, whipped off the chain, twisted the handle and pulled open the door.

I got it open halfway before Ren's hand landed palm flat on the door. I was pulling but he was stronger. Thus the doorknob slipped out of my hand and the door slammed shut.

Before I could take a breath, I was pressed front to the door with Ren's heat pressed in behind me. Further defeating any chance of retreat, his hand snaked across my belly and his arm turned to iron.

Great.

"Let me go," I snapped.

His lips came to my ear. "Baby—"

"*Let me go!*" I shouted, trying to yank away but his other arm wrapped high across my chest and he held me tighter, closer, his lips not leaving my ear.

"I was unconscious," he whispered.

I jerked harder but he didn't let go.

So I gave up but didn't give in. I strained against his hold, rested my forehead against the door and waited for this to be over.

"Listen to me," he urged.

I closed my eyes and stated, "You tell me, the situation was reversed, you wouldn't think the same damned thing."

"I was asleep."

I opened my eyes. "Bullshit. You were into her. You'd fought over her that night. You took her back through that whole thing, even *after* we had *our* thing."

"I see this, honey. I get you, why you'd think what you're thinking. But you gotta listen to me."

God!

Why couldn't he ever let it be *over?*

"Say it so I can get gone and this can be *done,*" I hissed.

His arms gave me a gentle squeeze. "Come sit on the bed with me."

I jerked against his hold again, clipping, "Fuck no."

"All right, Ally, baby, calm down."

I went still, not because he told me to, just because I needed my strength. I was holding on by a string.

When he didn't go on, I ordered, "Just say it so I can go."

I heard and felt him draw in a deep breath.

Then he said, "I get you're not in the place right now that what I'm gonna ask is gonna be easy, but I need to give you what you need and some of it isn't going to be what you wanna hear. What it is gonna be is honest."

I closed my eyes again and clenched my teeth.

"Are you gonna stick with me and hear me out?" he asked.

I opened my eyes and snapped, "Just get it done, Zano."

"All right, honey."

God.

Sweet.

Someone kill me.

"I was into her," he admitted quietly and my throat closed. "But that night, beer, bourbon and me tellin' you I like the Bears was not about her. It was about you and me. Then you snuck away and I get that, Ally," he said the last swiftly, his arms going tighter as he felt my body go solid. "I get why you'd do that. But I didn't get it *then.* I thought it was something else, honey, and you know what I thought it was."

"Yeah, you came over to my place in the middle of the night and made *that* perfectly clear," I reminded him.

"I also apologized," he reminded me.

Crap.

He did.

I shut my mouth.

"So yeah," he continued gently as well as cautiously. "I had feelings for Ava and I had to work through those. But, Ally," his arms gave me another squeeze, "she was with another guy. Deep in it with him. I had no shot. I knew that. We'd never been out on a date. I hadn't even kissed her. I was definitely never in love with her."

"You took her to Carmine's," I reminded him.

"That wasn't a date, honey," he told me. "And you know it. I took her to dinner and took her home to Stark. A man taking a woman to dinner and dropping her off with another man is not a date."

Okay, I had to give him that.

"I thought we'd connected," I found myself whispering then I found I couldn't stop doing it. "We were naked. You were holding me. And you were thinking about her."

"She had a lot of shit happening around her, and I was involved. So it's not surprising that shit was swirling in the back of my head. But I *wasn't* thinking about her. I wasn't in control of my thoughts. I was unconscious."

"You just said you were into her," I reminded him.

"And I found another woman I was into, we had a great night, the fuckin' best, and she blew me off. A man did that to you, you had no idea why, how would you react? What would you think?"

Oh crap.

That made sense.

And he thought that night was the best?

"Can we stop talking pressed to the goddamned door and move to the bed?" he asked.

"Let me go," I demanded softly.

"Ally—"

"Please let me go, Ren."

His arms got tight before they went loose and I stepped away.

I turned and saw him standing there, eyes on me, but they weren't pissed. Not even close.

They were warm and concerned.

I closed my eyes against that beauty and dropped my head.

I had one way to explain this and make him let me go. Only one.

Was I going to use it?

I opened my eyes and lifted my head.

I was going to use it.

"For Lee, it was Indy."

He did a slow blink before he asked, "Baby... what?"

"For Lee, it was Indy. Only Indy. It had always been Indy."

Understanding moved through his features and he made to come at me but I lifted my hand to him and he stopped.

I dropped my hand. "Eddie screwed everything that moved, but I swear, the minute he got a load of Jet, he was gone."

"Ally, let me—"

I cut him off. "I think you know I could go on."

"I know," he said quietly.

"I want that for me," I shared.

"Honey," he started carefully, "you weren't my first."

"I wasn't your first several things," I replied.

"I wasn't in love with her, Ally. Baby, I hadn't even kissed her," he told me.

"Yeah, Ren. But that doesn't mean anything. I know because I fell for you *before* you kissed me. It was just that I knew I'd done it the morning after."

His head jerked, his brows shot up, but his eyes stayed locked on me.

Then something moved over his face I didn't quite get, but it was more than a little alarming, and he growled, "Come here."

I had to get this done and get the hell out of there, so I shook my head. "No, I—"

"Ally. Get. Your ass. Over here," he ground out and I blinked.

Then my spine straightened again.

"Zano, don't you—"

"Fuck it," he bit off then he was on me and half a second later he was *on me* as in, I was on my back in the bed and his body was covering mine.

Macho Alpha Maneuver!

How had I not seen it coming?

"Zano!" I shouted, shoving at his shoulders

The shoving at the shoulders and shouting gig didn't work in the slightest (then again, it never did).

But this time, it was because Ren was focused.

Like, *really* focused.

"You're in love with me?" he asked.

"Well, I *was*," I snapped.

"So you *were* in love with me and then you spent a year sleeping practically every night at my side, every morning eating breakfast with me, even though you thought I had feelings for another woman, and you're not in love with me anymore," Ren replied immediately.

That sounded absurd.

Still, I was realizing that maybe I'd landed myself in hot water and perhaps silence was the key to the hungry Italian hothead that was lying on top of me not making a meal of me.

Ren didn't need me to participate in this discussion and give him more fodder to chew me up and spit me out.

I'd already given him plenty.

I would know this when his eyes narrowed and he noted, "A year I've been busting my ass to get in there and the whole fucking time I wasn't just in there, I was *in there*."

I kept my mouth shut and just gave him big eyes. Indy cuted her way out of things. She was good at it. It even sometimes worked on Lee.

I'd never tried it but I figured now was as good a time as any.

He took in my big eyes and didn't find them cute.

I knew *this* when he declared, "Christ, you're a pain in my ass."

He stopped talking.

I didn't fill the void.

He didn't either.

Finally I couldn't take it anymore and asked, "Can I go find Darius now?"

"No you fuckin' can't go find Darius now," he answered and I shut my mouth again. "Jesus, Ally, you just told me you're in love with me."

"Uh… I think I said *was*."

"So you're not in love with me?"

I didn't answer that.

"Ally," he growled.

God!

I knew one thing, he never let anything go so I had no hope in hell of him letting *this* go.

And since I was letting it all hang out it was time to go for the gusto.

But carefully.

"I didn't say that," I whispered.

Instantly upon my words, his eyes got heated. It was his angry heat warring with a totally different kind of his heat and he verbalized these conflicting emotions by sharing, "I don't know whether to fuck you or turn you over my knee."

I decided not to give him my input because the first option I was always up for and the second one might make me lose my mind and we didn't need any more emotion making things crazy.

Instead, I decided to change the subject and I did this by asking cautiously, "Um... what's happening here?"

"Um... you're officially ending this game we been playing by tellin' me you love me?" he asked back sarcastically.

I had already pretty much done that but I didn't point that out at that juncture because I decided at his words and tone that I felt we needed more emotion making things crazy.

And I was going to bring it.

"Seriously?" I snapped.

"Jesus, why can't you just say it?" he returned.

"Maybe because you're essentially ordering me to," I fired back then kept going in order to advise, "Don't think you can watch the Rock Chicks and think you're getting the same thing with me. This macho bossy shit does not fly with me."

"Clue in, Ally," he immediately volleyed, "Watchin' the Rock Chicks, I know *exactly* what does and does not fly with you, and just like every one of those men when their women serves up attitude, I don't give a shit. And, just sayin', that attitude, just like with them, is *why I'm with you.*"

"What?" I bit out.

"Babe, every one of those guys had pussy lined up at the door. Bitches were gagging for it. They'd do anything to get their hooks into those men and those men knew it. They didn't want a woman who'd do anything. They wanted a woman who knew her own mind and *wouldn't* do anything. Not a single one of your posse lets their man walk all over them. And not a single one lets them get away with shit. At least not without dishin' up a fair amount of attitude before they let them get away with it which is the definition of *not* letting them get away with it."

This, I had to admit, was true. At the very least, if one of the Hot Bunch got bossy, they'd get an eye roll, but usually they bought a whole lot more. Those boys might get their way but that didn't mean they didn't have to work for it.

I just never looked at it that way.

Ren wasn't done.

"With your crew, you get what you see, not some twisted version who's tyin' herself into knots to give you what they *think* you wanna see. And even if every one of you and your crew are totally fuckin' whacked in your own unique ways, it's just you and *all* you. Not some bullshit fantasy that will go up in smoke the minute you get your hooks in me."

There was a lot there, and all of it made total, if surprising, sense.

But I got stuck on one thing.

And being me, I called him on it.

"I'm not whacked!" I stated (loudly).

"Ally, you been fuckin' me for a goddamned year, in love with me since the night we met, and pushing me away that whole time. That's whacked."

"There *were* circumstances that led to all that, Zano."

"And you took your sweet time sharing those with me, and I'll add, did it in a goddamn motel hours away from home, after rescuing some random damsel in distress who got fucking *buried alive* that you met on your fuckin' computer, for God's sake, and you did it during a fuckin' drama. Baby, that, *all* of that, is *whacked*."

"Faye's not random. She's my friend!" I shouted.

"You met her in person last night!" he shouted back.

"So?" I asked, still shouting.

"Jesus, are we honestly *fighting* about the fact you're in love with me?" he asked.

"Words you'll never hear if you keep up this bossy in your face bullshit, Zano," I returned (again, loudly).

He scowled at me.

Then he rolled off, shifting to his back in the bed. He lifted his hands to his face and rubbed, muttering under them, "Fuck me."

I rolled to my side, got up on an elbow and requested to know, "If I try to leave and go find Darius, are you going to pin me to the bed again?"

He removed his hands from his face and locked eyes with me. "Fuck yes."

"God!" I exclaimed, falling to my back on the bed with a plop.

Within an instant, Ren was looming over me.

His hand came to my jaw and his face dipped close.

I glared.

"I'm in love with you, Ally."

I stopped glaring and my heart flipped.

"What?" I whispered.

He didn't repeat himself.

He said something a lot longer and almost (but not quite) as good.

"I knew it could happen when you were cool when I told you about my dad and you wrapped your hand around my thigh. I definitely knew it could happen when you went wild for me on my stairs. Shit went down and it took a while but I knew it *did* happen when you cried in my arms after Sadie had her thing. Anyone who would feel that badly about being mean and care so deeply about another human being's fucked up life I knew was the woman for me. You gave me a run for my money, and once I stopped finding it a pain in my ass and started enjoying it, I did nothing but. I enjoyed every fuckin' second, Ally. And every fuckin' second I've never doubted how I was feeling. And just to be clear, how I was feeling, every day through this game we've been playing, was that I was falling deeper in love with you."

Holy crap.

"Seriously?" I breathed.

"Seriously," he declared firmly.

I stared up at him, my heart beating hard, my stomach melting, my hands itching to touch him, words getting clogged in my throat.

With effort, I was able to let some out and the ones that came were, "I'll go to Ava and Luke's wedding with you."

When I was done speaking, I watched him close his eyes then watched as he dropped his head so his forehead was against mine.

Whoa.

Wow.

God.

Ren Zano loved me.

I got choked up again and put a hand to his chest, sliding it up to curl around the side of his neck. At the same time I lifted my other hand and wrapped it around his wrist at my jaw.

He lifted his head an inch and opened his beautiful eyes.

And there it was in all its glory.

God.

He *loved* me.

95

I so totally didn't see that coming.

But I was over the freaking moon that it did.

"Maybe I'm a little whacked," I whispered.

He said nothing which meant he agreed, just maybe not about the "a little" part.

Suddenly, for the first time in a very long time, I was uncertain.

But I'd very nearly fucked this up by being emotional and maybe a bit stupid (okay, maybe not "maybe" about that last part).

I had to stop doing that.

Therefore, I asked quietly, "Don't you think it's a little weird, a woman saying she fell in love with a man the first night they met?"

"No," he answered immediately as his eyes got warmer and more beautiful.

My nose started tingling.

I swallowed.

"Do you love me, Ally?" he asked in his sweet voice.

I stared into his eyes. I drew in a breath.

Then I answered, "Yes, Ren. I love you."

I didn't get to stare into his eyes as they responded to that.

Because his mouth and body were responding to it.

That was to say, I was in his arms and he was kissing me.

Hard.

My mouth and body, specifically my heart and my happy place, responded to his kiss (and the fucking righteous fact that he loved me) and I rolled him to his back with me on top. I shoved my hands under his shirt and yanked up.

He lifted up to sitting, forcing me to straddle him, and ended the kiss only to finish what I started, tug off his shirt and toss it aside.

Then he tugged off my tee and tossed it aside.

His arms closed around me, his mouth took mine again, and he fell back, taking me with him and twisting so I was on my back, Ren on me.

His hands moved on me and I liked it.

My hands moved on him and it was debatable but I might have liked that more.

His mouth took, mine gave.

This was our way. One place I absolutely didn't mind Ren being bossy and domineering was in bed. And he was both, he'd never been anything but both, and I got off on it.

Finally, his fingers curled into the cup of my bra and pulled it down. I bit my lip in anticipation for the delights awaiting me and he didn't delay. He moved his mouth there, sucked hard, getting what he was going for immediately; my moan that corresponded to the heat surging through me at the same time me driving my hands in his hair.

He swirled his tongue around my nipple then blew against it.

Oh God. I loved it when he did that.

I felt it pucker further and harden harder and whimpered as that shot straight to my happy place.

"Kick off your boots, baby," he murmured as his arm that was around me shifted up, his fingers honing in on my bra clasp.

With a flick, it was undone.

With a tug it was gone.

"Hurry, honey," Ren ordered softly then he went after my other nipple.

It was difficult, I wanted to concentrate on what he was doing, but I managed to toe at my boots until they were gone.

Ren heard the second one hit the floor. I heard my zip go down and suddenly my jeans, panties and socks were gone.

Lying down my side but up on an elbow, his hungry, heated eyes came to mine and my happy place convulsed.

"Spread for me," he whispered.

I held his eyes and did as asked. He held my eyes and slid his fingers through the wetness between my legs.

My hips jerked.

A growl tore from his throat.

Hearing it, my hips jerked again.

Ren delayed no further, slid down my body, rolled into me and his mouth was there.

I wrapped my legs over his shoulders and dug my heels in his back, my fingers in his hair, arching and moaning as my happy place spasmed.

"*Ren*," I breathed.

God, I loved this.

No, that wasn't right. I liked this before. But I *loved* the way Ren did it. Like he couldn't get enough of me. Like he'd waited lifetimes for a taste of me and now that he had me, he never wanted to stop.

It was amazing.

He kept going until my happy place was nearly as happy as it could be.

Then he was up and covering me, his eyes catching mine right before he slid inside.

As he filled me, my lips parted, my eyelids lowered and I wrapped all my limbs around him.

There it was. Everything I needed.

Holding my gaze, he started moving.

"Ren?" I called on a whisper.

"Yeah, baby," he answered, gliding, not thrusting.

He was making love to me.

He loved me and he was making love to me.

Thank *God* I didn't fuck this up.

I tightened my arms and legs, lifted my head, touched my mouth to his and dropped it back to the bed as my declaration of gratitude for what he was giving me.

Then I requested, "Can I change my answer?"

"What answer, honey?" he asked, still gliding, going faster, not harder, but touching me deep.

I arched into him, sliding a hand up his back and into his hair.

"To that question you asked last summer," I answered, my words hitching because he was again going faster, this time harder, and it was doing a number on me.

But I needed to get this out or I'd lose focus and not say it.

And I really needed to say it.

Again, that wasn't right.

I really needed Ren to hear it.

"Ally, baby, what are you talking about?"

"This," I said.

"What?" he asked.

I held him tight at the same time I lifted my head and put my mouth to his. No brush this time, just being close, all this while holding his eyes.

He sensed what I needed and—God, Ren, so awesome, always so freaking awesome—he stopped on an inward glide, filling me thus giving me what I needed.

All I needed.

"I'm amending my answer," I whispered. "This."

I gave him another squeeze, this time with everything I had, including my happy place, and I felt it as he bit his lower lip, showing he liked what I did to him, nipping my lip in the process, something so hot it made me shudder underneath him.

"This, baby," I kept whispering, "does *not* feel casual."

His eyes burned into mine.

I moved a hand to his jaw and finished, "And it never did."

I just got out the last word before Ren slanted his head and took my mouth, hot, hard and wet.

He also again started moving.

But not gliding.

Not even close.

And he kept doing it until we both found it.

Simultaneously.

It.

Was.

Righteous.

Chapter 8
Semi-Sweet

We were in Ren's Jag, nearing my apartment complex, when I pulled my phone out of my purse.

For obvious reasons, I elected to ride back with Ren.

When I called Darius to inform him of this fact and ask him to meet me at his truck so I could get my stuff, Darius laughed his ass off.

I did not take to this kindly but I was in a good enough mood I let it slide.

Letting it slide got harder when I met Darius at his truck and Brody was there.

He took one look at me and said to Darius, "She got her some."

I glared at Brody.

"She's anywhere near Zano, she always gets herself some," Darius replied.

I transferred my glare to Darius.

Darius took in my glare, lifted his brows and asked, "Am I wrong?"

Since he wasn't, I decided not to answer.

"So, are you guys *together* together, as in, you're gonna stop pretending to pull the wool over everyone's eyes and come out of the bedroom, or are you two still gonna keep dancing your dance?" Brody asked nosily.

"Ren and I had a meeting of the minds this morning." I decided to share.

"Sounded like the opposite," Darius muttered and I started glaring again.

"Yeah, when you fight, you guys are seriously loud," Brody put in.

Unfortunately, I'd discovered Brody and Darius's rooms flanked Ren's and mine.

Though, I had to admit, even if they didn't, they probably still would have heard us shouting.

I took in a deep breath, reminding myself Ren loved me and I'd just had a fabulous orgasm, and let it out feeling much calmer.

Then I told them, "We worked it out."

Brody leaned into Darius and mumbled loudly, "That'd be the part where she got her some."

Darius's eyes never left me through this, but when Brody was done, he grinned.

I practiced more calming breathing and requested, "Can I get in the truck?"

Darius beeped the locks.

I moved to the door.

"This sucks," Brody remarked as I yanked it open and reached in to get my purse and laptop bag. "The Rock Chicks have cost me a shed load of money. And now there's none left. I can't win any back."

I pulled out of the cab, slammed the door and looked at Brody. "You bet on Ren and me?"

"Sure," he replied and when I started glaring again, he added, "But I bet *on* you. I thought you'd hold out longer. But you caved."

My back went straight.

"I didn't *cave*," I snapped. "Like I said, we had a meeting of the minds."

"You've been having a meeting of a variety of things but you never caved," Brody pointed out. "Though, if it makes you feel better, you held out a whole lot longer than any of the other Rock Chicks. I did a spreadsheet. Sadie took the longest to win. You beat her by, like, eleven point five months. You should be proud. That's a lot."

Darius started chuckling.

"Do you *want* me to hurt you?" I asked the both of them and the both of them grinned.

They said no more and I didn't either. I was in for a lot of this, I knew. I bought it and I knew that too. I was just going to have to suck it up and take it.

"I'll see you guys back home," I muttered, moving away.

"Ally," Darius called and I turned back.

"Yeah?"

"Believe in it," he said softly, "and be happy."

God, I loved Darius.

I swallowed as my eyes started feeling hot.

Then I nodded and got the hell out of there.

I barely had the door to the room closed before Ren asked, "How much shit did they give you?"

He was sitting on the side of the bed tugging on his boots.

I dumped my stuff on the bed and turned to him. "I'm screwed."

He straightened, reached out, grabbed my hips and shifted me so I was standing between his opened legs.

I rested my hands on his shoulders and looked in his eyes.

This man loved me.

Seriously.

How lucky could I be?

"I'll make it worth it," he whispered.

Yeah.

He loved me.

And I was *very* lucky.

"I think, after acting like an idiot for a year, that's my job," I replied, and his warm eyes got warmer, his hands slid from my hips to my ribs and he pulled me down to him as he fell back so we were lying on the bed, me on top.

"How you gonna do that?" he asked as one of his hands drifted over my ass and the other one drifted up and into my hair.

"I don't know," I answered. "But I'll be creative."

He smiled.

My heart soared.

"Lookin' forward to that," he murmured.

"Would you like to start now?" I offered. "Or after we get back to Denver."

"Seein' as I'm takin' my woman on our first official date tonight even though she's been my woman for a long fuckin' time, I want to get back to Denver. So you can start there."

God. I'd been *such* an idiot.

I didn't admit that since I figured he knew. And, by the way, he was being very cool by not rubbing my nose in it.

Which made me love him more.

Instead, I replied, "Copy that," and got another smile.

Then I got a hot, heavy, wet kiss.

After that, I got my ass hauled to a sweet ride and Ren pointed the Jag toward Denver (after we checked in on Faye who, surprisingly, after being buried alive, was doing all right; then again, she had her own hot guy badass so maybe this wasn't a surprise).

I delayed until nearly the final moment to check my phone because I knew what I'd find. I'd even avoided looking when I'd called Darius.

But this was sissy behavior and not me. However, I allowed myself this bubble of happiness with Ren without letting the world intrude as he drove his sleek, high performance machine through the beauty of the Colorado Mountains.

He did this, by the way, almost the whole time holding my hand against his thigh. Yes, the fact that I loved this was more romantic girlie than Rock Chick, but who cares? A hotheaded Italian badass loved me. This required being romantic girlie on occasion.

And I picked that one.

But it was time to stop being a sissy and face the music.

So I hit the button to turn on my phone and found I had fifty-seven missed calls and thirty-three voicemails.

"*Shit*," I hissed.

"What're you lookin' at?" Ren asked, having been around the Rock Chicks enough to know what I was facing.

"Fifty-seven missed calls and thirty-three voicemails," I told him.

Ren started laughing.

I didn't find it funny and found it less funny when I went to my Recents list, scrolled down and saw the vast majority of calls were not from the Rock Chicks, snippy and calling to ream me because I didn't share.

They were from Lee, Hank and Eddie.

Not good.

Those three were also the vast majority of voicemails.

Also not good.

I turned off my phone and shoved it in my purse as Ren pulled into the parking lot of my complex. I did this deciding that maybe I could still be a sissy for a little while longer.

Ren parked. I put my hand to the handle but stopped and turned to him when I felt his fingers curl around my knee.

"We go up, you pack enough to stay at my place awhile, but you make sure you got a variety of dresses and heels," he ordered and I bit back a smart mouth retort at him being bossy. It took me so long to do that, he was able to keep talking. "And you do that shit fast."

At bossy part two, I failed in biting back the smart mouth and asked, "Should I salute when you issue an order? Or will nodding and instant compliance do?"

He grinned and replied, "No salutes. No nods. But you could kiss me."

I gave him a look.

He kept grinning.

I decided to throw out a deal that he couldn't refuse.

"I'll kiss you, and comply with your order, if you do me a favor."

His fingers gave my knee a squeeze and he asked, "What do you need?"

I dug in my purse, got out my wallet and opened it. I found the little pocket that had absolutely no use. A pocket I put a use to. I snapped it open and pulled out what was inside.

I dumped the wallet back in my purse, turned to Ren and lifted my hand between us.

Then I dropped the guitar pendant and it bounced between us from where I held the chain.

"What I need is for you to put this on me," I said quietly and Ren's eyes moved from the pendant to me.

His voice was rough when he stated, "You carried it with you."

"Yes."

"Always?"

I took a breath in through my nose.

Then I nodded and whispered, "Always."

His eyes stayed locked to mine, heated and intense, before he grinned and declared, "I was *so* in there."

I palmed the necklace and snapped, "Zano, do you *want* me pissed at you?"

"Semi-sweet Ally, just seein' how far she goes," he replied.

"You reached the end, mister," I returned, twisted to exit the vehicle but instead found myself in Ren's lap, wedged between him and his steering wheel.

Oh, and he was kissing me.

I decided to forgive him and kissed him back.

Then kissing turned into making out.

After we were done doing that, he put the necklace on me.

When the guitar was dangling in the dent of my collarbone, Ren touched it as his eyes watched.

He lifted his gaze to mine and stated, "You do know you aren't bullshitting me. There is no semi-sweet Ally. She's pure honey all the way through."

I slid my fingers along the dark stubble at his jaw and whispered, "Don't tell anybody."

"Baby, your secret's safe with me."

I smiled at him.

He smiled back, touched his mouth to mine and deposited my ass in my seat.

We got out of his car and walked hand in hand into my complex and up the stairs.

I was in my head. Precisely what I was thinking up there was which dresses and heels I was going to pack to take to Ren's.

On the way home, we'd made the deal that we were going to try this *together* togetherness, not fuck around and not delay. That meant me staying at Ren's (because, seriously, his house was awesome; he even had a sauna in his bathroom).

This also meant me meeting his mom and two sisters, him meeting my family not as Ren, a member of the Zano Crime Family, but as Ren, the boyfriend of me, and me sitting down to dinner with Vito and his wife Angela.

None of this scared me. Vito liked me. Ren loved me and he was the kind of guy who, if he made that decision, even if his mom and sisters didn't like me, they'd have to deal. As for my family, Ren was Ren and his family was his family and mine were who they were and usually this would be a Romeo and Juliet type of scenario. But I wasn't big on Shakespeare so my family was also just going to have to deal.

I was narrowing down my dress and heels choices when I felt his hand tighten in mine and he pulled us both to a dead stop.

I looked up and tensed when I saw The Kevster running our way down the hall.

"Bomb! Bomb! Bomb! Bo——!" he was shouting.

But he didn't get the last one out.

This was because my apartment exploded. The Kevster was taken clean off his feet and was blown our way. Ren and I rocked backward, Ren tugging my arm and curling me into him so when he landed on his back, I landed partly on his front but my left side slammed into the floor.

Instantly, he rolled me so I was on bottom and he tucked me low so he fully covered me.

Oh man.

Here we go.

Shit.

Chapter 9

Sixteen to Me

I was pacing Lee's office.

The Kevster, healthy and all in one piece (thank God), was sitting in one of the chairs in front of Lee's desk.

For some reason, the police cruiser we were loaded into took us to Lee's offices in lower downtown Denver (known as LoDo) instead of the station. We were escorted into Lee's office and locked in.

Yes.

Locked in.

When we left my place, the entirety of the Hot Bunch were milling about with police and firefighters.

And when we left, looking out my window with a totally freaked out Kevster at my side, Ren and Lee were nose to nose, and neither of them looked happy.

I was not either, being carted off like a girl (or a pothead) who needed to be protected.

What was *that* all about it?

I also wanted to know why Lee and Ren were in each other's faces, but neither of them were answering their phones. Sadly, before I could try to get to either by proxy, as in calling Indy to call Lee, my phone ran out of juice.

The Kevster didn't have one.

And Mace had destroyed Lee's office phone in a fit of (justifiable) rage during his and Stella's drama and Lee elected not to replace it. This meant Shirleen couldn't transfer annoying phone calls from clients that he didn't want to handle and therefore he could spend more of his time "in the field."

It also meant, since we were locked in (again, *locked in*), I was incommunicado.

And I was steaming.

My apartment had exploded!

What the fuck was that?

And here I was, pacing in an office across town, not knowing anything, and worse, not able *to do* anything, all because the macho alphas in my life deemed it fit I should be carted away.

I had been, at the time, semi-flipped out, seeing as my apartment had exploded, so I didn't argue.

I made a mental note to delay flip outs in future so I would not give the macho alphas in my life the opportunity to treat me like *a girl*.

After making this mental note, I eyed Kevin and decided I'd given him enough time to control his freak out, or get it together enough to converse with me (insofar as The Kevster could do either, even when things weren't exploding) so I moved to Lee's desk. I rested my hips against it and looked down at Kevin.

His wide eyes looked up at me.

Okay, maybe I hadn't given it enough time.

Still, I had to do *something*.

"Kevin, do you feel like talking?" I asked carefully.

"I nearly exploded," he told me instead of answering.

"I know. You may have saved Ren's and my life, and dude, I don't know how to thank you for that. That was way cool. I'll try to figure out a way to express my gratitude, but now we need to talk. I gotta know how you knew——"

The door opened before I could finish and my eyes went there.

Lee was prowling in, but looking behind him, arm raised, finger pointing at something or someone.

I watched him order angrily, "Keep the Rock Chicks back and I don't give a fuck what it takes to do it."

Then his eyes came to me and coming in behind him were first Ren then Hank, Eddie, Luke and Mace.

"What's——?" I started but Lee jerked his finger toward my face and interrupted me.

"You. Shut it," he growled then turned his attention to The Kevster and jerked his finger in Kevin's face. "You, tell us how you knew there was a bomb."

I clenched my teeth and my eyes flew to Ren.

He was looking at me and he looked even less happy than me. But he jerked his head in a negative shake once and looked to Kevin.

I did too and saw that The Kevster was fidgeting, his eyes darting from me to Lee to different men in the room then to Lee again and he said, "I, uh... dude, I——"

Lee leaned into him and roared, "*Tell me how you knew there was a bomb planted in my sister's apartment!*"

I pushed away from the desk. "Lee," I started cautiously. "He's freaked. Give him a minute."

Lee turned blazing brown eyes to me. "Your best bet right now, Ally, is to keep your mouth shut. I'll get to you."

He'd get to me?

I felt my eyes get big. "Excuse me?"

Lee turned fully to me and planted his hands on his hips. "One day, my sister gets up in the business of every dirty power broker in a hundred mile radius of Aspen. The next day her apartment explodes. You puttin' these pieces together or do I gotta do it for you?"

Oh I did not *think* so!

I leaned into him and started to snap, "Don't you——"

"It was Rosie."

That was said by The Kevster, and both Lee and my eyes shot to him.

"Say again?" Lee demanded.

"Rosie's back," The Kevster told Lee, and then looked at me. "I mean, dudette, he didn't plant the bomb. But he may have, um... dropped your name, to some, uh... *people* and, uh... well, that didn't go too good."

What the hell?

"Rosie's back?" I asked.

"Yeah. He's back and he might have, uh... brought some trouble with him."

Lee dropped his head and looked at his boots.

I stared at The Kevster.

I saw movement and turned to see it was Ren who was the one moving.

Taking one look at his face, belatedly I felt the weight of the air and I knew he was not just angrier than me. He was livid.

I moved quickly, got in front of him, put a hand on his chest and caught his eyes. "Let me, Ren. Please," I asked quietly.

"You got two minutes, babe. Then it's me," he replied.

I stared into his eyes.

Yep. Livid.

Hmm. Better get a move on.

I nodded, turned my back to him and looked down at The Kevster.

Kevin was looking up at us, so he saw it when Ren's arm curled around my upper chest.

Seeing that, his eyes lighted and he cried, "Dudette! You two finally comin' out?"

Jeez. Even The Kevster knew about me and Ren.

"Maybe we can discuss my love life over Cheetos and beer later. Right now, and fast, Kevin, you need to tell us about Rosie, what he's up to and how this concerns me."

"And how you knew there was a bomb in Ally's apartment," Hank butted in.

Kevin looked to Hank when he spoke and got visibly *more* uncomfortable (then again, Hank had had him arrested during the Premier Rock Chick Drama, which would be Indy's). When Hank was done speaking, Kevin's eyes came to me.

"Right. Well. You know he grows. Yeah?" he asked.

I nodded. "I know he grows."

"And you know things got hot here when he was growin' in Denver," The Kevster went on.

I nodded again, lifting a hand and rolling it because I knew that too. Intimately. I was the one who found his ass, and I'd also been there when Hank had The Kevster arrested for trying to save Rosie's unattended pot farm—a pot farm unattended because Rosie was in hiding.

"And I think I told you he's the maestro of pot," Kevin continued.

"Skip to the parts we don't know," Luke ordered, and Kevin fidgeted again in his seat as he looked to Luke then back to me.

"He kind of recently moved to New Mexico," The Kevster said.

Finally, something I didn't know.

"And?" I prompted.

"Well, he started growing," Kevin stated and I closed my eyes.

Rosie.

All that trouble he had the last time, and, I might add, brought down on Indy, and he was growing again?

What a fucking idiot.

I opened my eyes again when The Kevster kept at it. "He established a fanbase, like, *real quick*. So some dudes wanted in on the action. As you know, that's history repeating."

Oh, I knew this, too.

"Rosie was having flashbacks, not the good kind, and he'd heard word you were establishing yourself as the Badass Queen of Denver," Kevin stated.

At this, Ren's arm got tight and I sighed.

The Kevster kept going. "And so, you know, for protection, he dropped your name."

Ren made a noise that sounded like a growl and I was pretty certain I heard others, primarily from Lee and Hank. But fortunately The Kevster had finally found his mojo and was on a roll.

"The dudes down there tryin' to horn in on his action don't know you're a badass with badass backup. They apparently were unimpressed."

Great.

Kevin went on.

"So they stopped tryin' to horn in and just did it. Rosie got pissed. Told them he was comin' to get you to take care of business and he hightailed it up here. They followed him. He came to me because I knew where to find you. I didn't get a good feeling about things, because, you know, he was totally tweaked. And Rosie's usually mellow. When he's tweaked, dudette, that means bad things."

It *so* did.

Kevin carried on.

"I talked to him and got him to bare all. This included the fact that one of those New Mexican dudes blows stuff up in the New Mexico boonies all the time. So that Rosie didn't, like, lead them to you, I came to tell you this was all going down, and saw some dude who I knew was not your style comin' out of your apartment. I figured they found you without Rosie. He didn't see me, so I followed him and he was just sittin' in his car in your parking lot. But he had this little box in his hand."

"Fuck me," Ren murmured.

Kevin talked over Ren. "I figured he was waiting for you to get there so he could, you know..."

He trailed off. The room became stifling, so I urged him to go on, saying, "I know."

Kevin nodded. "So he wouldn't see me, I went in and kept an eye out. But you were takin' a long time to come home, so I went to the stairwell I thought you'd use and had myself a doobie to smooth out the rough edges and pass the time." His eyes went to Hank and he stated quickly, "It's legal now, you know."

"I know," Hank growled, his thoughts on that matter not hidden even in those two words.

Again, I sighed.

"What I don't know," Hank stated. "Is why you saw a strange man walking out of my sister's apartment and sitting in her parking lot, holding a box you knew was a detonator, and you didn't phone the police."

"The police?" Kevin asked, like the concept of law enforcement was foreign to him.

Hank said nothing, obviously realizing this conversation would lead to nothing good. But I saw his jaw clench.

The Kevster clearly also decided conversing longer with Hank would lead to nothing good, so he gave up, looked my way and kept going. "So, obviously, I missed you. Luckily I came up as you were comin' up and," he flicked out his hands, "we're all breathing."

"Where's Rosie now?" Eddie asked, and Kevin looked at him.

"My place," he answered.

"Mace, roll out," Lee ordered, but Mace was already moving to the door.

I looked back at Kevin. "Why would Rosie think I'd help him?"

"'Cause you guys are buds," The Kevster informed me.

"Since when?" I asked.

The Kevster looked confused. "You're not buds?"

"He got my best friend in a situation where she nearly got kidnapped to Costa Rica," I replied. "No, we're not *buds*."

"Dudette, that was like, *years* ago. Forgiveness is divine," Kevin told me.

"Kicking ass feels better," I replied.

At my words his eyes got big and he grinned a goofy grin. "You are so totally badass." Then he threw his arms up in the air and cried, "Rock Chicks rule!"

This was true, all of it, but I didn't get the chance to agree with him. Lee took over.

"There are uniforms in reception. You're goin' with Eddie now and making your statement. Then, until this shit blows over, you're in my safe room."

The Kevster's eyes stayed big, but for a different reason this time.

He bounced in his seat and cried, "Dude! No! You have a no-smoking policy!"

"Man, you nearly got blown up today," Lee reminded him. "You can stay here and stay off the weed or you can go out there and take your chances. Your choice. You got two seconds to make it."

"Can I crack a window?" Kevin asked.

"No," Lee answered.

Kevin slouched in his chair. "Bummed, dude."

"Are you accepting my protection?" Lee pushed.

"Things get hairy when a Rock Chick is under fire so... I guess," The Kevster accepted ungraciously.

But at his words, Ren's arm got tight again.

Lee looked to Eddie, but Eddie was looking at Kevin. "Up. Now. Let's go."

The Kevster pushed up and his eyes came to me.

"Stay alive," he advised as he walked by me.

That got another tightening of Ren's arm and another sigh from me.

The door closed behind Eddie and Kevin and all attention focused on me.

Or I should say Ren and me.

"Where's Darius?" Lee asked me.

"He and Brody started down the mountain before Ren and me so he should be in Denver," I answered. "Listen, Lee—"

He lifted a hand close to my face and shifted his eyes to Ren.

My body strung tight.

"I take it you two are makin' it official," Lee noted.

"Get your hand out of my woman's face," Ren returned pretty unhappily.

Lee dropped his hand but his brows rose as he remarked, "I'll take that as a yes."

"And I'll say now, I know she's your sister, but don't do that shit again," Ren replied.

Oh crap.

"Ren—" I started.

Hank moved closer to Lee and noted, "Not sure that's the way to win your way into the family."

"I pointed in Roxie's face and told her to shut it, what would you do?" Ren asked what I thought was a valid question.

Hank held Ren's eyes then he moved his to Lee.

Lee was looking at Hank and he shrugged.

Hank pressed his lips tight and looked at Ren.

Lee returned his attention to Ren.

No one said anything. This lasted a while. Long enough for me to lose patience.

"For God's sake, yes!" I yelled. "We're making it official!"

Hank looked to the ceiling.

Lee looked to his boots.

"Explains why apartments are exploding," Luke commented. "A Rock Chick has set her sights on a hapless male."

I felt pressure in my head. A lot of it. But I still managed to turn it Luke's way and declare, "*He* set his sights on *me*."

"Same thing," Luke muttered, one side of his mustachioed lips tipped up.

"Were *you* hapless?" I asked.

"Totally," he replied immediately.

"You *do* know what hapless means," I snapped.

"I didn't say I was hapless *now*," he corrected. "I was hapless then, while she was running me through the ringer."

"I'm thinking Ava saw it the other way around," I informed him.

"She'd be wrong," Luke informed me and his eyes went to Ren. "What've you had? A year? And the bombs are just starting?" He shook his head, stating eloquently that Ren was fucked. However, he did this without the half-grin thing going.

He was outright smiling.

Ren said nothing.

I glared at Luke then gave up and looked to my brothers. "Are we done here? Because Ren and I have a date."

"Ally, your apartment just exploded," Hank reminded me.

This was true.

Therefore I revised, "Are we done here? Because I have to go shopping for a kickass dress and sexy heels, and then Ren and I have a date."

I felt Ren's body moving like he was laughing, but I ignored that and raised my brows at my brothers.

"You got a room full of Rock Chicks, plus Tex, Duke, Tod, Stevie, Ralphie, Buddy and Smithie out there waiting to see if you're all right, and then to get your explanation," Lee's eyes slid to Ren then back to me, "about a lot of things."

"I love them, but I'm not sure that takes precedence over my first official date with my hot Italian American boyfriend," I replied, and Ren's body now *definitely* felt like it was laughing. I ignored this and kept speaking. "However, before we go, I'd like to know why you two were in each other's faces at my apartment, otherwise known as the crime scene."

Ren's body stopped shaking.

That didn't bode well.

"Thinkin' you two can talk about that on your date," Lee returned.

That didn't bode much better.

This brought me to the hard part, and I braced before asking, "Right, then now I'd like to know if anyone was injured in the blast."

"Blast was contained to your apartment," Hank answered. "One of your neighbors got knocked over and sprained a wrist. Shit fell off walls of other units. Yours was pretty much decimated. Other than that, nothing."

This time when I heaved a sigh, it was of relief.

"So now," Lee started. "We're done here." He looked at Ren. "Except to say, I think you get, we leave her in your care, you better take that seriously."

"Are you kidding me?" I yelled before Ren could say a word, and Lee looked at me.

"Ally, I'm your brother. Do you think I *wouldn't* say anything?"

"I'm thirty-two, not sixteen," I retorted.

"You'll always be sixteen to me," he shot back, and my body jerked as I blinked.

Oh God.

Oh shit.

Fuck!

It was coming on. My nose was tingling. My eyes got hot and my throat had closed.

"Fuck, she's gonna cry," Hank muttered, staring at me, lips twitching.

"Am not," I forced out.

Ren shifted me so I wasn't pressed back to front to him but tucked into his side and he spoke. "We all know she's not gonna get through the gamut out

115

there unscathed, so we're movin' on to that scene in this ongoing drama so we can then move the fuck out."

He started us toward the door, but stopped and I looked up at him to see him looking between Hank and Lee.

"And to answer your question," he stated. "Yes. I get you. And I take it seriously."

Oh God.

Oh shit.

Fuck!

I'd managed to control it and it was coming on again!

I looked away quickly so none of the men in my life would send me over the edge, and luckily Ren started us again to the door.

He opened it and let me precede him. The instant I did, I got hit by a wave of Rock Chicks.

"Christ." I heard Ren say.

But I was being pushed backwards down the hall and I saw him recede until he disappeared when Ava and Shirleen—who were the ones who had hands on me, the rest of them were just following—shoved me in the safe room.

Tex, the last one in, slammed the door and glowered at me.

He wasn't the only one glowering at me.

Again.

Here we go.

Shit.

Chapter 10
Show Me How Special

I tore my eyes from Tex and moved them through the Rock Chicks, but stopped when I saw Indy.

She was not head of the pack. She was at the back. This was not only not her usual place, but the look on her face as she stared at me made my lungs start burning.

"I... I... I..." Shirleen stammered, and I looked her way, stunned she was stammering. Shirleen didn't stammer. Then she stopped stammering and shouted, "I don't even know where to begin!"

"I know where to begin," Tex boomed from the back, and I looked at the mammoth wild-blond-haired, wild-russet-bearded man that stood head and shoulders over the Rock Chicks (and gay guys). "Woman, you know, you got action, you give some *to me!* I mean, you women have been quiet for fuckin' *months.* Some woman in the mountains was buried alive and I was cut out?" His face started getting red before he shouted, "*Unacceptable!*"

Brody.

It had to be Brody. Darius wouldn't talk. How I'd kept Brody's mouth shut as long as I did was a miracle. But that miracle had ended.

Not surprising.

I had no idea when the news hit what I'd get, if they knew about my activities, or Ren, or both.

I suspected both, considering the number of phone calls I had and the news Brody received that morning about Ren and me.

But, at the very least, a bomb blast was hard to miss.

Before I could reply to Tex, Daisy shoved up to the front. "And Ren was up there with you. And Ren was at your apartment with you when it exploded. And Ren was walking out of Lee's office two seconds ago and he was doin' it *with you.*"

At her last two words, her mass of platinum blonde hair was shaking and she'd planted her hands on her hips.

In other words, I'd hit the Daisy Danger Zone.

But Daisy wasn't done.

"And just so you know, you take a swing at a hot guy at a Rock Chick wedding then disappear—*completely*—we know you're off doin' the nasty, as in the *angry* nasty, which is some of the best nasty you can get," she declared.

She was not wrong. I knew this because Ren and I had existed almost entirely on the angry nasty for going on a year.

She was also *still* not done.

"And you *know,* when you're doin' the nasty, we know all about that nasty!"

She wasn't wrong about that either.

She kept going. "But you're zipped tight for months, like you totally forget you make everyone else spill. Well, sugar," she leaned in and her eyes narrowed, "the time has come for *you* to spill. Comprende?"

I'd already comprende'd.

Before I could explain this to Daisy, Tex started up again.

"Don't give a shit about that. Her apartment exploded," he said to Daisy then looked on me. "I'm in on whatever that shit is. Starting now."

I opened my mouth to say something to Tex or Daisy or all the Rock Chicks, but I ended up looking at Indy and just calling, "Indy?"

Everyone looked at Indy.

Indy just looked at me.

Then she opened her mouth to speak as the door flew open.

Ren was there and he didn't delay in cutting a swathe through the Rock Chicks, gay guys, Tex, Duke and Smithie.

He grabbed my hand and turned to the group. Everyone's eyes dropped to our hands. Some of them widened, some mouths fell open.

They looked back at Ren when he commenced in giving a Macho Alpha Speech.

"Ally and I have been together a year," he declared.

He also ignored the gasps, big eyes and Sadie whispering, "*A year?*", and kept talking.

"She had her reasons for keepin' that from you. She also had her reasons for doin' other things and keepin' that from you. Now it's all out and you want answers. But you'll wait until she's ready to give them to you, which will be sometime after I take my woman out to dinner. So you'll hold your shit until Ally's ready. Is that understood?"

Apparently it wasn't, and this was proved when Roxie asked, "Do you actually think that's going to work?"

Ren said nothing, but he leveled his gaze on Roxie.

Roxie pressed her lips together and gave big eyes to Stella. Stella bit her bottom lip, but that didn't mean both her lips weren't curled up in a big way.

So maybe I was wrong. It was going to work because no one else said a word.

Maybe that macho alpha gig wasn't such a bad thing. At least it was good to know it had its uses.

Or it had its uses until Smithie spoke up.

Smithie, by the way, owned a strip club. Jet worked there as a waitress during her drama. Jet's sister was currently the headliner there as a stripper. He was a big black guy gone slightly soft. And strip club owner or not, there was nothing "slightly" about his soft heart.

He was also a nut. Then again, the Rock Chicks, as a collection of nuts, collected their own.

"Are you sayin' her apartment just exploded not two hours ago and you two are goin' on a date?" he asked, brows raised, eyes big.

"That's what I'm saying," Ren confirmed, then muttered, "We're done here." And he made that statement true by dragging me through the Rock Chicks and out the door.

But as I went, I locked eyes with Indy and mouthed, *Are we cool?*

She just watched me go and gave me nothing.

In Ren's bathroom, I spritzed with perfume, set it aside and looked at myself in the mirror.

After the Rock Chick Confrontation, I'd spoken with the police in reception at Lee's office for five minutes, giving them my semi-statement, which was only semi seeing as I had no involvement in the activities, outside my apartment exploding, so I had nothing to give them that The Kevster hadn't already provided.

Then Ren had guided me to his Jag and we left.

He took me straight to Cherry Creek Mall, valet parked (total class) then dragged me to Nordstrom's. There, he found a comfortable chair, pulled out his credit card and handed it to me.

"You got an hour. Use it wisely," he ordered.

I knew what his wisely meant. I couldn't help but know. My apartment exploded, the only clothes I owned I was wearing. We were going out on our first date, he considered my dresses foreplay, and we were at a mall.

I just didn't know what the credit card meant.

"Zano, my purse didn't explode with my pad. I had it with me, and just saying," I pointed to it on my shoulder, "I still do."

Ren ignored this and replied, "Text me when you decide on something to tell me where it is. Give them the card so they can ring it up. I'll go and sign."

This didn't address my remark.

"What I'm saying is, I have my own money," I told him.

"Ally, we're not arguing about this," he told me.

I was trying to be confused and not pissed, though, in truth, I was both.

In order to acquire the information needed not to be confused, or pissed, I asked, "Are you saying my emergency provision purchases are on you?"

He looked at the card I was holding aloft and then at me.

However, he didn't verbalize his answer.

That was still an answer.

So now no confusion and I was stuck with trying not to get pissed.

I pushed the card his way. "I've got it."

"And I said we're not arguing about this."

"Zano, I make my own money."

To this, he asked strangely, "Was it you sittin' in that booth with me, beer, bourbon and the Bears?"

"Yes," I answered the obvious.

"And was it you cryin' in my arms over Sadie?"

"Yes, Zano, but—"

"And was it you who opened my Christmas present naked in my bed on Christmas morning?"

I narrowed my eyes on him. "Where is this leading?"

He didn't answer my question or wait for an answer to his. He kept up his bizarre interrogation.

"And was it you who told me you loved me in a motel room this morning?"

I crossed my arms on my chest. "You know it was."

"And who were you with all those times?" he asked.

"Zano. You!" I snapped. "What's the deal?"

"And do you know me?" he pushed, and I sucked in breath.

I knew him.

And I got him.

He knew I got him and this was why he said, "You know what you signed on for, babe. Now take my card, buy what you need and text me to sign for it so we can get outta this fuckin' place."

I had to admit, his desire to exit the mall without delay was a surprise. Ren dressed really well. Although it would be a hit to his alpha badass to be comfortable in a mall, the results of said comfort couldn't be argued.

Still, I found it interesting he clearly had an aversion to the mall.

This made me wonder where he got his clothes.

"Ally?" he prompted, and I focused on him.

Seeing as we were together *together*, I loved him, he loved me, I decided in that moment to try new conversational gambits that might result in actually conversing and not fighting.

Therefore, quietly, I pointed out, "You know what you signed on for, too."

"Yeah," he agreed instantly. "I also know my woman's apartment exploded. So I want to get her across from me at a nice dinner with booze so she can relax. Then I want her at home with me in my bed so I can make her *really* relax."

I was down with both of those.

Ren kept going.

"And she's facing a variety of shit, including a lot of shopping, which is going to cost a whack and take a lot of time. You can do that. I want no part of that. I'm doin' this. And I want this done quickly. But I also want you to have something nice that makes you feel good that's from me so that makes it special, so you can have something special on a *very* special day that, unfortunately, included your apartment exploding. Not something you like that you can afford that'll do. So, go, enjoy and," he leaned in, "*text me* when I gotta sign something."

Oh my God.

That was really nice.

As in, *really*.

"You could have explained it like that," I shared.

"I just did."

He did. Though belatedly.

In order to keep conversing and not fighting, I didn't point out the belatedly part.

Instead, I informed him, "You're freaking me out."

His brows shot together.

"Why?" he asked.

"Because you're thoughtful, or more thoughtful than I thought you'd be."

"If you'd let me in a year ago, by now you'd know intimately just how thoughtful I can be," he replied, and that was when *my* brows shot together.

"Just saying right now, you have precisely two more opportunities to throw that in my face, and then you're done," I snapped.

He looked at the ceiling.

Then he looked at me, his hand snaking out, hooking around the back of my neck and his mouth came down on mine.

In Cherry Creek, at Nordstrom's, he laid a hot, heavy, wet one on me.

Then he lifted his head and I blinked, trying to remember what we were talking about, at the same time trying to make certain my knees didn't fail me.

"Go. Shop," he urged softly. "And don't freak if you see Lucky or Santo trailing you. They're both on you unless I'm with you and they're both here."

This was news.

Lucky and Santo were Zano family sidekicks. I'd met them both during Ava's Rock Chick Ride. I also didn't know what to make of either, as in, if they were buffoons or if they concealed crafty under a thick veneer of moron.

Since he was kind of their employer so hopefully didn't think they were buffoons, I didn't ask Ren his opinion on this.

Instead, I asked, "They are?"

Ren nodded.

"Since when and... how?"

"Since I called between you getting corralled by the Rock Chicks, then saving you from the Rock Chicks, and I told them to haul their asses here to watch *your* ass."

"You know I can take care of myself," I told him.

"I know I'll feel better if you got backup," he told me.

"I'm uncertain, since *you're* here, why *you* aren't my backup."

"If I was your backup, I couldn't use this time to return the fifteen messages *I* got while we've been dealing with this shit." His eyes started heating and he concluded, "And if I was with you when you bought what you're about to buy, I wouldn't get the surprise I suspect I'll like later."

This was a very good answer.

"I think it's time for me to go shopping," I announced, and he smiled.

Getting his smile, I leaned into him but lifted up to my toes.

He touched his mouth to mine before he murmured, "Go."

"'Kay," I murmured back and pushed away.

I got two steps in before he called, "Ally?"

I turned back.

Eyes holding mine, he stated, "I don't need those two opportunities. That one was one too many. It was also out of line. That's done."

I stared at him, knowing what I was feeling but unable to put it into words.

Then I found the words.

"You do know I think you're the shit, right Zano?"

They were the right words.

I knew this when he gave me another smile and replied, "I know."

I tipped my head to the side and lifted the credit card I was still holding. "Do I have any limits?"

His answer was a question. "Is tonight special?"

I started feeling warm(er) inside.

"Yes," I replied.

He looked beyond me, then at me, and finally answered, "Then show me how special."

I smiled at him. He jerked his head so I'd get a move on.

I got a move on. I shopped, texted, shopped more and got an LBD, fabulous shoes, equally fabulous undies, a phenomenal nightie, a plethora of makeup, perfume, shower stuff and a few other bits and bobs to get me through the next couple of days.

We loaded up and Ren took me to his place.

At that point, it was well into the afternoon so I headed to the bathroom with my bag and Ren headed to his office upstairs with his phone.

We had the same charger. He had one in his bedroom so I hooked my cell to it before I did my going out gig.

But now I had smoky eyes, sleek hair and I smelled good.

And the only jewelry I was wearing (because it was the only jewelry I now owned) was my guitar pendant. It didn't exactly go with my slinky dress with its tunic-style, v-neck top, empire waist, ruched short (*short*) skirt that was skintight and my strappy stilettos. Then again, what it was and who it was from, it was my opinion that it would go with everything I owned.

After I gave myself a once over and walked out of the bathroom, I didn't go to Ren.

I'd given it time, and not just the time my cell needed to charge.

So I went to the phone.

I scrolled down and dialed Indy.

I got voicemail.

I took in a deep breath and disconnected. It wasn't unheard of I'd get voicemail. If Lee had Indy's attention or she was neck deep in coffee, she wouldn't answer her phone.

The thing was, her BFF had her apartment bombed. This was not a time when she wouldn't take a call from me.

I hit go on her contact again.

I got voicemail again.

This time I didn't disconnect.

Instead, after her message, I left one.

"Hey. I figure you're pissed and just to say, you have a right. I kept a lot from you, but I had a lot going through my head. I kept that from you, too. But if you'll let me, I'll explain everything. I had my reasons, chickie. And hopefully, when you hear them, you'll understand." I paused, then whispered, "Love you."

Then I hung up.

I was unplugging my phone from the charger and pushing thoughts of Indy being pissed at me to the back of my head by lamenting the fact I hadn't bought a bag to go with my slinky dress when I heard Ren mutter, "Christ."

I straightened and turned.

While I was in the bathroom, he'd changed into dark blue trousers and a light blue shirt with dark blue and gray stripes.

Nice.

"Hey," I greeted.

He said nothing, but his eyes were glued to the vicinity of my hips where my dress was *very* tight and didn't leave a lot to the imagination, even through material.

I took this as indication he liked the dress.

I smiled big inside, but my lips only tipped up slightly on the outside.

His gaze drifted to my shoes and locked there.

"Zano, I'm hungry."

He looked at my face.

"If I tell you to get your ass over here, are you gonna give me shit?" he asked.

"Yes," I answered. "Though, I will warn you, you unwrap this package now, you spoil the surprise I have planned for later, and I'll note that whatever you might make up in your head from now until then, the reality is better."

His eyes heated but his lips quirked.

"Baby, just to say, I'm likin' how special you're showin' me this night's gonna be."

My tipped lips tipped up higher.

Then his head cocked to the side and the heat went out of his gaze, but it stayed fastened on me and changed to probing. He studied me a moment before walking to me, lifting both hands to either side of my neck and dipping his face close.

"You have insurance?" he asked gently.

I wasn't following from our sexual banter to that question, so I asked back, "What?"

"Insurance, personal property. You covered?"

"I don't know *how* covered I am, but I do have a policy," I answered. "Why?"

"You've got something on your mind. Not surprising since your apartment exploded. And maybe we should talk about that."

Oh. That.

I blew it off. "It'll be okay."

His scrutiny, already acute, got more so right before his thumbs moved to stroke my throat.

Both of them.

He'd never done that before.

It felt delicious.

So delicious, I wondered if I threw a tizzy about my apartment, what that would get me.

"You haven't talked about that hardly at all, honey," he noted.

"What's there to talk about?" I asked, genuinely curious, and his thumbs stopped.

"Ally, baby, you lost everything," he said quietly and carefully.

"Yeah," I replied and he blinked.

"Yeah?" he repeated after me, but his was a question.

I shrugged. "It's just stuff. I had my phone and my laptop on me and the backups of both were at my pad so it was good I had them. Clothes, furniture and kitchen implements can be replaced," I told him, but finished on a mutter, "though I'm gonna miss my towels and sheets."

When he said nothing and this lasted awhile, I focused on him, not my incinerated sheets.

"That's it?" he pushed. "You're gonna miss your towels and sheets?"

I shrugged again. "Sure."

Then I stopped being an idiot and realized he was concerned for me. And it was sweet, as Ren could be.

Therefore I leaned into him and lifted both my hands to wrap my fingers around his wrists.

"Stuff is stuff, Ren," I told him softly. "If someone wiped my memory clean of the Whitesnake concert Indy and I got in shitloads of trouble sneaking off to Vegas to go see but was totally freaking awesome, that would be bad. Or if someone wiped away me standing in a bridesmaid dress watching one brother, then another, take the women that were made for them as their wives, that would be bad."

I leaned in closer, gave his wrists a squeeze and kept going.

"Or if I hadn't watched an Italian American hothead in action in a parking lot brawl and sensed he was the one for me, *that* would be bad. Losing my sheets sucks. They were awesome. But they don't mean anything. People mean something. Memories mean something. Things mean nothing."

Ren stared down at me, but his thumbs were sweeping my throat again and his gaze was unwavering.

When this lasted some time, I asked, "What?"

"You do know I think you're the shit, don't you, Ally?" he asked back.

I got to feeling warmer and leaned even closer, which was to say, I pressed my body to his and replied, "I know."

He moved in and brushed his lips to mine, but he didn't move away or take it further.

He stayed close and stayed on target.

"So what's on your mind?"

"Dinner," I answered, and that was partially true.

"Baby," he whispered, said no more and didn't move.

I sighed.

I knew what he wanted.

Okay, this was us now and I figured it was time I started sharing.

The problem with that was, I didn't share. Not with anybody. Not even sometimes Indy. That just wasn't me.

But I had seen the way my mom was with my dad, and Marcus with Daisy, and any of the Rock Chicks with their Hot Bunch boys and learned that give and take was key.

If I wanted this to work with Ren, who had indeed busted his ass to get *in there*, then I needed to let him *in there*.

Starting now.

And anyway, he was being all kinds of sweet.

Shit.

"I think Indy's pissed at me."

His hands left my neck so he could wrap his arms around me. When he did, my hands left his wrists so I could rest them on his chest.

Through this, he spoke.

"You two have been through more thick and thin than anybody. She's gonna bust your chops, babe. She's also gonna get over it. And you know that."

Okay, that required more sharing.

Shit!

I pulled in a breath and whispered, 'I don't like her mad at me."

He nodded and his face got soft. "Sucks when anyone you love is mad at you. But if they love you, they get over it. And Ally," he gave me a squeeze, "that woman *loves you*. She'll get over it. You just need to suck it up and let her bust your chops."

He was right.

And he was definitely all kinds of sweet.

Because of that, I slid my hands up his chest to wrap my arms around his neck and I pressed in, saying, "I'm suddenly not hungry."

"Anticipation," was his reply.

I rocked back on my heels, but kept hold of him as I asked, "What?"

"Honey, the next two hours I get to sit opposite you wondering what's under that fuckin' phenomenal dress. Then I get to peel that fucking phenomenal dress off and find out. Anticipation. Makes something sweet all the more sweet. You gonna take that away from me?"

"I'm thinking that would be selfish," I answered.

"It would," he replied on a smile.

"The problem is, I'm in the mood to be selfish," I shared, then I got to watch and feel as he burst out laughing.

Both his hands also slipped down to my ass so I thought I was going to get my selfish way.

I didn't.

He bent his neck, kissed mine then pulled away, as in, *entirely*, letting me go and ordering, "Get your bag. The sooner I get food and champagne down you, the sooner we can see just how special this night's gonna be."

Champagne?

I liked my tequila. Definitely.

But Ren in a suit *I* got to peel off later, good food, just us, our first date, and champagne?

I was all for that.

Ren tagged his suit jacket from the bed and shrugged it on.

I grabbed my bag.

Ren grabbed my hand.

We were out on the landing, Ren one step down the stairs, when I tugged on his hand. He stopped and looked up at me.

It was time for more sharing.

"Thanks for making this easy, honey."

Instantly, his eyes got so hot, they burned through me. He pushed back on my hand so I took a step back and he took the step back up. Then his hands were at my ass, his mouth was on mine, and he was shuffling me backwards.

Quickly.

I landed on the bed.

Ren landed on me.

His mouth went to my neck and his fingers went to my zipper.

My lips went to his ear. "What about anticipation?"

He didn't answer.

He pulled down the zip.

No, I wasn't right. He *did* answer. *That* was his answer.

And I liked his answer.

Jeez. This sharing stuff was easy.

Or, at least, Ren made it be easy.

I hooked a leg around his thigh and slid my hands inside his jacket.

We'd never know if we gave it a couple of hours if the anticipation would have made it sweeter.

Then again, with the sweet Ren gave me, that would be impossible to beat.

Chapter 11

Come to Jesus

I slid up, then down, slowly filling myself with Ren.

Ren's hands moving over the fabric of my new peach silk and cream lace nightie, his head back, his eyes moving over my face, my arms around his shoulders, the fingers of one hand in his hair, he murmured, "Faster, Ally."

Riding him with him sitting up and close, number one of my five most favorite positions to do the nasty with Ren, I gave him what he wanted.

One of his hands slid down to cup my ass, the other one slid around my ribs to cup my breast over the silk and lace.

This was incentive to move even faster, so I did. I liked it a whole lot, my happy place clenched around Ren and my head fell back.

Both Ren's hands gave me a squeeze. "Unh-unh, give me that," he ordered, his voice rough.

I knew what he wanted.

He liked to watch.

I tipped my head forward, tried to focus and caught his even white teeth sinking into his full lower lip.

He liked what he saw.

I did too.

Okay, so I also liked to watch.

So much, I whimpered and moved faster. Ren wrapped his arm around my hips. It tightened and he started lifting me and slamming me down on his cock, even faster and way harder. He did this while the thumb of his other hand dragged across soft silk and hard nipple.

Nice.

At that, I moaned and my head fell further forward so my forehead was resting on his, my eyes looking into his heated ones, shivers sliding over the tops of my thighs.

Using my momentum and his strength, Ren pulled me up and drove me down even faster and way, *way* harder.

Seriously nice.

"*Ren,*" I breathed.

"Fuck yeah, baby."

Oh God, it was coming.

"Ren!" I gasped and it hit me.

Powerful.

Mind-boggling.

Soul-enriching.

Amazing.

I tried to grind down, but Ren was stronger and kept yanking me up and pounding me down as his hand drove into my hair and held my head to his so he could watch it sear through me.

And it did. My mouth open and a whisper away from his, my eyes open and locked to his, my breath caught and stayed that way as I clamped my man tight with everything I had.

A minute later, it was Ren who ground me down. His hand fisted in my hair and I watched his sear through him.

Okay. Yeah. This together *together* thing was easy.

Sure, we'd always had this part. But something about having it *and* the other made it even better.

And it got better when Ren's breathing eased and he gently pulled my head back by my hair. I felt his lips at my throat right before I felt his tongue touch there. Then I felt him guide my pendant into his mouth with his tongue and the chain tightened around my neck as he sucked it deeper.

His mouth was working my pendant, but it felt like it was working every part of me. My thighs tightened on his hips, my arms around his shoulders. In fact, everything tightened everywhere (and I mean *everything*) and I mentally went back on what I said the day before.

Yes, people and memories meant everything and things meant nothing.

Except that pendant.

That pendant meant the world.

He released it, kissed my chest and tipped his head back as he moved mine forward to catch my eyes.

"Want breakfast?" he asked and I grinned.

"Yeah," I answered.

"Then kiss me and get off me, baby."

In bed, Ren still inside me, it was these occasions and only these occasions I always did what I was told.

So I did what I was told.

But the first part of his order, I gave it my all.

⊱⊰

I was sitting on Ren's kitchen counter, Ren leaning against the one kitty corner to me.

I'd swallowed the last ketchup covered tater tot and put my plate in the sink. I was sipping at my coffee when Ren pushed away from his place, dumped his plate in the sink and moved in front of me.

He took my cup from my hand and set it aside. Hands at my knees, he spread them. He moved in and wrapped one arm around my waist, curving his fingers under me to cup one hand to my ass, and hauled me a couple inches forward on the counter so my happy place slammed into his happy place and stayed nestled there perfectly.

He'd never done that before. Breakfast time was when I reestablished the boundaries I blew apart when we fucked each other's brains out and Ren had always given that to me. He didn't hide that he found it amusing. But he still gave it to me.

This was tons better.

I curled my arms around him.

Totally better.

"You work tonight?" he asked.

I nodded. I'd called off the night Faye had her thing so I could take care of Faye's thing. Last night was my night off. Tonight, alas, I was back at it.

"Date night, your next night off," Ren declared.

Oh yeah.

I nodded. I also smiled. I did it small on the outside, *huge* on the inside.

"Tonight, you wanna eat before you go or when you get home?" he asked.

God, *God,* my man was sweet.

"Before," I answered.

"Lasagna or chicken parmesan?"

Seriously? He had to ask?

I mean, his lasagna was the bomb, but he made his chicken parmesan from scratch and the first time I had it—and every time since—I'd had a culinary orgasm emanating from my mouth. And this orgasm was loud. Ren couldn't have missed it. He didn't miss anything.

"What do you think?" I asked back.

"Chicken," he muttered, his lips quirking. They stopped quirking, he held my eyes and his voice was gentle and sweet when he queried, "She call?"

I pressed my lips together. Then I shook my head.

I'd checked my phone and Indy hadn't called during our mind-blowing, soul-enriching, together *together* sex-a-thon last night.

This worried me.

So I did something about it while Ren was downstairs making breakfast and I was upstairs freaking that my best friend was mad at me.

"I called her," I shared. "Left a message for her to meet me this morning and chat."

"Right, honey," he replied. He gave me a squeeze and dipped in for a brush on the lips before he went on, "Don't worry about it. She'll hear you out. It's sweet you care, but she does too, so you two will get past it." I got another brush of the lips before he muttered, "Now, I gotta get to work."

He moved to let me go, but I tightened my thighs on his hips and my arms around him and regained his focus.

"We got busy last night and conversation was limited," I noted. "I didn't get the chance to ask you about your conversation with Lee."

"Rather have more time than we got right now to explain that to you," he said, and I didn't get a good feeling about that.

"Zano—" I started, but stopped when one of his hands came up and curled around my neck.

"You're lettin' me in and you already know you're in, Ally. But I'll let you in more when I have time to explain. But just to say now, Lee and I are cool, or as cool as we can be. However, he was not a big fan of you heading off to the mountains and gettin' involved in that shit, and he was even less of a fan of your apartment exploding. You know what kind of man he is. You know how he feels about you. And if you don't know, you can guess he wants the kind of man he is, which includes the ways he looks after his woman, for you. This means he feels all that shit is my responsibility. So we had words."

This was understandable. Lee was wrong about it being Ren's responsibility, but I knew my brothers, both of them, so regardless, Ren was right in what he said. So it was understandable.

Ren went on, "And there's shit going down at work between Vito, Dom and me. Lee's in the know about it, and since he was pissed about other shit, he took that opportunity to get in my face about that. That's done between your brother and me too."

This was not understandable, seeing as I had no idea what he was talking about.

Therefore I asked, "What?"

"That's the part I need time to explain," Ren replied. "And I don't have that time now, but I'll explain it, honey. It's not bad. But it is somethin' you gotta know."

Oh shit.

I was not good at waiting for information. Especially if it was juicy. *Especially* if it had something to do with someone I cared about. And this sounded juicy and it definitely had something to do with someone I cared about.

"Uh... Zano," I started. "Something to know about me——"

I stopped speaking because he smiled and that took all my attention.

Then he pulled me deep into his body and dipped his face close to mine.

"Curiosity killed the cat," he noted, still smiling.

"Cats have nine lives," I replied and his smile instantly died.

"How many of those you gone through?"

Uh-oh.

We were hitting a conversational danger zone. This was because, counting nearly being blown up the day before, I suspected I was close to the end of my quota. I also suspected Ren knew that and didn't like it all that much.

In an effort to prevent this talk from becoming a Talk, I stated, "I'll wait until we have time for you to explain."

"Good choice," he returned.

"Now kiss me and go to work so I can go meet Indy," I ordered and got the smile back.

Then I got his mouth back, another squeeze and a sweet, soft, "Later, baby," before he let me go.

I watched him walk away.

And when he disappeared, I gave myself a moment to kick my own ass (mentally) for not initiating this *together* togetherness ages ago.

Then I got over it because it happened, I fucked up, it was over and there was nothing I could do about it. Except live in the now and make that now the best it could be, for me *and* for Ren.

I jumped off the counter, did the breakfast dishes and headed out to make amends with my friend.

Hopefully.

⚡

I was sitting outside a Starbuck's in Cherry Creek North.

In other words, I was taking my life in my hands.

No joke.

This was not because there might be snipers (don't think I'm kidding—I *was* a Rock Chick; anything goes when you're a Rock Chick, the scarier, the more possible).

This was because, if Tex knew I was at a Starbuck's, he'd lose his mind.

Tex felt, and shared this philosophy liberally, that the coffee counter at Fortnum's was like your momma's dining room table at Thanksgiving. That was to say, on Thanksgiving, your ass was at that table. You didn't tell your mother you were going to a Chinese restaurant with your friends or suggest you have Thanksgiving catered at your house or explain you were taking that longed for, once in a lifetime vacation to a five star resort in Antigua.

You sat your ass at your momma's table.

And you got your coffee from Tex. Even if you had to go out of your way, you went to Fortnum's and Tex handed you your cup.

No excuses were accepted.

If you didn't do this, things could get ugly.

So although I had a lot on my mind, I was also scanning the area just in case Tex's radar pinged and sent him on a mission to ream my ass, throw away my latte and drag me to Fortnum's to make me a coffee.

I knew this sounded weird. It was also true.

But outside of being unfaithful to Tex's coffees and the possible consequences of that, what was on my mind wasn't that I'd been waiting over an hour for Indy to show. It also wasn't that none of the Hot Bunch were taking my calls so I could ask what was happening with Rosie. It further wasn't the fact that this informational lockout pissed me off, considering I might not be a member of their team, but it *was* my apartment that had blown sky high because Rosie dropped *my* name, so I had the right to know.

What was on my mind was that my boss had called and told me not to go into work that night.

This was because I was fired.

He was nice about it, and truth be told, I was expecting it. He'd put up with me a lot longer than I would have put up with me, that was certain.

Suffice it to say, I wasn't a stellar employee. Shit went down with the Rock Chicks, not to mention my cases, and there were only so many times you could call in when your friends had been kidnapped or you'd been in a high speed chase and totaled your car or you needed to stake out a cheating husband.

That shit no longer flew, even if my friend was buried alive and I was a key player in her rescue and the next day my apartment had exploded. Drinks needed to be served. I got that. And it had to be said, these excuses, although honest, were frequent. So I also got that would be a little alarming for any employer.

So now I had a lot to do, including serious shopping, which would have been made easier by the gift cards at my pad that were probably melted. My insurance would undoubtedly not cover everything, and my income had been significantly reduced. Fortnum's sold a shitload of coffee and the tip jar was never light. Then again, the tips at Brother's were a whole lot better, so that was going to be a hit.

I also had a decision to make because I'd known for some time a career as a bartender/barista was not for me.

Now I had an excuse to make things official.

But, although licensing was voluntary for investigators in Colorado, to be taken seriously and charge that way, I needed a license. And this might be a problem. I no doubt had the hours of investigation logged to get it. I just did not have those hours in any official capacity. Lee, Hank, Eddie or my dad would have to vouch for me, and the prospect of that happening was not rosy.

I also now had a boyfriend, and always had a family who would not take kindly to this career shift. And by "not take kindly" I meant their reactions would be volatile.

But it was what I wanted to do, and not on a whim. I'd been doing it for a long time, and loving it, and now I had the opportunity and the time to go for it.

I just had to manage the reactions of those around me.

On that thought, I activated my phone, checked the time then scanned the area.

Still no Indy.

Fuck.

It wasn't like we didn't disagree or even fight.

But this kind of silent anger was not her thing and it unnerved me.

I was about to hit buttons to call her again when my phone rang with the display saying, "Zano Calling."

I took the call and put my phone to my ear. "Hey."

"Hey, baby. She show?"

My insides warmed. He was checking in because he was concerned for me. Totally sweet.

"Not yet," I replied.

"She will."

Totally supportive, which was also sweet.

On this thought, I saw her blue Beetle drive by, Indy's redhead at the wheel.

I let out a breath and said, "She just drove by."

"Good," he murmured.

"It'll take half an hour for her to find a parking spot, which is plenty of time for me to get her a coffee," I told him as I left my table and headed inside. "So I'm on that."

"It's gonna be okay, Ally."

Jeez. This together *together* shit with Ren was *so* easy.

And awesome.

"Thanks, babe," I whispered.

"See you tonight."

"Later, Zano."

"Later, honey."

We disconnected, and by the time I came out with the coffees and resumed my seat, Indy had found a parking spot and was walking up to my table.

She made it to me and stopped.

I looked up at her through my kickass, gold-framed, orange-lensed Ray Bans that had been payment on a "job" and also had luckily been in my purse when my belongings exploded. She looked down at me through her righteous, huge, black-framed, black-lensed Hollywood Starlet shades.

I opened my mouth to speak but she got there before me.

"Tex knows we're here, he's gonna go ballistic."

This was a promising opening.

"This is clandestine because we need privacy, and that's because I need to know I'm cool with you before I take on the Rock Chicks," I explained.

She said nothing and didn't move.

This was not promising.

I slid her cup toward her. "I bought you a skinny vanilla latte."

Her shades dipped to the cup then came back to me. Other than that, she said nothing and didn't move.

This was definitely not promising. India Nightingale was Queen Coffee. I didn't think I'd ever seen her turn down a cup. Definitely not a vanilla latte. In fact, during road trips, I made sure we had a bottle of tequila for when we reached our destination. Indy made sure we had travel mugs filled with java.

I closed my eyes.

Then I opened them and stated, "That night Ren fought with Luke, in an effort to calm him down, I suggested we go for drinks. He took me up on that offer. We went to Brother's but when we got there, it wasn't about Ren and Luke and Ava. It was about Ren and me. And it was good. So good, he took me to his house. That was better. *Way* better. Out of our stratosphere better."

Indy remained silent, another bad sign. She got me. I was talking about sex. And the Rock Chicks existed on a conversational diet heavy on sex talk, Hot Bunch bitching and skincare tips.

Time to pull out the big guns.

"I fell in love with him, chickie," I whispered and watched her lips part.

There it was, thank God. I was getting in there.

So I kept at it.

"In one night, I fell in love."

She bit her lip.

Yes. Getting in there.

"I woke up in his arms in his bed and I was happy. Totally happy, babe. So happy I was lying there smiling. And he curled me closer, shoved his face in my hair and said Ava's name."

That did it.

Her body jolted before she yanked out a chair, sat her ass in it and leaned toward me, exclaiming on a horrified hiss, "Oh my God! Seriously?"

I nodded. "Seriously."

"Holy crap," she breathed.

"It killed," I admitted.

"It would," she agreed.

"Ren was asleep when he did it," I explained. "I snuck out. He got pissed that I did, came over that night and that didn't go very well. I didn't share why I left so he didn't know until yesterday why I established stringent fuck buddy boundaries. Boundaries, I'll add, that he didn't really adhere to and, looking back, I didn't either. Since he was asleep, he didn't know he did it and was pretty upset when I threw it in his face. He explained, we worked it out. I love him, he loves me and it's all good."

Something moved over her face that I could read even behind her shades.

Surprise.

And warmth.

"You love him?" she asked quietly and I felt my lips tip up.

"Yeah," I answered just as quietly.

Her head tipped to the side. "He loves you?"

I nodded and full-on smiled. "Oh yeah."

No surprise that time. Just warmth.

"He's good to you?"

My smile got bigger as my hand lifted to touch the pendant at my neck. "Definitely."

Her shades dropped to my throat. Her mouth got soft but she didn't say anything. I knew she'd like the pendant. I knew she'd know it was from Ren. And I knew she'd know, just looking at its kickassness, that it was thoughtful and generous and said it all.

She took in a breath, looked at me, and asked, "Why didn't you tell me any of this?"

Right. The hard part.

"He said Ava's name," I told her.

"And?" she prompted when I said no more.

"And that hurt," I answered. My voice was quiet, but there was a tremor in it that was not me.

140

And Indy knew me. She knew what that tremor meant. She knew exactly how much it hurt.

This was why her hand shot across the table and grabbed mine as she murmured, "Oh, Ally."

"I didn't want to share. I didn't want to relive. It haunted me enough as it was. And I didn't want Ava to get wind of it," I told her.

"I see that, but you know I would never—"

I cut her off.

"I know. And I know it isn't the same. You've been in love with him since you were five, but it still kind of is, so what would you do if Lee was holding you in his arms in bed after you had a great night, the best you ever had, and he said another woman's name in your hair?"

Her hand gave mine a squeeze. She didn't answer, but she didn't need to. Her face, even with shades, said it all.

She let me go, grabbed her coffee, sucked some back and put it on the table, her shades again locking with mine.

She got me.

"And all the other stuff?" she asked.

This time I got her. Conversation about Ren was done. We were moving on. She wanted to know about my activities.

Another hard part.

Crap.

I leaned forward.

"I'm good at it," I told her.

"I know you are," she replied, and no doubt about it, hearing her say that and do it instantaneously felt *great*.

But I expected nothing less. That was pure Indy.

"No, Indy, *I'm good at it*," I stressed. "It's in my blood. It's who I am. I think I needed to prove that to myself, and the other night in the mountains, I did. What happened there was extreme, and Darius, Brody and me, we kicked its ass. It was awesome. So now, I need to prove to Hank, Lee, Dad, and probably the hardest, Ren, that this is my thing. I'm good at it. And I'm going to keep doing it." I took in a breath then made my point. "Now, do you think I'd get the chance to do that if I did my thing with the Rock Chicks tagging along?"

She saw the wisdom of this statement, and I knew it because she sat back and sucked back more coffee.

"Right. No," I answered for her.

"I would have kept that secret, too," she told me something I already knew.

"I dig that," I replied. "But honestly, think about it. If I shared—you, me, our history, the way we are—can you sit there and tell me you wouldn't have finagled a way to get involved, or at least take my back somewhere in the last two years?"

She saw the wisdom of this statement too, and I knew it when she didn't answer.

Tacit agreement.

"Right, no," I repeated. "And if you did, Lee would lose his mind, you'd lose your mind with Lee for losing his mind, and all that would land on me. I'd have a choice. Stop doing what I love to do, something I'm good at, something that's *in me,* or be responsible for friction between two of the most important people in my life. And Indy, I'm not going to stop. So I had to manage that situation another way. And I picked secrecy."

She nodded. She got this, too.

Thank God.

Then she asked, "So what are you going to do?"

"I'm going to get licensed and put out a shingle."

Her head jerked. "Seriously?"

"Totally seriously."

Her lips spread in a big smile. "That's freakin' awesome, honey."

Again, pure Indy.

There was a reason she was my BFF, and it was not because we'd been thrown together as babies because our parents were best friends and we had no choice.

It was because she was the absolute shit. We clicked. She was not yin to my yang. She was not Laverne to my Shirley.

We were cut from the same cloth. She might be a redhead and me a brunette. She might have curves where I had angles. And she might be a tad bit less crazy than me (a *tad*).

But other than that, we were sisters.

To the core.

I did not share any of this deep crap with her.

I didn't need to.

She already knew it.

Instead I guided the discussion to something (else) that was important.

That was, I warned, "No Rock Chick involvement. I don't tell Roxie how to design websites. I don't tell Jules how to counsel runaways. And you need to back me on that."

She lifted a hand, palm my way.

A Rock Chick Promise.

"You got it. I'm all in on backing you on that."

"That includes you," I added. She dropped her hand and I knew what was coming, so I started, "Indy—"

"What if you need a decoy or something?" she asked.

Yep. I knew that was coming, and it was precisely why this conversation was two years late.

Fuck.

"If I do, that decoy won't be you."

Her head twitched. She was offended.

"It's always me."

That was true too, but now it couldn't be.

I leaned in further in order to lay it out.

"This is the deal and you know it. My brother, your husband, runs this town. What he doesn't run, Marcus or Vito do. And Hank and Eddie protect it. In that mix, there are allegiances and there are alliances. Some of them are unholy, but for some reason, all of them work. And if you think you don't come with Daisy, Jet, Roxie, Jules, and I could go on, and those men won't shut me down because you do, you're wrong."

I put my hand flat on the table between us and kept talking.

"Honest to God, Indy, this is the first time I understand what I want to do with my life. And if I'm going to be taken seriously doing it, *I* have to do it. I have to be professional about it. I have to be smart about it. And I have to make my own allegiances and alliances, and the most important ones I can make are with Lee Nightingale, Marcus Sloan and Vito Zano. You get involved, Indy, *any* of you, I'm done. Lee will see to it, and even if he didn't, any member of the Hot Bunch has enough cred on the streets to make that happen, and any one of them wouldn't hesitate. I don't want to be done, and I need to do everything I can to avoid that. Are you with me?"

"I'm with you," she said softly.

"I need to believe in that," I told her, then continued with the honesty. "I love you, but I can't be making my plays in that game, focusing my attention on that and dealing with you or any of the Rock Chicks at the same time."

Her hand came out again and curled around mine. "I'm with you. I get you. I understand. And you can *believe* in that," she stated firmly.

Yeah. I could believe in that. Indy wouldn't lie to me.

Or she would (told you we were cut from the same cloth), just not about something like this.

I drew in breath and let it out, saying, "Thank you."

She grinned and replied, "Our next come to Jesus, should there be one, which I hope there isn't, but if there is and you feel the need to court the wrath of Tex, let's do it at Paris on the Platte so I can get a Café Fantasia and make it worth it."

Shit. I should have thought of that. Paris had the second best coffees in Denver.

I grinned back. "Agreed."

Her hand tightened on mine. "Love you, honey."

Again with the breath, this one going in deep and coming out deeper. "Right back at cha, sister."

She let me go, let the tough part go, and I knew this because she again sat back and she changed the subject.

"So. Ren Zano. He's hot. You're hot. You look great together. And bonus, he doesn't seem to mind you throwing a punch at him at a wedding, which is good news for you."

I laughed because this was true.

She continued after I stopped laughing and she did it smiling, "So you love him. He loves you. Are there Catholic classes in your future?"

My brows drew together. I wasn't following.

"What?"

"They're Italian. They're Catholic. You're not. You're Presbyterian, and the last time you were in a church, the reverend had to stop services to shout at you to turn your headphones off because AC/DC's 'You Shook Me All Night Long' was screwing up his message."

This was true.

And I'd learned from this to sit in the back.

"In other words, I'm not sure you're going to convince them your gig is more important than theirs. What does Ren say about that?" she asked.

I didn't know what Ren said about that. Ren and I had been too busy breaking a commandment to discuss religion.

Or pretty much anything.

"We haven't gotten that far," I answered, and I saw her brows draw together over her shades.

"Okay," she said slowly. "So what about the families? How are you going to handle that?"

At least I had that sorted.

"They're just going to have to deal," I announced, and Indy stared at me.

Then she repeated, but in a question, "They're just going to have to deal?"

"Yep," I replied nonchalantly.

"Ally, honey, you *have* met your father, haven't you?" she asked.

I waved my hand between us. "Indy, it'll be cool."

She ignored me.

"And Hank."

"Hank wants me happy," I reminded her.

"He does. With a cop, a firefighter or marine."

This was true, too.

"Well, he isn't getting any of those," I pointed out.

"So what you're saying is, you're telling them you're getting in the family business at the same time hooking your star to a man who's already in the family business, but his family business is *family business,* and you think it'll all be cool?"

"Not immediately," I conceded. "Eventually."

"I'm thinking you might need to add nuances to your plan," she suggested.

"And I'm thinking I'm me. They all know me and have my whole life. They know I do what I want and find a way to get what I want. I want Ren. They love me, they'll deal. They give me shit, I'll deal... for a while. It continues, they make a choice. But I've already made mine."

"Lee was broody last night, and in his many levels of broody, it was beyond the my-sister's-apartment-exploded broody, which is at the top of the scale. I think you get that's a little scary," she shared, and she would know his many levels of broody. She'd lived through them all, repeatedly.

But I understood what she was saying.

Ren and I had made it official. This meant it wasn't a fling those around us could pretend wasn't happening and wait for it to be over.

It meant it was something they had to deal with.

I was a little sister to two alpha male brothers. Me finding a man was going to be something they would not dig dealing with normally.

Ren being a Zano didn't make matters better.

"Not to be a bitch or anything, but that's not my problem. It's Lee's," I replied.

"It's his and what's his is mine," she returned.

I was hitting another conversational danger zone. I could feel it.

So I moved to avoid it.

"Indy, babe, I told Ren I was worried that you were mad at me. He called me just before you showed to check in. He was concerned about me and didn't hesitate showing it. That's sweet. That's also Ren. He does that kind of thing all the time, even when I considered us fuck buddies. I'll admit he and I have things to discuss. I've been closed down for a year so we haven't done much of that. We'll also do it. And with the families, I get this road is going to be rocky. What I'm saying is, when they see the way he is with me," I leaned in, "I promise you, *they'll deal*." I leaned back and finished, "It'd help if you had my back on that, too."

"Last time I saw you with Ren, you aimed a punch at him," she reminded me.

Shit.

"So," she went on, "I think I need to delay my answer to that until *I* see him with you."

I could give her that.

Totally.

"Deal," I agreed.

She shook her head but muttered, "Deal."

I sucked back some coffee and asked, "How much shit am I facing with the Rock Chicks?"

"They've had a whole night to rip it to shreds so they've mostly burned it out. They'll get over it," she answered. "Tex is beside himself, though. He's going stir crazy without anything exploding or anyone getting kidnapped. He likes to be a sidekick and he's got grenades and tear gas that are going unused.

146

He doesn't need to use them, but he prefers living a life where that might be a possibility."

She was not wrong.

She kept going.

"Duke's being quiet so, heads up on that. I think he's hurt. And Smithie's pissed because he knows no way he's ever gonna get you to dance for him if you've hooked up with a Zano. And you were his last hope."

There was no way Smithie was ever going to get me to dance for him anyway, even though he asked—frequently—so that last was a relief.

I summed up. "So, not bad. Except Duke."

"You need to find your time to connect with him," she advised.

I could do that. Duke had been so much of a fixture in my life, I didn't remember a time when he wasn't in it. He also cared about me a lot, showed it, and I returned the favor (in my way).

I nodded then declared, "Brother's also let me go so we gotta get to Fortnum's. The tip jar just became my livelihood."

Her eyebrows shot up. "You were fired?"

"How I lasted this long was a miracle."

She didn't agree verbally, but her smile did it for her.

Then it faded and she asked, "You gonna be okay?"

"Right now, all my belongings would fit in a carryall and I'd have room to spare. Still, I've got everything a girl needs. So yeah, I'll be okay."

"Yeah, you will," she said softly.

She was one of the reasons I'd be okay, so she should know.

"That doesn't mean I don't need to hit Fortnum's, but before, we gotta dash through the mall. I have two changes of clothes. I need to stock up and then we gotta bounce."

She nodded again as she rose, taking her coffee. I went up with her, doing the same. We left our cars where they were and moved down the sidewalk heading out of Cherry Creek North toward the mall.

"You know, it would go a long way to smoothing things over with those three if you sent Roxie, Tod and Stevie to the mall to deal with your wardrobe emergency," Indy noted.

I stopped dead on the sidewalk and turned to her.

She was *so* right. And I was a Rock Chick, which meant I was a shopper. But I had shit to deal with, and as much as it killed, the time suckage of buying new jeans and tees was suckage I didn't need.

"Why didn't I think of that?" I asked.

"I don't know," she answered, grinning. "Maybe because you were worried about me, your apartment exploded and you got fired."

I grinned back. "Oh yeah. That took some headspace."

"I see that," she replied as we made to turn back.

But as we did, my eyes caught on something through a shop window and I again stopped dead.

Then I stared.

Then I whispered, "Holy shit."

"What?" Indy asked.

"Holy shit," I repeated, not answering, still staring, and also not believing my eyes.

"*What?*" Indy also repeated, but I knew she saw it when she whispered, "Holy crap." And a nanosecond later she shouted, "*Holy crap!*"

In unison, we ran to the door of the store and then we ran through the store to the display.

And without a window separating us making the sun play games with our eyesight, there they were proving we weren't having a mutual solar hallucination.

Stacks of them in an upright display, at the top of which was a starburst sign that announced *New Series by Local Author.*

And under it were dozens of hot pink books that included the Denver skyline, a film strip filled with pictures, and the white title in (what I had to admit was) a kickass font:

Rock Chick.

Chapter 12

Did I Mention the Suits?

"Oh my God."

"Holy crap."

"I don't believe this."

"Blooming heck. Did that really happen?"

"This pink color is the bomb."

The Rock Chicks were reacting to the book.

We were at Fortnum's and we were holding an impromptu Rock Chick Powwow that Indy had hysterically called to order while riding shotgun with me on our way to the store. She was too freaked to drive. And anyway, she had a strict rule against driving and dialing and she was doing a lot of that.

As usual, no one wasted time hauling ass to Fortnum's.

Now there were stacks of pink books that we'd bought in Cherry Creek on the low table in the seating area in front of the big plate glass window where we were congregated.

The good news was, a published (maybe) fictionalized account of Indy and Lee's courtship took precedence over anyone giving me shit for being secretive about my non-Rock Chick activities as well as not sharing details as I was carrying on a fuck buddies relationship with Ren Zano for a year.

The bad news was, a (maybe) fictionalized account of Indy and Lee's courtship had been *freaking published.*

"Oh my God," Tod chortled, and everyone looked to him to see his book open, his eyes to it, a huge smile on his face. "I remember that. That was hilarious!" He looked to the group. "And this is fab...you...*las.* I'm famous!"

"Tod, this is not fabulous," Indy snapped.

"Yes it is," Tod disagreed.

"It is not," Indy retorted.

"You're famous, too," Tod pointed out. "Or, you're already famous with those newspaper articles, but you'll be *more* famous with this book."

"I don't want to be *more* famous," Indy shot back.

Tod stared at Indy like she'd just declared the sparkly fringed crochet dress Tina Turner wore for her 1971 Beat Club performance of "Proud Mary" was in bad taste.

Then he asked, his voice pitched high, "Why on earth not?"

Indy brandished a pink book at him and yelled, "Tod! They have the kitchen counter scene in this! I don't need the world knowing about the kitchen counter scene."

"What page is that?" Shirleen muttered to Sadie, frantically flipping through a book.

"I'm looking," Sadie muttered back, doing the same.

"That scene was hot," Tod said to Indy.

"That wasn't a *scene*, Tod," Indy returned. "That was my life!"

"I remember hearing that story," Roxie whispered to Ava. "Tod's right. It was hot."

I looked to Roxie, my gut clenching, as Daisy asked, "Who's this Kristen Ashley person?"

"My guess," Tod took his attention off Indy and looked at Daisy, "it's a made up name. Kudos to whoever picked that, *great* romance novelist name. But totally fake. No one's named Kristen Ashley."

"It's not a strange name, Tod," Stella pointed out.

"How many people with romance novelist's names do you know?" Tod asked Stella.

"Ava Barlow," Stella answered.

"Hmm," Tod mumbled.

"India Savage. Allyson Nightingale. Roxanne Logan. Juliet Lawler. Sadie Townsend," Stella carried on.

"Point taken," Tod murmured.

But I was listening with half an ear.

The rest of my focus was on Fortnum's.

I saw a lot of faces I knew. This was because Tex's coffee was revered, thus practically everybody came back for more. It was also because, with the newspaper articles, as Tod noted, Fortnum's, the Rock Chicks and the Hot Bunch were already famous in Denver.

Therefore we had a lot of regulars, and those regulars didn't always just pop by for a coffee. Fortnum's had been around a while. It had that feel that was real. That feel that invited you to stay. That feel that assured you you were welcome. That feel that many gave in to and hung out.

Sometimes for hours.

Right then, the place wasn't packed, but the seating area in front of the espresso counter was full and there were people in line for coffees. And Jane, Indy's other employee outside Duke, Tex, Jet and me, was even ringing up a book.

The kitchen counter story had been talked about, more than once, in that space.

I obviously hadn't had time to read the book, though I'd skimmed parts, but it was safe to say most of what was in it had been discussed, at length and in some detail, in that space.

And easily overheard. The Rock Chicks weren't about quiet. Not even close.

That meant it could be any regular that spent time there.

Why I hadn't thought of this when wondering who spilled to the papers, I did not know.

But I was thinking of it now.

My gut clenched further as I remembered something.

During Indy's Drama, Lee had put bugs and cameras in Fortnum's. These fed to Lee's surveillance room at his office in LoDo. After Indy's drama, he didn't take them out. This was because Lee's surveillance room was manned 24/7, and those feeds provided comic relief for the boys.

And Brody Dunne was not the only computer whiz who could hack into anything.

Someone could have hacked into those feeds.

Someone could be watching us now.

I jumped out of my chair, digging in my back pocket for my phone and heading to the door.

"Where're you goin'?" Tex boomed.

"Gotta make a call," I shouted back.

"Sidewalk, woman. I have eyes on you all the time!" Tex kept booming.

I lifted a hand and waved my assent, head down, phone up. I pushed open the door and stopped on the sidewalk, but before I could call Brody to tell him to check to see if he'd been hacked, it rang and the display told me Ren was calling.

Kristen Ashley

I put it to my ear but didn't say "hey" because Ren was speaking when I got it there.

He was not speaking to me but he *was* pissed.

"I don't give a fuck. Do it. *Now.*"

Uh-oh.

"Ren, what's up?" I asked cautiously.

His attention came to me. "Ally?"

"Yeah, honey. Is something wrong?"

"Santo was tailing you," he stated strangely.

"Okay," I replied.

"He called Lucky, did a hand off, and now I got this pink fuckin' book on my desk."

Hmm. He seemed as angry as Indy. The thing about that was, her having sex with Lee on his kitchen counter and everyone reading about it was (maybe) something to be angry about.

But why was Ren angry?

In order to give him the opportunity to explain his emotion, I repeated, "Okay."

"And this bitch has a website," he told me.

"What bitch?" I asked.

"Kristen Ashley."

My head shot up and I blinked at Broadway.

"What?" I whispered.

He didn't repeat himself. Instead he said something a whole lot scarier.

"Coming soon," he spoke like he was reading. "*Rock Chick Rescue,* the story of Eddie and Jet."

Oh shit.

Unfortunately he kept going.

"*Rock Chick Redemption,* the story of Hank and Roxie."

Oh shit!

He went on, "I'll cut to the chase, babe. The last on this list is *Rock Chick Revolution,* the story of Ally and Ren."

Fuck!

Chills slid down my spine and I whispered, "Our story hasn't been written."

"Babe, our story isn't *a story,*" Ren clipped.

152

This was true.

"They have them all?" I asked.

"Every last one," he answered.

"This isn't good, Ren," I said quietly.

"No, babe. It is not fuckin' good. It's *really* not fuckin' good. You and your girls got eyes on you from somewhere and I don't need my woman to have eyes on her. I also don't need eyes *on me*. Especially not now."

Especially not now. What did he mean by that?

I opened my mouth to ask, but he got there before me.

"Your brother on this?" he asked.

"Which one?" I asked back.

"I don't give a fuck. One, the other, but both would be better," he answered.

"Well, we were kind of busy freaking so I'm uncertain that information has filtered down. Though, Fortnum's is wired to Lee's offices so I expect incoming Hot Bunch imminently."

Ren was silent.

"Zano?" I called.

"That place is wired?" he asked in a scary soft voice.

Oh man.

"Well..." I paused. "Yeah."

"How long has it been wired?"

Oh man!

"Uh... since Indy's thing."

The receiver was not at his mouth when he bit out, *"Fuckin' fuck me,"* but I still heard it.

He came back to me and asked caustically. "You think you might have wanted to mention that?"

"Zano, you've hardly ever been here," I pointed out.

"You think your girls haven't discussed my shit, your shit, our shit, my shit with Ava and anything in between?" he returned.

Hmm.

He had a point.

I heard the roar of a bike, looked that way and saw Vance approaching on his Harley.

I watched Vance (Vance was very watchable), but into the phone, I said, "I need to call Brody, get him on it, see if the feeds were hacked." My eyes on Vance, and particularly the unhappy expression he was wearing, I told Ren, "Vance just got here, and I'm getting the sense this is not a random drop in. I'll phone Lee and Hank after Brody, but I suspect they're already on it and likely both heading this way."

"I'm also on it," Ren told me. "This shit needs to get shut down. You see your brother, Ally, you tell him he needs to find the source before me. Are you with me, babe?"

I had a feeling I was, though I thought it might be prudent to get particulars.

"Maybe we can discuss this tonight over dinner," I suggested.

Vance was in the store and my eyes were aimed down Broadway, where I spotted a black Porsche approaching.

Luke.

"I'm not in the mood to cook," Ren replied. "I'll pick up Chinese."

"That works for me. But I can also pick it up," I offered.

"That works for me," Ren agreed. "You know what I like."

I was feeling weird, freaked, something was gnawing at my gut, but still, Ren pointing out I knew his Chinese preference still made my insides warm.

"Yeah, I know what you like, honey," I murmured.

"Gotta go. Shit to do," Ren stated.

"Okay, but just an FYI, I got fired today so we have time to talk tonight."

This got me nothing.

So I called, "Zano?"

"You were fired?" he asked.

"Yeah."

"From Brother's?" he requested further details.

"Well, Indy's not going to fire me," I noted.

"Babe, your apartment just blew up," he reminded me.

"Zano, that isn't something I'll forget."

"There's eyes on you. New Mexican lunatics after you. We don't know the fallout from your activities in the mountains. Your apartment is rubble. And you tellin' me you just lost your job is an *FYI*?"

"It isn't like I don't have another one," I told him.

Or two.

"Fuck, does anything shake you?" he asked.

"Not really," I answered.

A beat of silence before he shared, "Right now, I don't know what to do with that."

"Admire it?" I suggested.

It was then his voice went sweet.

"Baby, I do admire it. And that is no lie. It's one of the many things I love about you. But that doesn't mean you don't need to keep sharp, and nothing keeps you sharper than you bein' smart enough to be freaked."

"I didn't say I wasn't freaked," I told him. "I just said nothing shakes me."

"We'll get into the nuances of what the fuck is the difference between those two things over Chinese," Ren said, and although a long sentence, the whole of it sounded like it was uttered on a sigh. "Now, I gotta go."

"Okay, but I want your promise that you'll enumerate the other many things you love about me over Chinese," I said.

"Only if you return the favor," he replied.

Instantly, don't ask me why, I launched in.

"Your hair. Your eyes. Your body on the whole, incidentally. Though, if pressed, I could pinpoint a top ten of your anatomy. The way you wear a suit. Actually, the way you dress in its entirety. The way you cook. The way you make sure to cook enough for me. You having tater tots for breakfast. Your voice normally, but more when it gets sweet. The things you do to me in bed. The fact my nighties are appreciated. The fact you're a maximum contact sleeper. Your ability to give perfect presents. You've only given me one, but it was the most perfect present I ever received. You're taller than me. You think I'm funny. You admire me being unshakable. You love your family. You say I love tough and stubborn, and I like that you think that of me. You pay attention. And you never gave up on me." I took in a deep breath and asked, "Did I mention the suits?"

Ren said nothing.

"Zano?"

More nothing.

Just in case I hadn't given him enough, I informed him, "That wasn't exhaustive list. You said you had to go. Those were just the highlights."

"Shut up, baby."

My entire body went still at his tone. It was one I'd never heard. One that slid through me, and if I thought he'd made me feel warm with his sweet, that tone, even using it to say those words, gave me a new kind of warm. The kind

155

of warm that settled in and made you feel found and safe and loved in a way you knew you would never lose any of those things.

Not ever.

For the rest of your life.

"Ren," I whispered.

"I don't know what I did to deserve a whispered Ren, honey, but you can explain that to me later, too. Call me when you're headin' home and I'll do what I can to wrap shit up and get there when you do."

"'Kay," I replied just as a shadow blocked out the sun, and I looked up to see Hank standing there, scowling at me.

Another unhappy member of the Hot Bunch, but one that was in my space.

Shit.

"I have to go," I said to Ren.

"Later, babe.'

"'Bye, Zano."

I did not take it as a good sign that Hank's jaw got tight when I said Ren's name.

I shoved my phone in my pocket and held my brother's eyes.

"What?" I asked when he said nothing.

"You think it's a good idea, you standin' out here on the sidewalk?"

I pointed across the street where Santo had eyes on me and a hand to his mouth, working his teeth with a toothpick.

"Fuck, Zano put his goon squad on you?" Hank asked, studying Santo with a look on his face that stated what I'd previously thought of Santo and Lucky, and that was that he wasn't quite certain if they were idiots or brilliant at playing them.

"Apparently," I answered.

Hank's eyes tipped down to me. "How 'bout you do your brother a favor and get your ass inside?"

"I'll do you that favor, but only because you asked," I answered magnanimously.

Hank looked to the sky.

I sashayed to the door.

I was caught just inside when Hank's fingers curled around my bicep to stop me. But before I stopped, I saw that not only had Vance and Luke joined the party, Hector and Marcus were there as well.

156

No one looked happy.

Except Tod and Shirleen. And it appeared Roxie was fighting a smile. And I couldn't tell because I had her profile, but it looked like Ava was giggling behind her hand.

I wondered what they'd think if they knew they were "coming soon."

This thought exited my head when my brother said into my ear. "Dad wants a family meeting."

This was not a surprise. When Ren and I made it official, I didn't figure Dad would delay.

I pulled away, but not too far, and told Hank, "I'll call him. Set it up."

"He won't want Zano there," Hank told me.

"That might not be his choice," I stated.

"Ally, you want this, you gotta play it smart," he warned.

"Hank," I leaned in and said quietly, "I want this and I don't have to play at anything. You would no sooner ask for approval of the woman you chose to be in your bed than Lee would. Or Dad would. And I will not be happy if that's expected of me. I get your concerns. Totally. What I will not get is if you make a decision before you give Ren a chance."

"We know this guy, Ally, we know his family," Hank replied.

"You don't know how he is with me," I returned. "And you all knew Darius and Shirleen. And when they turned to the dark side, not one of you turned your back on them. Deep down, you got exactly who they were and you accepted how they had to be. You didn't like it. I know it, Hank. Especially you. But you didn't wash your hands of people who mattered because you cast judgment on them. You may know Ren, but you don't *know* him, and all I'll ask of you and everyone is to give him the chance to get to know him. If that doesn't swing my way, so be it. It'll be then I'll ask you to trust in the fact that I know him better than you and *I* know he matters."

Hank held my gaze before he gave in (in a macho alpha way) by jerking up his chin.

Then he declared, "There's more to talk about."

"There is," I agreed.

"We're worried," he stated.

He was talking about my soon-to-be legit business.

"You've no need to be," I assured him.

"Ally—"

Kristen Ashley

I leaned in further and got up on my toes to get (kind of) eye to eye (my brother was seriously tall; then again, so was everyone in our family). "Hank, babe, love you, you know it. And I love it that you're worried. Says a lot. But we'll talk about it later. Okay?"

Another macho alpha chin jerk, which meant *okay*.

Jeez. These guys.

"Now," I continued, deciding to let that go and rocking back to my heels. "Tell me what's happening with Rosie."

This got me a clenched jaw, complete with muscle jumping in his cheek.

Not good.

"Hank?" I prompted.

"By the time Mace got to Kevin's, Rosie had bailed," Hank shared.

I felt my gut get tight.

Not again.

"You're shitting me," I snapped.

"We got a BOLO on him, and Ally," he got close, "you lay low. We also called down to New Mexico. These guys who want his action, they're not good guys."

"I kinda put that together, bro," I replied.

"No, I mean, these guys are not your garden variety assholes," Hank returned.

"Wiring a bomb to a detonator to take out a woman who's an undetermined threat told me that already."

Hank nodded, then informed me, "Darius is on that. And you let him work that without your help. You deal with all the other shit that's going down."

Bossy.

Gack.

It was all around me.

Before I could call him on it, we saw movement and turned to watch a stony-faced Lee approach and yank open the door. The bell over it rang and I knew attention came to us, but I didn't take my eyes off Lee.

"You okay?" I asked, and he tore his gaze from where it was pointed in the store, and without turning to see if I was accurate I knew he was looking at Indy, before he looked down at me.

"Fuck no."

Well, that didn't leave any room for interpretation.

"So I'm not in the mood for you to piss me off," he went on then finished, *"More."*

I lifted my hands, palms out. "Dude, I'm just standing here."

He scowled at me. Then he looked at Hank.

Then he prowled into the store.

Hank and I watched him, and then I called Hank's attention back to me.

"You know you and Roxie are volume three."

"I know. Brody found the website and sent the word out."

"Is he looking into a hack of the feeds?" I asked.

"As we speak," Hank answered.

I studied him. He didn't look happy. I didn't like my brothers unhappy so I leaned into him, bumping his arm with my shoulder and staying close.

"You know," I said softly. "It might be a good idea to adopt Tod's attitude. He thinks it's hilarious."

"Not sure I can get there, honey," Hank said softly back.

I nodded. I was with him.

"Oh my God!" Tod yelled and Hank and I both looked his way. "Cherry and the Chinese restaurant!" He kept yelling, his book open in front of him, his face lit up with humor, his lips smiling and his eyes on Indy. "Your outfit that night, girlie... *lush.* Too bad it got covered in hot and sour soup and fried rice."

My eyes slid to Lee, who was not smiling. Then to Indy, who was glaring at Tod.

But my mind went to Girls Night Out two years ago when Indy got in a catfight with Lee's ex, Cherry.

Her outfit *was* lush (Indy's, not Cherry's; I hated Cherry, she was a lying, bitchy skank, though it was kinda harsh she nearly exploded in a car bomb— karma, totally a bitch).

Indy's outfit did get covered in soup.

That had been a good night.

The best.

Or, as it was with the Rock Chicks, one of many bests.

And now it was laid out on pages for all the world to read.

And I couldn't stop that small part of me thinking that wasn't such a bad thing.

Because it wasn't perfect, none of it.

But it *was* a fairytale.

And people needed to believe in fairytales. Even flawed ones. Maybe especially flawed ones.

And they needed to believe always.

Chapter 13

Lotus, Cowgirl, Scissor and Doggie

I put the plates on the dining room table and adjusted the cutlery.

I'd called Ren ten minutes earlier and lied to him that I was heading home with food. This was a lie since I called when I was already at his place.

It's important to point out it was a little white lie. One I forgave myself for because I needed time to do all I needed to do (not that I didn't forgive myself for all of them). And all I needed to do was get the champagne and the chocolate candles I bought from Pasquini's in the fridge, set the table and arrange the bouquet of flowers and candles there and wash the champagne flutes I also bought.

I'd timed it so all would be ready, but the food would not be cold and I hoped he could wrap things up at work and get home in time to fit in with my plan.

It was a bummer that I didn't have a fabulous dress and heels he hadn't already seen to change into. But after leaving the Rock Chick Powwow, I only had enough time to deal with my plans for dinner and not enough time to do some shopping.

The good news was, I'd taxed Roxie, Tod and Stevie with the mission to kit me out with clothes and other items any girl needed to exist and they were all over it. So I suspected I'd have way more than two pairs of jeans tomorrow.

The bad news was, although my insurance company was on top of working through the process of getting me a check, when I'd called my landlord, he'd communicated to me he was not a big fan of keeping me as a tenant.

He communicated this by saying, "Ally, darlin', you pay your rent on time. You got a lot of visitors, but you're quiet." (This, by the by, was only partially true, and indicated to me that none of my neighbors had complained when I played my rock 'n' roll.) "And once that stuff hit the papers about your friends, gotta admit, I was expecting this to happen. But, gotta say, I wasn't expecting it to be *this bad*."

I couldn't argue that. There had been a lot of kidnappings and stun gun usage was not unheard of, but only Stella and me shared our pads getting blown sky high.

"For the safety of my other tenants, maybe we can make arrangements for you to be let out of your lease," he went on. "Full security deposit back and you don't have to pay this month's rent, seeing as there's no apartment to rent."

I translated this to mean: *It would be a good idea that you let me let you out of your lease so I don't have to be an asshole and evict you.*

It must be said, I didn't like it when assholes were assholes normally (who did?). Forcing someone who was trying not to be one *into* one was not my gig. So I agreed to vacate the premises. Figuratively, of course, since currently there were no premises to vacate and I had no possessions actually *to* vacate.

But this sucked. I couldn't say I was emotionally attached to my apartment, but I didn't need to be looking for one at this juncture. I had tons of other shit to do.

I also couldn't argue with his reasoning. If the unknown jerkoff from New Mexico was a little more gung ho, something already bad could have gone way worse, and I didn't need that on my conscience or to force the issue and put it on someone else's.

So maybe I'd look for a house to rent. One with land. Like ten acres. On ten acres, Tex could set a shitload of booby traps.

Therefore I was planning a nice dinner with Ren that was more than just Chinese takeout because I needed a nice dinner with Ren, seeing as I'd been fired and made homeless on the same day. I figured from our phone call earlier he needed a nice dinner too. I also wanted to break the seal on his dining room table doing something special.

But it was mostly that I wanted to do something special. We hadn't had our first official date and he clearly wasn't in the mood for that tonight, but that didn't mean we couldn't celebrate.

And I'd nearly screwed us up and I needed to make it up to him.

He was sweet. He needed to know in not giving up on me that he'd get that back.

And it wouldn't hurt that, if I buttered him up with my sweetness, he might take the news I was going to officially become a private investigator without losing his Italian American hotheaded mind (too much).

162

I heard someone at the front door and quickly snatched up the lighter on the table so I could light the candles. I pointed the flame to the wick and looked to the left.

Ren was walking in, eyes on me, shrugging off his suit jacket.

Mm.

Yum.

I flicked off the lighter and straightened when it dawned on me Ren wasn't walking in, eyes on me, shrugging off his jacket.

He was *prowling* in, eyes on me, shrugging off his jacket.

Jacket off, he tossed it to a chair he passed without taking his eyes off me and kept prowling.

I dropped the lighter, turned to him, and since his gait was not slowing in the slightest, I started backing up.

"Zano, what the——?"

I kept backing. He kept coming, and I stopped talking when I tripped on the rug that was under his dining room table.

He shot forward and caught me around the waist before my stumble became a fall, but didn't quit moving until my back slammed into the wall and Ren slammed into me.

He drove his fingers into my hair, fisted them and tilted my head one way while his arm tightened around my waist, his head slanted and his mouth landed hard on mine.

Then he kissed me, wet, deep, long and *rough.*

My inner thighs quivered, my happy place rejoiced and both my hands lifted so I could sift my fingers in his hair and hold him to me.

It took some time but he finally (alas) tore his mouth from mine and I stared, breathless, into his heated eyes.

"What was that for?" I asked in a quiet voice, mostly because there was no way in hell I had it in me to speak louder seeing as I could barely breathe.

"That was because I like, a fuckuva lot, all the reasons you love me. But more, I like that you laid it out, no hesitation, all real, and didn't make me work for it."

I made a mental note to do that again, and often, as my insides warmed in a way that had nothing to do with the heat created by his kiss.

"Just to keep that goodness coming, right now, would you like me to give you my top ten of your anatomy?" I offered.

He smiled, but he did it while pressing his body into mine (and, incidentally, that meant nearly all of his top tens were pressed tight to me, including my number one). And since my back was to the wall, that meant I felt him deep.

I liked the feel.

Then again, I always had.

"We'll wait on doin' that when we're naked," he replied.

"Sounds like a plan," I muttered.

His smile got bigger and my happy place got happier. He tipped his head, touched his lips to my jaw and pulled us from the wall, turning.

He got to facing the table and stopped dead.

"Christ," he whispered.

Apparently, he'd been all fired up to show me his appreciation about what I'd said earlier and hadn't noticed my preparations for the evening.

"Baby, what——?" he started, dipping his chin to look down at me.

I interrupted him to ask, "Was last night the only night I get to show you special?"

He said not one word. He just stared at me, his arm around my waist, his body unmoving.

"Zano?" I called.

"I love this. This is beautiful," he said in his sweet voice. "And hear me, honey, I get what you're doing, but I need you to know that you have nothing to make up for. You gave me you and that's all the special I need."

God!

Seriously?

This guy was unreal.

I loved it at the same time it was undoing me. The thing was, I didn't mind the idea of coming undone and that freaked me.

To communicate this to Ren, I curled into him and shoved my face in his chest.

His hand came up and curled around the back of my neck.

More sweet.

I couldn't hack it.

"I need to pick a fight," I told his shirt.

His body jolted slightly and his voice held a vein of humor when he asked, "What?"

I dropped my head back to look at him.

"I'm Ally. I'm not the romance and candlelight and flowers and champagne and sweetness and soft words that mean everything kind of girl. We need to pick a fight. This is freaking me out. And anyway, you're an alpha badass hothead. You're not supposed to notice flowers and candlelight. And no alpha badass hothead has the capacity to say the right thing at the right time and do it repeatedly. I know. I've been witnessing them in action for a while now. Counting Dad and Indy's dad, Tom, it's safe to say I've had a lifelong study."

"Maybe your girls don't share everything," he suggested.

He clearly hadn't been around to overhear the Rock Chicks gabbing.

I decided not to reply as that information might freak *him*.

"I'll do my best to ignore it from here on out," he offered.

"Appreciated," I muttered.

He grinned, bent his head to brush his lips to mine then he let me go and ordered, "I'll get the champagne, you get the food."

Since this was an acceptable arrangement, I complied.

He got the champagne. I went to the table to light the candle I didn't get to when he'd rushed me. Then I set out the food. Ren set out a champagne bucket filled with ice and the opened bottle. He handed me my glass as we both sat.

I stared at the champagne bucket.

"Babe," he called and my eyes drifted to him.

"You have a champagne bucket," I told him something he knew since it was him that filled it with ice and put it on the table.

His head tipped to the side. "Yeah."

"I'm not sure what to do with that," I shared.

"And I'm not sure why you'd have to do anything with it," he returned.

"Um... I don't think I know anyone with a champagne bucket, except my parents, and they got theirs for a wedding present thirty-nine years ago."

"Which would stand to reason this is the bucket Ma and Pop got at their wedding thirty-eight years ago."

"Oh," I mumbled. I tipped my head to the side and proceeded cautiously, "Why do you have it?"

He took a sip of champagne, set his glass aside and picked up his fork. He did all this not looking at me, which was all kinds of strange with Ren. He was a straight talker and a big fan of eye contact.

And he did all of it while he answered, "Ma couldn't let go of shit, but she had to get rid of it. She bided her time for years, keeping it for her kids, and when we left home, she divvied it out. I got a champagne bucket I never needed until now, and 'cause she had to unload that shit, I didn't argue. What I did do was keep it just in case she changed her mind and wanted it back."

I remembered during Brother's, beer and bourbon he said his mother couldn't deal when his dad died and I was curious to know more. Most especially why Ren relayed this seemingly tame, though sad information without looking at me.

But I sensed now was not the time to dig into that.

So I just said, "Right."

He dropped his fork on his plate, went back to his flute and held it up to me. "Toast, baby."

Oh shit. A toast could mean anything and that anything could include more of my undoing.

In order to ascertain whether or not to prepare, I asked, "Are you going to say something that's going to make me feel warm inside?"

His beautiful espresso eyes lit, his lips quirked, and he asked back, "I make you feel warm inside?"

Like he needed me to confirm that.

I gave him a look as answer.

He gave me a grin.

"Okay, how's this?" he began, lifting his flute half an inch. "To my top ten. Eyes. Ass. Pussy. Hair. Tits. Lips. Neck. Legs. Backs of your knees. Ankles. In that order."

My brows shot up because I was shocked.

"My ass is before my happy place?"

At that, his beautiful espresso eyes were actually *dancing* (no joke), his body was shaking and his words were rumbling with laughter when he asked, "Your happy place?"

"Dude, totally happy."

He let fly and burst out laughing.

I watched, enjoyed the show, and when it waned, I lifted my glass and said, "To your top ten."

We clinked. We drank. But before we set our glasses aside, Ren's hand snaked out, hooked me behind the neck and pulled me to him for a hard, closed mouth kiss.

When he was done, he turned his attention to his food and I followed suit thinking I really liked his dining room table.

I'd had a bite when he demanded, "Right, let's get the bad out of the way. Update."

I forked into a piece of kung pao shrimp and gave him what I knew he wanted, which was what I'd gleaned from a variety of phone calls I took while shopping.

Though it wasn't much.

"No hack. Brody was affronted it was even suggested that could happen. But it hasn't. The author's website is registered to a non-existent address somewhere in bumfuck Wyoming. The name it's registered under is not the author's name, but it's also a person who doesn't exist."

"Dead ends," Ren murmured, sounding displeased.

"Sorry, honey," I murmured back. His eyes caught mine and he nodded. "They're widening the net," I assured him.

He nodded again while turning his attention back to his plate.

I took a bite, swallowed and kept to our current theme of getting the bad out of the way by saying, "I got some more bad news today."

His eyes came to me and, seriously, no joke, I could do nothing for a year but stare into those eyes and I'd be totally cool.

Maybe two years.

Or three.

"What?" he asked when I said nothing.

I stopped focusing on his eyes and focused on him.

"Called my landlord to check in. He's letting me out of my lease, which is his nice way of saying he's evicting me."

The easy we'd fallen into being together *together* disintegrated when his anger hit the room with a heavy weight, and I felt my back straighten.

"Say that again," he ordered.

"It's okay, Ren. If you're okay with me hanging here awhile, I'll find a new place."

"No, Ally, it isn't fuckin' okay. Everything you own is ash in an explosion that was not your responsibility. It had nothing to do with you and everything to do with a pot-addled moron in New Mexico you haven't seen in two years. So it's not okay that you pay further for that guy bein' a moron. You've tolerated too many knocks in too short a period of time. Your landlord isn't going to land another one."

He reached to his champagne, threw some back and finished his alpha badass statement while placing the glass on the table.

"I'll have a word with him. You're good to stay here until they repair the damage."

"Ren, I'm down with being let out of the lease."

He again turned his gaze to me. "I'm *not* down with it. I'll have a word."

"But—"

"Ally, no."

I waited for him to say more. But it seemed he figured, *Ally, no,* was the end of it, and I knew this because he resumed eating.

I took in a deep breath. Then I ate more shrimp. Then I took a sip of champagne. After that, I took another deep breath.

Nope.

None of that worked. I didn't feel calm. I felt like mouthing off, being a smartass and making a massive point.

However, that was not an option open to me during a special dinner with my hot guy.

So I turned my eyes to Ren and did everything I could to break our pattern of fighting instead of conversing.

That was to say, I struggled to sound calm when I said, "It's both cool and hot, this gig of you wanting to protect me and stick up for me. But I just want to make it clear right now, honey, that you don't get to make and carry through decisions about my life without discussing them with me. And just to be *crystal* clear, discussing is a courtesy I extend to you. My life is my life, and in the end, I make the decisions."

His head had turned to me while I was talking and I was feeling pleased with myself for dropping the "honey" in my statement, thinking that softened it nicely.

"Your life is not your life," he replied, and I expected a lot of things, particularly him saying something in Asshole or him dismissing me.

That I didn't expect. I also didn't understand it.

"I don't follow," I told him.

He shook his head and stated, "I've changed my mind. I won't talk to your landlord."

That was better.

Surprising. Surprisingly easy. But better.

Maybe he wanted to break the pattern of shouting at each other too.

"Thanks, honey," I said softly.

"Because you're movin' in with me."

I blinked.

"What?"

He put his fork down and turned fully to me and I didn't suspect this boded good things.

I would be proved right.

"Ally, your life is not your life. We love each other, and in case you missed it, that means we've committed to each other. So your life and how you lead it affects me. So yeah, we discuss things. But you don't make decisions we disagree on about shit that affects me—in other words, your life. You also need to have a mind to my need to protect you. I know this is not news that I have this need. You picked me, you signed on for that. But all that's moot. We already decided you're gonna stay awhile. Yesterday, you lost everything. Today, you found out you can't go back. Backed in a corner by circumstances, thinking on it, shit often happens for a reason and even bad shit leads to good things. And this particular good thing is that there's absolutely no reason not to make the arrangement we already agreed on permanent."

"Zano, making that permanent is a big leap from what we had to roomies."

"Baby," his voice (and expression, I'll add—double whammy) turned sweet, "there is *never* a time we're gonna be just roomies."

My eyes narrowed, not because I didn't like what he said (a lot).

They narrowed because I was getting a sneaking suspicion he turned on the sweet in order to get his way. I'd missed it for months because usually by the time he turned on the sweet, we were shouting at each other.

Things were now coming clear.

I tried to keep the sarcasm out of my, "Maybe I think there are absolutely *some* reasons not to make the arrangement we agreed on permanent."

It should be noted, although I said it, I couldn't think of a single reason not to make it permanent.

If pressed though, I'd make something up.

He leaned into me. "Tell me, since Sadie's thing, when you're not working or gallivanting, when have you been at your apartment and I haven't been there with you?"

Uh-oh.

He was making sense.

And I wasn't fond of the word "gallivanting."

Sure, one could say I gallivanted. My net was not wide, but I got around.

Still.

"And tell me," he continued, "when have you had downtime at all when you were not in your apartment, with me, or you weren't here..." He paused to drive his point home. Then he drove it home. "*With me.*"

More sense.

Gack!

"Babe, we already live together, and we've been doin' it for eight months. It's just that our clothes were in different closets," he finished.

Jeez, we were so totally not fuck buddies. No wonder Ren found that amusing.

This thought and his words meant I kept glaring at him, mostly because he was right and that sucked.

But as I did this, something stole through me.

And what that was was the fact that Lee essentially moved Indy in with him the day her thing started. They never separated after that.

And now they were married.

Jet had succeeded in keeping a hint of distance between her and Eddie for about a week. Then he moved her in and she never left.

And now *they* were married and *she* was pregnant.

Much the same thing happened with Roxie, Jules, Ava, Stella and Sadie.

And when I said "much the same thing" I meant near on *exactly*.

Holy crap.

I wasn't a Rock Chick.

I was a *Rock Chick!*

That meant...

That meant...

That meant Ren and I were getting married!

Holy *crap!*

I fought hyperventilating and did it by sucking back champagne.

This was a stupid move because, once done, I started choking.

"Ally? Baby?" Ren called, and I saw him move and then he was leaned into me, hand rubbing my back. "You okay?"

I sucked in oxygen, twisted my neck to look at him, and declared, "We're getting married."

His chin jerked back and his brows shot up. "Now?"

"Not now!" I cried, falling back in my chair. He straightened to standing, but I tipped my head back so I could keep my eyes glued to him. "During her thing, Indy and Lee moved in together. The same with Jet and Eddie. Roxie and Hank. Jules and Vance. You get my drift. Now all of them are married. Ava and Luke are getting hitched on the weekend. And three weeks ago, Sadie strolled into a Girls Night Out with a diamond on her finger." I stretched my torso up to him and announced, "Ren, we're screwed."

At that, his brows knit.

"You don't want to get married?"

"No," I answered, and completely ignored his expression shutting down in order to continue to have my nervous breakdown. "For the next five years I want to engage in copious amounts of hanky-panky until my biological clock starts ticking so loud I can't ignore it anymore. Then I want to engage in copious amounts of hanky-panky in order to get pregnant. Prior to part two, I want to get married."

He sat down but didn't take his eyes from me as he stated, "This doesn't sound like a bad plan."

"It's not. It's a righteous plan."

"Then why are you freaked?" he asked.

"Because no way am I falling into the pattern of meatloaf, Letterman and missionary, and with practice, that's a possibility."

His head jerked before he asked, "Ally, *what?*"

"I like meatloaf but it's boring," I explained. "I like chicken parmesan way better. Letterman rocks but I'd prefer to do other things when he's on. And missionary is my fifth most favorite position behind lotus, cowgirl, scissor and doggie."

It was Ren's turn to blink.

Then he again burst out laughing.

When he was done laughing, but he was still chuckling, he calmly picked up his fork and speared some sesame chicken before he said to his plate, "So you're movin' in."

Shit.

"Yeah," I answered, spearing another shrimp.

"Baby?" he called, and I looked at him.

Oh God.

The look on his face was a new look. It corresponded with the tone of his voice earlier that day. And it was so beautiful, my heart skipped a beat and I lost the ability to think.

And speak (mostly).

"We're never gonna have meatloaf, Letterman and missionary," he said softly.

"'Kay," I replied breathily.

"And if you can pare down that five year fuck-a-thon to two or three, I'd appreciate it," he went on.

"'Kay," I repeated.

"Though, during that two year fuck-a-thon, you may have one, then two of my rings on your finger."

Oh shit.

Even me, Ally, Rock Chick, that didn't make me warm inside.

It made me melty.

"'Kay," I breathed, and his eyes warmed.

"Just to give you something to look forward to, we'll stop the fuck-a-thon when we have to, but we'll resume soon's we can after you give me healthy babies."

Oh *God*.

I felt my eyes get hot.

Ren and I were getting married.

Not now.

But eventually.

Oh.

God.

"You really love me," I whispered.

"Do not ever doubt it," he whispered back.

"How did that happen?" I kept whispering.

"You accepted my devotion to the Bears only dishin' out minimal shit."

He was such a liar.

But what he said said it all.

And it meant everything.

He started falling when I did.

I closed my eyes.

I opened them when I felt the backs of his fingers sweep my jaw.

"It doesn't take much with you, does it?" I asked, trying to be funny.

I didn't get a smile.

I got heated eyes and *the look.*

"Yes it does. It takes a fuckuva lot."

That said it all, too.

Jeez. He needed to stop.

Before I could tell him to do that, he did it.

And he did it by saying, "And most of that fuckuva lot has to do with the fact that you're a woman who placed cowgirl at two and doggie at four."

I got over being a big, starry-eyed, head-over-heels-in-love-with-a-hot-guy *girl,* started laughing and asked through it, "So you approve of my rankings?"

He turned his attention back to his plate, saying, "Cowgirl one. Doggie two. Missionary three. Lotus four, but you're close enough."

I kept laughing and through it watched Ren grinning before he took a sip of his champagne.

I quit laughing, grabbed my own champagne and was taking a sip when Ren's voice—not sweet, instead all kinds of sexy, the kinds that got my full attention when he declared, "Three, one, two."

I looked at him. "Come again?"

"Tonight," he replied. "Three, one, two. Maybe during one we'll also do a four, but I'm finishing you off on your knees."

My happy place spasmed, my breasts swelled and my mouth got dry.

"That is, after you go down on me," he finished as he reached for the champagne bottle.

That was when I started salivating.

A knock came at the door.

I stopped salivating and was thankful I hadn't begun panting as I looked to the door.

Ren threw his napkin down and pushed back his chair, muttering, "Fuck."

"Are you expecting someone?" I asked as he walked away.

"Are you in my house?" he asked back.

"Yes," I pointed out the obvious.

At the door, hand on handle, he turned to me and answered, "Yes."

What did that mean? I'd never had visitors at his house.

Then again, I frequently got visitors at my apartment. Ren knew that because he'd been there a lot when I got them. So clearly he expected this to go on and I made a mental note to do something about that since it sounded like he didn't like it much.

And it must be said, when it interrupted dinner and discussion on the later positions in which Ren would be giving me the business, I didn't like it much either.

He looked through the double row of three square windows set high in his door. I heard his sigh all the way across the house (his sigh was that big) and he opened it.

I couldn't see anything since Ren was standing in the door and hadn't fully opened it, but I did hear a deep, somewhat familiar voice I couldn't place ask, "Is Ally Nightingale here?"

When I heard Ren's answer of, "You wanna explain why you want that information?" I pushed back my chair and threw down my own napkin.

"We need to have a chat," the familiar voice answered.

I walked that way as Ren replied, "And you're lookin' for her here, how? How is it that you're *here* lookin' for her?"

The voice had turned guarded, probably with caution and maybe a little irritation, when it returned, "Man, she's yours and her apartment is a black hole. Where else would I look for her?"

I made it to Ren's back and put a hand there, but it was clear the voice's answer was acceptable because he was moving back to open the door.

I then saw how I knew the voice.

Jacob Decker. And Jacob Decker was Chace Keaton's friend. And Chace Keaton was my girl Faye's hot guy badass.

I'd met him briefly during the brouhaha up in the mountains. And when I saw that mountain of muscle, thick dark hair and intelligent hazel eyes, I lamented there were no Rock Chicks left I could toss in his path. He looked like a man who could handle a Rock Chick. Even a man who needed one. The more

174

fucked up her life, the better. And if there had been one left, it would be me causing mayhem in order for him to get one.

"Deck, hey," I greeted as I stepped back with Ren and Jacob Decker stepped in.

His eyes went to the table, flowers, food and candlelight, then they skimmed through Ren and me.

"Interrupting. Apologies," he murmured.

Ren slid an arm along my shoulders, moved us into the house and out of the entryway, and Deck followed.

What he didn't do was accept Deck's apology, though his moving us all in probably didn't need words. I suspected Jacob Decker spoke macho alpha so he likely wasn't offended.

"This won't take long," Deck assured as we settled in the living room and his eyes settled on me. "I'm cleanup in Carnal," he announced.

I didn't get it.

"Sorry?" I asked.

"The situation in Carnal. I'm batting cleanup," Deck said the same thing with more words.

Therefore, I still didn't get it.

"Uh... those dudes buried Faye to force Chace to get the dirt other dudes were holding on them. My crew got that dirt. We turned it over. They have it. No cleanup necessary."

"You did do that. You also turned over enough to the cops they took down two of those guys," Deck replied.

I did do that. Or Brody, Darius and I did that.

I shrugged.

"Them's the breaks," I stated blithely. "Anyway, added deterrent to the others not to fuck up. It should all be good."

Ren got closer and his arm got tighter when Deck's face went way scary.

"You don't understand me," he said on a growl. "Nothing is good. My boy's woman got buried alive. I'm *cleanup* in that situation in *Carnal*."

I finally got it.

Those dudes were not going to get away with burying Faye alive.

I was down with that. Those shitheads deserved whatever this mountain of man had in store.

And anyway, that meant I could tick one thing off my watch list.

I didn't speak macho alpha, therefore could not communicate telepathically, via chin lifts or through actions to other macho alphas, so I felt it prudent to agree verbally. I did this by mumbling, "Okeydokey."

"You got anything that will help me do that in a timely manner," he stated, "It'd be appreciated you turn that over to me."

"What we have, you'll have by tomorrow," I told him, adding a call to Brody on my to-do list for the next day.

He nodded, reached in his back pocket, pulled out a wallet and then a card that he handed to me.

"Email," he said.

It was my turn to nod as I shoved his card in my back pocket.

Deck looked at Ren. "No blowback."

Why he told this to Ren, I did not know, but I suspected it was because I had a vagina.

I decided not to throw a hissy fit and I did this for two reasons. One, a hissy fit took time and I wanted to finish dinner, drink more champagne, eat my chocolate candle then do three, one, two (and maybe four) with Ren. Two, Jacob Decker could break me in half and he seemed to be fired up to accomplish his mission, so I didn't feel it was wise to waste his time which might make him testy.

"Grateful," Ren murmured.

I fought an eye roll.

"I'll leave you to dinner," Deck said.

He nodded to me, gave a macho badass chin jerk to Ren then disappeared through the door.

Ren let me go to walk to it and turn the locks.

He claimed me again and guided us back to the table.

Once there, after refreshing our champagne, he shared, "Jacob Decker. Qualifies for Mensa. Occupation, hazy. Reputation, not a guy you fuck with."

I stared at Ren. "You checked him out?"

"I checked out everyone close to Faye Goodknight and Chace Keaton."

I kept staring at Ren. "When did you have a chance to do this?"

"When I texted Dom to get his ass on it about five minutes after Keaton shook my hand and said, 'Nice to meet you, I'm Chace Keaton,' which was about two seconds before I laid into you."

I continued staring at Ren. "Okay, *why'd* you do this?"

"Because you got your ass on radar for that guy and his woman, and since your ass is *my* ass, I protect that ass, both proactively and retrospectively. I do that by gathering any and all information on anyone who might be involved, even unintentionally, in threatening that ass." He looked back to his plate, muttering, "Though I prefer proactively or not having to do it at all."

I didn't know what to do with this. It wasn't a surprise, really. It also wasn't an invasion, exactly.

Before I could make a decision about what to do with it, Ren swallowed a bite and kept talking.

"One good thing, you with me, all that shit is over."

Uh-oh.

He reached for his glass, but before he took a sip, he looked at me and stated, "And Decker's visit means that shit'll be shut down. His occupation may be hazy, but his reputation also says he gets a job done." He took a sip, put his glass back and finished, "Finally something good happened today. A line drawn under that mess. And if you got any other shit goin' on, you work with Tucker and Dunne to finish it, then you're free to find a real job and settle in with me."

Oh man.

He picked up his fork.

"Uh... Zano," I called.

"Yeah, honey?" he answered his chicken.

Shit.

I stared at his profile, his square jaw, the line of his full lips, the spikes of his thick eyelashes. Then my eyes slid through the food, the champagne bucket, the flowers, the candles.

I took this all in, but my head was filled with promises of three, one, two (with the possible inclusion of four) and the way it felt when he drew my pendant in his mouth that morning.

Then I decided we'd both had enough for the day and tomorrow would be a better time to explain to Ren about the "real job" I was finding.

So, I scooped up some peanuts and mumbled, "Nothing."

Crap!

Chapter 14

Hit Play

Darius stared at me.

"Well?" I prompted.

We were sitting in his truck outside Fortnum's the morning after Chinese with Ren (and, by the way, after chocolate candles, we did four along with one, as well as three and two; it was *righteous*).

I'd just told Darius my future career path.

"You got instincts I haven't seen except in men trained and experienced or earned on the streets," Darius stated.

Well that was good.

"I still don't like it," he finished.

Hmm.

"It would mean a lot if I had your support," I said quietly.

He shook his head but said, "You have my support, Ally. I know you enough to know no one's gonna be able to talk you out of it, but that isn't it. Seen it time and again, takin' your back, you got your shit tight. But your girls are nuts. The reason I don't like it is because those women don't have their shit tight."

"They won't have anything to do with this," I assured him.

"How you gonna manage that miracle?" he asked.

"I explained it to Indy, she gets me. They will too."

He shook his head again and looked forward. He also looked reflective. And lastly, he didn't say anything.

"Darius," I called, and his head again turned to me.

"You need to get licensed, and for that you need bona fide investigative hours. And the way to get them is workin' with Lee," he announced.

I blinked at him, something funny, but by no means bad, moving through me.

Before I could pinpoint what that feeling was, he kept talking.

"And no way your brother is gonna take you under his wing. He's been on my ass now for months to find a way to shut you down. He doesn't give a shit you close cases, you're trained, you shoot, you run, and you take this shit seriously. He knows the dangers and he wants you nowhere near that. Your dad and Hank agree."

"Maybe I can convince them," I suggested, but when Darius's expression turned from pensive to dubious, I tried something else. "Maybe I can work my next case with one of the Hot Bunch and whoever that is can vouch for me."

"You're workin' your cases with Brody and me and that hasn't worked. Brody thinks you're the shit, Ally. And he's shared that with Lee. Repeatedly. Lee isn't swayed."

Okay, as annoying as Brody could be, at Darius's words, I remembered why I loved him.

"Then I'll work with another investigator," I proposed.

"Sylvie Bissenette," Darius said immediately.

I knew of Sylvie. I'd never met her, but she was a private investigator in town who had a reputation, a good one.

And this idea was a good one, too. Badass bitches take on Denver.

I liked it.

"She had a partner," Darius went on. "He re-enlisted, died overseas. That means she's used to workin' with somebody. But Lee also contracts with her occasionally, so she might not be big on takin' you on if that makes things shaky with Lee."

God.

Lee.

Every time I turned around it came back to Lee standing right in my way. And he was my brother. I loved him, respected him, admired him. I needed to finesse that, not try to find my way to blow through it.

"That said," Darius carried on, "she's a chick in the business and knows it isn't easy breaking through. She might be down with workin' with you because of that."

A ray of light.

"Uh, dude," I started, "there *is* another way."

"That would be?" he asked.

"You're in the biz, so *you* could vouch for me with the Licensing Board."

That expression I did not like crossed his face before he hid it and replied, "Ally, I'm not licensed, and I'm not gonna be. Workin' with Lee, I don't gotta be. But still, it isn't going to happen."

I didn't get this.

Sure, he had a rap sheet, but as many times as he got arrested, nothing ever stuck. He'd never done time.

And it wasn't like he was the only human being who did wrong and turned his life around.

I wasn't certain how the Colorado Licensing Bureau felt about it, but he'd been working under Lee now for over a year. He was on the crime-free wagon and hadn't once even teetered, much less fallen off.

I could tell by his face that this wasn't the time he was going to share, and I wondered if there would be a time he would do that voluntarily.

I suspected there would not.

So that meant it was soon going to be *my* time to get out the tequila and have a sit down with my brother of another color. He lived. He breathed. He worked. He even smiled and sometimes laughed.

But something about him made me feel he was on hold. Waiting.

For what, I didn't know.

But it was becoming clear it was time I did what I could so Darius Tucker would stop existing on pause and hit play.

"I'll talk with Sylvie," he offered.

"That'd be cool, Darius," I accepted.

Darius changed subjects.

"Now, you know both Hank and Lee have been in my face to keep you out of this Rosie shit, but I know if I tried, you'd lose your mind and you'd get in it. So I'm gonna keep you briefed."

Seriously.

I loved Darius.

I grinned.

He kept talking.

"He's smoke. His shit was good shit and he's still got fans here, so I'm workin' my way through who I knew was partial to his product. The boys from New Mexico have no ties here. This is not good. No known associates, nothin' to go on. Brody's workin' that book thing and he's also workin' hotel/motel registrations for me. I'm takin' this on two angles, shuttin' down Rosie and shuttin' down the source of danger by findin' those guys. It's not gonna be easy so Lee has also assigned Hector to work with me."

I nodded.

Darius carried on. "Because of their relationships with you, Hank and Eddie can't work this case officially. They've assigned it to Jimmy Marker. Jimmy's keepin' them briefed, they're briefin' me."

Poor Jimmy.

A colleague of my dad's, I'd known Jimmy Marker since I was a little girl. And Jimmy was batting a thousand. That would mean he'd picked up every Rock Chick case, now including mine.

"You got Santo and Lucky on your ass," Darius continued. "You still carry, keep your stun gun and pepper spray on you. Vigilance, Ally."

"Always, honey."

This time, he nodded.

"Shit to do," he muttered, which meant we were done.

"Darius?" I called, even though he was looking at me.

"Right here, Ally."

"I love what I do. I'm going to love doing it for a living. But the thing I love most is that you always believed in me."

Darius held my eyes a beat before he looked down to the seat.

When he lifted his eyes again, I took in a hissed breath at the unconcealed pain there.

"And I love it that you always believed in me," he whispered.

Oh God.

I leaned toward him. "Darius——"

"Get outta my truck, Ally."

"Darius——"

"Out, sweetheart."

It was him calling me sweetheart *and* doing it in a voice that was rough with emotion that made me nod and exit his vehicle immediately.

I stood on the sidewalk and watched him drive away.

Definitely time for tequila and a sit down between Darius and me.

I looked across the street and gave a wave to Lucky who was standing outside a sedan and leaning into his forearms on its roof.

He lifted a hand and gave me a salute.

I gave him a chin lift that was probably not macho badass and walked into Fortnum's.

It was a hair after opening, which meant the place was packed.

Duke was behind the book counter, and when I caught his eyes, he scowled at me, turned and disappeared into the rows of shelves behind him.

Okay, so, tequila with Darius. And also beer with Duke.

Tex and Jet were behind the espresso counter and I headed there, even though both of them being there left little room for me. Not because there wasn't enough room for three people. Just that, with the addition of Jet's seven month's pregnant belly, it made it a tight squeeze.

We got to work, but I knew I was operating on borrowed time caused by the coffee rush and this was confirmed when it slowed and immediately Tex turned to me.

"Not happy," he boomed, even though I was three feet away.

I was not surprised by this announcement. Not because I ticked everyone off with my secrecy.

No, because Tex was rarely happy.

"What now?" I asked.

"You're hooked up with Zano."

Shit.

Here we go.

"Tex——" I started.

"That means you got Zano Family protection. So that means no one's gonna fuck with you. So that means you're gonna do whatever it is you're gonna do, but still, shit's gonna stay boring."

I stared.

Tex kept booming. "That apartment explosion was a fluke. Those New Mexicans get wind you've got family protection, they're gonna back off. Then where we gonna be?"

"Safe and happy?" Jet suggested, and Tex turned a narrowed gaze and knitted bushy brows to her.

"What fun is that?" he asked.

"Just pointing out," I entered the conversation, "the other Rock Chicks had Nightingale and police protection, not to mention Sloan and Zano protection in some cases, and shit happened to them."

Was I assuring Tex of impending danger and mayhem?

"You women burned your way through anyone stupid enough to spit into the eye of those tigers. There's no one left," Tex replied.

"Maybe those New Mexicans won't get wind of all that," I proposed. "Out-of-towners with no local known associates, they may be slow to cotton on."

Yes, I was assuring Tex of impending danger and mayhem.

"It's thin," Tex muttered. "But it's something."

He turned back to the espresso machine and jerked off a portafilter with such force, the entire machine (and it was not small *or* light, not by a long shot) moved sideways half an inch.

He also kept muttering.

"And we got that book thing. Those badasses were beside themselves yesterday. Got a feeling that shit's gonna get interesting."

I had a feeling he wasn't wrong

I looked to Jet.

Jet rolled her eyes and shrugged.

I got close to her and asked, "How are you feeling about the book thing?"

Her head tipped to the side before she replied. "I can't find it in me to get worked up about it. Sure, there's more detail in Indy's book, but it isn't like it wasn't mostly all laid out in the papers." She righted her head and went on to inform me, "Eddie's not pleased."

That wasn't a surprise.

"So I'm thinking I should probably devote my attention to not getting wound up about it." Her hand went to her belly. "He's not big on me getting worked up about stuff."

I knew that. If Eddie adored Jet before (and he adored her, in his macho badass way), he doted on her now. He was ecstatic (again, in his macho badass way) that she was having his baby, thus he treated her like porcelain. No Eddie Chats that pissed her off. No being bossy. It was all about soft looks and sweet touches and handling her with the utmost care.

It was pretty righteous.

Then again, Eddie had always been a really good guy (in his macho badass way).

So that wasn't a surprise, either.

I dipped my head to her belly. "How's preparations for the blessed event coming?" I asked, and she gave me her knockout smile.

"The addition is done," she told me, referring to the new kickass laundry room Eddie and Hector added on to their house so Jet didn't have to walk down to the basement to do laundry. "The nursery is done," she went on. "Now he's starting on refinishing the basement so we can move number one out to a bedroom downstairs," she patted her big belly. "And move number two into the nursery upstairs when the time comes."

"Forward planning," I noted and got another big smile.

It was safe to say Jet, as well as Eddie, were looking forward to having a big happy family.

I pulled in a breath and got to the hard part.

"Okay, so how are you doing with me?" I asked, and her smile changed. It didn't fade, but it grew softer.

"You're Ally," she answered.

I was.

"You do what you do," she continued then her smile re-brightened. "I'm just bummed out I didn't get the chance to tell you not to fight it."

"I wouldn't have listened," I told her.

"They never do," she replied, and that was so true, we both giggled.

The bell over the door rang.

I turned and watched Daisy charge in wearing a skintight baby pink Juicy Couture track suit with the hoodie unzipped so far you could see the lace of the cups of her bra. This was not a fashion option she chose while she zipped up that morning. This was a necessity as the fabric didn't stretch enough to zip over her bodacious ta-ta's.

"Yo," I called my greeting seeing as her eyes were glued on me.

She didn't reply, and I knew I was getting it from Daisy when she kept up her charge right behind the espresso counter, grabbed my hand and dragged me out toward the bookshelves.

Down the aisle we went and she turned right at the W-X-Y-Z section.

She stopped us in the middle of the row, turned and tipped her head back to me.

"I'm workin' with you," she announced.

Fuck!

"Daisy—" I began.

She lifted a hand palm out, pearl-painted, lethally-long fingernails pointed to the ceiling, and I could see the tips were brushed with hot pink on the diagonal and every one had a little heart of rhinestones affixed to it.

I didn't usually allow people to shut me up, especially giving me The Hand. And Daisy was not carrying a purse and her tracksuit didn't afford any opportunities to hide anything, but even without a stun gun handy, Daisy found ways to get her way and I wasn't in the mood for a catfight in the W-X-Y-Z section.

So I shut up.

She dropped her hand.

"After you left, Indy told us on the hush-hush you're puttin' out a shingle," she declared and I took a calming breath.

I hadn't even told Ren. Or my family.

But Indy had told the Rock Chicks.

I was seeing that I needed to be far more thorough in my instructions in the future as Daisy kept talking.

"She explained we gotta keep our traps zipped. And sugar, you know we will."

I knew no such thing.

She kept going.

"She also said we gotta keep our noses out of your business. We all agreed."

I wasn't certain I believed her, especially since she just told me she was going to work with me. As for the rest of them, that remained to be seen.

"But I'm workin' with you," she repeated.

"Daisy, I can't—"

Her hand went back up and she immediately started talking.

"Not *with you*, with you, like, in the field. I'm gonna be Shirleen to your Lee."

I stared.

Then I felt that feeling I felt earlier start to move through me and again it was far from bad.

This was because Daisy's idea was far from bad.

"You know," she continued, "I tried the society gig and the charity gig. Both of those did not work for me."

I did know that. I also knew that neither of those worked in a big way. The one and only charity function Daisy gave ended up in a standoff complete with firearms. The crème de la crème of Denver society wasn't hankering for another such escapade, even if it was for a good cause.

"And no one wants me to do their hair for some reason, so the salon idea I had is out," she stated.

At that, I tried (and failed) not to look at her hair which made her four inches taller than she was, but she still had two ponytails sticking out the back and they were both tied with baby pink satin ribbons.

In other words, if big hair made you closer to God, Daisy's hair was touching the Pearly Gates.

And that was the only way Daisy knew how to do hair. So if you weren't up for the Southern Woman Style, you were screwed. And let's just say that the vast majority of women in Denver fit in two groups. Those who mountain biked (and not with big hair). And those who drank cosmos (and they might have big hair, but not Daisy big).

Thus no one championed her salon idea.

"And sugar, I need to find a way to spend my days," she kept going. "The Rock Chicks are petering out. There's no hands to hold and no need for me to turn my home into a safe house. The other day I noticed my stun gun had a cobweb on it. After I had a word with my cleaning lady, it made me think. And what I think is, I can send an email *and* an invoice. So we're teamin' up."

"Daisy, honestly, this isn't a bad idea," I told her, and her blue eyes lit up. "But I don't have any clients yet."

She waved her hand in front of her face, dropped it and leaned in.

"To get clients, you gotta have *infrastructure*," she stated authoritatively. "So, that's why I got Roxie on designin' your website. And Ava's mockin' up a couple ideas for a logo for you. She's gonna do our business cards and letterhead."

Our?

"And I'm lookin' for some office space. Marcus knows some people and I told him to put us in touch with the people he knows. In no time," she snapped her long-nailed fingers, "we'll get you *set up*."

I decided to focus on the Rock Chicks finding ways to be involved and provide support that would not lead to their Hot Bunch boys losing their minds, and not scary words like "our," and I smiled at Daisy.

"It's cool the way you guys are all kicking in, chickie. But I have to have your solemn Rock Chick Vow that, if we do this, you answer phones and send invoices. You don't get involved and you also help me make certain the other Rock Chicks don't horn in in a way that'll make things difficult for me."

187

Her eyebrows shot up. "Girl, do you honestly think Marcus is gonna let me get myself into a situation where my fat could be in the fryer?" she asked but didn't let me answer. "No way. One thing, the RC's findin' trouble through no fault of their own. Another, *lookin'* for it."

That was a relief.

She moved into me and hooked her arm through mine, starting to guide me out of the W-X-Y-Z's, stating, "I'm gonna be the best PI receptionist ever. I'm gonna have you so organized, shit'll get done before you even know it's happening. I'm gonna kick receptionist ass so good that Lee's gonna wanna recruit me, because I even file and Shirleen don't do that shit."

Something tentatively good just got better. I'd chipped in to help file at Lee's office once. It wasn't a fun activity.

We made it to the center aisle when I heard Tex boom, *"Ally!"*

This was not his usual, "Ally, quit fucking around and help with coffee" *Ally.*

This was an *Ally* that made the skin at the back of my neck prickle.

I looked down at Daisy, she looked up at me and we hustled out of the books.

I had no idea what I would find, but someone standing there wearing a bomb vest was a possibility.

But it was Annette, Roxie's best friend; a Rock Chick by association (thus not getting laid by a Hot Bunch guy; she was getting laid by a guy name Jason who was a vegetarian). She was also the owner of the head shop across the street. And last, she was standing amongst the tables and chairs at the front with five women who were gazing around, faces filled with wonder, lips parted.

As the nuts the Rock Chicks collected go, Annette occupied the upper echelon. Then again, she had a lot of company.

"Get her and those women outta here!" Tex boomed, and I looked in confusion at him then I looked back at Annette and saw that the women with her now had cameras to their faces and they were taking pictures of Tex.

What the fuck?

I moved toward Annette as she called encouragingly to Tex, "Sock it to us, big man! Give them the Rock Chick Experience!"

Again.

What the fuck?

I approached her from the back. "Annette?"

She turned to me, took in both Daisy and me, and cried, "Fuckin' phat!" She motioned to us and looked at the women with her. "Sistahs, this is Ally Nightingale and Daisy Sloan."

"*Ally,*" one of them breathed.

The rest of them took pictures, the flashes exploding in my face one after the other.

I had no choice but to look away and when I was able to focus, I saw Daisy had not missed a beat and was standing beside me striking a pose and giving them a face set in "smolder."

Jeez.

I looked back at the women. "Stop taking pictures."

Immediately, five cameras dropped.

My eyes went to Annette. "What gives?" I asked.

"Rock Chick Tour," she answered.

"Oh my God, sugar, that is *such* a good idea!" Daisy squealed.

But I stared.

Then I repeated, "Rock Chick Tour?"

"Yeah," Annette replied. "We start here at Fortnum's for coffee. Then we go to Sissy and Dom's house, where Ava and Luke got caught in a drive-by. Then we go to the alley where Jules kicked those drug dealers' asses. Then we go to that bar where Jet got shot at the poker game. Then we go to the mansion where Stella's apartment exploded. Then we go to Sadie's art gallery because it's all okay now, but it wasn't okay when it was torched. Blah, blah, blah," she rolled her hand in front of her and finished, "We eat lunch at Lincoln's and end with cocktails at Smithie's."

I kept staring at her.

"You need to take them to Thornton to the haunted house thing where Billy caught up with Roxie," Daisy advised. "The haunted house ain't runnin', but they still got all the buildings there."

"Phat!" Annette shouted. "I'll add that to our itinerary."

"I'm not part of no tour!" Tex boomed, and the five women again turned to him, lifted their cameras and started taking photos. "*Put down those fuckin' cameras!*" Tex roared on a ferocious scowl.

The women dropped their cameras again, but they weren't offended or frightened. They were all smiling, giving each other happy looks, and two of them were even giggling.

I remained focused.

"Annette, you can't do Rock Chick Tours," I told her.

"Bitch, I *so* can," she told me. "I got the idea when the articles came out. I set it up, then Roxie told me about the book yesterday so now I *have* to do it."

"I've read the book, like, five times," one woman said.

"I've read it three," another woman put in.

"You're my favorite character, Ally," a third told me.

I was her favorite character?

"I read it last night," Daisy said, moving into their huddle. "Stayed up all night. My favorite part was when Lee caught Indy and Tex during their B&E. Laughed myself sick, and when I did I woke Marcus. He was not happy."

The women closed ranks on the huddle and one remarked, "My favorite is the living room tussle."

"Mm-hmm, that one's good too," Daisy agreed.

"The Head Olympics discussion and the ensuing wrestling match," another one said, and Daisy emitted her tinkly bell laugh.

"Oo, sugar, that one's *way* good," Daisy again agreed.

"Ohmigod," the woman breathed to the one at her side, "Daisy called me 'sugar'."

"Sure I called you sugar, sugar," Daisy said on a huge bright smile.

The woman lifted her shoulders up to her ears and her eyes went dreamy, not like Daisy was calling her sugar, but like Channing Tatum had just kissed her cheek.

I looked to the ceiling.

Then I looked to Annette.

"Does Roxie know about this?" I asked.

"No," she answered.

"Indy?" I went on.

"No," she said.

"Anyone but Daisy, Tex, Jet and me?" I pressed.

"No," she repeated.

"Do you see how this might not be taken positively?" I kept going.

"No," Annette replied.

I drew in breath.

One of the women moved to the coffee counter and declared, "I *need* a Tex coffee."

"Me too," another one said as she followed.

"Totally!" a third one cried.

"Tex, will you be in a picture with me holding one of your coffees?" the fourth one put her life in her hands to ask as she approached.

Tex's angry glower shifted to me and he boomed, "Do something!"

All the women looked to me.

"What do you want me to do?" I asked.

The women looked to Tex.

"*Something!*" he shouted.

The women looked to me.

"Tex, they're buying coffees. And it's likely they're gonna tip. That's more cat treats for the kitties," I pointed out.

The women looked to Tex.

"The cats got enough treats."

The women looked back to me.

"You do realize that you're giving them the show they came for and if you just shut your trap and made them coffees, it would probably be over a lot faster."

The women looked at Tex.

Tex's mouth snapped shut.

Finally.

Still behind the counter, Jet moved toward the group of women, introducing herself with, "Hi, I'm Jet."

One woman breathed, "*Jet.*"

The other four lifted their cameras and started taking pictures. Jet looked startled a moment, then she smiled her killer smile that took your breath away and more flashes lit the scene.

I felt Annette get close and I looked at her.

"Can you call one of the Hot Bunch and ask them to drop by?" she asked, might I add, *insanely.* "They don't have to say anything. Just stand there so the girls can take their picture."

"Do you want to survive until tomorrow?" I asked back.

"Yes," she answered.

"Then no. I can't call one of the Hot Bunch so he'll drop by and pose for pictures."

"Bummer," she muttered.

"And just a reminder," I started. "The place is bugged. This means Lee probably already knows this is happening. And the rest of the Hot Bunch. And that means I'll say good-bye now because you're probably gonna disappear in the night and never be seen again."

"That. Would be. The *bomb!*" she exclaimed. "Tell your brother, if he sends someone to kidnap me, I pick Luke. But if he's busy, Vance. No, wait!" she yelled. "Hector!"

"Hector?" one of the women called from her place at the coffee counter, but her eyes were scanning the space. "Where's Hector?"

I couldn't help it because, seriously, it was totally whacked, but I'd lived whacked for two years. It was also all kinds of funny.

So I burst out laughing.

And as I did so, I saw the camera flashes against my closed eyes.

⚡

"Baby."

At Ren's call, I whirled the tip of my tongue around the tip of his cock. I wrapped the hand I'd been using to stroke him tight and looked up his molded abs, his wide chest, to his face.

He was sitting up, back to the headboard, and I got a tingle in my happy place from the hot, dark look on his face as well as the knowledge he'd been watching my activities.

I no sooner caught his eyes when he curled toward me, grasped me under my arms and hauled me up his body.

His hand in my hair cupping my head, he slammed my mouth down on his and kissed me hard and wet while shifting and rolling so we were down the bed. We ended with me on my back, Ren on top of me.

No sooner had he got me there than he slid off and curled an arm around me, making me do a partial roll so my back was to his front. I felt my panties dragged over my ass and I held my breath as my happy place convulsed.

"Give me that," he growled into my neck.

I gave it to him. I *so* did.

Tipping my booty so he could have access, he didn't delay. One of his hands slid between my legs, his middle finger hitting me right where I needed it.

His other hand slid up my chest so he could wrap his fingers around the underside of my jaw, holding firm, keeping me where he wanted me.

And last, he drove into me.

I'd forgotten about spooning, and right then that was top of my list of positions with Ren.

And serious to God, I loved this. Held captive by him, powerless to do anything but take what he gave me, but knowing he'd work to give me what I needed to take me *there* so I got it first before he took what he needed to get *him* there.

Amazing.

So amazing, I held still, whimpering and moaning, until it started to burn through me.

Then my neck arched back. I felt his lips at the side and I breathed, *"Ren,"* right before it blistered through me.

He thrust hard, fast, deep, and his hand between my legs continued working me, taking, even as I came down. He kept going until I felt his mouth open on the skin of my neck and he sucked deep. A tremor ran through me and I felt and listened as he got what he needed.

As it left him, he settled, still buried inside me. His hand between my legs moved so he could wrap his arm around my belly. His hand at my jaw gentled and his fingers started stroking.

His mouth still at my neck, he whispered there, "Love you, Ally."

"Love you too, honey," I whispered back.

He kissed the side of my neck, shifted, kissed the back of my neck and we lay there connected for several long, happy, silent minutes until he pulled out and rolled to his back. He took me with him, positioning me tucked to his side with my forehead in his neck and his hand cupping my ass.

"Shimmy outta your panties, baby," he murmured.

Using just my legs, I shimmied out of them, caught them with my toe and used my foot to toss them over Ren to land at the side of the bed.

When I settled in, he drew random patterns on my ass as he said, still murmuring, "Not done with you tonight."

Ren was feeling energetic.

Right on.

I smiled against his skin.

It was after work at Fortnum's where, fortunately, nothing else happened, except Roxie, Tod and Stevie showing with about five hundred bags from various stores at Park Meadows Mall (okay, maybe four hundred). It was also after Ren got home late from work, but he still made me chicken parmesan.

But the dishes were still on the dining room table. The pots in the sink.

This was because, once I'd taken my last bite, Ren said to me, "Thinkin' about it all day, couldn't get my mind off it, so now I want your mouth on me."

I hadn't been thinking about it all day, but I was thinking about it right then. And what I thought about it was that it was a fantastic idea.

Therefore I immediately got up, sashayed to and up the stairs and into his bedroom.

He followed me, hitting the room, eyes hot but lips quirking.

I'd then commenced in obliging.

You know the rest.

That brought us to now.

I lifted my head and looked down at him. I felt my insides warm at the contentment in his expression, and asked, "Do I have to turn Catholic?"

His face blanked, his hand at my ass stilled, and he did a slow blink.

Then he demanded, "Say that again."

I didn't say it again.

Instead, I explained, "You're Catholic. I'm not. And you're Italian. And seeing as the Pope lives in a sovereign city-state in your homeland, I'm thinking that's important. And since we're committed and you've promised we won't be about meatloaf and missionary, I've gotta have some detail about what else the future has in store for me."

His hand not at my ass lifted to cup my jaw before he said quietly, "That's not something you tick off a to-do list, honey."

"No. But it is something you consider and look into if it's important to the man you love."

Ren closed his eyes.

A second later, I found myself on my back with Ren looming over me, but he did this with his chest pressed mostly on mine and his hand still cupping my jaw.

His eyes moved over my face and his face had *the look*.

My insides got warmer.

Then he stated, "It's not necessary you convert, Ally. But it's important to me that my kids are raised in the faith."

"Wouldn't it be important, to raise kids in the faith, that I knew about said faith at the very least, but better, practiced it?" I asked, and *the look* intensified so my insides got melty.

"You'd do that?" he whispered.

"I don't know. Is here an initiation ceremony where I have to drink blood of the calf or something?" I asked and he grinned.

Then he answered, "No."

"Okay," I replied. "Then maybe you can set it up so I can talk to somebody."

He dropped his head so his forehead touched mine, all the while muttering, "Fuckin' fuck me."

That meant a lot to him.

I loved that. I loved that I gave that to him.

But I didn't tell him that.

I shared, "I'm obviously no expert, but my guess is the Pope frowns on the f-bomb, Zano."

I saw his eyes smile.

Then I didn't see anything because he was kissing me, slow and sweet.

Then he did other things to me slow and sweet that I wasn't sure the Vatican approved of.

Much later, drowsy, sated, happy, my man's arms around me, his body curled into me spooning, I decided we'd had a good day without anything exploding and another day without us fighting (so far, a record). Further, his breath was evening, which meant he was heading toward sleep.

So I'd tell him tomorrow about my plans for the future that didn't have to do with me discussing conversion with a priest.

Chapter 15
I'm Good at What I Do

Ren moved to the sink, dropped his plate in it and moved to me sitting on the counter.

He pulled my coffee mug out of my hand and set it on the counter. Then he pulled my legs apart and moved between them. With a hand at my ass, he yanked me close.

His face dipped to mine and his voice was sweet when he noted, "You got lots of bags upstairs, baby."

"Yep," I agreed.

"You got a dress for me?" he asked.

"Yep," I repeated, and this was true. Roxie, Tod and Stevie bought me four of them and they were all smokin' hot.

"Good. Date night tonight."

I grinned.

Ren kissed me.

Then he kissed my neck.

After that, he let me go and on a, "Later, honey," and walked to and through the front door.

I watched.

Smiling.

⌦⌫

It was mid-morning when the bell over the door rang.

I was in Fortnum's with Indy, Jet, Tex and Jane. Stella and Mace were also there, both of them at the counter. Stella was shooting the shit and sipping a latte. Mace was being silent and badass as he held his woman in a casual-but-affectionate embrace at his side.

Duke had not showed. I told myself this wasn't because he was avoiding me, but because he'd hopped on his Harley with his wife Dolores for an impromptu ride of the Rockies.

However, even as I told myself this, I wasn't very convincing.

Everyone looked to the door to see Tod walking in carrying two big thick scrapbooks.

One was stuffed full with copious pieces of paper and fabric swatches protruding from the sides. The other one looked new.

The first was Ava's wedding planner.

The second, seeing as she'd only been engaged for a little over three weeks, was Sadie's.

Tod was a drag queen and a flight attendant. He was also the unofficially-official wedding planner to all the Rock Chicks. This meant a lot of headache, arguments, browbeating and unnecessary powwows sprinkled with a few hissy fits.

It also meant every single Rock Chick had the wedding of her dreams that went off without a hitch.

Nevertheless, Tod, with the planners in tow, did not bode good things.

The door closed behind him and his eyes came to me.

"Good to see you alive, girlie," he called.

"Good to be alive, Tod," I called back.

"Do me a favor," he kept talking loudly, "stay alive until Saturday. And a call to the bomb squad to do a sweep of the church and function room would come in handy."

"That's not a bad idea." I heard Mace mutter, and I looked to him to see his expression was serious.

Then again, the way things were, he and Tod were right.

"I thought we had the final read through of Ava's shindig last weekend, Tod," Indy noted, moving his way.

Tod dumped the books on a table and looked at her. "That *was* the final read through. Now we're having the final *final* read through. And tomorrow, before the rehearsal, we're finalizing the final *final* read through. But also now, we're deciding Sadie's wedding colors."

Indy looked around the store and then back at Tod in order to point out the obvious. "Sadie isn't here."

"I know, she's busy at the gallery," Tod replied, slapping open the smaller album and I saw a plethora of colors on the page. But he said no more.

With experience of the planning stages of Tod organizing a wedding, it was understandable that Indy's tone was cautious when she stated, "Honey, we can't pick Sadie's wedding colors without Sadie here."

Tod looked up at Indy and I felt everyone brace (except Mace, he sighed). But I grinned.

"Not another word," Tod warned.

Indy opened her mouth to give him another word.

He gave her The Hand. "No. Sadie's a millionaire. I have no budget. None at all. I'm pulling out all the stops. She told me I could. And anyway, Stella and Mace are going to be married on a beach in Hawaii."

"We are?" Mace muttered to Stella, and I heard Stella's throaty laugh.

Tod must not have heard any of that because he kept going.

"And everyone knows Ally's going to do something like elope to Vegas. So this is my last shot at greatness. Not that I didn't kick butt with your wedding," he said to Indy, then turned his attention to Jet. "And yours too, girlie."

He had, indeed, kicked butt with both of their weddings. It seemed practice made perfect because Indy's was awesome, Jet's was fantastic, and Roxie and Hank's was the bomb. Not to mention, plans for Ava's were far from shabby. So without a budget, Sadie's was undoubtedly going to *rock*.

It also should be noted that going to Vegas *was* what I had always wanted to do.

However, I wasn't certain how Catholics felt about Vegas.

I added this on my mental list to discuss with the nun or priest who Ren set me up with for my literal come to Jesus (and Mary, God and the Holy Spirit) meeting and shared, "I'm thinking it might be a full mass."

Tod's head snapped to me, his eyes alight.

"You shouldn't have done that," Jet, the voice of experience, said under her breath to me.

"*Seriously?*" Tod cried.

"Unless there's a Catholic priest who dresses like Elvis and has a wedding chapel in Sin City, yeah," I answered.

"Oh girlie," Tod's eyes were getting bright, "you've made me so happy."

Don't think I was crazy. I was a Rock Chick. In for a penny, in for a pound.

Tod lifted his hands to the sides of his head and wriggled his fingers, announcing, "I feel it! It's coming over me! You!" He suddenly pointed at me.

"Buttery yellow, the creamiest of creams and a bright grass green. You," he pointed at Stella, "a white bikini, I'm thinking crochet, a lei, maybe a band of flowers around your forehead, and a fabulous sarong."

Again with Mace muttering, this time through a smile, "That works for me."

"Tropical island paradise will be your theme," Tod kept at it and looked at Indy. "And Sadie, ice blue and shimmery glittering winter white."

That wasn't bad for Sadie. In fact, perfect.

But no way I was doing yellow and green.

Red and maybe black.

If the Pope approved.

I didn't share this with Tod. Mostly because the door opened, Ava blasted through it and sauntering in on her heels was Luke with a half-grin going.

Ava did not have a half-grin. She was fuming.

"Tod," she snapped. "I'm here, but not for the final-*final*-read-through-preliminary-to-the-finalized-final-*final*-read-through."

Clearly she'd got the memo.

"I'm here because the wedding is off!" she finished.

"No!" Tod exclaimed, then proceeded *not* to react to the dire news that it appeared Ava and Luke were at odds (then again, that happened occasionally; she busted his chops often and Luke, having chops of steel, got off on it) but to something else. "It's too late to get any of the deposits back!"

"Calm down, man, the wedding isn't off," Luke announced.

"It is," Ava retorted angrily, whirling on her man.

"It isn't," Luke replied calmly, staring down his nose at his woman.

"Are you going to dance with me?" she asked.

"Vertically?" he asked back, and I pressed my lips together in order not to laugh.

"Yes!" she snapped.

"Yeah, baby," he said. "I'll dance with you vertically, in the bathroom on the plane on the way to Bermuda."

This was not the answer she was looking for, therefore she whirled back to Tod and ordered, "Start making calls. It's over."

"I'm not... I can't... it's..." Tod stammered, hand to his throat, eyes wide and filled with panic. Then he shrieked, "*The custom order baby blue, aqua and teal M&M's have already arrived!* There's nine pounds of them already parceled out and ribboned up for wedding gifts! *What am I going to do with nine pounds of baby blue, aqua and teal M&M's?*"

"Give them to me," Ava retorted. "I intend to eat them all in one sitting."

"Don't make any calls, Tod," Luke contradicted Ava's order as he also ignored her response to Tod.

Ava again whirled on Luke. "I'm not marrying a man who can't set aside the badass for three minutes in order to dance at our wedding."

"Yes you are," Luke replied.

It was at that, Ava had had enough.

I knew this when she shouted, "I've been in love with you since I was eight! And I've been dreaming of dancing with you at our wedding," she leaned toward him, "*since I was eight!* And if you can't give me three minutes of that drea—"

She didn't finish.

This was because Luke's hand flashed out, caught her behind the neck and pulled her to him so she landed face first in his chest. He then bent his neck and his face disappeared from my view as he spoke in Ava's ear.

But I saw Ava's face get soft. Then softer. Then the hands she had curled in his tee at his sides uncurled so she could wrap her arms around him.

Luke's head lifted.

Ava's neck twisted so she could look at Tod. "Don't make any calls, babe."

Tod heaved an audible sigh of relief prior to collapsing into a chair by his albums.

I did not know if this meant Luke was dancing with Ava at their wedding or not.

I just knew that whatever he said made Ava happy.

And seeing that, thinking on how Eddie was with his pregnant wife, and knowing Mace was standing with Stella only a few feet away and she'd barely been out of the curve of his arm in the fifteen minutes they were, what Ren said in that motel room two days before hit me.

And it hitting me made me reach to my back pocket and pull out my phone. I started it up, touched the button to send a text and typed in, *Tonight. Post date. Cowgirl, lotus, doggie.* Then I hit send.

With the most recent crisis in Fortnum's diverted, I shoved my phone back in my pocket and moved out from behind the counter to do a sweep of the tables to gather empties when I heard the store phone ring just as my phone at my ass binged.

I yanked it out and saw I had two texts from Ren.

The first, *Not positions. Locations. Stairs. Wall. Bed.*

His plan was way better than mine.

The second, *Love you, baby.*

I smiled and sent back, *Back at 'cha* just as Jane called, "Phone for you, Ally."

My brows drew together as I looked at her.

No one called me there. Not friends, definitely. And my informants and "clients" all knew my cell was the only acceptable form of communication.

I walked to the book counter, took the phone and put it to my ear. "Yo."

"You want Rosie to stay alive, you deal," a man's kinda whiny, definitely weasely voice said to me, and my back went straight. "We want Rosie alive 'cause we want him growin' for us. We wanna talk about what it'll take to buy him outta your protection. You don't deal, face to face, you comin' alone, we find a farmer who can take over the crops and his pain in our ass gets dead. You hear me?"

My heart pumping, blood singing, I made a split second decision. I lifted my head and hand and snapped my fingers, my eyes moving from Luke to Mace.

They were both already studying me and they immediately moved my way, their hands going to the back pockets of their jeans.

"You'll understand I'm not big on a meet seeing as your last approach was detonating a bomb in my apartment," I replied, eyes to Luke.

"That was before we knew your connections," the voice returned. "We want no beef with you. We just want Rosie."

My eyes moving to Mace, I said into the phone, "I may have misunderstood. Do you currently have Rosie?"

"Not yet. But you askin' that means you don't either. Which, gotta say, has us confused as to why your crew is searchin' for him when he has your protection."

I decided not to share with Lee that these idiots thought his crew was my crew and stated (mostly lying), "Rosie knows I'm not a big fan of explosions. Firefights, okay. Car chases, I dig. Rescues, a specialty. Shattered kneecaps, not my gig, but I got a guy who does that. Everything me or those under my protection owns burning to a cinder, not so much. He brought that down on me, he knows to avoid me for a few days."

"We apologize for that error, and you can tack reimbursement onto us buyin' out your protection on Rosie," he offered.

Thinking on the check I wrote to Roxie the day before to reimburse her for the bags of clothes currently sitting on the floor in Ren's bedroom, I thought this actually wasn't a bad deal.

I heard a snap. I focused on Luke, saw he had his phone to his ear and he jerked his head to Mace.

Mace was bent over the counter, phone to his ear, other hand scribbling. He straightened and turned a pad of paper around to me.

On it, it said, *Take the meet. Tell them you're sending an intermediary.*

I shook my head.

Mace jerked a finger at me then down to tap the pad.

I slid my eyes away and said into the phone, "Lincoln's Roadhouse. Today. Three o'clock."

"Fuck." I heard Luke bite out quietly.

"Nowhere public," the voice said in my ear.

"It's public or it doesn't happen. If it doesn't happen, I have more time to focus on getting Rosie under my wing, unleashing the dogs to deal with you, and moving his operation back to Denver where I can keep an eye on him."

This was obviously a partial lie. The first two were already happening. The last one, never.

I kept going. "You're on my turf and you don't sound entirely stupid, so you gotta know you've got no hope of locating Rosie before me. But given time, Rosie knows I'll calm my shit and he'll come to me. Then I can focus all my energies on you. And I had a lot of really sexy underwear in that apartment, all of it with fond memories. I'm feeling a little grumpy I've got to start from scratch."

"*Fuck,*" I heard Luke bite out again, this time less quietly, and I looked at him to see him scowling at me.

I held his eyes as I said into the phone, "Lincoln's. Bring your checkbook. Rosie's a pain in my ass, but he's mine. You make an offer that's motivating and reimburse me for your error, he belongs to you."

Then I hung up.

The minute I did so did Luke. Mace walked away, phone still to his ear.

Luke instantly launched in, leaning toward me growling, "Jesus, Ally. What the fuck's the matter with you? Talkin' about your underwear? Christ. You *never* sexualize yourself to guys like these."

"You do when they think you're a badass who isn't scared of them, which I'm not because you nor Lee nor anybody would let anything happen to me," I shot back. "You lose the upper hand if you act like anything they can do puts the fear of God in you. And newsflash, Luke. They knew where I lived, they know where I work. It's a possibility they've had eyes on me. Therefore, unless they're blind, they know I'm a girl. They don't need me to sexualize me. They're guys. They've already done it."

Luke's mouth got tight, which was silent macho badass for *point taken*.

"You need to set up for a takedown at Lincoln's," I ordered.

"Lee's already on that," Mace stated, walking back to us. "And you better prepare, woman, 'cause he's also on his way here and he's not real happy."

Whatever.

Lee wasn't real happy when Indy and I bottle rocketed Nina Evans's front yard when she spread that rumor I had herpes, her brother went ballistic and he had to step in.

And he wasn't real happy the sundry times I'd gotten a bit past tipsy and interrupted his evening for a ride.

I could go on.

He always got over it.

He'd get over this too.

"I'm gonna go see if my stun gun is charged," I told Mace and Luke.

Luke frowned at me.

Mace frowned at his boots.

I barely got three steps before Tex was there.

"I'm in," he declared.

"This is team play," Luke declined.

"I'm in," Tex repeated.

"This'll take three seconds, we don't have to deal with a wildcard," Luke returned.

"I'm,' Tex leaned in and finished on a boom, "*in!*"

Luke stared him in the eyes.

Then he muttered, "Fuck."

By the way, that was verbal macho badass that meant Luke was giving in.

A second after that, the bell over the door went and I looked that way to see Lee stalking in, eyes on me.

Yep.

Unhappy.

Whatever.

⌘

"Tex and Brian are already in place," Lee said to me.

We were in the biography section of the bookshelves.

It was near go time for Operation Takedown New Mexican Baddies.

Tex, you know. Brian was Brian Bond. He was a uniformed cop who had been a rookie when Indy had her Rock Chick Drama, but now he had some experience under his belt. He was also partner with Willie Moses who, aside from being a seriously fine black man, was a friend of the family and a very good cop.

"I know," I answered Lee.

"You go in, you keep an eye out. You do not look at Tex or Brian, even a glance. They do not exist for you," Lee ordered.

I fought rolling my eyes and saying, *Duh.*

"You gotta keep this guy, or guys, occupied for five minutes, ten tops. Mug shots we got on them are years old so don't rely on those pictures I showed you, and even the police in New Mexico don't know the extent of their crew so keep alert. Brian and Tex will be casing inside, seein' if they're alone or if they come with sentries. My crew will be workin' outside. You will get no go sign. If inside and outside are clear, Willie will come in and he and Brian will do the takedown. They're not, we'll neutralize the threat outside. You'll see Ike, Bobby and Matt inside workin' with Willie. You sit at a booth opposite the bar. Brody's in the van and he'll have eyes on that row. You have two jobs. Keep them occupied while we clock who's in play and then gettin' the fuck outta the way when the takedown begins. You got that?" he asked.

"Yes, kemosabe," I answered and his eyes narrowed.

"This isn't a joke, Ally," he gritted out.

"No shit, Lee."

His face got dark and after hours of planning this crap, he got down to what was really bugging him.

"You should not have taken the meet."

"And wait for however long it is for this situation to be dealt with?" I asked. "Luke and Ava are getting married in two days. I don't want to have to take the time to call the bomb squad to ask them to do a sweep. I take the meet, this is done and all I have to do is wonder with everyone else if Luke's gonna dance with Ava at the reception."

His lips got tight.

Although I knew that meant he was going to give me no further shit, which was usually an opening for me to give him some (or some more), I passed on that opportunity in order to get this done.

"Is there anything else before we move out?" I asked.

"Yeah," he answered. "They give you any indication they got a weapon trained on you in a way we can't see, like under the table, you run your hand through your hair startin' at the top and going back. Yeah?"

I nodded, not liking that part, but knowing, seeing as they blew up my apartment, they could come in carrying and have no problem switching from negotiation to threats—and other much less fun possibilities—to get what they wanted.

Lee got a lot less intense and moved a few inches away from me.

But he did this saying, "Dad wants a family meeting tonight."

At that, I shook my head. "Ren and I have a date."

His chin jerked back. "You had a date two days ago."

"That didn't happen seeing as we got sidetracked," I shared and this time, Lee shook his head.

"Go no further," he ordered.

I wasn't going to so I complied.

"We get this done, Willie and Brian get whoever we take down to the station, they're interrogated, processed, Hank gets briefed, he's free, the family sits down," Lee decreed.

"I just said I couldn't do it tonight because Ren and I have a date," I reminded him of something he couldn't have forgotten in the three seconds since I said it.

He got close again. "Ally, it's not gonna surprise you that Dad—and Mom, I'll add—are upset and worried. They need a sit down with you and you need to show them the respect of givin' them that time and listening."

He was right about that so I had no choice but to nod again but queried, "Can I ask why this meeting is being called through you and Hank?"

"Because by upset and worried I meant hurt and pissed."

Oh man.

That was not good.

I loved my mom and dad. They were the shit.

Malcolm and Kitty Sue Nightingale weren't perfect human beings or parents.

But they came really, *really* close.

Part of me was being nonchalant about all that was happening with me and how it would affect my parents because, as crazy as I was, they not only always loved me but expected, when it got down to the important shit, I'd do the right thing. And save for some lying and underage drinking and a few other things (okay, maybe not a few but nothing that was important), I did.

So I knew two things. The first was that whatever decision I made, if it wasn't stupid, they'd back it (eventually). The second was that they knew they raised a woman who would not be stupid.

But hearing what Lee said sucked. And it pained me. Because I didn't want to hurt or piss off my parents. And I'd done both.

So I needed to attend this meeting and see to sorting that out.

I drew in breath.

Then I let it out and nodded once again, mentally planning to send a text to Ren that was a lot less fun than the earlier ones to explain the change in plans for our evening.

Now, however, I had a job to do.

Therefore I asked Lee, "We ready?"

He stepped to the side for me to precede him, answering, "Let's roll."

I followed Lee out of the books and to the front.

Lee went to Indy.

I went to the door.

But as I did, I had eyes on my BFF.

She also had eyes on me and she mouthed, *Be safe.*

I mouthed back, *Always.*

Then I walked out the door.

I'd chosen locations wrongly.

This was because Lincoln's had two rows of stationary tables down its front room, at the end there was a bar, an entrance at the front, a door to the smoking area at the back. That meant that there was no way to sit without your back to a door.

I picked facing to the front but turning my back to the wall so I had eyes either way.

I'd also clocked Tex sitting at the bar with a bottle of Bud in front of him. I didn't look at him, but I clocked him. Then again, with his mass, that would be hard not to do.

Brian, I didn't see and I didn't look. I knew Brian enough, if he told Lee he was in place, he was.

I ordered a bottle of Fat Tire and waited, phone on the table by my beer, pepper spray in my back pocket.

At three seventeen, I was getting antsy.

It was then the front door opened and they came in.

I knew it was them right away. I knew this not because they looked like their mug shots (they didn't), but because there were two of them and one was slight, wiry and looked as whiney and weasely as he sounded on the phone.

But the other one was big, brawny and I knew instantly he was not only the muscle, he was the brains.

And he was not to be messed with.

I also felt it. The prickle at the back of my neck and the charge of my adrenaline flowing.

They were not here to negotiate. I had no idea what they had planned but they offered deference in an attempt to outfox me and get my ass right where it was. This meant, regardless of any connections I had that they'd put together, they did not take me seriously.

It also meant they had something up their sleeve.

And last, it meant it was highly unlikely I had five to ten minutes to give to Lee.

I turned to face their way on my stool at the same time I casually ran my hand through my hair from top to back then let my hand fall to the table. I wrapped the fingers of my other hand around the beer bottle which, if broken against the side of the table, could be used as a weapon.

And I didn't take my eyes off them.

They no sooner got their asses on their stools than I felt a presence at my back, close, and something that couldn't be mistaken pressed hard to my ribs.

They had a soldier inside, and he wasted no time moving on me and jamming the barrel of a gun into my flesh.

Not.

Good.

I gave no headspace to what this might mean—this soldier free to make his move—if Brian or Tex didn't clock him or if they did and they had some plan.

I needed to remain clearheaded and calm.

I also needed to remain alive so I could have my red and black Pope-approved nuptials then give Ren babies.

In my head I whittled the length of Ren and my fuck-a-thon down to two years prior to making babies and whispered to the men at my table, "You don't waste any time."

"No woman fucks with me," the big-guy-brains-of-the-crew growled at me.

"Uh, just saying, I didn't fuck with you. You fucked with me," I pointed out.

"Okay then, I don't waste time fuckin' around with women unless I'm actually *fuckin' them*," he amended.

Well, he'd proved that.

"Now, you're gonna come easy. Leave your phone," Whiney Guy ordered.

"And if you're thinkin' your backup is gonna see to things," Brawny Guy added. "The black dude with the tattoo outside is outta commission."

Fuck.

Fuck!

That was Ike, one of Lee's men. And I did not like to think with the cold dead I saw in Brawny Guys' eyes what his definition of "outta commission" could be.

Fuck.

I let go of my beer and slid off my stool.

The presence behind me moved with me.

Calmly, I cleared the table and headed to the door as Whiney Guy and Brawny Guy flanked me.

Suddenly the presence behind me disappeared. I took this as what I hoped it would be, Tex or Brian instigating their plan, and I flew into action.

As Tex pounded a fist in the face of the guy who had been behind me and he went flying into a table, losing purchase on his gun, I turned to the primary threat, Brawny Guy. I got my hand around his package. Once there, I twisted and squeezed and I did this with no mercy.

He made a high-pitched noise that made the backs of my teeth ache before his knees buckled and he went down hard. I bent with him, let him go then came up, at the same time jerking up my knee and catching him hard under his jaw.

He flew back and I roundhouse kicked him in the cheekbone with my boot. It was then he flew to the side, and I knew by the way his face hit floor without him trying to break his fall he was out.

Before I could turn my attention to him, Whiney Guy caught me by my hair. It hurt like a mother but I yanked it loose, turned on him, and aimed a hard punch at his throat.

He also went down on his knees, hands to his throat, wheezing.

By the time I took three steps back, I saw Tex with a knee in the chest of a big guy on his back on the floor. Brian was there, gun out aiming between the three as he pulled his badge out of his back pocket and shoved it into his belt.

"Police. You're under arrest," he announced.

We had onlookers and we also had company as Lee, Hank, Eddie, Mace, Luke, Willie, Matt, Bobby and Jimmy Marker joined us.

My eyes went to Lee. "Ike?" I asked.

"Vest," he answered. "He gets his breath back, he'll be fine."

The grip on my insides released.

"Are there more?" Tex asked.

"Only these three," Lee answered.

"So this is it?" Tex asked, sounding peeved.

Lee just stared at him.

Tex looked at me.

"Told you, woman. *Boring.*"

Whatever.

I felt fingers wrap around my arm and saw Lee had hold of me. He propelled me to the front door and out of it, Hank following.

We stopped on the sidewalk. He let me go and I looked up at him.

"I'm missing the fun part of cuffing and hearing them get their Mirandas," I complained.

"How'd you know?" Lee asked bizarrely.

"What?" I asked back confusedly.

Hank got close and reiterated Lee's question. "How'd you know?"

I looked at Hank. "Know what?"

"You ran your hand through your hair before they sat down. Brody sent word the situation had deteriorated about two seconds after they walked in. Last report, which was five seconds before that, their man inside was nowhere near you," Lee explained, and I looked back at him. "How'd you know?"

Oh. I got it.

How did I know they were a danger.

I shrugged. "Felt it."

"You felt it," Hank said.

I nodded to Hank, but Lee was again talking.

"They had no witnesses outside, so I reckon they intended to do you here or get you to a car and do you somewhere else. As long as you were inside you were safe, and Tex had the element of surprise. You gave him the heads up. He moved, got the drop on them. They had five seconds more, they could have got you to a place where Tex couldn't get to you fast enough, including outside where they had the upper hand," Lee said.

I knew what this meant.

I knew *exactly* what this meant.

So I held his gaze and said quietly, "I'm good at what I do."

Lee looked at Hank.

Hank started, "Ally—"

My eyes went to him.

"I knew they were who they were the minute I saw them, and I knew they were not there to negotiate. I didn't waste time. I also," my eyes went to Lee, "took two down. I know I had surprise on my side, but I still kept my shit together and I didn't fuck around and do it like a girl. I did it like I meant it and incapacitated them both without hesitation." My eyes moved back to Hank and I repeated, "I'm good at what I do. And what happened in there is only part of it." Again I looked to Lee. "And if you'd listen to Darius and Brody—not like a brother, but like a colleague—you'd know exactly how good I can be."

I left it at that. They were macho alphas. Drama only worked on them if it ended in them giving and receiving an orgasm.

This was going to be my livelihood, and these two men who happened to be my brothers were integral in me making a go of it.

So, like an alpha badass, I let my actions speak for me, moved around Hank and walked back into Lincoln's to give my statement to Jimmy.

Chapter 16

I'm Me

I parked in front of Ren's and I was a little freaked.

This was because I'd texted him after Operation Takedown Baddies and told him our plans for the evening had to change. I also asked him to phone me when he had a few minutes to talk so I could explain.

He didn't phone, and when I phoned him he didn't pick up.

During the Not-Really-Fuck-Buddies phase of our relationship, we didn't text or call to shoot the shit, be funny or flirty.

But we did text and even call to sort things like his place or mine or tell each other we were on our way.

This had obviously intensified since our time in Carnal, but even before Ren had never ignored a text or phone call from me. If I called, I couldn't remember a time when he didn't immediately answer. Not even one. And he might not return a text instantly, but I never had to wait more than an hour to get a reply.

So the fact that he didn't do any of that and hours had passed freaked me.

I didn't want our relationship to fall into a pattern of taking each other for granted. This wasn't to say that I expected him to hop to the minute I tried to connect with him. But I also didn't want to slide into a place where he assumed it was cool to delay connecting with me because he knew he had me where he wanted me and I could fit into the schedule of his day. Especially not if something I had to say was important.

Which this was.

I folded out of my car, threw the door to and beeped the locks, crossing the street and making my way up to Ren's.

I'd never asked, but looking around on my way up to his house, distractedly I figured he had to have a gardener. Denver was arid, but that didn't mean yards could not be lush and green. However, for them to be so, you had to put a shitload of effort into it. Ren's front *and* back yards were amazing. Thick and flourishing, mostly plants and grasses, but here and there was a hint of color that made it interesting.

And it wasn't him slaving away to make it that way.

I put the key in the lock, turned it and walked in, kicking the door closed behind me. Then I stopped dead.

The front of Ren's house was one long room with two seating areas. One was just a seating area. The other was the TV area.

He was sitting on a couch to my left in the TV area. The TV, however, was not on. His suit jacket was off, but he had not changed out of his shirt or trousers. The cuffs of his shirt were rolled back, though. He had one arm slung across the back of the couch. The other hand was upending and touching his cell on his knee.

Upend, slide, touch it to his knee and repeat.

This was weird.

His eyes were on me.

They were angry.

I felt the air in the room was heavy and I knew I was in trouble.

"You have a good afternoon?" Ren asked quietly, but not in his sweet. Not even close.

It was then, belatedly, it hit me.

Shit, shit, *fuck*.

I had not told him about Operation Takedown Baddies, and Lucky was on me so he'd know and report that to Ren.

I hadn't really thought about that, what with having a gun jammed into my ribs and being given the opportunity to end this crap in plenty of time to fully enjoy Ava and Luke's wedding without it hanging over anyone's head.

It was good Lucky didn't get involved because that could have been bad.

But even though he was currently angry, I thought it was going to be okay that I did not share this with Ren. Evidence was suggesting that if I kept calm and explained things, this was taken positively.

I also had an explanation, so I hoped once I gave it to him, he would take it positively. Or, at least, with a minimal amount of yelling.

"I texted and phoned," I reminded him carefully.

"Yeah," he returned immediately. "*After* you got a .38 shoved in your ribs."

Oh man.

"Ren, honey, I'm so sorry," I said, taking a step to him. "I didn't think. I've been on my own awhile, doing this gig awhile, and I've never had to report in to anybody but Darius or Brody. In fact, even when I was with Carl, I never really reported in to anybody about anything. But what happened this afternoon went down as a surprise and I had to stay focused. But I should have called and next time I will."

He hadn't moved in the entire time I spoke, but when I was done, he asked, "Next time you will?"

Okay, it was time to get down to this.

That was to say, it wasn't an *optimal* time seeing as he was pissed. But it was time.

I took another step toward him. "Yeah, babe," I said softly. "Next time I will."

He said nothing and kept staring at me.

I took a further step toward him.

"I should have explained my decision earlier, but things between us had changed in a really good way. A way I liked. We weren't fighting. We were working things out, getting to know each other better, understanding what was in our future. I didn't want to mess it up because I knew you wouldn't be happy with the decision, but the decision I made was important to me."

"And that decision would be?" he prompted, brows up, when I stopped talking.

I took in a deep breath, and on the exhale, I announced. "I'm officially going into the family business."

Again he was silent.

I took yet another step toward him and explained, "I decided it when I got fired from Brother's. I don't have it all planned out, but things are falling into place. After Luke and Ava's wedding, I'm going to get down to doing that."

"Two days ago, we had a discussion about you making decisions about your life and how those decisions affected me," Ren reminded me.

"And we're having that discussion now," I told him quietly.

"It's not a discussion, Ally, when you're telling me it's a decision already made and that you're making plans to carry it forward."

This was true.

Time to take this in another direction.

"This is important to me," I whispered.

"And it's important to me to be with the woman I love, the woman with whom I intend to have a family, and do that without the possibility of her getting

215

riddled with bullets or comin' back from getting ice cream with the kids and finding our home has been leveled."

"Those things aren't going to happen, Ren. It's not—"

Ren cut me off.

"Jules was shot twice, stickin' her nose into shit that was not her business. You're all livin' the relief that she's breathing so you don't let your minds go there. But the truth is, she got it in the gut and chest, and the fact she still exists on this earth is a fuckin' miracle. And both Stark and Crowe have taken bullets during jobs your brother contracted to do. And both those men have years of experience and training. It's not going to happen?"

"I'll be careful with the cases I chose to take on," I assured him.

"In that line of business, you can't *be* that careful," he shot back. "It's an impossibility. Your brother knows every risk he and his men face when he takes a case. They plan every move they make and every operation they undertake considering all the variables. And they've got enough time in on the job, they know every fuckin' variable they gotta consider. And the one they always plan for, the most important, is they always know it's a possibility in every job they take that there's one variable they won't have covered."

"I've been doing this for a while, Ren. I've been watching my brothers, both of them, and Lee's guys. You learn from doing and seeing, and I have. And I'm good at it. But the bottom line is, I love doing it. It's in my blood. It's *me*."

"You've said that before, but I see you aren't takin' into consideration that it's important *to me* that you do not do this shit. You do not put yourself out there. You do not get into a situation—or *situations*, repeatedly—that might take you away from me or, later, our family."

Okay, maybe another tactic was in order.

"So what do you propose I do?" I asked.

"Find something you like, or enjoy your time at Fortnum's then turn your focus to raising our kids."

I studied him closely, hoping he was joking.

It appeared he wasn't joking.

Nevertheless, I thought it important to seek clarification.

"You want me to be a barista and then a stay-at-home mom?" I asked.

"Honestly?" he asked back, and I nodded. "Yeah. I got my wish, that's what you'd be. But if that isn't what you want, we can discuss it and you can find something to do that doesn't include maybe pissing off husbands you caught cheating or putting you on radar with pimps and dealers."

I stared at him and said nothing. Not that I didn't have things to say. Lots of them.

Just that he was sitting there, unmoving except for upending his phone, eyes on me, totally calm and saying this shit to me, which for all intents and purposes was ripping my heart out and tearing it to shreds.

So my voice was strange in a way I'd never heard it be, not even in all the emotional ups and downs with Ren Zano I'd experienced for over a year, when I asked, "In all the time we've been together, have you paid even the slightest attention to me?"

I knew it was my tone that made his face turn guarded as he straightened out of the couch, keeping his eyes locked on me and starting, "Ally—"

I interrupted him. "This is me."

"Honey—"

"This has always been me and you are one of a very select few who have always known it."

"Yes, I have," he agreed. "Not that you shared that with me openly. Just that I found that shit out."

This was true, but at this juncture, it also didn't matter.

"What I'm sayin' is," he continued. "For us and our future, it's important to me to know you're safe, but more, to know me and our future plans are important enough to you that you yourself do what you can to *stay* safe."

I shook my head. "No, Ren, what you're saying is, to be with you, I have to prove you're important enough to me to change everything about me."

He took a step toward me.

I took a step back and he stopped.

"Ally—" he started again.

I cut him off again. "You don't want me."

He shook his head and I saw his eyes flash with irritation when he clipped, "Baby, that's just not true."

"Really? Am I having a conversation in a different dimension than the one you're in?" I asked sarcastically. "Because the Ren in my dimension is telling me I can't be me and instead, to be with him, I have to be someone who is so, so, so, so, *so not me.*"

I knew it would happen. It was actually a shock he'd kept his shit tight for as long as he had. And me switching to sarcasm didn't help.

But at my words, the Italian hothead badass broke through and he lost it.

And this made his voice loud and his eyes cold when he chose a tone like he was talking to a small child, and one who was not all that bright to boot.

"What I'm trying to impress on you, Ally, is that I understand this is important to you, very important. But we're talkin' about you showing me that *our future* is important enough for you to do something as simple as havin' a job where you're *safe* and stay *healthy* and don't bring shit into our lives that's *uncontrolled*."

"I'm not some maverick with a death wish, Ren. I always do everything I can to stay safe and healthy, and it's part of my job to keep shit *controlled*. I've been doing this *for two years* and none of this has leaked back into my life."

That was when he really lost it.

"For fuck's sake, Ally!" he shouted, "Your apartment exploded!"

Fuck.

I had to give that to him, and unfortunately it was a biggie.

"Rosie was a one-off. He was never a client, but I'll admit he's a wildcard."

"Babe, the people you will connect with day to day in that business are all gonna be wildcards," he returned.

He was right about that, too.

But it also wasn't the point.

"Okay, Ren. You're correct. That's true. That said, what I'd ask from you is to trust me to know what I'm doing."

"Since I don't, that's a problem," he bit out, and I felt each word like he'd landed a blow.

So it came out breathless, and not the good kind, when I whispered, "Right."

"Ally—"

"No."

His chin jerked on that one word and I knew why.

Because it was quiet and filled with so much pain, it permeated the air, threatening to choke me.

I powered through that because I was Ally. That's what I did.

And I had no choice.

I took in another deep breath and told him, "The reason our date was off was that Mom and Dad called a family meeting. I was going to talk to you to see how you felt about coming. Obviously, that isn't an issue anymore."

"Baby——" he took a step toward me, but I again stepped back.

He stopped moving and I kept talking.

"Still, they want to talk and I need to listen, so I have to go. I'll be back later to get my stuff."

"Honey——"

"I'll text you when I'm on my way and it would be really cool if you weren't here when I got back. I'll leave the key in the kitchen."

"Ally, don't——"

"There's nowhere to go with this," I hissed, and he shut his mouth. "We've been around this and around it and it leads nowhere. I have no *fucking* clue why you worked so hard to get in there with me when you didn't want *me*. But you did. Now, you need to move on. Because I'm me. And if you can't accept me as I am, then we're done."

After that, I moved slowly to the door, through it and to my car.

Ren didn't follow me.

I walked up to my childhood home in Bonnie Brae and walked right through the front door without knocking (seeing as it was my childhood home, this wasn't rude; and anyway, they were expecting me).

Lee's Crossfire and Hank's 4Runner were at the curb, so I knew the gang was all there.

When I got inside, I found they were all hanging in the living room.

Dad, Hank and Lee had beers. Mom had, what looked to my practiced eye, a margarita in a regular glass.

I could use a margarita, *sans* the margarita mix, of course.

But I didn't have time to ask. I wanted this done. I wanted to get back to Ren's. I wanted to get my shit. Then I wanted to get somewhere no one could see me and have a complete mental collapse.

It didn't escape me when I walked in that no one with two eyes in their heads would not click that we were a family. We all had the same hair, even Mom and Dad. Hank and I had whisky-colored eyes while Lee had chocolate brown, but other than that we were all tall and lean. The men had more bulk, but we all had the same frames.

I'd always liked this. Even as a kid. Belonging to this family. Belonging to these people. And knowing no one could mistake that they were a part of me.

And also knowing what I knew was in them when their eyes turned to me.

Whatever this was going to be changed the instant every single one of them got a look at me.

They knew.

They knew inside I was bleeding.

"Honey, are you—?" Mom started, and I straightened my shoulders.

"I suspect," I cut her off to start, "that part of the reason I'm here is because you're not happy I'm with Ren Zano. So, in order not to waste anybody's time, I'll let you know that doesn't factor anymore because before I came over here, I ended things with him."

"Jesus," Hank muttered, studying me closely.

"Ally—" Lee started.

Dad and Mom just stared at me.

As for me, I kept talking.

"The rest, so you can target your comments, I got fired from Brother's two days ago and decided to start a private investigations agency. This is why Ren and I are no longer together. He's violently opposed to that idea and wants me to consider a career as a barista before I move into my tenure as a stay-at-home mom."

Dad's eyes moved to Lee and Hank.

Mom's mouth got tight.

I kept speaking.

"I'm not down with that. He's unwilling to see my point of view. So that's done. What's not done is the fact that Daisy is looking for office space to rent and I've tentatively taken her on as my receptionist." I looked to Hank. "And you may or may not know, but Roxie has started designing a website for me." I looked to Mom. "And Ava is mocking up logos. So it's all a go. I'll be sitting down with Daisy after Luke and Ava's wedding to organize a business plan, and shortly after we'll be actively recruiting clients."

I took in a breath and kept going.

"I intend to get licensed eventually, and Darius is approaching Sylvie Bissenette so I can work with her and acquire the hours I need to approach the

Licensing Board. Until that all takes off, I'll continue to work at Fortnum's with Indy."

I threw out a hand and moved to my conclusion.

"If I'm willing to lose Ren for this, the man I love, the man who loves me, the man I fell in love with the first night we met, then I'm willing to do anything for this. In other words, you won't talk me out of it. But because I love you all and respect you, I'll listen to what you have to say."

After that, I shut up.

Dad looked at Mom.

Mom only had eyes for me.

"Maybe you and me can go into the kitchen, get you a drink and have a chat," Mom suggested gently.

This meant she wanted to ascertain just how cut up I was about ending things with Ren.

I had no intention of going there. Not until I was alone with a bottle of tequila.

"I have things to do tonight, so thanks Mom, but that's gonna be a no," I replied.

"I'm thinkin' we should delay this meeting until you're in a better state of mind, honey." This came from Hank and it was also suggested gently.

I looked to him and saw his expression was just as gentle.

My brother was awesome. Both of them were.

Still, I shook my head. "I'm thinking we should get this over with."

"You, Hank and me, we're going to The Hornet," Lee stated and I looked at him. "And I'm calling Indy."

This meant he was worried about me and didn't want to discuss my career path, but wanted to call in reinforcements (namely Indy) who could see to my broken heart while he and Hank paid for tequila shooters.

See?

Awesome.

"Thanks, bro, but that's also a no," I whispered.

"Sweetheart—" Dad started, and my eyes got instantly hot just hearing that word.

When you're a kid and a girl, dads had superpowers. They could heal any hurt, usually with a word said just like that one. Or, if shit was extreme, if he added a hug, it would all go away.

221

My dad's superpowers were finely honed.

But they didn't extend to this kind of healing.

"No, Dad," I whispered. I looked through my family and requested, "Can we please just get this done?"

"We'll talk Monday," Hank declared. "You come to Lee's office. We'll all be there."

"Hank, we're here. Why can't we just do this now?" I asked.

"Because we're not doing it now," Lee said. "We're doing it Monday. Five thirty. My office."

I looked from one brother to the other.

Fuck.

"Fine," I snapped. "Now I gotta go." I looked through my brothers again and finished, "I'll see you tomorrow at the rehearsal."

"Ally, why don't you stay and eat dinner with your dad and me?" Mom asked, and I looked to her.

"You're cool with it, I'll come over for dinner on Sunday," I offered an alternate, which might appease her even if it would not do it totally.

At least it was something.

She looked to Dad then back at me and nodded.

"Later," I murmured, turning and giving them a low wave.

"Allyson," Dad called, and I sucked in breath and turned back. When I caught his eyes, he said softly, "You're loved, sweetheart."

I pressed my lips together and nodded, keeping my eyes to Dad because I knew I couldn't cope with them all at once showing me Dad's words were true through the expressions on their faces.

I then turned again and got the fuck out of there.

❦

I clenched my teeth as I sat in my Mustang outside Ren's house.

This was because, regardless of the fact that I texted him before I drove away from Mom and Dad's, Ren's Jag was at the curb.

During our Not-Really-Fuck-Buddies phase, I'd always wondered but never asked why he didn't park in the two car garage he had out back. It was in good repair and had a kickass wooden garage door with these interesting windows at the top.

I figured it was because the front was closer and had easier access to the house since his backyard was long. Some of it was terraced so he had a boatload of steps to climb up. That wouldn't be all that fun for lugging in groceries, even if you were a tall, strong, fit hot guy.

Then again, the front required, without fail, parallel parking, which was something I, like only three point two seven percent of the population (my estimation, not based on a study or anything), had the skills to do. Still, that didn't mean it didn't suck having to do it.

I was sitting there thinking I would never get an answer to this question at the same time I was thinking there was nothing for it. I had to go in, even with Ren there. I needed clothes, and my clothes were in Ren's house. So even if he wasn't going to be cool and let me get in and out without hassle, I had to get my meager belongings.

But before I did that, I knew I had to make a clean getaway. Therefore I had to have somewhere to get away to, and I'd made my decision on the drive there where that was going to be.

I pulled out my phone, found the contact and hit go.

On ring three, Daisy answered, "Everything good, sugar?"

"I ended things with Ren and I need a place to stay," I announced and ignored her sharp gasp. "Can I crash with you and Marcus for a couple of days?"

Silence before she asked, "You ended things with Ren?"

My eyes got hot and my voice was husky when I requested, "Please, Daisy. Not now."

This bought me more silence, but it lasted a lot less time before she said, "Absolutely, darlin'. I'll go up and make sure one of our guest rooms is ready for you and I'll be doin' that right now."

I *so freaking* loved Daisy.

"Thanks," I whispered.

"No problem, baby," she whispered back. "Now, you get here when you get here and we'll sort you out."

"Okay, Daisy."

"See you soon, sugar."

"Right."

I hung up before she could keep being sweet. I didn't have a lot left in me before I lost it, and Daisy had a lot of sweet and that would undo me. So I had to cut that off. Pronto.

I twisted his key off my ring in order to be ready, angled out of my car and hoofed it to Ren's.

Get this done and get gone.

Done and gone.

I tried the door, found it unlocked and walked right in.

The TV was on and Ren was in jeans and a tee, lounging like the hot guy he was on the couch, watching it. But the minute I entered, his eyes turned to me.

My mouth filled with saliva.

I tore my eyes from him and made a beeline to his kitchen.

I heard the TV go off.

I didn't take this as a good sign.

I dropped the key on his counter and moved out of the kitchen.

He caught me at the doorway. Arm hooking my waist, he shuffled me to the side and closed in so I was back to the wall and Ren was pressed to me.

I looked up at him and his face was set to sweet.

Somebody.

Please.

Kill me.

"We need to talk this through, baby," he said in a voice set the same way.

But this time there was no way he was going to get to me through his sweet.

"We haven't talked about much in all the time we've been together," I replied. "Except this. And we never agreed. I'm thinking we never will. You've got a life to lead, so do I. So I also think we should get on with doing that."

His free hand came to my jaw and I fought swallowing because I didn't want him to get anything from me. He already had enough.

In fact, everything.

"You love someone, you compromise. We'll find a way to compromise," he told me.

"What you mean is, *I'll* find a way to compromise," I told him.

"Ally—"

I was losing it, so my voice was scratchy when I asked quickly, "Why are you doing this?"

His fingers flexed into my flesh and his face got closer when he answered, "Because I believe in us."

224

"There is no us," I returned.

"There's always been an us, but I get you needed not to believe in that and why. That said, you can't deny there's been an us the last three days, honey."

"That was all fantasy."

He blinked and whispered, "What?"

"That Ren and that Ally don't exist. That was just you and me wanting to believe we could. But we couldn't. We fight. We don't agree on important things. We want the same thing in different ways. We don't work, but for those three days, we pretended we do. We can't pretend anymore, Ren. We have to be honest, see this isn't going anywhere and move on."

"So you're saying right now you're going to get your shit and leave and not sit down and see if we can work on finding a future we both believe in?" he asked.

"What I'm saying right now is that I think all that's been said has said it all."

"Right, then, you're not in a space right now where you're up for talkin' about this, so I'll ask you don't make any decisions. Stick with me, sleep beside me, and tomorrow when we're less raw, we give each other that time."

I shook my head. "Nothing's going to change, Ren."

"It won't if you don't give it a shot, Ally."

I held his eyes and laid it out. "You don't believe in me."

His jaw got tight.

Yep.

He didn't believe in me.

Fuck.

Again my fucking eyes got fucking hot, but *again* I powered right the fuck through to end this.

"Even if I could talk you around, I can't live with a man who doesn't believe in me. And I can't do what I have to do out there with half a mind to wondering what you'll think about this case or that decision or a client or how you'll react when I come home and tell you about my day. I wouldn't have to worry about any of that shit if you trusted me. Believed in me. But you don't and you won't, because you don't want this for me, or for you, or for our future. So what is the *fucking point* of dragging this shit out now when it already hurts in a way that if we even gave it days, it would *kill?*"

He took that as an in. I knew it when he pressed deeper and his face got closer.

225

So I moved to end it.

"You're not the man for me, Ren, and I'm not the woman for you. We're done and when I say that it is not a Rock Chick done where you can be badass or cool or whatever and talk me into changing my mind. I mean that in an Ally Nightingale way, where I know what I want and I've found the path that leads to a future that's exciting to me. So when I say we're done, I mean *we're done*."

With that, I pulled away, sliding out from in front of him and walking quickly up the stairs.

I had not had time to scatter my shit to the four corners of Ren's house.

Which was good.

It meant what I had to gather took little time.

But it didn't matter.

Because I barely hit his bedroom before I heard the front door slamming.

When I had it all gathered, I went to the window and looked down to see the Jag was gone.

So the coast was clear.

Nevertheless, I wasted no time double checking that I had absolutely everything.

And then I got the fuck out of there.

Chapter 17
You're Ally. And I'm Ren.

I opened my eyes and stared at the early morning light peeking through Daisy's curtains.

I knew I hadn't slept long. This was because I cried most of the night.

Yes. Me.

But I did it in Daisy's pillow so she nor Marcus would hear.

When I arrived the night before, she took one look at me and gave me space. That was, she took me to a room, asked my preference and brought me a glass and a bottle of tequila.

Then she touched my cheek and whispered, "We'll talk in the mornin', sugar."

She closed the door on her way out.

I didn't take even a sip of her top shelf tequila.

I'd never been heartbroken, not like this, but I'd stood behind a bar countless times listening to those who were. And I'd noted, repeatedly, imbibing didn't much help. Although that had been my preliminary plan, with the bottle and glass available to me, I instead chose the pillow and giving myself the opportunity to let loose the shit crawling inside me in an effort to get it out.

This didn't much help either.

I'd had two calls in that time. One from Indy, the other from Roxie.

This meant Daisy nor Hank and Lee had shared with anybody, except my brothers told their wives. But Indy and Roxie told nobody. If they had, my phone would never quit ringing and The Castle (or Daisy's house, which looked like a castle; no joke, complete with moat), would be descended on by Rock Chicks.

I was grateful for that, so much you wouldn't believe. And I texted both Indy and Roxie to tell them I'd connect with them later, I needed some time, and they texted back that they'd give that to me.

By the way, Ren had not phoned. He had also not scaled the wall and broken in the window in order to press his suit.

This was not a surprise. I'd been pretty inflexible with the way I ended things.

But this meant I definitely wasn't a *Rock Chick*. None of their men ever gave up.

That wasn't bitching. It was just an observation that didn't feel real great. Anyway, with the way I felt, I was glad Ren didn't do this. This was mostly because, when I had time to let myself feel all the things I was feeling, I knew if he came back to me and pushed it, I'd cave.

Again.

Yes. Me.

Ally.

Caving.

That was how much I loved him.

So I told myself maybe it indicated how much he loved me that he was going to let me go, which was the only way he could give me what I needed.

And although this thought was cool (kind of, in a rip your heart out way), it didn't make me feel any better, mostly because it ripped my heart out.

But now was now and I had a day to face.

I also had money to make. I had to find somewhere to live. And I had to find a way to get through Luke and Ava's rehearsal and dinner without totally losing it in front of everybody.

So I got up, got a shower, sorted through my bags and got ready.

I did this being careful. Not externally. Internally.

I was vulnerable. I knew this.

Yes, me.

Ally.

But I was.

I'd been shown the life I wanted. Tasted the fairytale. Then I let it slip away from me. I had doubts, second thoughts, and carried pain you wouldn't believe. Hell, I didn't even believe it.

So I had to forge ahead but handle me with care.

And that was what I was going to be doing.

My first trial was when I hit Daisy's huge kitchen to find Daisy at the counter beating something in a bowl and Smithie and Shirleen sitting at Daisy's kitchen table.

All eyes came to me and I knew they knew.

Whatever.

"Yo," I greeted, strolling in.

"Ally," Smithie replied, eyes never leaving me.

"Come sit by Shirleen, child," Shirleen called, also keeping her gaze locked on me.

"You want pancakes, sugar?" Daisy asked as I moved toward the table.

I didn't. The idea of food made me want to hurl.

"Sure," I said and walked right up to Smithie.

Then I leaned in and kissed his cheek, muttering a distracted, "Hey," as I moved around him and did the same with Shirleen.

After that, I sat down.

I looked out the window knowing that these people were nuts, but they loved me and they'd be careful with me. It'd be far easier to handle if they acted normally. But they were too kind to even think of doing that.

Therefore, I was bracing.

And in bracing, I didn't see Daisy, Shirleen and Smithie giving each other wide-eyed looks.

"Uh… Ally," Daisy called.

I tore my eyes away from the window and my mind away from noting there were ducks in her moat and I looked at her.

"Yeah?"

"Know you had a tough night, honey bunch, but Shirleen and Smithie are here for a reason," she told me.

Fabulous.

I looked between them and asked, "Which one first?"

"Me," Shirleen said so I focused my attention on her. When I did, she didn't delay in declaring, "Your brother declines cases."

My head jerked.

I didn't expect to hear this. Demands to know what happened between Ren and me. Or how Ren wasn't good enough for me. Or alternately how I should maybe give it more than three days of together *together* before I ended us. Or just kindness, and maybe sympathy.

Not a random detail about my brother's business.

"Okay," I replied cautiously.

"He does what he does. In other words, he makes decisions and doesn't share why with me. But I see a pattern," she went on. "He declines when we have a full caseload and the boys are stretched to the max. Usually, though, he declines if it isn't enough of a challenge for their badasses to bother with."

Suddenly, what she was saying cut through my melancholy.

I straightened in my chair.

"And?" I prompted.

"And part of my job is takin' down the preliminaries of a possible case and reporting those to him. If he's going to decline, usually he does it without a meet. That means he doesn't decline, I do."

I nodded.

She kept talking.

"He never says no without givin' them a referral. Most of the shit goes to Dick Anderson. Occasionally he'll want something referred to Sylvie Bissenette. There's a player in town called Hawk who has specialties that aren't Lee's specialties and he'll punt shit to him, too. This is rare. Most of his refusals go to Anderson."

"Okay," I again said cautiously.

"And now, some of them will go to you," she finished.

Oh my God.

This was righteous!

"Shirleen——" I started, and she lifted a hand.

I swallowed annoyance at getting The Hand and shut up.

"Darius has talked to me and he says you're good. He also says he's gonna keep workin' with you. Brody says the same. Lee has not come down on this and I'm waitin' to see if he will. But regardless, my nephew doesn't talk shit to me. He says it straight. So if he says you're good, and I've seen the way you are, girl, I know you got somethin', then I'm good with punting refusals to you. But Lee trades on his reputation, and the reason he refers to Anderson, Bissenette and Hawk is that he trusts them to take care of the business he refuses. Referrals reflect on him. You fuck up, that reflects on your brother. Not only 'cause you got the same name, but you got the business because of his referral. But his referral is one given by me. You make me regret that once, that will be the only time I regret shit."

"Shit happens, Shirleen," I told her. "But whatever shit happens, I'll bust my ass to be sure you won't regret this. And I sure as hell won't do anything that will reflect poorly on Lee."

She nodded. "I hear you. I believe you. Now, take into account that he's not gonna know I'm doin' this until he finds out I'm doin' this. And he knows pretty much everything, so I figure it'll take him about a day to find that shit out. I'll handle him. In other words, I'm throwin' myself in that lion's den. For you. Don't make me regret that shit either."

There were two people who could "handle" Lee. Indy. And Shirleen. Mom couldn't even do it and had given up trying years ago.

Though Indy's batting average was better with that.

Still, what Shirleen was saying was that she intended to go to the mat for me.

"Thank you, chickie," I murmured on a smile.

She smiled back, reached out a hand, took mine and gave me a quick squeeze.

Then she let me go and announced, "I need a refill. Java, Ally?"

I nodded to her and watched her get up, grab her mug and give me rolled eyes before she took the mug Smithie had lifted her way in silent demand for more coffee.

She headed to the pot.

Daisy was at the grill of her massive, restaurant-quality stove flipping pancakes.

Smithie spoke to me. "Shirleen can give you business. I already got some."

I looked at him and the chill that was left on my insides after ending things with Ren started warming.

"No shit?" I asked.

"None at all. I got a situation at the club," he told me. "And I ain't payin' Lee's prices 'cause that shit is highway robbery. And anyway, he don't got no bitches on staff and he took this job, Lord knows what he'd find me. I gotta have a girl backstage, which means *onstage,* so she's gotta be right." He tipped his head to me. "You're right."

Oh fuck.

This didn't sound promising.

"What's going on?" I asked.

"I don't know. That's what I'm gonna hire you to find out," Smithie answered.

"Okay, what's happening?" I amended my question.

231

"What's happenin' is, bitches are quiet. My bitches are never quiet. None of 'em. Waitresses. Dancers. Even the one female bartender I got bends my ear so much it's a wonder it ain't torn clean off. They got boyfriend problems. They got car problems. They got childcare issues. They're on the rag. They didn't *get* their rag—"

I rolled a hand at him and said, "I get it. Move it on, Smithie."

"Right. Now?' He shook his head. "None 'a that shit. Not one thing," he stated.

"You got an idea why?" I asked as Shirleen slid mugs in front of Smithie and me.

"Got a bouncer. Hired him, good guy, checked out. I think he snowed me 'cause my girls... they're scared of him."

The skin at the back of my neck prickled.

"Usually," he went on, "that kinda shit happens, it's because he's creepin' and I just fire the asshole. But he wasn't creepin', not that I could see."

I nodded.

Smithie kept talking. "But I fired him anyway. When I did, he told me he was filing a wrongful termination suit. I have no idea what that shit is. I just know I don't want that kind of bullshit hassle. So I kept him on, kept my eye on him and set Lenny on him. Lenny's close to graduating from DU so he's got other shit on, but it don't matter. Neither of us is findin' anything. We need a girl in there to keep her eye on shit and either give me a valid reason to can his ass or give me reason to beat his ass until he's close to not breathing. I prefer number two. But I could live with the number one, long's it happens fast."

"So you need me to waitress," I tried.

And failed.

"I need you to dance."

Oh shit.

"Uh, Smithie—"

He cut me off. "The waitresses don't often go backstage. Whatever's happening is happening back there. Bouncers will go back, provide presence, protection or so they can walk the girls to their cars. I usually ask another one to do that shit, but he comes up on rotation 'cause I gotta be careful not to single him out and give him shit that he can give *me* shit about."

"I don't dance," I told him.

"Daisy'll teach you."

She would. She'd taught Lottie, Jet's sister, Smithie's headliner, and the premier stripper in the western half of the United States (not kidding).

Shit!

"We have another problem, and that is that I'm a regular there so your guy has probably seen me. He'll know my name, particularly my last one, and he might figure out what's going on," I shared.

"I already got that covered, seein' as I been hearin' about what you do from Darius and I been thinkin' about talkin' to you," Smithie replied. "So I set it around that you got your apartment exploded and lost your job. You need money, and it ain't like you got judgment on the girls for what they do since twice a month your ass is at a table by the stage cheerin' them on. All 'a them are where they are 'cause they got in tight places. No doubt about it, you're in a tight place. Not one a' them will blink, your ass hits my stage."

He had it all covered.

Crap.

I drew in a breath, sat back and grabbed my mug to take a sip, my eyes on Smithie, my mind whirling.

On the one hand, this sounded like a juicy case the likes I would not hesitate sinking my teeth into (if it did not require me taking my clothes off in front of an audience). On that same hand, Smithie was in the posse; he meant something to me and he cared about his girls. He wanted them protected, he was worried about them, was powerless, and I knew this was likely striking deep. So I wanted to help him.

On the other hand, this job required me taking my clothes off in front of an audience.

Well, at least this gave me one good reason that I ended things with Ren the day before. If we were together and he heard about this, he would lock me in his bedroom and not let me out until I was his pregnant love slave.

That might seem overkill, but trust me, with this, it wasn't. Love slave wouldn't be enough. Pregnant wouldn't be enough. Both of these would mean I was tied to him in a way I couldn't come untied, and therefore both would be the only acceptable requirements for release.

Then he'd probably ask a priest to marry us there, standing by his bed with its wine-colored sheets, me wearing a cream nightie.

Then he'd let me out.

Alas, at that moment, all of this seemed good to me.

233

Ugh.

So it was decided.

"Right, I'll take on the job," I told Smithie. "I'll dance, but only if it's up to me if I go all out with that in a top off kind of way. Your girls and customers will have to deal if I go with keeping on the bra. It might be I'll rise to the occasion or the stripper vibe will carry me away and I'll go all in. But right now, that's freaking me, so you're going to have to ride that with me."

"Done," Smithie immediately agreed, and that was when I knew how deep this was striking.

He was *way* worried.

"I have to be all about Ava the next couple of days, Smithie. But soon as I can, I'll work with Daisy. I'll also set Brody on an electronic search, Darius on looking into things. I'll need a name, address and social and if you got it, car info, including the plates," I told him.

"You'll get it within an hour," he told me.

I looked to Daisy to see her making her way to the table balancing three plates up one arm with the other hand carrying a bottle of syrup.

I looked back at Smithie, "You need to set up an account with Daisy. She'll discuss rates and payment information."

Daisy gave me a huge smile, set the syrup down and placed a plate in front of me.

"Done," Smithie muttered, his eyes on the plate she was setting in front of him.

But it was then, it hit me.

And it hit me hard in a good way that at that moment in my life I really needed.

This wasn't happening.

It had happened.

I had my first official client.

I was an investigator.

I grinned down at my plate and picked up the fork and knife Daisy put there.

"I'll get the butter," she murmured and I looked up to her to see her moving away.

But she was doing it looking at me.

And when I caught her eyes, she winked.

She'd done this, my kickass Daisy. She'd planned and instigated this so my morning wouldn't totally suck.

God, freaking *loved* Daisy.

I kept grinning.

Shortly after, I ate five of Daisy's pancakes.

I did this because I hadn't eaten the night before.

And I was hungry.

※

"You good, honey?" Stevie asked in my ear.

It was early afternoon. I'd made my calls to set Brody and Darius on Smithie's case. I was working at Fortnum's and Stevie had just called me.

Also, word had gotten around about Ren and me. I knew this because not only were Indy and Jet at Fortnum's (like normal) but Roxie, Sadie, Stella and Ava were also there. Jules was at the shelter for runaways where she worked, and since we were all heading out early to go to the church for the rehearsal, she had to stay there and sort some stuff before she left. I knew this because she called and told me.

They knew, but no one got in my face or space.

But that didn't mean all of them, including Tex (Duke was still a no-show), weren't being watchful, though cool.

It felt nice.

I knew that the word would spread, but I was glad the ones who knew last night gave me that time, and when they let the word out, they made it what it was.

Safe for me.

And I knew by Stevie's tone he was going to do the same.

"I'm hanging in there, Stevie," I told him.

This was when he proved me right by letting that go and asking, "T minus two hours and twenty minutes before rehearsal. You're there?"

"Absolutely," I answered.

"You still in for dinner? Because I can call the restaurant and change our numbers without them charging us. Tod will be cool. We have a big enough party and folks are ordering off the menu. It'll be good."

"I'll be at the dinner too, honey. Wouldn't miss it for the world," I replied.

"Okay, sweetie. See you soon."

"'Bye, Stevie."

"'Bye, baby."

I smiled into the phone, slid it into my back pocket and my head snapped up when I heard Indy breathe, "Holy crap," and felt the vibe all around change.

But I made no move and uttered not a sound.

This was because Ren had entered the store and he was currently stalking to me.

Then he'd stalked to me.

Then he'd grabbed my hand and tugged me from the table I was about to clear and he yanked me down the center aisle.

He turned us at the self-help section and tugged me down the row to the side aisle which had a wall of books.

Once there, he pulled me around, pushed me into the shelves and got in my space *and* my face.

Deep in the first, way close to the other.

"You kissed Smithie?"

I was not following. I had no idea how I was one second in one place, another second standing with Ren in my space. And I had no idea because I was totally freaked due to his actions breaking a very important breakup law.

Maybe the most important there was.

That was, if you shared friends and acquaintances, during breakups any guy who wasn't a dick didn't show their faces for ages. Ren was also classy. And classy guys gave you plenty of time to get over it so the hit when you saw them again didn't kill you. It just maimed.

So by my estimation I had at least five months and twenty-nine days before I saw him again.

And anyway, what he asked made no sense whatsoever.

"Come again?"

He pushed deeper into me and growled, in a statement this time, "You kissed Smithie."

Was he suggesting I'd made out with Smithie?

And thus, was he high?

"I... no, I..." I trailed off.

Pull it together Ally!

"You kissed him on the cheek," Ren gritted out.

Oh.

I did do that.

"Well, uh, yes. I did that," I confirmed.

"You don't kiss people's cheeks," he stated.

This was true.

But why had he come all the way there and broken the most important breakup law there was in order to tell me this?

"Zano—"

He pressed so close, I stopped speaking. I also lost my ability to breathe when his hand cupped me under my jaw and gently pushed my head back as his face came so close he was all I could see.

Once he had me in position, he bit out, "*Ren*."

I blinked, and in that instant, I pulled myself together.

Therefore, I put a hand to his abs, firm and communicative, and snapped, "What the fuck is going on?"

"You wanna be a PI, there's office space across the hall from me. Dom enquired about it. The way shit is with this economy, it's been vacant for six months, no one even sniffing. They're desperate to make something on it, so they offered a large discount for the first year. It's not big; reception, big office, small office, small kitchenette and decent-sized conference room. I signed the lease, bought your first year."

My mouth would have dropped open if his hand wasn't at my jaw.

So instead I just felt my eyes get wide and stared.

He kept talking.

"I wasn't going to make a big deal out of it because I want you however you come to me. But I'll say it now, it's important I bring up my family in my faith and it's important my future wife is a part of that. You offered me that possibility without me even asking."

At that, I would have swallowed if his hand wasn't at my jaw.

So instead I just kept staring.

He got even closer so it was only his eyes that I could see, and his voice dropped near to a whisper.

"You know what I do. You come from who you come from, and I know your meeting with your family last night was about that. And you wanted to give me the opportunity to be a part of that meeting, also givin' me the shot to start without delay in showin' your people what you mean to me. I do not know how you feel about what I do because you just let me do it. My guess, I forced that issue, I'd learn you didn't like it much. You still just let me do it. You could have thrown that shit in my face last night, but you didn't utter a single fuckin' word. Which shows me that it's so embedded in what you give me that it wasn't even a consideration to draw that blade. Which tells me you take me as I come."

It was then, I was breathing heavily.

But Ren wasn't done

"And I didn't return that favor."

Oh my God.

Was this happening?

Hot hit my eyes and he kept right on going.

"I'm not a maximum contact sleeper, Ally. *You* are."

I gasped because this wasn't true. I wasn't.

That was, not with anyone but him.

Before I could sort that in my head, Ren kept going.

"Never held a woman all night in my arms in my life... until you."

Oh shit.

I felt the wet in my eyes because I was thinking this was happening.

He kept at me.

"And last night, because I was a fuckin' dick, I didn't have you in my arms. I didn't like that. Even when you thought we were fuck buddies, you gave me that."

Oh God.

"Ren," I whispered.

"You want this. And what you want to do means so much to you that you would let me be who I am, look into accepting my faith, love me that much, but walk away. Then you take that hurt so deep, you're on autopilot, lettin' out the woman inside you hold close and only dole out occasionally, but give to me. And you do shit like kiss Smithie to say hello when you never would do that shit. It means that much, then you can have it. *And* me. I'll worry, but I'll learn to trust you. All I ask is, when you got my babies inside you, you take cases you know are safe, and once we got kids under our roof, you proceed with the same caution. You with me?"

"I... are you... are you saying...?" I took in a breath. "Are you saying that you're okay with me starting a private investigations agency?"

"No. I'm not saying that. I'm sayin' I'll work at it and try to be."

Oh *God.*

I couldn't stop it. A tear slid out of the side of my eye.

Ren's hand finally moved from my jaw so it could cup my cheek, but his thumb kept moving in order to sweep away the tear.

But his eyes never left mine as he whispered, "I love you, Ally. I was pissed and worried. Lucky said you had a gun on you and that undid me. You not callin' and tellin' me that shit was gonna go down didn't make things better. You came home and were immediately cool. I was not in a place where I could be cool so I was a dick." He dipped his head, his mouth touched mine and he kept his lips there when he finished, "I'm sorry, baby."

Yep. Not only was this happening; it happened.

I hiccoughed back a silent sob and shoved my face in his neck.

Both his arms closed around me. They did this tight and I felt this jaw press to the side of my head.

He was going to give himself to me at the same time take me as me.

This.

Was.

Righteous.

Oh shit.

This was a disaster!

I took two deep breaths to pull myself together, but kept my face firm in his neck when I started, "Uh... Ren——"

"Smithie's got an issue and you're dancin' for him," he stated matter-of-factly.

I blinked against his skin.

Then I pulled my face out of his neck and stared at him.

He didn't look happy. He didn't look pissed, but he didn't look happy.

"You're on that case and you come home from work, baby, I don't wanna know," he stated.

Was this Ren?

Or *was* there another dimension, and the Ren from that dimension slid through?

"Do you feel okay?" I asked and he grinned.

Then he said, "I shouldn't. I got shit sleep. And last night, I also got calls from both your brothers, up in my shit."

Uh.

Say *what?*

Ren kept going.

"Then I got a call from Daisy, up in my shit. This means I got a call from Marcus, also up in my shit. And this morning I got a call from Shirleen, again, up in my shit. And last I got a call from Smithie, tellin' me you're workin' a case for him and he would not be happy if *I* got up in *his* shit. Then I hauled my ass over here to sort our shit. Now, you gotta call and let whoever know I'm gonna be at the rehearsal dinner tonight, because I missed dinner with my woman last night and that shit isn't happening two days in a row."

Our first semi-official date was going to Luke and Ava's rehearsal dinner.

How freaking cool was that?

I didn't tell him I thought that.

I muttered, "I best call Tod."

"And don't bother calling Daisy. She already sent your bags back to my place."

God.

Totally *loved* Daisy.

"Last," he went on, "you gotta be a badass and call me Zano, that's cute. I like it. But if things are deep with us, shit's raw, emotional or important, I'm Ren. I've asked a lot from you Ally, and you from me. But you're not a badass with me. You've let me into that place in you that you don't give anybody. So you don't put up that shield to hold me back when shit's important. You're you. You're Ally. And I'm Ren."

This kind of weirded me out how much he'd figured out about me.

I also didn't share this.

I whispered, "Okay."

"Okay," he replied.

"Can I ask what my brothers said to you?"

"No," he answered. "Just know those two men love you. They'd break important alliances to take your back. And they'd likely lay their lives down for you."

Those must have been intense conversations.

Nevertheless, I already knew all that.

So, my insides so warm they were melty, I smiled.

"Uh, sorry," a voice said from our side, and we both looked that way to see a thin woman wearing a brightly colored tunic and jeans and lots of jewelry standing there. Her eyes were on me. "I know you work here. Where can I find *Eat, Pray, Love?*"

"Are you shitting me?" Ren asked low, which meant dangerous.

Her eyes went from Ren to me and she lifted her brows.

Clearly a regular.

"Have you looked in the G's?" I asked her.

"The G's? It's called *Eat, Pray, Love*. I looked in the E's," she answered.

"It's written by Elizabeth Gilbert, and books are shelved by author in biography. So try the G's. But, heads up, we're a used bookstore and that's a popular title. Odds are we've had about fifty of them and sold that same fifty, unless you're lucky."

She nodded. "I'll look in the G's."

"Do that now," Ren ordered.

She gave him a look, rolled her eyes at me, and sauntered away.

Definitely a regular.

"Fuck me," Ren muttered, and I looked at him to see he was staring at the space the woman used to occupy.

"Ren," I called softly, and he immediately looked at me.

And thus I got his eyes.

Jeez, those eyes.

"Are you gonna kiss me, or what?" I asked.

That was when I got his smile.

A second later, I got his kiss.

"Uh... just to say..." We heard, and Ren growled into my mouth before he broke the kiss and we both looked to the side to see Indy standing there.

She looked to Ren then to me.

And she smiled huge.

"I approve," she declared and disappeared.

She'd so totally been listening.

Before I could process this, Ren's hand was again at my jaw. He turned my head back to him and then his mouth was again on mine, his tongue again in my mouth, and I wasn't up for processing anything.

"You good?" Ren asked.

Oh yeah.

I was good.

So good.

My plethora of shopping bags were in Ren's bedroom.

And I was in Ren's arms in his bed after he gave me two orgasms.

So. Totally. *Good.*

"Yeah, honey," I muttered sleepily.

"No, baby," he replied, pulling my back deeper into his front and nuzzling his face in my neck where he went on, "Ava and Luke's thing. You and me. That history. You seemed okay tonight at dinner. I just wanna make sure that's where you are, not what you want people to see."

I closed my eyes.

Seriously.

So.

Totally.

Loved this man.

Then I opened them and turned my head to look at him.

"That's done, Ren. I don't even think about it anymore."

"Promise?"

"Yeah."

"Nothing buried that will come out and bite either you or me?"

I bought this after burying what was between us for a year.

So I sought to pay up, and fast.

I turned a little in his arms and put my hand to his jaw. "That's done. Now it's just you and me. And honestly, cross my heart, I haven't thought of it once since we had it out in a moderately priced motel in a small Colorado mountain town."

I heard a deep, short chuckle before, "A moderately priced motel in a small Colorado mountain town?"

"AKA, my favorite place on earth."

His body went still.

Then his mouth growled, "*Ally.*"

Right after, that mouth was on mine, I was on my back and Ren was on me.

I guessed we weren't settling in to sleep.

Righteous.

Chapter 18

Love Was in the Air

I sat on Ren's kitchen counter, Ren standing between my legs, our happy places touching, my phone ringing in my ear, my eyes on my man.

Mom answered, "Hello?"

"Hey Mom. You got two seconds?" I asked.

"Yes, he's invited to dinner tomorrow, Ally."

I bit my lip and gave big eyes to Ren.

Her knowing Ren and I were back together wasn't a surprise. I was thirty-two, but she'd been in my business since I was born, and as far as she could be, never got out. Even so, it wasn't exactly a secret, what with Ren charging me at Fortnum's and us being at the rehearsal dinner together. Her informants were in attendance at both of these events. And her informants were big on informing.

I let my lip go and asked quietly, "You sure?"

"You love him?" she asked back.

"Yes," I whispered.

"Then your father and I best get to know him."

So totally told you my mom was the shit.

"Thanks, Mom."

"See you in a few hours, honey."

She disconnected. I did too.

I set my phone aside and addressed Ren.

"You're invited to dinner tomorrow."

He stared at me.

Then he asked, "How did that happen in the two seconds you were talking to her?"

"It's Mom's way." I curled my arms around him and pressed closer from happy place to chest, and assured him, "It's gonna be okay."

His arms tightened. "I know, baby." He then gave me a touch on the lips before he said, "You gotta get goin'."

I did. I needed to be primped and trussed in preparation for two people I loved tying the knot.

Therefore, I smiled.

Ren smiled back at me.

⇛⇚

"Oh God, honey."

"Hurry."

"*God, Ren.*"

"Hurry, Ally."

We were in a cloakroom at Hotel Monaco where Luke and Ava were having their reception.

I had my back to the wall, my arms and legs curled around my man, and Ren was exploring the functionality of the deep slit up the front of my killer aqua column bridesmaid dress with a chiffon overlay that exposed a pure Ava rock 'n' roll stretch of midriff.

Ren and I were doing the business.

In other words, love was in the air.

Totally good luck that Tod had picked up and kept hold of all the bridesmaid dresses until the big day. If mine had been in my apartment, semi-tragedy.

But my mind wasn't on escaping a semi-tragedy.

It was on something way better.

"I'm... it's... *Ren,*" I gasped, whimpered, then came.

Glorious.

"Fuckin' fuck me," Ren growled. He shoved his face in my neck, thrust deep and groaned.

I held on tight as his shuddered though him and mine me.

After it was over, I kept holding him until he kissed my neck, indication to let go.

I did. He slid me up, sliding out of me. His mouth came to mine, his eyes glued to mine, as he put me to my feet. He held me against the wall and I felt him do up his trousers.

Then he touched our lips together before crouching in front of me and ordering, "Foot, baby."

I lifted a silver strappy, stiletto-heel shod foot and he slid one side of my discarded thong over it. I lifted the other and he repeated, then slid my thong up my legs.

This caused another shudder.

He settled my panties on my hips and rearranged my skirt so it fell properly, but before he got to his feet in front of me, he kissed the inside of my right knee.

And another shudder.

Then he was on his feet and I was no longer leaning against the wall because I was in Ren's arms.

"You got sex hair, honey," he told me, eyes moving around my head.

"So?" I asked, and his gaze came to me.

That got me a smile, which led to another touch on the lips. This one harder, it lasted longer and it included our lips opening and both of us adding tongue.

Yummy.

Ren ended the kiss, landed one on my jaw and grabbed my hand.

He led me to the door, opened it and shoved me in front of him, still holding my hand as he pushed us out.

And thus we ran headlong into Sadie and Hector.

Sadie, in a baby blue dress the same style as mine, stared up at me.

Her face got red.

Hector muttered, "Fuck," and pulled her back. He gave a chin jerk to Ren, and then sauntered away, clamping an arm around her waist and disappearing around an opening to the corridor.

I looked up at Ren.

Ren's eyes were to where Sadie and Hector disappeared, but when he felt mine, they came down to me.

When they did, I burst out laughing.

Ren's arm slid along my waist and he propelled me forward as he joined in my hilarity.

Yep. Love was in the air.

After hitting the bathroom for a necessary errand due to Ren and my cloakroom activities, I entered the function room and scanned the crowd looking for Ren.

My eyes stopped on Luke, who was standing with his mom and Ava's mom.

Ava's mom was clearly babbling, and it was clear she'd been doing this for a while because Mrs. Stark was nodding but the smile was fixed on her face and it was obvious her mind was miles away. This was also clear because Luke looked like he wanted someone to shoot him. But still, he was standing there holding his mother's hand, and I thought this, particularly from badass Luke, was all kinds of cool.

I continued my scan and my eyes stopped again when I saw Tex and Duke standing close, Tex looking weird (and not just because he was wearing a suit instead of his uniform flannel shirt and jeans) and Duke smiling and clapping him on the shoulder.

Tex had a personality set to crotchety and Duke worked with a bunch of crazy women and had for decades. Thus they did not get along in a normal way. They got along by bantering (sometimes heatedly), bonding when shit got crazy and they agreed that the women amongst them were loons, and the rest of the time ignoring their own craziness in order to focus on the crazy around them.

This did not mean they weren't tight. They'd known each other awhile and had both ridden the turbulent waves of the Rock Chick/Hot Bunch Courtships from the very beginning, and those kinds of rides formed unshakable bonds. Trust me.

But they were men. They didn't have heartfelt conversations or hug it out. I'd never seen one touch the other. I didn't think I'd even seen them smile at each other.

Now Duke was smiling big.

However, Tex wasn't.

He just nodded, said something, turned jerkily away and his eyes caught on me.

He then lumbered toward me.

When he got close, I greeted, "Yo, Tex. What's up?"

His eyes moved over my hair then back to me and he noted, "I think sex in a public place is illegal."

"That's only a problem if you get caught," I returned.

"This, the Ally Nightingale Life Philosophy," he muttered on a low boom.

I grinned. "You bet your bippy."

He stared at me, and it was then I noticed he still looked weird.

So I asked, "You okay?"

"Need to talk to you," he told me.

Uh-oh.

This could mean anything.

"About what?" I asked cautiously.

"What're you doin' on Wednesday?" he asked back.

I was likely taking pole dancing classes from Daisy.

I didn't tell him this.

"Nothing... yet," I answered.

He lifted his hand to his throat, where the tie that was there earlier was now gone and likely in some trash receptacle. His fingers encountered no tie so he lifted his hand to wrap it around the back of his neck and he rubbed.

Oh man.

This was not a good sign.

"Tex—"

"Indy's standing up with me," he cut me off to say bizarrely. "Trixie's doin' it for Nancy. We only need two witnesses, but I still want you and Duke standin' beside me. Indy and Duke already agreed. I need you at the Justice of the Peace on Wednesday when I marry Nancy."

Ho.

Lee.

Crap!

"What?" I whispered.

"On Wednesday, me and Nancy're gettin' hitched," he stated, and I felt my body lock and my eyes get hot in that way that this was the kind of stuff I knew would take a miracle to hold back the tears.

Nancy was Jet's mother. Nancy was the bomb. Nancy had also been Tex's girlfriend for a good long while.

But Tex and a Justice of the Peace?

I started teetering and Tex started talking.

Fast.

"It's no big deal. We just do our thing, get the fuck outta there, and Blanca's givin' us a little shindig in her backyard. Just family. You don't even have to wear a dress. You can wear jeans."

"I... you... Nancy..." I stammered, stopped and felt the wet hit my eyes. "Tex," I whispered.

He stared at me, looking agitated, then more agitated then finally he declared, "The cats like her."

I burst out laughing.

Still doing it, I threw myself at him and wrapped his massive bulk in my arms (as best I could, my arms didn't go around).

His arms closed around me and they did this tight.

Tex and I had also never hugged it out.

Now that we were doing that, it felt amazing.

My body bucked as the emotion shoved itself up my throat and I barely managed to force it back down.

I felt his bulk bow as he put his lips to my ear and that was when Tex—yes, Tex—whispered, "I take it you'll be there."

I turned my head to get to his ear and my voice was croaky when I whispered back, "With bells on."

"Thank you, darlin'." He kept whispering.

My body bucked again and the swallow was audible, and loud, when I beat back the sob.

"What's goin' on?"

That was Ren.

I twisted my neck to look at Ren as Tex's hold loosened and one of his massive mitts hit the small of my back in order to direct me into Ren's arms.

When Ren had me, Tex answered, "Nuthin'. Gotta go."

But he didn't go.

He caught my eyes and held them before he lifted a beefy hand and rested it on the top of my head.

Warmth flowed through me.

Only then did he take off.

Quickly.

"Baby?" Ren called, his hand coming to my jaw and tilting it up.

"We have plans Wednesday," I declared. "I'm standing up with Tex while he marries Nancy, and then we're going to Blanca's for an after party."

Ren did a slow blink at me before his head turned and he looked in the direction where Tex took off. Then he looked back at me.

"I'm gettin' a feeling that, you in my life and not just my bed, my social calendar is gonna be busy," he noted.

"You might want to buy a whole new calendar with lots of blank space," I suggested and got a lip quirk and arm squeeze. Then I shared a colossal understatement. "The Rock Chicks like to party."

"Right," he mumbled, lips still quirking.

"So," I started, "Would you like me to quit avoiding them and take you to my parents to introduce you?"

His brows shot up and he asked disbelievingly, "You doin' that shit with sex hair?"

He had a point.

"Uh…" I mumbled, but did it beginning to laugh.

"No," he answered and dipped his face to me. "Tame that mane, honey, and the answer changes to yes."

Time for another trip to the bathroom.

I was about to tell Ren where I was going when Roxie, in a dress like mine but in teal, rushed up and stopped on a wobble.

"Did Uncle Tex ask you?" she queried excitedly.

"Yep," I answered as Ren let me go, but tucked me into his side with his arm around me.

"Did you say yes?" she asked.

"Yep," I answered.

"Did you have sex in the cloakroom?" she went on.

"Yep," I answered, that word shaking with humor, and my body shook with it when I heard and felt Ren sigh.

She looked over her shoulder in the direction of where Hank was standing and talking to Tod and Stevie.

And she did this muttering, "That's out."

"Please, do not tell me where you and Hank have sex during this reception," I begged.

She looked back at me. "You're one of my closest friends. Friends talk sex. Everyone knows that."

"And he's my brother," I reminded her.

"It's not like you don't know we do the deed," Roxie returned.

"I do know that," I retorted. "I just don't want details. I've already had so many details, it's a wonder I'm not in therapy."

"Location isn't a detail," she shot back.

God!

"La, la, la, I'm not listening, la, la, la," I chanted.

"Oh God, Roxie's talking about Hank and her doing the business."

This was said by Indy (in aqua, like me) who, when I turned my head, I saw was approaching with Lee.

"Then we're leaving," Lee muttered.

Indy giggled and pulled him to us, sharing, "Well, don't use the handicapped bathroom upstairs."

"Fuck." Lee kept muttering.

I bit back laughter.

Roxie didn't.

"Or the cloakroom." Stella's kickass husky voice came at us from the side, and I turned to see her (in teal) and Mace (like Lee and Hank, in a tux), joining us.

"That's two for the cloakroom," Roxie stated.

"Who else?" Stella asked.

"Ren and me," I told her.

"Ah," she mumbled.

"Jesus," Mace grunted.

"What are you talking about?" Jet (in baby blue, though she didn't have a chiffon-exposing midriff; she had a figure-skimming, kickass pregnant lady's bridesmaid dress) with Eddie (in a tux) asked.

"Rock Chick/Hot Bunch wedding assignations," Indy answered.

"Oh shit," Eddie murmured.

"Handicapped bathroom," Jet shared.

"Fuck me," Eddie clipped at the same time Lee bit out, "Christ."

Jet turned to her husband. "What?"

I didn't bite back laughter then. I couldn't. I just let it fly.

"What's funny?" Jules (in teal) asked, and we all looked to see her and Vance coming in around Indy and Lee.

"Cloakroom or handicapped bathroom?" Roxie asked.

Jules knew exactly what we were talking about and answered instantly, "Cloakroom."

"Popular choice," Stella put in.

"In about fifteen minutes, we can get Sadie and Hector's info. But my guess, handicapped bathroom since they ran into Ren and me on our way out of the cloakroom," I told them.

The women nodded knowingly.

Eddie requested, "Can we stop talking about this?"

"No," Daisy (in baby blue) stated, dragging Marcus to our group and stopping. "Or at least not until you tell me what you're talkin' about."

"Cloakroom or handicapped bathroom?" Jet shared at the same time she asked.

"Oh, sugar," Daisy waved a hand with silver polish on her long nails tipped with aquamarine rhinestones in the shapes of hearts, "Me and Marcus got a room. All access all the time. Comprende?"

I leaned up to Ren and whispered, "We're doing that next time"

"What?" he asked, looking down his nose at me. "Did you say something? My ears are bleeding."

At that, I burst out laughing.

"What's funny?" Shirleen queried, also in aqua (a Rock Chick wedding party stretched long, believe you me). "No, don't tell me. I don't give a shit. What I give a shit about is that I'm about to whale on those bitches Ava calls sisters so someone needs to calm me down. With brandy. Or bourbon. I don't care which. I just spent five minutes with those two where they ripped every woman here's outfit to shreds along with complainin'—at length—about not bein' in the weddin' party, when every fool knows those two treated their sister like trash for years. So how do they think they're gonna get a pretty dress? Don't answer that. The answer is, no one here knows how bitches' minds work."

She sucked in a huge breath.

Then she admitted, "I was beginning to get scared—*me... Shirleen*—that suddenly their fangs would come out and those vampires would lay waste to the entire guest list."

We all looked toward Ava's sisters, Marilyn and Sofia, who nobody liked. Even Ava.

They were in a huddle, clearly whispering, lips set in sneers, eyes to a woman I didn't know, but I thought she was Luke's aunt (or something). Which meant she was in her fifties. And there was nothing wrong with her outfit. She looked great.

Then again, Marilyn and Sofia could talk trash about anybody. They'd cut their teeth honing that skill through a lifetime of abuse piled on Ava.

And obviously they hadn't stopped.

Also, neither of them had a steady man.

That said it all.

"What's happening?" Sadie asked, pulling Hector into the group.

Jules looked at Hector, whose black eyes were still burning, then at Sadie, who totally had sex hair (like me), before she wisely stated, "We'll tell you later."

"Okay," Sadie replied and leaned into her man as he slid his arm around her shoulders.

Her eyes were bright and happy.

A shrill whistle pierced the air and we all looked in its direction.

When we did, we saw it came from Luke (also in a tux, obviously; black with black shirt and a long black tie, unlike his groomsmen who all had white shirts and ties to match the women's dresses).

He was standing on the dance floor.

He was also crooking his finger at something.

Our heads swung in unison to the direction he was crooking, and we watched Ava wending her way through tables, her face soft, her eyes locked on her new husband.

She was wearing an ivory, chiffon column dress with a ruched strapless bodice and rows of soft, wispy, vertical ruffles falling down the skirt. The whole thing was covered with a sheen of what looked like glitter. The sides of her hair were pulled back with teacup ivory roses behind her ears, the back falling in curls.

Her dewy, peachy makeup was applied by Jet.

Her hair was done by Indy.

She made it to Luke on the dance floor. The minute she did, he grabbed her hand, turned his head to the DJ and jerked up his chin.

His intent could not be missed.

And none of us missed it.

"Holy crap," Indy breathed.

"Oh my God," Jet murmured.

"Holy cow," Roxie whispered.

"Damn," Jules sighed.

"Lordy be," Stella husked.

"Aces," Sadie mumbled.

"Oowee," Shirleen chortled.

"Well, all right," Daisy chimed.

"Righteous," I muttered.

Luke pulled Ava into his arms.

Ava shoved her face in his neck.

Tom Petty's "Alright for Now" started playing.

My insides melted.

Luke swayed to the music, his neck bent, cheek pressed to Ava's hair, his new wife held close in his arms.

I curled into Ren's front and both his arms closed around me.

Hank approached and claimed Roxie.

We all watched.

Silently.

The song lasted two minutes.

And those two minutes were two of the best minutes of my life.

Because in a function room in a kickass hotel in Denver, Colorado, watching two people I loved, two people in love, dancing to a simple beautiful song, was two minutes of experiencing sheer beauty.

Chapter 19

We're a Fuckin' Pair

The morning after Luke and Ava's wedding, I walked into Ren's bedroom carrying a tray.

That morning, for the first time since our first night together, I woke up before Ren.

And I decided that this time was going to go a whole lot better.

So I walked in seeing Ren still asleep on his stomach, the bedclothes down to his waist, the smooth olive skin and defined muscles of his back bared to me.

I smiled at the sight, set the tray aside and put a knee in the bed. Then I put a hand between his shoulder blades and leaned in to kiss the indent of his spine at the small of his back.

He shifted and turned.

I lifted and looked toward his face.

"You sleep any longer, Zano, breakfast is gonna get cold," I said as my good morning.

The brows over his sleepy eyes went up (hot) before his gaze slid to the nightstand.

I'd made French toast Roxie's way. That was to say, with powdered sugar sweetened cream cheese sandwiched in the middle (we could just say it was good Ren cooked—he had everything in his kitchen). I'd also fried up some smoky links and cut up some strawberries with the stem still on so I could fan them on the plates, two of which, with mugs of steaming coffee, were on the tray.

It looked and smelled awesome.

His eyes came back to me. "You cook?"

I felt my brows knit. "Sure I cook."

"You've never cooked for me."

This was true. I hadn't. I'd made toast, but that didn't count as cooking.

I smiled, leaned in and whispered, "Lucky boy, you have a plethora of delights awaiting you."

His eyes got hot, his arms closed around me and I found myself back to the bed, Ren on me and his tongue in my mouth.

Nice.

When his lips slid to my neck, I noted, "Baby, this gets any hotter, breakfast is gonna suck."

He kissed my neck, lifted up, looked at me and mumbled, "Right."

Then he touched his lips to mine, rolled off and away. I turned to my side and got up on an elbow to watch his ass as he went to the dresser and pulled out a pair of gray drawstring pajama bottoms. He tugged them on (hot) and I then watched the muscles in his back move as he walked to the bathroom (also hot).

I was in a new satin nightie the color of lemon chiffon with light blue lace (which was also hot; Roxie, Tod and Stevie set me *up*) as well panties. I was sitting cross-legged on the bed and had a coffee mug in my hand when Ren returned.

He joined me, back to the headboard, legs stretched out, ankles crossed, one of his thighs touching my knee. He grabbed some coffee, sucked it back then handed me a plate. I stowed my mug snug in the bed beside my hip as he nabbed his own plate, picked up the fork resting on it and looked at me.

His brown eyes were still slightly sleepy. They were also still totally hot.

"Breakfast in bed on a Sunday, baby. I like it," he said quietly before he commenced eating.

"I'm buttering you up," I admitted, and that was when his eyes narrowed on me.

"For what?" he asked.

"Twenty questions," I answered.

His eyes unnarrowed, he looked back at his plate and forked into the French toast, saying, "Fire away."

That was it. *Fire away.* Nothing to hide. Not with that reaction. He didn't tense. He didn't evade. He just said, *Fire away.*

I liked that.

"Actually, it's just three questions, not twenty," I amended, and he looked at me, chewing.

When I said no more, mouth still full, he prompted, "Yeah?"

"Why do you park in front?"

His head jerked and he swallowed. "What?"

"You have a perfectly fine garage out back. Why do you park in front?"

"Because it's half a football field away from the house," he answered the answer I'd guessed.

I grinned at my plate because I liked being right, and I liked it more when Ren was witty, then I forked into French toast.

"Do you wanna park in back?" Ren asked, and I looked at him. "Got remotes for the opener. You should have one anyway, and when you do you can park where you want."

"Okay. But I'm fine in the front. I just didn't know why you didn't park there," I shared.

"And this is important?" he asked.

"No," I answered.

He stared at me then he grinned. "You always wanted to know."

I said nothing.

"And badass Ally Nightingale, holdin' me at arm's length, wouldn't let herself ask."

I rolled my eyes even though he was right.

"I was *so totally* in there," he declared.

"I think we established that, Zano," I replied.

"Just good to know how in there I was," he murmured, still grinning even as he bit off half a sausage link. Bite in his mouth, he asked, "What else you always wanna know, honey?"

"Do you have a gardener?"

"Yes."

Ren Zano didn't mulch.

Why did having that confirmed make me feel melty inside?

I didn't ponder that.

I kept going.

"You seem to have an aversion to the mall."

His answer to that was, "Do I have a dick?"

I felt my lips curl up and I replied, "Yes, baby. You have a dick."

"Then, yeah. I got an aversion to the mall."

"Okay. Then how do you dress so well?" I asked.

He went back to his plate and answered, "Personal shopper." He dug into French toast, lifted it to his mouth, chewed, swallowed and looked at me as I tried to process this surprising information. "Gotta have clothes. Don't like shoppin' for them. There you go."

Interesting.

And an excellent solution to every badass's problem of having to be clothed and being allergic to the mall.

"And, we gotta talk about this, so might as well do it now," he started. I bit off part of my own smoky link and focused on him. "My woman's her own woman, so I get that it's likely gonna be important for you to feel you're contributing. I'll say now I'm good with covering everything until you get on your feet. I'm also cool with you making a contribution, just as long as it isn't you making a statement that overextends what you can actually afford."

I got what he was saying, so I told him, "I wouldn't be good with living here without doing something, honey."

"Right," he replied. "Then come up with something you think you can afford, and we'll talk about it. Yeah?"

Clearly, we were back to the easy part of this *together* togetherness.

Thank God.

"Yeah, Ren," I said softly.

He grinned and went back to his plate.

I did the same and kept doing it until I heard him say, "This is delicious, baby."

I looked at him. "It's Roxie's recipe for the French toast."

"Your hand that made it."

Again I felt melty.

God, I was totally becoming a *Rock Chick*.

Nevertheless, I decided breakfast in bed every Sunday until that day long in the future when Ren and I were both in a nursing home where we didn't have kitchen privileges.

"You done with your questions?" he asked, and I nodded. When I did, he stated, "Right. Then we got something else we gotta talk about."

I hoped whatever it was stuck with the easy vibe of our *together* togetherness because I was still riding the high of Ava and Luke's wedding, the fact that I introduced Ren to Mom and Dad (eventually, between Ava and Luke's dance and cake cutting) and they'd both acted genuinely nice instead of stiffly polite, and breakfast in bed with Ren was the bomb. I was digging easy. We hadn't had a lot of that. And, with our personalities, this was as easy as I suspected it would get.

"What do we have to talk about?" I asked.

"What I've been needin' to get down to talkin' to you about since we got back from the mountains, just haven't had the time." He sucked back some coffee and finished, "Now we have the time."

Okay.

Good.

I was happy we were getting to this. So much had been going on I hadn't thought about it that much. That didn't mean I wasn't curious. Then again, I was always curious.

"Shoot," I invited, grabbing my mug and leaning over him to deposit my plate on the bedside table.

Ren followed suit, lifted one knee and twisted partially to me.

"Shit's goin' down at work," he announced.

Oh man.

This was sure to take us out of easy.

Denying what Ren and I were, having my apartment explode and the rest of all that went down, it didn't hit me in our together *togetherness* that an official Ren and Ally would not only include us sharing mundane things like why he parked out front, but also non-mundane things, like how his day was at the office where he was in charge of the legitimate side of a crime empire.

Fuck.

"Okay," I said slowly.

"And you gotta know what it is," he went on.

"Okay," I repeated.

"You also gotta know *why* it is what it is," he continued.

I didn't repeat an "okay." I just nodded.

He looked away and took a sip of coffee, but something changed in his face that I did not like.

Then he looked back at me and I saw whatever it was I *really* didn't like.

But it was familiar. I'd seen it before whenever he mentioned his dad.

"My mother wasn't in the life," he shared. "She came here from Chicago after college for a job and met my pop."

Yep. This was going to be about his dad.

I took in a breath and nodded.

"The way Aunt Angela told it to my sister Jeannie, Ma didn't know shit. Not until Pop took over the business from my grandfather and two weeks later got whacked."

Holy shit!

"Then she knew," he said.

"Wow, I, uh... honey," I stammered, reaching out and curling a hand around his thigh. "I hadn't heard about that. That's terrible. Awful. I don't know what to say."

"Yeah. It was awful and there's nothin' *to* say. I was three. Jeannie was five. My younger sister Connie was barely a year old. Ma was fucked. She didn't have a job. Gave it up to be a wife and mother. Young. Three kids. Then she sorted it out, why Pop was dead from a bullet to the head, and it set her reeling. She packed us up and went back to Chicago to be with her family."

Now it was becoming clear why he wanted me to be a stay-at-home mom. That was what he knew, and I knew he loved his mother; she'd done a good job with him, so that was what he wanted for his kids.

"That's understandable," I murmured, squeezing his thigh.

"She made a mistake though. She took family money."

Uh-oh.

Not good.

"In the meantime," Ren kept going, "Vito and Angela, they couldn't have kids. Dom was around, but he's a fuckup and he didn't start fuckin' up when he started usin' his dick for more than jerkin' off. Vito's all about family, in good ways as well as not so good, so he looked after Ma. He also came to visit. And he had his eye on me. Time came when he had to start to think about who'll take over when he's ready to retire. Me and Dom the only males, Vito old school, he decided it would be me."

As much as this sucked, I didn't blame Vito. I knew Ren's cousin Dominic. He *was* a fuckup.

I also knew his wife Sissy. Dom had fucked around on her and treated her like garbage. Ava's Rock Chick Ride dragged Sissy along with it and Dom woke up, saw he was screwing over a good woman and got his head out of his ass. Now they had a baby and were happy.

I wasn't Sissy. He didn't cheat on me, so it wasn't up to me to judge.

Still, I wasn't his biggest fan, even if he now seemed a devoted husband and family man.

Ren brought my attention back to his story.

"Uncle Vito leaned on Ma to come back to Denver. She didn't like it, but since she was still mostly a stay-at-home mom with only a part-time job—

but a nice house and nice car all paid for by Zano family money—she was in a tight place. She couldn't say no. She also had a lot of misplaced gratitude. So we came back."

At this juncture, it must be noted, as whacked as it was, I'd always liked Vito. He was outspoken and funny, and he'd stepped up for two of the Rock Chicks.

But I didn't like this.

"And Vito started grooming you to take over," I guessed.

"Not right away, but yeah," Ren confirmed. "So, in one ear, I got Vito. In the other, I got Ma, who wants me to have nothin' to do with that shit."

It was all coming clear.

"That's why you're the legitimate side," I said quietly and his focus intensified on me.

"Yeah," he replied just as quietly.

"And now Vito wants to retire?" Again, I was guessing.

"No. Now, I got a mom I love and respect who had to be both parents to me for as long as I can remember. And I don't remember my dad, Ally. Not what he looked like. Not a touch. Not a smell. Not even a feeling. He's gone. The only thing I got is pictures, and they mean shit to me. He's a phantom that haunts my mother to this day. So we'll also say, I don't remember him, but I don't like him either."

With a dad like my dad and thinking everyone should have a dad like my dad, his words made my heart bleed. I'd hate that. And obviously Ren hated it, too.

I leaned closer, squeezed his thigh harder, and whispered, "Ren, honey."

His jaw got tight before he said, "He lied to her. Brought her into the life and didn't say dick. You don't do that to a woman. Not with that life. Not with any fuckin' life. You don't hold shit back. Ever."

I sure was glad he thought like that.

I nodded. "I get it."

"What I also got is hooked to a woman whose father and brother are cops."

This surprised me so much I leaned back and took in a sharp breath.

"Yeah," he stated, still watching me intently. "So Vito's mutterin' about me makin' inroads into the other side of the business, my ma will lose her mind if I take over and the woman I was fallin' in love with is tangled up in blue."

"Tangled up in blue?" I asked.

"Cop blue," he answered.

"Right," I mumbled.

"So what do I do?" he queried.

"I don't know, honey. What do you do?"

"It's not what do I do. It's what I *did* do. And what I did was told Vito we're movin' the whole thing to legit. He eventually bows out, Dom tows my line or he gets another job, and we're done with the business."

Holy shit!

I knew my mouth had dropped open, and I knew Ren didn't miss it because he was still watching me closely, but he ignored my reaction and kept going.

"That didn't go over too well."

Oh man.

I bet it didn't.

"What happened?" I asked.

"Vito lost his shit is what happened," he answered.

I pressed my lips together.

"The good news is, he loves me. I get out of the life, he won't order a hit on me."

Oh my God!

A hit?

"The bad news is, he's all over me to change my mind, and if I don't, I'm excommunicated."

Okay, that was bad news. But a hit was a whole lot worse.

"I know you're tight with your family, Ren, but is that really a bad thing?" I asked hesitantly.

"Yeah, honey, because I'm tight with my family. But it's better than dead."

It totally was.

"But, even with this and all the shit before, bottom line, Vito has been good to me, my sisters, my ma. He's the only father I ever had, Ally. He's fucked up along the way, like now, bein' stubborn and tryin' to bend me to his will. But mostly, he's been a good one. I don't wanna lose him and it looks like he's givin' me no choice." He paused then finished, "It also means I got no job."

Oh *man!*

"That isn't good," I noted, again cautiously.

"No. We do well, Ally. When I say that, I pull down high six figures," he told me.

Yowza!

High six figures?

I made eight hours of a couple bucks above minimum wage and fifty dollars from the tip jar the day before yesterday.

I couldn't wrap my mind around high six figures.

No wonder he drove a Jag, had a gardener and a kickass pad in Cheesman Park.

"So I got some put away, and we're good in a live-real-good type of way for a while. We're good for a live-content type of way for a longer while. I'm just not the kind of man who golfs."

Thank God.

Nothing against golf. I was just not the-man-who-golfed-being-my-man type of woman.

"So what're you thinking of doing?" I asked.

"I know what I'm doing. I'm settin' up with Marcus."

I blinked and my voice squeaked when I asked, "What?"

"This is not popular with Vito either," Ren noted.

I didn't understand.

"So, let me get this straight. You're going out of the family business, but staying in the business?"

He shook his head. "No. Marcus has been pullin' back for a while now. He has one thing on this earth he gives a shit about, and that's his wife. I don't have to tell you she had a tough life. They got together, with his social set, she had a tough go. She hasn't had anything solid, anything at all, not her whole life, except Marcus..." he grabbed my hand, "and the Rock Chicks."

I knew this.

"Chavez hates him because of what he does," Ren continued, letting my hand go and taking a sip of coffee before he went on, "Hank also wouldn't hesitate to take him down if given the opportunity. Marcus feels that tension. The truces made to deal with Rock Chick shit are tentative, baby. And that also means with my family. You women settle in, focus will shift. And when it does, it will not be good. So that Marcus can give Daisy what she needs, the family that comes with the Rock Chicks, without that tension or any shit hangin' over their heads, he's been growin' the legit side of things, lettin' go of the other.

He's almost there. The thing is, his talents lie in the other. But my talents lie with the legit."

I had also always liked Marcus.

Now I liked him more.

Suddenly, I smiled huge.

"Perfect fit," I decreed.

He smiled back. "Yeah."

Just as suddenly, I was again confused.

"Was this what you were talking with Lee about after my apartment exploded?"

"Yeah," he confirmed.

"This isn't bad, so why were you in each other's faces?"

"Because I was with you and Lee suspected where that was going, which is where it is now, and he wasn't pleased with the pace the other shit was going."

Yep, that was Lee.

"You go at whatever pace you wanna go, honey," I told him.

"I intend to, baby," he said on a grin.

I took a sip of coffee and asked, "How does Dom feel about all this?"

Ren shook his head, but replied, "He's calmed his shit since all that went down with Ava and Sissy, but he's still a fuckup. It's just that now, he knows it."

"And that means?"

"That means he doesn't want to be at the helm, because Vito's gonna retire but still be up in his face all the time. He also doesn't want the helm because he's got a wife and kid, his wife got roughed up in some bad business, and he doesn't want any of that shit ever to touch his family again."

I didn't get a good feeling about this.

"So it's crumbling," I remarked.

"Yeah, Ally, and I can't get worked up to give a shit about it," Ren said, and his voice had gone harsh. "I gave them an out. Everyone connected to us does well with what I do. They don't need that other shit. It's just stubbornness and fear of change that's makin' him hold on. Vito's a few years from retiring, so that makes even less sense. What does he care?'

Good question.

Ren kept going.

"And I didn't grow up in the life. Until we got back to Denver, I had no fuckin' clue. Then when I had a clue, I didn't want it and that shit was forced on me. I didn't like that. They pulled me in and I worked my ass off to keep my shit as separate as I could," his eyes locked on mine, "but I'm not clean, Ally. Far from it. I know what they do. I'm in on meetings where decisions are made. And I've made decisions. I've also carried them out. I'm removed and I'm not."

"I know," I whispered.

"Yeah, you know," he said, eyes still holding mine. "Before you knew any of this, you accepted me. And that was not a test, baby. Just circumstances that prevented you from knowin' where I was at. But gotta say, I'm glad to know it."

I leaned in and touched my mouth to his.

He put a hand to my neck and slid it up into my hair to hold me there so my mouth touch lasted longer and included some tongue.

Only then did he let me go, but when I resumed my position, I did it closer.

"So how's that all gonna go for you? Disconnecting from the business?" I asked.

Again his eyes caught mine in an intent way that made me brace.

"Your brothers know. Lee's men know. Marcus knows. Now I'm gonna tell you," he said softly, but his soft voice was not his sweet voice.

It was a voice that was telling me to brace.

Luckily, I already was. I just did it more.

"What are you gonna tell me?" I asked.

He leaned into me and his hand went back to the side of my neck and stayed there when he declared, "You do not fuck with me, Ally. This disconnect with Vito is gonna go fine, because the people who I deal with in my business understand that." He paused. "And why."

"You're a made man," I whispered my guess.

His head moved back an inch and his eyes narrowed. "What?"

Why was he asking "what?"

"You're, uh, *not* a made man?"

Ren said nothing and stared at me.

"Ren?" I prompted when this went on a while.

"We're Sicilian, babe, but we're not *Cosa Nostra*."

My head jerked. "You aren't?"

"Fuck no. If we were, I'd never get out."

Wow.

I did not know this.

How did I not know this?

I mean, I didn't know everything that went down in Denver and I'd purposefully never gotten into Zano business, but I knew a lot.

Just not this.

"I just assumed—" I started.

"We aren't clean," Ren interrupted me. "Vito's into a variety of shit that his father was into and his father's father started. But they left New York to come to Denver to leave that shit behind and do their own thing."

"Oh," I mumbled.

"Fuck, you thought my family was mafia?" he asked, his voice getting louder. Which, by the way, was not a good sign.

What it was was a sign that we were moving out of easy.

"Actually, I—"

"Jesus," he clipped. "I was gonna say this is gonna go fine, not because if it doesn't, I'll whack anybody who fucks with me. Just that they all know I know how to take care of myself and my family. I've proved that in a variety of ways. I've also not hesitated proving it *or* getting creative. So they've learned not to fuck with me." He scowled at me and repeated, "Jesus."

I didn't know what to say. I personally didn't think that it was a huge leap to make, him being Sicilian and the nephew of a third generation crime boss, but it was also an assumption that didn't shine a great light on me.

"Ren, your family does certain... *things*. And they're Italian. *Sicilian* Italian. Your dad was whacked. And Vito can be scary. I put two and two together—"

"And made twelve."

Oh man.

I put a hand on his chest and leaned in. "You're right. I'm sorry. That was totally uncool. *Totally*. Really, I'm sorry." I tipped my head to the side and pressed my hand into his chest "Forgive me?"

"For thinkin' I'm an underboss?"

Hmm.

Time to shut my mouth.

See, I'd been stupid and I'd apologized.

And he hadn't accepted.

I offended him and maybe his acceptance was going to take a few minutes.

So I was going to give them to him before I lost my patience and pointed out (in a perhaps snotty or sarcastic way) that he should accept my apology.

"I'll just take the dishes down to the sink," I muttered, moving to exit the bed.

Instead of getting out of the bed, my coffee mug was pulled from my hand, put on the nightstand, and I was shoved back into position facing Ren.

"All this time, you thought you were fuckin' a wiseguy?" he asked.

"Um..." I mumbled, because I did. It was just that he was angry and I didn't want to say it out loud.

"You did. You thought you were fuckin' a wiseguy," he pressed.

I pushed my lips to the side.

"And you let me in there," he went on.

"Yes," I whispered.

He stared at me.

I fought squirming.

Then he burst out laughing.

I stopped fighting squirming and glared.

"What's funny?" I snapped.

His hand shot out and hooked me behind the neck, pulling me into him even as he leaned close.

"Christ, you love me so much, I was so damned *in there,* you accepted me as a wiseguy."

I had a feeling I was never going to hear the end of that.

"Just saying, Zano, if you're looking for new career paths, I'd prefer you veer from that one," I returned.

"Babe, you thought I was already on it."

This sucked, but it was true.

"Whatever," I muttered, yanking at his hand at my neck and looking anywhere but at him.

"Ally," he called.

"What?" I asked the bedpost.

"Baby, give me your eyes."

He was talking sweet.

I heaved a sigh and gave him my eyes.

"So, I want a stay-at-home mom and you give me a badass PI. You accepted a wiseguy and got whatever I am. We're a fuckin' pair."

We were.

I looked into his eyes and wondered how on earth we were working.

Then it hit me I shouldn't think on that too much. We were. That was all that mattered.

"I suppose I should thank you for giving up your six figure part of a criminal empire for me," I said somewhat ungraciously.

This made him smile and pull me closer as his eyes dropped to my mouth and his lips murmured, "You're welcome, honey."

"Now, I need to go out and run off my French toast," I informed him.

His eyes came back to mine just as his lips hit mine and he replied, "Oh, we'll work it off."

A shiver slid over my skin and my happy place got happy.

His head slanted, his lips pressed to mine and his tongue slid inside.

We then proceeded to work off the French toast *and* the sausages.

I wasn't sure what we did would help me stay in shape should I have to outrun bad guys.

But it was *a whole lot* better than running.

Chapter 20
Welcome to the Family

"You good?" Ren asked, and I looked from my place in the passenger seat to him behind the wheel of his Jag.

"I'm good," I answered. "You good?"

He grabbed my hand, gave it a squeeze and rested it on his thigh. "I'm good."

I looked out the windshield.

Even though we were heading to have dinner with Mom and Dad, I *was* good.

This mostly had to do with the fact that Ren instigated Operation Two Year Fuck-a-Thon today. Ren got out of bed to make us these awesome toasted roast beef sandwiches with peppers, mushrooms and melted cheese for lunch, and we both got out of bed about an hour and a half ago to take a shower. The rest of the time was in bed making love or holding close, touching and whispering, or snoozing to prepare for more making love.

It was righteous.

So since we had no fights or breakups and nothing exploded, but I'd had seven orgasms, I was all set for dinner with my man and my parents.

"Date night tomorrow night, baby," Ren said on another hand squeeze, and I looked at him.

"Okay, but I have a meeting at Lee's office to discuss my future career plans tomorrow evening, so we'll have to go after that."

"What the fuck?" he asked, eyes narrowing on the road.

"It'll be cool," I assured him. "I'll talk them around but if I—"

"No, babe," he bit out. "What the *fuck?*"

I looked forward.

My parents lived in Bonnie Brae, which was just off the very popular 'hood where I lived, Washington Park. Wash Park surrounded a massive park-slash-hotspot that even in the winter was teeming with activity. It was practically impossible to find a parking spot in Wash Park. Bonnie Brae, unless you were close to Bonnie Brae Tavern, didn't have the same problem.

But lining the curbs outside Mom and Dad's house were not only Lee's Crossfire and Hank's 4Runner but also a shiny black Caddy, a semi-sporty Hyundai coupe, a Chevy SUV, a Honda Accord and a GMC Acadia.

"There's a space in front of the Acadia, Zano," I pointed out, and it was only two car lengths down from Mom and Dad's, so I wasn't certain what the big deal was. Still, maybe Ren was feeling nervous so I said, "Sorry that Lee and Hank are here, even though we didn't know they were coming. But they'll be cool. And all these cars mean one of the neighbors is having a little get-together."

"One of your neighbors isn't having a get-together, babe. The Acadia's Dom's. The Honda is Connie's. The Chevy, Jeannie's. Hyundai, Ma. And the Caddy belongs to Vito and Angela."

I stared at the lineup of cars.

Holy shit!

Ambush!

"Are you serious?" I asked, sounding like I hoped to God he wasn't, mostly because *I hoped to God he wasn't!*

"Yes, unfortunately," he answered, putting on the brakes to swing in in front of the Acadia, which would mean he intended to park.

"What are you doing?" I yelled.

He stopped the car and looked at me. "Parking."

"Don't park. Do *not* park. Drive on. I just got a really bad headache, period cramps and I think that French toast gave me food poisoning. I'll text Mom. She'll understand."

Ren didn't listen to me. He swung into the spot, and while looking over his shoulder to reverse closer to the bumper of the Acadia, he spoke to me. "Of all that, I really hope you're kidding about the period cramps."

Like I'd have sex during a bout of food poisoning.

"Zano!" I snapped.

He put the car in park and turned his attention to me.

"Is this my Ally, scared of nothing?" he asked, sounding slightly pissed, but also slightly teasing, and I knew the former was for his family, the latter for me.

Still, I gritted my teeth.

He reached out a hand and curled it around the side of my neck, and when he spoke again there was no more teasing. "Do you think your mom planned this?"

270

"Absolutely not," I answered.

"So I mentioned to Dom at the wedding yesterday I was havin' dinner with your folks tonight. Dom opened his mouth and Vito did what Vito does. He horned in," he deduced.

"Probably."

His voice was just pissed when he said, "Don't worry. I'll get rid of them."

"Do that fast," I ordered, then explained my eagerness for him to be rude, "See, Mom and Dad will be cool with you because I love you. I don't love Vito and Angela, and Dad *really* doesn't love at least Vito. So he's probably in there, about to have an aneurysm because Mom won't let him be mean to guests. Even surprise ones. Even ones who engage in criminal activities. And anyway, knowing what you mean to me, he definitely won't want to be mean in front of your mom and sisters. The problem is, Mom likely instigated the Lee and Hank being here thing without telling us, which means Dad also doesn't have the upper hand. So he's screwed, and he won't like that."

To all that, Ren's answer was simply, "Like I said, Ally. Don't worry, I'll get rid of them."

He let me go and turned to his door, but a thought occurred to me, I grabbed his wrist and yanked.

He turned back to me.

"You can't get rid of your mom and sisters, so you just have to get rid of Vito, Angela, Dom and Sissy."

Something else occurred to me and I yanked again at his wrist.

"No. Not Sissy, because she's a sister, so you can't get rid of her, which means we're stuck with Dom, too. Which also probably means were stuck with Vito. Shit!"

Ren twisted his wrist to grab my hand and hold it tight as he leaned into me, and I noticed his eyes studying me.

Intently.

"You're freaked," he whispered, and his voice sent a chill over my skin.

"I... well, a little bit," I admitted.

"You're totally freaked," he stated.

His family was in there with my family, and some of his family engaged in criminal activities and my family was a cop family.

Not to mention, without warning, I was meeting his mother and sisters.

Of course I was freaked.

Kristen Ashley

"Okay, maybe more than a little bit," I allowed.

His eyes moved over my face in the waning sunlight, the air in the car got heavy then, again with the scary whisper, "My woman doesn't get freaked."

Uh-oh.

"Ren—"

"Let's go," he clipped.

Before I could say another word, he let me go, turned to his door and angled out.

I rushed to do the same thing. I barely got to the sidewalk before my hand was seized and Ren half walked with me, half dragged me toward my childhood home.

The dragging part had to do with the fact that I couldn't keep up with his pace. I had on a pair of high-heeled bronze sandals that were awesome and went great with my new brown-washed jeans and kickass Stevie-Nicks-meets-Olivia-Newton-John batwing dusty blue top shot with bronze and silver that had a deep vee. But even the reminder that I had on great jeans, shoes and a kickass rock 'n' roll top didn't unfreak me (as it usually would do).

We were at the base of the walk when the door opened and expelled Roxie and Indy.

Roxie had her hands up, palms down, pressing the air and she was calling out (but quietly), "Calm. Calm. It's all going to be okay. We got out the leaves for the dining room table."

This did not make me feel better, and not just because Mom didn't have that many leaves.

Indy just lifted a hand and stated, "No worries. It's under control."

I couldn't tell if Ren even looked at either one of them before he hauled us through them.

As for me, I had just enough time to give them a wide-eyed, warning-danger-is-imminent look they both totally understood before he tugged at my arm, pulling me in front of him. He did this while reaching beyond me to yank open the storm door, push open the front door then shove me in front of him.

I took two steps in, Ren one, and we were faced with a tense family room filled with people holding cocktails or bottles of beer; none of them, I noticed on a quick scan, having a good time.

Except Vito looked like Vito always looked. Expansive and happy.

Shit.

272

The Montagues and Capulets were never congregated in anyone's living room. If they were, I had a feeling from the vibe in my parents' house right then, *Romeo and Juliet* would be a much shorter play.

Crap.

"Malcolm and Kitty Sue," Ren greeted my parents tersely with a chin jerk, and then his eyes immediately went to Vito. "Vito, a word outside."

"Son, we're havin' a drink," Vito returned, lifting up what looked like a Manhattan.

"A," Ren started, his voice on that one syllable rumbling and another chill ran over my skin, "*word.*"

Vito and Ren went into a staredown.

Indy and Roxie squeezed in through the limited space Ren left at the door, but they didn't move in much further, just because movement in that kind of volatile environment could mean bad things.

I held my breath.

Surprisingly, Ren won the staredown when Vito turned to Mom and Dad and said, "Mal, Kitty Sue, my nephew needs a word."

Mal?

Oh God.

Dad's lips got tight.

Oh *shit*.

Mom murmured, "Of course."

Dad just looked between Ren and Vito and nodded.

Vito moved toward the door.

Ren moved us out of his way and looked at Dom. "You too."

Dom, incidentally a man with looks that could make him Ren's brother, not cousin (except he had wave in his hair and his confidence had swagger), was playing it smart for once. I knew this when he immediately made his way toward the door.

They disappeared behind it.

Mom spoke. "Ally, honey, I had another pork tenderloin that I just popped in the oven, and you know I always have backup Pillsbury crescent rolls. It's okay."

Pillsbury crescent rolls could be served at peace talks to put the negotiators in good moods. However, I was thinking their magic wouldn't work here.

273

I looked at Mom and told her, "He's a hotheaded Italian American badass. I think he needs to do what he needs to do."

"He needs to do what he needs to do," an attractive, petite, stylish woman who was sitting on one of my mom and dad's couches confirmed.

She rose.

I took in Ren's mother, then his two sisters who had been flanking her on the couch.

His sisters looked like female versions of Ren, long, lean and attractive.

His mother had silver hair, lots of it, and it was fashioned in a becoming style that curled in at her shoulders. She also had fabulous cheekbones and exotic features that had not dimmed with age. Looking at her, it came semi-clear why Ren's dad didn't share with this woman that he was what he was. Because she was currently a knockout; erase thirty-five years, she would be breathtaking. So even with just her looks, a man would do a lot to keep hold of that.

But I knew she was much more than just beautiful. Therefore Ren's dad likely would do anything.

And he did.

She stopped in front of me and offered her hand. "You must be Ally."

I took her hand and held it. "Yes. And you're Mrs. Zano."

"Amalea," she corrected on a hand squeeze.

"Amalea," I repeated on my own hand squeeze.

"As I told your mother," she went on. "I was under the impression we were invited."

Vito.

Jeez.

"I'm really sorry for the misunderstanding," I replied.

"No misunderstanding," she returned, letting my hand go then finishing on a sigh, "Just Vito."

It was clear that there had been a lot of *Just Vito* times in her life.

I forced a smile.

I mean, what else could I do?

"We've met your lovely family." She turned and held out a hand. "Meet Lorenzo's sisters. Giovanna and Concetta."

At their mother's unspoken command, both women were approaching me, hands raised.

When I took her hand, the taller one muttered, "Jeannie."

And when I took her hand, the one with the longer hair muttered, "Connie."

They were uncomfortable. Then again, it would be impossible not to be.

We all stepped back but stayed in a loose huddle as I felt Indy and Roxie close to my back, and I tried to figure out a way to break the tension. Alas, my usual ways to do something like that were things you didn't do when you first meet your man's family.

I decided on, "It's nice to finally meet you. Ren talks about you and it's all good."

It was lame but at least it was polite.

"Then he's lying," Jeannie stated. "At least about Connie."

I blinked.

Connie glared at her sister. "Hardly. If he's lying, it's about you."

Holy crap.

"Connie works his nerves," Jeannie told me.

"He actually disowned Jeannie once," Connie told me.

"Pfft," Jeannie made a noise with her mouth. "He was eight."

"He wasn't eight, and I can't repeat what he said the last time you crashed your car, called him and told him you'd forgotten to re-up your AAA *and* you needed a loan to get another car," Connie retorted then looked at me in order to share, "She crashes her car a lot."

"Is three times in three years a lot?" Jeannie asked me.

I thought it was, but luckily Connie saved me from replying by snapping, "*Yes.*"

"Girls," Amalea said quietly, and they both clamped their mouths shut.

Yowza.

Impressive.

And evidence was suggesting I'd like Ren's sisters.

"While we wait for that situation outside to sort itself, I'll get my daughter a drink," Dad announced, getting close and leaning in to give me a kiss on the cheek. "Beer? Margarita? Something else?" he asked.

I did a quick scan and knew from what I saw that Mom had a pitcher filled with margs, so I put in my order, biting back my real order, which was a tequila shooter with a valium chaser.

Then I did the rounds, greeting everybody.

Lee and Hank also seemed pissed but holding it back.

Sissy whispered in my ear, "Sorry."

"It's cool," I whispered back. "How's the baby?" I asked.

"Light of my life," she said on a big smile.

He would have to be for her to smile that big during this disaster.

Dad brought me a marg. I took a healthy slug, trying not to appear like I was taking a healthy slug, and I was pleased when I was done and it seemed I accomplished this feat.

The door opened and Ren, Dom and Vito walked through.

The minute Vito hit the family room, he looked at Dad and announced, "Lorenzo just reminded me I have some business to see to tonight. Unfortunately, Angela and I can't stay for dinner."

"Holy crap," Indy breathed beside me.

I just stared.

Vito was not a man to back down.

This was a mini-miracle.

"I'll need Dom with me, so he and Sissy will also be leaving," Vito went on.

I moved my stare to Ren, at this point wondering if I should contact the Pope to report this miracle.

Ren was scowling at his uncle.

"You're more than welcome to stay," Mom said courteously.

"It's urgent," Ren bit out.

Mom shut her mouth and nodded.

Vito glowered at his nephew.

The room grew tenser.

Sissy made a move to her husband.

"Again, Vito, it's urgent," Ren said when Vito made no move.

Vito kept scowling at his nephew for a few beats before he rearranged his face and looked at me in order to declare, "Just want to say before we go, you with my boy Lorenzo, it's a good thing. I've always liked you and I see a happy future. Much love. Big family. And I know I speak for Amalea and Angela as well when I say we're extremely pleased you're turnin' Catholic."

Oh shit.

The room went wired, and even just with my family, this was bad. Add a bunch of Italian hotheads, this was *very* bad.

As for me, I avoided Mom and Dad's eyes. It wasn't like he was a deacon and she led a Sunday school class, but they went to church on Sundays (mostly). So me staying in the faith I was raised in was probably important to them.

Crap.

"Vito," Ren gritted.

"What?" Vito asked him, fake innocently.

"What?" Ren asked back, not-fake sarcastically and turning fully to his uncle. "You think maybe Ally wanted to discuss that with her family? And furthermore, she's not *turning* Catholic. She's *considering* it. For me. Which is what I told you outside. But either way, it was not up to you to share it now since she hasn't discussed it with her family."

"Turning. Considering. Same thing," Vito retorted.

"It isn't," Ren returned. "Reflecting and deciding are two different things. And my woman is gonna do her reflecting with no pressure, say, like the shit you just piled on her. And whatever she decides, she'll have the backing of this family."

"If she decides Catholic," Vito stated.

"If she decides Scientology," Ren shot back, and I heard Roxie and Connie giggle and Hank clear his throat to disguise a chuckle.

"I'm uncertain how the Pope feels about Scientology, Lorenzo," Vito replied.

"The Pope doesn't make my woman breakfast," Ren countered.

God.

Seriously.

Was my man awesome or what?

I pressed my lips together and felt Indy's hand curl around my elbow, her body getting close and it was shaking.

"How about we give this some time, see how things go," Angela suggested, moving toward her husband and bravely entering the fray.

"I know how it's gonna go," Vito stated, sliding his arm around his wife's waist.

"I do, too," Ren returned immediately. "And if it doesn't go the way *I* want it to go, the issues we already got get bigger."

Thus another staredown commenced, which lasted until Sissy began the process of saying her farewells, adding more excuses about how she wanted to get back to her baby and dragging Dom with her.

Kristen Ashley

Vito and Angela were forced to do the same. We all did cheek kisses, gave awkward hugs, and said see you laters. Ren, clearly wanting to make sure Vito followed his directives, followed them out the door.

Roxie, Indy and me ran to the window.

On the other side, we were joined by Mom, Amalea, Connie and Jeannie.

We watched Ren prowl down the walk behind Dom, Sissy, Vito and Angela, and then we watched Dom stand close as Vito gesticulated wildly. Ren stood there with a hard jaw, a closed mouth and arms crossed on his chest. I didn't know what all the girls were thinking.

Personally, I was thinking my man was hot.

"Indy, come away from the window," Lee ordered, and I looked away just long enough to see Indy wave at him to shut up, but she said nothing and did not move.

"Kitty Sue, the man doesn't need an audience," Dad called.

I didn't look at Mom, but she didn't say anything. She also didn't move.

"Jesus," Hank muttered.

"Fine to say that, but don't take L. Ron Hubbard's name in vain," Lee muttered back.

All the women giggled.

Then we all dashed away from the window as Vito climbed into his Caddy. Dom took off toward the Acadia and Ren turned to come up the walk.

I sucked back more margarita and didn't bother trying not to look like I was sucking it back this time.

Ren came through the door.

Before I could make a move to get to him, Dad did.

I knew my Dad. I (mostly) knew Ren. However, I had no clue what was about to happen.

But if you'd asked me to guess, what happened would be so far down on the list, it wouldn't even make the list.

And what happened was that Dad lifted his hand, Ren took it, and Dad announced, "Welcome to the family."

Indy grabbed my hand. Roxie put hers to my back.

As for me.

I melted.

The women (all of us, including Ren's mom and sisters) were in the kitchen doing the dishes.

After the Vito fiasco and Dad welcoming Ren into the family, things went a whole lot better. It became clear very quickly that Ren didn't blink at much of my or the Rock Chicks behavior because his sisters might not be as nutty as us, but they weren't far behind. It also became clear Ren got his class from his mother because she was brimming with it.

Conversation, understandably, started stilted, and also understandably got less so as time went on and drinks were consumed.

So dinner wasn't a disaster and now we were cleaning up.

Or, I should say, the women were.

"Can I ask why it's always the women in the kitchen doing the dishes after, I'll add, it was the women in the kitchen doing the cooking?" I queried.

"Have you seen your brother let loose in a kitchen?" Indy asked, drying a platter.

"Not recently," I answered.

"It's not pretty," she returned. "He doesn't even rinse his dishes before he puts them in the dishwasher. I've given up and told him just to put them in the sink."

"You do know he does that so you would do that. In other words, he does a crap job so he won't have to do the job at all. Or, in your case, anything," I educated her. "He did that when he was at home, too."

"This is true," Mom, at the sink, muttered to Amalea.

"Well, it was a smart move because he doesn't have to do anything," Indy replied. "And it takes longer to complain about it than it does just to rinse his bowl and put it in the dishwasher."

"Caving," I stated.

"You'll see," she retorted.

"No I won't," I told her. "Ren cooks *and* does the dishes *and* he does both well." I looked to Amalea. "Thanks for that, by the way."

Amalea smiled at me and opened her mouth to speak, but Indy got there before her.

"You're joking," Indy said, and I looked back her way.

"Not even a little bit." I grinned. "*And* he serves tater tots with breakfast."

I knew that would get her.

It got her.

Indy's eyes got wide and she whispered an envious, "*You're joking.*"

"Nope," I replied, still grinning.

"That's... that's like... that's..." she stammered.

"Righteous?" I gave her a word.

"Totally," she agreed.

"Hank does the dishes *and* he's good at it," Roxie put in. "He also makes great eggs, and he's a grill master."

"Whenever I suggest we grill something to Lee, he says we should go to a steak joint or invite ourselves over to your place," Indy said to Roxie.

I took the rinsed serving bowl Mom handed to me and started wiping while saying, "You're letting Lee get away with too much. You need to crack down."

Indy shoved the platter in the cupboard. "I'm not sure cracking down works with Lee."

In mixed company, I couldn't suggest what would, so I didn't say anything

"Just sayin'," Connie put in. "Ren does all that stuff because Jeannie and me were like Lee."

"This is true," Amalea murmured to Mom.

"He was a brownnose, always suckin' up to Ma," Jeannie stated, and Amalea's back snapped straight.

Uh-oh.

"He was *not* a brownnose. He was a good son," Amalea stated. "After slaving in the kitchen to feed a family of four, it was nice to have someone do the dishes. And, I'll add, nice to have someone who saved me from having to slave in the kitchen every once in a while."

So that was how Ren learned how to cook.

"Total brownnose," Jeannie muttered, wiping the stove.

"This is what I wish," Amalea started. "I wish for you both to have sons and daughters, sons that look out for you, daughters who don't, so you'll understand precisely how it feels."

Oh man.

Seriously set down.

She was *good*.

I bit my lip and gave big eyes to Mom.

Mom grinned huge at me.

Jeannie began concentrating closely on cleaning the stove like Mom was performing surgery on it later, while Connie shoved more leftovers in the fridge but did it without speaking,

With excellent timing, Dad ended our discussion by walking in and announcing, "I'm taking drink orders. Any of you gals want a refresh before you join us?"

"I have to get behind a wheel, Malcolm," Amalea said. "Nothing for me."

He got yeas from Roxie, Mom and me, nays from Connie and Jeannie. We finished up the dishes, Dad brought our drinks and we wandered back to the family room, me bringing up the rear and Amalea poorly pretending she wasn't trying to position to bring up the rear with me.

I slowed my gait as the others forged on. I stopped, turned and looked down at Ren's mom.

"Did you want a word in private?" I asked quietly.

"Was it that obvious?' she asked back.

"Yes," I answered on a smile.

She returned my smile before hers faded. Then she tipped her head to the side and studied me for a moment before speaking.

"It's just that..." she hesitated then said, "I'm really very sorry to barge in on your family dinner, Ally."

"That's okay, Amalea. Mom invited my brothers and their wives without telling Ren and me, so it evens out."

She grinned.

Then she looked down, reached out and touched my hand briefly, before she looked up and caught my eyes.

"He says he's moving on," she said softly, her words confusing me.

"I'm sorry?" I asked.

"From Vito," she explained, and I pressed my lips together. "Some months ago, he told me he met a girl, he cares a good deal for her, so now it's time."

Some months ago.

Ren made this decision *some months ago.*

How cool was that?

Again she reached out and touched my hand before she whispered, "I certainly am happy to meet you, Ally."

I got her.

She lost a husband; she was terrified of losing a son.

And she was giving me credit.

I didn't let her move her hand, but caught it and told her, "He's doing it for you, too."

"He's been going to do it for me for years now, honey."

Interesting.

"Now he's *doing* it," she continued. "Angela has been talking about it. Dom's mother, Ramona has been talking about it. Vito's angry about it. But Lorenzo isn't backing down."

I nodded. "He's got his mind made up and he already has plans for the future."

Her eyes grew intense on me and they were far from unhappy. "This, I can see."

I got that, too.

Again with the melty.

Jeez. What was up with me and the melty?

"As crazy as this night started," I told her, "I'm glad you and the girls were here."

"Me too, Ally."

I grinned.

She grinned back.

"Ally, sweetheart, are you and Amalea coming?" Dad called, and I rolled my eyes at Amalea because Dad was likely calling because he was worried she caught me and I wouldn't want to be caught.

See?

A good dad.

I pulled her hand up, tucked it in the crook of my arm and we walked with our drinks into the family room.

I stopped because everyone was lounging, except Lee and Indy were standing, Lee's arm around her shoulders, hers around his waist.

This was not weird, entirely. Lee didn't often have Indy close when he wasn't claiming her in some way.

It was just weird they were standing.

My eyes went to Ren to see his eyes were doing a sweep of his mom and me. They stopped on his mom's face, where it was clear he approved of what he saw, before he looked to me. He was also sitting in an armchair and he tipped his head to the armrest.

Seems another alpha hot guy wanted to claim his woman (yes, again, *melty*).

I let Amalea go and moved across the room to him. I sat my ass on the rest, felt his arm slide around my hips, and looked up at Indy to see she was looking at me.

But it was Dad who spoke.

"We had a lot of surprises tonight, but now I'll explain one. And that is that Lee and Indy and Hank and Roxie are here because Lee asked that they be."

What?

My gaze shot to Roxie who was giving me a wide-eyed look, then we both looked to Indy.

Lee was holding her closer, now with both arms, tucking her front to his side, and Indy had wound both arms around my brother.

"We have something to tell everybody," Lee took over.

Oh my God.

Oh my God!

Oh my God, God, *GOD!*

"We already told Tom," Lee went on, and I felt my eyes get hot as I glued them to Indy.

She looked happy. Not her usual run-of-the-mill, I-married-the-man-of-my-dreams-who-I-loved-since-I-was-five happy (which was pretty freaking happy).

But *happy*.

Oh.

My.

GOD!

"We're having a baby," Lee finished.

At his words, I hurdled from the chair, clapping and shouting, "Oh my God! Oh my God, God, *God!*"

I made it to Indy just as she pulled away from Lee. We collided and wrapped our arms around each other. I bounced her up and down with me as I kept shouting, "Oh my God, God, *God!*"

"I know!" Indy shouted back.

I stopped bouncing and pulled away an inch, declaring, "You know it's a girl—"

Indy interrupted me. "She's named Allyson."

I smiled.

Indy smiled back.

My eyes got hot.

Her eyes got wet.

"Oh my God, God, God," I whispered.

"I know," she whispered back.

We stared at each other for a long time before Mom asked from our side, "Can I hug my daughter-in-law?"

I didn't want to let her go.

Then again, I never wanted to let Indy go. My BFF. My partner in crime. My sister of the heart and sister by the law. The soon-to-be mother of my brother's baby.

No, I never wanted to let her go.

Not ever.

"Sure," I said, my voice husky, and it took some effort to tear my eyes from Indy's as I let her go and let Mom move in.

Dad called out, "Champagne."

"I think we have some in the fridge in the garage, Mal," Mom told him, hugging Indy.

I moved in after Roxie moved out and hugged Lee.

"Pleased for you, bro," I said in his ear.

"Not as pleased as me," he said in mine, his arms going tight.

That was not in doubt.

I pulled back and grinned at him.

He let me go with one arm so he could lift a hand and touch my cheek.

Then he said, "When he or she gets here, do me a favor. Don't try to convert them to Scientology."

I burst out laughing, and when I was done, my brother was still holding me close and smiling down at me.

I heard Amalea murmur, "An unexpected honor, but one nonetheless, to be here to hear this joyous news," thus proving she was total class.

But I was listening with half an ear because I was fully feeling the vibe, looking at my brother's smile and experiencing it again, almost exactly twenty-four hours after I'd just felt it.

That feeling you get only a handful of times in your life, if you're lucky.

That feeling that I was lucky to get often.

That feeling of sheer beauty.

⌖

I was curled up in Ren's armchair in his non-TV seating area downstairs.

It was the dead of night and I'd twisted the chair so I could look out the window at a sleepy street disturbed only by the occasional car.

I couldn't sleep, and not for the reasons people normally couldn't sleep.

No, mine were different.

"Jesus, Ally."

I turned my head to see Ren's bare chest, pajama-bottomed legs (and the rest of him) through the shadows walking down the stairs.

"Woke up, you gone, not in the bathroom, you worried me," he kept talking as he moved across the room toward me.

"I'm cool. Just couldn't sleep," I told him.

He stopped by the chair and looked down at me.

A nanosecond after his eyes hit me, he crouched in front of me and reached out a hand to wrap his fingers around my ankle.

"Is everything okay, baby?" he asked in his sweet voice.

He'd read me.

"Yes, Ren," I said quietly, then explained just how okay it was. "Jet is having Eddie's baby. Ava and Luke are on their honeymoon. Stella's recorded an album that's coming out soon. Tex is marrying Nancy. My man has accepted me as I am and I'm looking at office space tomorrow to start the job that I was meant to be doing. Your mom and sisters like me. My dad likes you. And my best friend, who I made a blood pact with when we were kids that she was going to marry my brother, we'd be real sisters and she'd name her daughter after me, is carrying my brother's baby." I shook my head. "So maybe it's no. Everything's not okay." I leaned into him. "It's *very* okay."

"And that makes you not able to sleep?" he asked.

"I don't know how to feel this happy," I answered, and his fingers around my ankle tightened.

Then he let me go, got to his feet, but did it bending over to pluck me out of the chair. He turned, sat in it and arranged me in his lap.

"Ren, it's okay. I'll be——"

His arms around me gave me a deep squeeze and his voice was thick when he said, "I want you this happy for the rest of your life."

Oh God.

Again with the melty!

I lifted a hand to his jaw, but tucked my forehead into the side of his neck.

"You willin' to work on that with me, Ally?" he asked.

"Absolutely," I answered.

"Good, baby," he whispered.

He held me close.

I slid my hand from his jaw to press it against his heart and lay in his arms, feeling it beat.

After some time, Ren spoke.

"My girl, she feels deep."

He was not wrong.

I said nothing.

He gathered me closer. "So fuckin' deep."

I pressed my forehead into his neck.

We again lapsed into contented silence.

It was me who broke it the second time.

"I wondered what it would be like, when the Rock Chicks and Hot Bunch settled in and the drama stopped."

"And what's it like?" he asked.

"Sheer beauty," I answered.

His arms got tighter again and his lips growled, "Mouth, Ally."

I pulled my forehead out of his neck and tipped my head back.

Ren took my mouth.

Then he took me on his living room rug.

After, he carried me up to his bed, leaving my nightie, panties and his pajama bottoms on the living room floor.

When we got there, neither of us had trouble falling asleep.

And we slept tangled up.

Maximum contact.

Sheer beauty.

Chapter 21

The Majestic

The next morning, breathing heavily as I jogged up Ren's front steps after my run, I shoved my key in his lock and pushed open the door.

I used my wristband to wipe away the sweat from my brow as I huffed to the kitchen. Once there, I went direct to the fridge and grabbed a bottle of water.

Closing the fridge and turning, I caught Ren sauntering in wearing a suit. Excellent timing.

He saw me and stopped dead.

"Hey, babe," I semi-panted.

His eyes slid down and up my sweaty body in my awesome Lucy running threads that the gang did a great job picking for me, and I knew they did a great job because I watched his eyes get hot.

I twisted off the cap of the bottle of water and grinned at him.

He came unstuck and moved to me. I thought goodness would commence, but he reached beyond me to open the fridge.

I stepped to the side, leaned against the counter and belted back some agua.

"How was the run?" he asked before he took a slug of orange juice, and I noted that Amalea was a good mom who raised a good son who cooked, did the dishes and was thoughtful, but she hadn't taught him not to drink out of the bottle.

Whatever.

"Run was great," I answered (lying; it was good, but that didn't mean it was fun—what was great was that it was over).

He put the orange juice back and focused his attention on me.

"You comin' to the office after your shower?" he asked.

I nodded.

We'd made plans before I went out to run that I'd come in that morning and look at the space he rented me.

"Good," he muttered, moving to the coffee.

"We didn't have breakfast so I'll bring Danish." I changed my mind. "No, LaMar's."

"Whatever you want," he said, turning toward me.

I moved into him, leaned up and kissed his jaw before I moved away, saying, "I'm just gonna shower and then—"

I got turned and only a step in before an arm hooked around my belly. I was pulled back, pressed forward and ended facing where I usually sat on the counter eating the breakfast Ren cooked me.

Arm still around my belly, his other thumb hooked into my running capris and yanked down.

Holy crap.

My inner thighs quivered.

"*Ren*," I breathed.

"Hands to the counter. Spread your legs. Tip for me."

Oh *God*.

Hot.

I did as I was told. Ren's arm at my belly slid down and his fingers curled in as his other hand slid up my chest to wrap around my jaw.

His fingers hit the spot. My head flew back and hit his shoulder.

His hand at my jaw kept it there as he buried his face in my neck.

His fingers between my legs coaxed orgasm one out of me (*nice*).

While I was still experiencing that, his hand at my jaw moved to between my shoulders as I heard his zipper. He pressed in, I bent, my ass moving back and up, and he slammed inside me, hard, fast, rough, doing this until orgasm two rocked through me (*very nice*).

He barely finished driving into me through his orgasm before he pulled out and crouched low, dragging my workout capris the rest of the way down my legs in a way that I could not misinterpret.

I did as he wanted and stepped out of them.

Ren turned me and, hands at my waist, he lifted me and planted my bare ass on his counter, moving in so my legs were forced to part, his arms closed around me and we were tucked close.

"Just sayin'," he started when he caught my eyes, and my happy place did a happy spasm at the heat still in his eyes, "you need a fuckuva lot more of these outfits."

Told you I totally rocked my running duds.

"Copy that," I whispered, scratching that on my already very full agenda for the day.

His eyes moved over my face and hair. "Your hair looks cute in that band, honey."

Yep. Going to Lucy for more running gear was going to happen post-new office inspection and pre-meet with Darius and Brody to see what they had on the situation with Smithie.

Maybe I could get Darius and Brody to meet me at Lucy. It was an outside chance that Darius was such a badass, his skin might catch fire if he entered a woman's clothing store without a woman he was fucking in attendance, but he loved me. Maybe he loved me enough to take that risk and help me multi-task.

We'd see.

It was then I noticed Ren's hot eyes had gotten hotter just before his mouth moved to mine. "Been waitin' a year to have that ass bared and sittin' on my counter."

Yowza!

A different kind of melty.

"Now I gotta go to work. Kiss me, Ally," he finished.

I wrapped my arms around his neck, leaned in and kissed him.

Ren kissed me back, deep and wet. He broke the kiss, moved away and gave me a hot sexy grin as he let me go, but slid one finger over my bare hip, in and along at the inside juncture of hip and thigh then down my inner thigh.

Another happy place spasm.

I grinned at him.

He leaned in for a touch on the lips, turned and walked away.

I watched.

Still grinning.

As I walked down the hall toward Ren's office, I did it smiling.

This was because I'd never been to his office and if the inside of the building was anything to go by, his space, as well as my space, was going to be the bomb.

Holding a carrier with two of Tex's coffees in one hand and a bag of LaMar's in the other, I turned left at the tall, wood door with the burnished silver plaque at the side that said *Zano Holdings Ltd.* and juggled the bag as I pushed the fancy handle down.

I was curious to see where Ren spent his days. But as I walked in, I didn't look around his office.

I looked at the woman behind his reception desk.

Dawn was sitting there.

Dawn.

Dawn, Lee's ex-receptionist.

Dawn, who I hated because she hated me (and everybody, except Lee and his boys; until they were picked off by the Rock Chicks that was).

Dawn, who got fired because she got caught on in-house surveillance badmouthing Jules while she was in the hospital after she got shot. Lee lost his mind, Luke lost his mind, and they dropped what they were doing in order not to delay in returning to the office and terminating her.

Dawn, who, until that moment, I was certain had crawled into the dark, damp, inhospitable holes beautiful but exceedingly bitchy women retreated to when they got their asses whupped (even figuratively).

Dawn, who was not hiding away in an inhospitable hole but instead sitting in Ren's offices, glaring at me.

"What the hell?" I whispered.

"I heard you had a thing with Ren," she snapped, totally still bitchy.

"What the hell?" I repeated, louder this time.

"I prayed it wasn't true, but apparently God doesn't listen to me," she went on.

"What the hell!" I shouted.

"The only thing I can say is, I still have hope for Dom because everyone knows he has a wandering eye," she kept at it.

"*What the hell?*" I screeched.

"Ally, Jesus, what's the matter?" Ren asked, exiting a hall to my side.

For once, his powerful frame in trousers and a dress shirt did nothing for me.

"Dawn works for you," I snapped, and it came out an accusation, as it *should*.

He didn't glance at Dawn as he headed to me, but his face said a lot and all of what it said made me feel better.

Slightly.

In other words, he didn't like her.

He got close to me, took the carrier of coffee then took my hand and spared Dawn a glance to order, "Hold my calls."

"Of course, Ren," she said, sweet as sugar on an eyes-hooded smile that said—*right in front of me*—she'd hold anything he asked.

Bitch.

Ren led me down the hall and into an office, which I again did not take in, mostly because I was fuming. He then led me to a big desk. He put down the coffee, grabbed the donut bag from my hand, tossed it with the coffee then pulled me loosely into his arms.

When he had me there, he said quietly, "Dom hired her."

That explained a lot.

"*Before* he reunited with Sissy," Ren went on.

Well, that was a relief.

Ren kept talking.

"I'll admit, her attitude often leaves a lot to be desired. Lucky and Santo hate her. And she does not hide she's attracted to Dom or me."

Great. Just *great*.

Ren wasn't done, unfortunately.

"She has also given us no reason to discipline or terminate her. I know she worked for Lee. but I saw her resume and personally checked her references. Although Lee said he had issues with her which led to her termination, he didn't share those with me but did share they had nothing to do with her performance. Her other references were stellar. The other applicants didn't come close. We were in a jam and needed somebody. So I agreed to take her on."

His arm tightened and he dipped his face close.

"I see you aren't fond of her, though I had no idea until now you weren't, but she's very good at her job, honey."

"She's a bitch," I declared.

"That may be so—"

"No, Ren. She's a *bitch*," I cut him off to say. "The reason Lee terminated her was because she was on the phone in his office with one of her friends, who's also likely a bitch, and she was talking trash about Jules *when Jules was in the hospital*."

His jaw got hard.

I kept at it.

"Lee was not down with that so he got shot of her ass. And, heads up, you might wanna check your phone logs because they have cameras everywhere at Nightingale Investigations, and she was caught catting with her friends repeatedly."

"Noted," Ren murmured.

"And last, remember when I told you I wouldn't hesitate to get into a bitch smackdown with a sister who was a bitch?" I asked.

He bit his lip and I knew it was to stop both from quirking, but I ignored that and he stopped biting his lip to answer, "Yes."

"Well, just saying, she even looks at me funny, in your reception area you're gonna have a knockdown, drag out, hair pulling, nails scratching bitch smackdown catfight that might be so extreme, it'll make the papers."

"That's noted, too," Ren replied immediately, but now his lips were actually quirking.

"I'm not being funny," I informed him. "She already gave me a nasty look and nasty words and told me since you were taken, her only hope was Dom, who everyone knew had a wandering eye."

All amusement fled his face and his eyes narrowed.

Finally.

"She said that?" he asked.

"Absolutely," I answered.

"Fuck," he muttered.

"You got that right," I told him.

"What nasty words did she give you?" he asked, and I felt his vibe beginning to weigh down the air, but I didn't care. If that meant Dawn would be out of his office, life and *my* life—*forever*—I'd bear the beast.

"She said she heard I had a thing with you and she prayed it wasn't true, but God doesn't listen to her."

His jaw got hard again, this time the muscle jumping there. He looked toward the wall that separated his office from reception, murmuring, "I'll check the phone logs."

"You might want to check company email, too," I advised.

He looked back at me and nodded.

"Now that I've had a run-in with Dawn, I need coffee and donuts about seventeen thousand times more than I normally need coffee and donuts," I shared.

The mood in the room shifted. His lips quirked again then he moved in to brush them to mine and let me go.

Ren saw to the coffees while I disbursed the donuts and after I'd snarfed down half of my Bavarian cream, he asked, "When's your meeting with your brothers tonight?"

"Five thirty," I answered through cream and dough.

He grinned as he watched me speak.

I took a swig of coffee and another bite.

Then he stated, "I'll make a reservation for eight. Will that give you enough time to do that and get ready?"

Something hit me and I panicked.

He noticed it immediately. Then again, I'd stopped snarfing down my donut and froze, staring at him.

"Ally?" he called.

"Uh..." I mumbled.

Shit!

"What?" he asked.

"Well, um..." I started but trailed off.

His brows knit. "Is something the matter?" he asked.

Fuck. I had to tell him.

Whatever. We were living together. He'd find out eventually.

"It's Monday," I declared.

"Yeah," he prompted.

"Monday night is *Castle* night," I told him, and his head jerked.

"It's what night?"

"*Castle* night."

"What the fuck is that?" he asked.

"It's a TV show," I answered, and he blinked. I hurried on. "If we do a late dinner, we might not be home in time to watch it."

He stared at me.

"Though, we can DVR it before we go, which would work," I allowed grudgingly. "But I usually try to watch it as it airs."

He kept staring at me.

Then he queried slowly, "We've had our first date delayed for over a year— so long we're actually living together and committed to each other before we actually have it— and you want to delay another night for a TV show?"

"It's *Castle*," I explained simply, because *no way* was I going to explain why I *really* didn't want to miss it.

"Is it that good?" he asked.

It was. But mostly it had Nathan Fillion. That was, it had tall, funny, talented, good-looking (did I mention funny? And tall?) Nathan Fillion.

My celebrity crush.

Do you feel me? No way I was going to share *that*.

I just said, "Yes."

"Can you wait to watch it until tomorrow?" he asked.

I might be working a pole tomorrow.

I *totally* didn't share that.

"Sure," I said and took another bite of donut.

Ren studied me.

I swallowed, washed donut back with coffee and threw him a smile to throw him off track.

This failed.

"Are there any other TV shows you feel this way about?"

"Um..." I started, because there were.

Luckily most of them were cancelled, but unfortunately my collection of series DVDs had been incinerated in an apartment bomb.

I decided to answer, "The most important one is *Castle*."

This was true. Mostly because that was the only one still airing that had Nathan Fillion in it.

I made a mental note to hit a computer and order *Firefly* from Amazon and ate my last bite of donut.

"Maybe *I* should ask *you* twenty questions," he suggested on a mutter, balling up the donut bag and tossing it in a bin behind his desk.

"Shoot," I invited.

He looked at me. "Tonight. Sexy dress. Heels. Champagne. And twenty questions."

"You got it, babe," I murmured then licked Bavarian cream residue from my fingers.

I finished this then found myself plastered against Ren where he went about tasting Bavarian cream on my tongue.

He tasted of cinnamon twist.

It was an awesome combination.

He lifted his head and whispered, "Let's go see your new office."

"Righteous," I whispered back.

He gave me a squeeze then let me go, but grabbed my hand. We carried our coffees out of his office, down the hall and into reception.

However, he stopped us there, somewhat close to Dawn's desk.

With a bright smile pinned on her lips, she looked up at him. "Anything you need, Ren?"

"We're goin' across the hall to check out Ally's space."

"Right," she chirped.

"And one more thing," he started, and she tipped her head to the side, eyes avoiding mine but glued to Ren, all ears.

Bitch.

"I'm livin' with Ally, so obviously I will not take kindly to you bein' rude to the woman who shares my home," Ren stated. Her face froze and my body jerked in surprise. His hand tightened in mine and he kept going. "But just to say, no matter who walks through those doors, rudeness will not be tolerated. You can take that as a verbal warning. Next time, it'll be written. Do you understand me?"

Her face was getting red, from embarrassment or anger, I had no clue.

I also didn't care.

Inside my head, I was doing cartwheels while outside I was struggling with gloating.

Her voice sounded strangled when she replied, "Of course, Ren." Her eyes came to me and she tried to cover by stating, "I'm sorry if something I said was misconstrued as rude, Ally."

Misconstrued.

Hardly.

"Apology accepted, Dawn," I replied magnanimously.

Ren was done and I knew this when he tugged me to the door.

But I was me. Ally. So I went with him.

But I also turned back and gave Dawn a huge smile. I lifted my coffee to my lips then out, making a smoochy face in a modified blowing of a kiss.

Dawn glared.

I grinned.

Ren pulled me through the door.

It closed behind us and he walked me to the door across the hall while muttering, "Was that necessary?"

"Totally," I answered.

His eyes on the door, his lips quirked again then they stopped doing that and he whispered, "What the fuck?"

He pushed down the handle as I heard why he was asking that question.

There were voices coming from inside.

He opened the door, pulled us through and we both stopped and took in the activity.

Daisy was on hands and knees on the floor, arranging big carpet sample squares.

Shirleen was at a wall, taping up paint chips; or more accurately, taping up *more* paint chips to the dozens already taped there.

And then there were Buddy and Ralphie who'd joined our tribe during Sadie's Rock Chick Ride. They were a gay couple who clicked right in like they'd been there years. Ralphie was male-model gorgeous (but better groomed). Buddy was bald, African American and a nurse at Swedish Medical Center. They had a tape measure and they were measuring the floor.

"How'd you get in?" Ren asked instead of saying hello, and all eyes came to us.

"Did a stint in juvvie 'cause of the skills I got to get us in," Daisy answered.

I decided that I needed to discuss this with Daisy so she could teach me those skills, then she motioned to me.

"Good you're here, sugar. I'm thinkin' oatmeal. But I really like this gray. It says class to me. We want warm, but we want classy. We also want professional. It's a difficult balance and the walls and carpet are the foundation so we gotta get it right."

I looked down at her adjusting her carpet samples then I looked through the space and that feeling swept through me again. The good one. The excited one.

The happy one.

Two offices along the back, both with room-length windows to the outside, and both had windowed walls facing reception. The conference room down one side, also with a glass wall facing reception. An opened door sharing a wall with the outside hall and one with the conference room that I could see was a small kitchenette, which could take a little fridge and a coffee pot. It also had a small sink.

Perfect.

Utterly.

"Ally?" Daisy called.

"No oatmeal," Shirleen said before I could answer Daisy. "Beige," she stated, ripping off a paint chip with six shades of beige on it. "That's the only thing that goes with oatmeal." She tossed the paint chip over her shoulder and it fluttered to the floor. "Boring," she went on and ripped another paint chip off, this one more shades of beige, sent it sailing and decreed. "No." Again with the paint chips, one (beige again), two (greens), three (blues), four (grays), as she repeated, "No, no, no, no."

Daisy was waving her hands around her head fending off the raining paint chips, snapping, "Shirleen, quit throwin' them chips. You're gonna give me a paper cut."

"*Sweet 'ums!*" Ralphie squealed, making an excited approach then reaching in and clasping his fingers around my wrist.

He pulled my hand from Ren's grasp and yanked me further in. As I gave a smile to Buddy, who was smiling back at me, Ralphie pushed me, adjusted me and stopped us facing the blank wall across from the inner offices.

He lifted his arms in front of him, hands up and fingers splayed wide, floated them out and stated in a weighty voice, "*The Majestic.*"

I turned my head to look at him. "The what?"

"*The Majestic,*" he repeated. "You *must* come to the gallery and see this painting we have. It's *perfect* for this space. *Utterly.*"

"I've seen it, Ally," Buddy called, and I looked over my shoulder at him. "It actually is."

Ralphie moved away from me and snapped at Buddy with his fingers. "Give me your phone, sweets. I'm calling Sadie right now. She needs to close up, get over here and see this space. She'll *totally* agree."

Buddy zipped up the tape measure, reached to the back pocket of his jeans and asked, "Where's your phone?"

Ralphie assumed a look that could only be described as *aghast*, dragged a hand down his side and asked, "Put a phone in my pocket and destroy this line?"

It had to be said, Ralphie, in fabulous skinny trousers and a tailored pink shirt, looked like he'd just stepped out of a *GQ* magazine. A phone *would* destroy that line.

He'd made a good call.

"I called Ralphie to get some interior design help," Daisy said, and I looked to her to see she was gaining her feet.

She had also been hiding her outfit in her earlier position, and as it fully hit me, it took a while for it to process through my system so I didn't hear her next words.

This was because she was wearing a jeans mini-skirt with a little poofy ruffle at the edge, a pink tank top that should get a medal for its act of heroism by stretching itself nearly to the limits in keeping her bosoms contained, a bolero vest that was edged in what looked like silver rope, and a hot pink, champion-boxer-wide, buckle-at-the back leather belt covered in rivets that formed the shapes of lassoes, wagon wheels and cowboy boots.

And, not to forget, her feet were encased in pink cowboy boots with wagon wheels stamped in the toe and lassoes decorating the sides.

A theme.

"Comprende?" she asked, and I focused on her face.

"What?"

"Ralphie is gonna help us decorate and get this place *stylin'*," Daisy said to me. "I have office furniture catalogues that'll be comin' in the mail in a few days. I figure your office, the big one." She waved behind her. "I'll be out here." She waved to her feet. "We'll set up a desk and computer in there for Brody and Darius to use when they're around." She waved to the small office. "And obviously that's the conference room," she finished, tipping her platinum locks toward the conference room.

"Daisy," I took a step toward her, "I think Dad's got an old desk in the garage. I can get him to unearth that and get it here. We'll get you a decent desk. Other than that——"

I said no more because Daisy snapped, "What?"

"Oh no, child," Shirleen entered the conversation. "You got a choice spot here. You don't move some old desk into it, slap a computer on the top and say 'I'm in business.' You gotta send the right message. And that message is you ain't Rockford. You're Allyson Nightingale, a fine piece of badass ass with class who can take care of *biz-nezz*."

"And the right message is also cherry wood," Daisy proclaimed.

"Oak," Shirleen countered immediately.

"Black," Ralphie stated and looked at me. "It'll set off *The Majestic*."

"Uh… guys, I don't have any money for carpet, paint, office furniture or fancy paintings," I shared.

"Sadie will give you a discount," Ralphie assured me on a big smile.

"Okay, let me amend," I began. "I have some clothes. Someday hopefully soon, I'll have an insurance check that will need to be used to buy me more clothes and various and sundry other items, like jewelry, roller brushes and CDs. And whatever paltry sum I have after that I'll need to use to live on until Daisy and I make a go of this."

Daisy chimed in, "Me and Marcus'll—"

"No, honey," I cut her off gently. "You won't."

Daisy's face fell.

"A minute," Ren said, and then I found myself dragged into the hall with my hand in his.

I knew what was coming, so the minute he stopped me in front of him, I started, "Baby—"

"You got twenty-five thousand dollars."

My mouth dropped open.

Then I snapped it shut and closed my eyes.

I opened them and leaned in, putting my hand with the coffee cup to his chest.

"That's very sweet, honey, but no way. I haven't even talked to you about paying you back for the year's rent. I can't take—"

"You aren't taking."

I blinked. "What?"

"I'm investing. We can discuss distribution of your profits when you make them. Until then, it's an investment."

"You're investing?"

"I'm investing."

"In me?"

"Yes."

I swallowed, feeling good things, *really* good things, but unsure.

"I don't know," I whispered. "What if I can't—?"

His hand dropped mine so he could wrap it around the side of my neck and he dipped his face close, ordering, "Don't."

"Don't what?"

"Don't doubt yourself. Not now. Until this moment, you were sure. Very sure. *Be* sure. Take the investment, make those offices something that anyone walking into them will trust you'll get the job done, then *be sure* and get the job done."

Well, one could say Ren was succeeding wildly in trying to be okay with me opening a private investigations agency.

Still.

"This is too much," I whispered.

"It's investing in your future, which is tangled with my future. How is that too much?" he asked.

I said nothing.

"If I didn't have a plan and was at odds and you were in the position to invest in something I wanted to do, would you do it?" Ren pressed.

"Absolutely," I answered.

"So because you're a badass, you can't take the same from me?" he pushed.

Seriously.

Totally.

Completely.

How awesome was my man?

To share this with him, I muttered, "Okay, okay. You've convinced me."

"Good, then kiss me and go in there and tell them they got twenty-five K to blow on makin' my woman's space right for her."

I stared into his beautiful eyes.

Then I whispered, "You're totally the shit, Zano."

"I know," he whispered back.

I leaned in and up and kissed him.

He kissed me back, wet and deep.

When he broke the kiss, I didn't move away, so I could say, "Though, as awesome as it is, you doing this for me and investing in our future, it was awesomer, you giving shit to Dawn."

Ren burst out laughing.

I pressed close and watched, smiling the whole time.

When he was done, I got up on my toes, touched my lips to his, pulled back and moved away.

But I blew him a real kiss before I walked into my new kickass offices to tell the gang they had twenty-five Gs to blow in making them killer.

And it was with no doubt that Ren heard the shrieks and squeals when I did.

By the way, we decided on gray carpet, gray walls and black furniture.

And when Sadie sent a text picture of *The Majestic* to me and offered the Rock Chick Discount (in other words, free) with a text that said, *Remember. I'm loaded,* we decided on that, too.

Chapter 22

Never Forgive

I'd found a parking spot three blocks away from the Lucy in Cherry Creek North but as I was hoofing it up to the store I saw Darius's Silverado parked three cars down from the front door.

Lee and his boys always managed to do that. It was some kind of voodoo but they had parking magic.

It was annoying, especially after driving by Lucy (twice) to find a parking spot that Darius obviously got after me and hoofing three blocks.

Darius was sitting behind the wheel of his truck. I stopped outside Lucy, where Darius and Brody were supposed to meet me, and sent a salute his way to get his attention even though it looked like his wire-rimmed shades were aimed my way.

He lifted a hand and did a full finger curl indicating I should haul my ass to his truck.

Badasses.

Save me.

I sighed and moved to his truck, yanked open the door, climbed in and turned to him.

"I have a full day and I need to shop," I said by way of greeting. "So if we can multi-task, that'd work in a big way for me."

"Then it's good this meetin' is gonna go fast because my ass is *not* gonna be in that store," Darius replied by way of his.

I knew it.

Whatever.

"Is Brody coming?" I asked. "I texted him and he hasn't replied."

"He's neck deep in used energy drink cans, his eyes are bloodshot and he's glued to the computer. He's on a mission to find out who's writin' those books and he's runnin' up against wall after wall. He's taken this on as a personal challenge. I think the only break he took since this all went down was to go to Luke and Ava's thing."

This surprised me.

"He's made no headway?"

Darius shook his head. "None at all. He hacked the publisher's systems and they don't have that woman on their books. Not electronically. Whoever she is, she obviously knows about Brody and took precautions. Calls to them brought nothin' back either. They say Kristen Ashley is a penname, the author is adamant about anonymity and they're not at liberty to give out further information."

Stymied.

Shit.

"Is there a legal route?" I asked.

"Lee looked into that," Darius answered. "His attorney asked if there was anything untrue or defamatory in the book. Unfortunately, there's not. So he's fucked."

"What's Brody doing now?"

"Checkin' blogs, reviews, anything that might give some hint or start a trail to the author. He's also tryin' to pick up a thread on financials since the bitch is local and she has to be gettin' paid."

I thought it prudent to inform him, "Just to say, Ren has mentioned he's also looking into this. He's not happy it's gone down and he and I are up eventually so, no pressure on Brody, but I think it would be good if Lee found whoever she is before Ren does."

"Zano is no way gonna find her before Brody," Darius spoke what was very likely the truth. "But, advice. You gotta brace. This woman, whoever she is, knows this crew. She knows us well and she's taken precautions. She's covered her shit so deep there may be no answer to that question, even for Brody, definitely not for Zano, and all you all might just hafta suck it up."

I was actually okay with that. Truthfully, though I would never share this with my BFF and brother, I was itching to dig into their book. Though I'd likely skip the sex parts.

"Right, movin' on to Smithie," Darius said.

I nodded.

"Seein' as when I asked Brody if he could take some time to run Smithie's guy, he threw an empty can of Red Bull at me and Lee would probably get up in my shit if I tore his head off, I let him be."

I grinned.

"So I ran him."

"Okay," I replied.

"Man's thirty-three and established a career as a bouncer startin' at twenty-one. Not much on him. He's got one speeding ticket that he paid. He also got a DUI at nineteen that he beat. I talked with Eddie, Eddie talked with the arresting officer and that guy remembered our guy. The officer said our guy was a smooth talker, even back then. The kind who could talk his way outta anything. So much so, fourteen years have passed and he still remembers him."

This was not good.

"What kind of clubs has he worked?" I asked.

"Normal shit, no strip clubs. Know a coupla the owners at places he worked, talked to them on the down low. Solid track record. Long tenures. Movin' on only for more money."

This gave us nothing.

"So I got eyes on him last night," Darius told me.

"And?" I prompted.

"So he wouldn't tag me, I stayed outside. Don't know what he does backstage, but whatever business he's doin', he's also doin' it in the parking lot."

I perked up. "What does that mean?"

"That means he has conversations with the girls he escorts to their cars. Not long ones. But not comfortable ones. Least not for the girls."

My mind started working.

"We need to get one of the girls wired," I murmured.

"Yeah. And you need a sit down with Lottie," Darius stated.

"She's after I drop a bundle in Lucy," I told him.

He nodded then asked, "When you goin' in?"

"I have my first stripper class this afternoon."

He grinned.

I rolled my eyes.

"Tex and Nancy are getting married on Wednesday. My aim is to be in Thursday, but I have to confirm that with Smithie," I shared.

"Want you covered," he replied. "So you keep me in that loop. I'll be there, but you won't see me."

I nodded again then told him, "You need to keep track of your hours and get in touch with Daisy to set up a contract. I'm billing them to Smithie and I'll be paying you."

"Unnecessary."

Argh!

I loved my friends, but this was getting crazy.

"Totally necessary," I returned.

"Ally, I'll keep track of my hours. You bill him, but I do this shit for you, not money."

God, Darius was great.

And everyone was being way cool, but enough was enough.

"Darius, this is my business now and I intend to do it right."

"To get set up, you need capital. Bill Smithie. Invest that in your agency."

"Darius—"

"This job," he cut me off. "We'll discuss what goes down with future jobs. Jump off on this one, Ally. You sort his shit, Smithie'll talk you up and half of Denver's male population strolls through his doors. Shirleen's puntin' you business. And Daisy's got Marcus droppin' your name. Me workin' for free is just this job. Take it, pocket it, we talk when we got the next one."

That I could do. I didn't love it, but I could do it. Not to mention, agreeing meant we'd stop discussing it so I could get shopping, get to Lottie, get to Daisy's to take my stripper class then get to my brother's office for the meeting.

"This one job," I agreed.

"Right, now got other shit to do," Darius ended our meeting.

But I wasn't done.

"We need to talk," I declared.

"About what?" he asked.

I held his eyes and stated, "About you."

His chin jerked back.

"Ally—"

I shook my head. "No. You. Me. Tequila. As soon as we can sit down."

"There's nothin' to talk about," he told me.

"You don't even know what I want to talk about," I told him.

"You said it was about me. And I know me." He leaned in, his face got hard and his voice got kinda scary. "And when it comes to me, there's nothin' to talk about."

Luckily, I didn't scare easily.

"We're talking, Darius," I contradicted. "And we're doing it soon."

"This conversation is over," he decreed. "Outta the truck."

"Darius—"

He leaned in deeper. "Outta my fuckin' truck, Ally."

I leaned right back.

"I love you," I hissed, and his face behind his shades blanked but I didn't stop. "And something's not right with you. You're holding back and I'm gonna find out why that is and help you get things right."

"Outta the truck."

"You know me, honey," I said. "You know I won't give up."

"How's this?" he asked, leaning back at the same time retreating. Not physically. Emotionally. "What's wrong with me can't get right."

Fuck.

I had a feeling, and my feelings usually were right.

Still, I returned, "That isn't true."

"You know?" he asked.

"Yeah. I know. That isn't true. It's never true. Anything wrong can be made right."

"You don't know dick," he bit out.

"Darius—"

"Outta my truck."

"Darius!"

He leaned back in and rumbled (definitely scarily, even to me), "Get the fuck outta my truck."

I sucked in breath but I didn't get out of the truck.

I leaned in deep so we were nose to nose, shades to shades, and I declared, "I won't give up on you. I'll *never* give up on you. What I'll do right now is get outta your truck. But I'll do it with you knowing me doing it does not mean I'm giving up on you." My voice dropped to a whisper. "Brace, brother. Because I'm gonna knock myself out to heal what's broken in you. And I won't quit until I've done it."

On that, I didn't give him a chance to reply.

I got out of his truck and sashayed into Lucy.

But I did it not thinking about the kickass running gear I was going to buy that would make my man lose control and give me orgasms in his kitchen (or elsewhere).

I did it worried.

I drove into the underground parking lot of Lee's offices, my mind on a number of things.

One was trying to figure out what dress I was going to wear out to dinner that night with Ren. I hadn't had a chance to try any of the four on that Roxie, Tod and Stevie bought me, but I knew just looking at them they were all on par in hotness so there wasn't an obvious frontrunner.

This meant I needed time to try them all on and make a decision.

Another was the fact that my sit down with Lottie got me nothing. Whatever this guy was doing, he was not doing to her.

She did tell me she felt the vibe and had talked with some of the girls even before Smithie approached her to talk to the girls. They were closed up tight.

Even as the headliner, she didn't have her own dressing room, although Smithie offered it. But she was social; she felt they were sisters and didn't want to foster that kind of thing with the girls so she was in with them. Though she was, she hadn't seen this dude do anything or heard him say anything.

Nothing there.

But she was also worried.

She came with me to Daisy's house to help with my stripper classes. Once at The Castle, I discovered that Daisy had one of her many rooms set up with a stage that had a couple of poles.

"Gotta keep up my skills, sugar," she said after she led us there and I stopped and stared at the set up. "Anyway, how do you think I keep this killer body?"

I had actually never asked how she kept her killer body, though I knew she power-walked regularly.

Thus commenced my stripper instruction, and even with two women I cared about the only ones in attendance, I felt awkward and danced stiffly.

After both of them showed me some moves, however, Daisy put on some music.

That did it.

Then again, music always did it for me.

Thus, three hours later when I finally hopped off the stage, Lottie gave me a huge-ass grin and declared, "You're a natural. You're even gonna give me a run for my money."

I had no idea why that compliment made me feel warm inside. It just did. So I went with it.

After hugs and setting up my next class the next day, I headed out to my car but before I took off, I sat in it and called Smithie to tell him we were on the case, were amassing a file and I would be making my debut on Thursday.

He was ecstatic. Not about the file, about me dancing.

I ignored that and the not-so-great flutter that it sent shifting through my stomach, hung up and called Duke.

He wasn't at Fortnum's, so I phoned his house.

Duke had always been the kind of guy that, if you wanted to connect with him, you did that on his terms. In other words, face to face. Therefore, until Indy bought him and Dolores an answering machine last Christmas, there was no way to get a message to him.

Thanks to Indy's intervention, I was able to leave a message at his place. That said, it was a crapshoot if he actually listened to it.

What I said was, "Hey Duke. Please don't erase this without listening. I know you're pissed at me and we need to talk about that. You know you mean a lot to me so you gotta know I don't like that you're pissed at me. But more, something's up with Darius. I need to sit down with you about that and get your wisdom. So please, stop avoiding me so we can talk things out." I paused then finished, "Hey Dolores." Then I hung up.

It was slightly manipulative to drop the Darius thing, because Duke might be rough and gruff but he looked out for the crew. He probably already had his eye on Darius and was worried. So sucking him into that was totally making a play.

But I told Darius I would stop at nothing.

So I was going to stop at nothing.

I parked in Lee's garage, got out of my car and made my way into the building and to the elevators. After running, shopping and stripping, I couldn't face the stairs.

Truth be told, I didn't know how I was going to face my getting ready preparations and a late dinner with Ren. I really wanted our date, as in, *really*. But I'd been running around all day, was facing what would likely not be a happy conversation with my family, and would rather go home, eat Ren's delicious food and curl up on the couch and watch Nathan Fillion (and, of course, the rest of the cast of *Castle*).

The elevator expelled me on Lee's floor. I made my way down the hall and into his office.

Shirleen was not behind the reception desk, but Vance was standing beside it, tossing a file on the top.

When I entered, he turned to me.

"Hey," I greeted.

"Ally," he replied.

"What's shakin'?" I asked.

He grinned his shit-eating grin and seriously—he was Jules's; I loved Jules and I had Ren who I loved—but I had to admit that it wasn't just once in the time I knew Vance that I wondered what it would be like to be horizontal and have him aim that shit-hot grin at me.

"Everything," he replied. His grin faded and he said weirdly, "Tomorrow night."

I stopped advancing to the door that led to the nerve center of my brother's operations and turned to Vance. "What?"

"Tomorrow night. You're ride along with me."

My mouth dropped open, but the rest of my body jolted with pure, unadulterated glee.

"Got a security system I wanna show you how to bypass," he went on.

That feeling stole through me, that one I liked, but I still didn't move.

"You know how to pick a lock?" he asked.

I forced my mouth to move. "Um... not yet."

"We'll go through that tomorrow night, too."

Holy shit!

"I—" I started, but Vance kept going.

"We document those hours, I sign off on them for the License Board."

Holy shit!

"I... uh," *Pull it together, Ally!* "Why?" I asked.

"Saw the tape," Vance answered as I heard the door to the inner sanctum open.

But I didn't look there.

I kept my eyes to Vance. "What tape?"

"You, cool as shit, dealin' with those guys in Lincoln's."

"Impressive." I heard muttered, and saw Hector standing with us, the strap of a workout bag over his shoulder. He was looking at Vance. "You offer ride along?"

"Yep," Vance answered.

Hector looked at me. "You need help on a case and someone to sign off on your hours, call me."

I stared.

Was this happening?

Hector did a chin lift to Vance and me and sauntered out.

I looked from the door that closed on Hector back to Vance. "What's going on?"

"What's goin' on is the team saw the tape. Darius and Brody both talk you up. But we saw evidence of what they've been sayin'. You want this. You're good at it. You should have it. So some of the guys are up for backin' your play."

Oh my God.

I didn't know what to do.

I did know what to feel.

Ecstatically *freaking* happy.

I also knew what to ask.

"Is Lee okay with this?"

"None of us work here to have someone tell us what to do unless we need direction. So it doesn't matter. He knows we do what we do. He also knows we won't work here anymore if he gets up in our shit about what we do."

This, I knew, was true.

However.

"But you're offering me ride along on one of his cases," I pointed out.

"Yeah. And after he trained me or if we're not workin' a team operation, he does not send me out, micromanaging how I deal with a case. And he's fuckin' smart. Definitely smart enough to know it would not go down good if he started doin' that shit."

Before I could reply, the inside door opened again and I watched Ike move out.

He gave a chin lift to Vance, a mini-smile to me and walked by us to the door.

But at the door, he stopped, turned and said to me, "You need backup with that Smithie gig, you got my number."

I had no chance to say anything before he was gone.

"I'm outta here," Vance murmured, and I looked back at him. "Text you tomorrow when to meet me. We'll meet here and move out."

"I... uh, okay," I agreed.

Kristen Ashley

"Don't be late," he returned, then he, too, was gone.

I stared at the door.

I did this for a good long while.

Then I smiled.

I was still smiling when I tested the door to command central and found it unlocked, which was unusual, but likely left open for me.

I made my way to Lee's office and entered it, yep... *still* smiling.

In it were the expected. Dad, Hank and Lee with the not expected but not surprising addition of Tom Savage, Indy's father, my second dad and my dad's best friend.

What was surprising was that Monty, another of Lee's guys was there.

Monty took one look at me then looked to Lee and declared, "Vance offered the ride along."

I looked to Lee and saw he was studying his boots, jaw hard.

I decided not to confirm this. If Lee's boys were offering help, I'd take it. What I wouldn't do was cause friction between Lee and his men. If they made their decisions and carried them out, that was one thing and they had to deal with that and any ramifications. If I stuck my nose in, say to gloat (or the like), that was another.

So I kept my mouth shut.

"Ally," Monty called, and I looked back at him. "The men in this room are here because we know your plans and we're askin' you, with respect, to think long and hard about carrying them through."

I held his eyes.

I'd known Monty a long time. He was the oldest member of the team, an ex-Navy SEAL who didn't work in the field often for Lee due to an injury he sustained during his time in the military.

I liked him. He was solid guy; nice, funny, a family man. I also respected him.

But this pissed me off.

My father, second father and brothers, I'd show them respect and listen to what they had to say.

But Monty?

What the hell?

It must be said, I failed at not getting pissed-off, but I succeeded in keeping my shit together and therefore pointed out (somewhat) calmly, "I've been thinking on this for two years."

"We'd like you to think on it longer," Monty replied.

I drew in a deep breath.

"Monty's here because he gives a shit, Ally," Lee put in.

"I get that," I said to my brother, then looked at Monty, "And due respect to you, what I do with my life is none of your business."

"I've been doin' this awhile, longer than your brother, and I've seen women chewed up and spit out in this business," Monty returned.

"Yeah? So every man you know who tried his hand did spectacularly?" I shot back.

"Honey," he started, and I fought back being even *more* pissed-off; not at the endearment, but at his patronizing tone. "Your first case has you stripping."

"Yes. I'm working for Smithie. And to get the job done, it requires me doing something that's uncomfortable. But you do what you have to do to get the job done, and I shouldn't need to tell you that. Marcus Sloan has you on retainer, and don't try to bullshit me that the things he pulls you boys in to do are the like of acting as crossing guards at the local school."

Monty shut his mouth and looked at Lee.

In silent badass speak, that meant *That was a good point. I said my piece. It's now up to you.*

It was then I got it. Monty was there as the objective voice of reason.

And this definitely pissed me off more, because it inferred they thought I was being unreasonable.

I slid my gaze through everyone in the room and stated, "Due respect to all of you, and I'll note, that's a lot of respect and it's not just out of love. I know you all are skilled and experienced and exceptionally good at what you do." I pinpointed Dad. "But you did not have a chat with Hank before he entered the Academy. You did not have a chat with Lee before he went into the Army *or* when he got out and built his team. You let them do what they had to do and you did that proud. The only reason I can think that I'm standing here is because I'm a woman. And that does not fly with me."

"Ally," Tom cut in, and I looked his way. "If Indy was doing this, I'd be worried."

"Indy's about coffee, books, family, friends, Lee and rock 'n' roll. In other words, Indy is not me," I retorted and kept at it. "We've also sat down and she knows that she will not ever be involved in my business. She's down with that." I moved my gaze to Hank. "All of the Rock Chicks understand this and are down with it. So if that's a concern, I assure you, that's covered."

"What Tom's saying," Dad put in, "is that, as fathers and brothers," he tipped his head Lee and Hank's way, "we're worried."

"As they go about their business, are you worried about Hank and Lee?" I asked.

"Every day," Dad replied quietly, and my body locked. "It's what fathers do, sweetheart."

There was no retort to that.

So I didn't give him one.

Instead, I said, just as quietly. "I get you and I love you for it. But this is what I want to do and I want to do it because I'm good at it and I *like* it. You know I've struggled to find my calling. I'm not struggling anymore. I've found it, Dad."

And Dad had no retort for that. I knew because he didn't give me one.

"Hector, Vance, Ike and Bobby, as well as Darius and Brody are backin' your play, Ally," Lee said, and I turned my attention to him, surprised and pleased at the unknown addition of Bobby. "And I'm not gettin' in their shit about that. But they're not your brothers and—"

I interrupted him. "Darius is."

"You know what I mean," Lee replied.

"And you know what I mean," I returned softly.

His jaw clenched.

I held his eyes and kept speaking softly. "You can try to stop me. But you won't. I know you have the means to do it. But I'll keep going. Ren's behind me. Daisy's behind me and that means Marcus has my back, and you know Daisy's support means I have Marcus's support. You won't sway him your way if Daisy is standing in between."

His jaw clenched harder.

He knew.

"The Rock Chicks are backing this too, so if you think the rest of the men won't fall, or at least won't stand in my way, you're wrong about that, too," I went on.

A muscle jumped in his cheek.

He knew that, too.

"And I'll finish with this," I told him, still soft but firm, and my eyes went to Hank, Dad, Tom and even Monty but they ended back on Lee. "If you make moves to shut me down," I looked to Hank, "Or you," I looked through Dad, Tom and Monty again, "Any of you." My eyes went back to Lee. "That hurt will dig deep. So deep I may get over it, eventually. What I won't do is forgive you."

Lee held my eyes.

I returned the gesture.

Since I had preparations to do and a date to make, I couldn't do it for what it seemed it would take to win it.

Eternity.

So I broke the staredown and I moved to the door, but turned at it and swept a glance through them all again, my eyes ending on Hank and Lee.

"One last thing. There's something wrong with Darius, and if you two haven't clocked that, color me stunned. But I figure you have, and since you're dudes and dudes don't get up in the business of other dudes, you're steering clear. A heads up: I'm done steering clear. I'm gonna sort that, and if I had your help, I'd be obliged."

On that, I left.

And by the time I got in my car, I felt my throat burning. My eyes were hot and my hands were shaking.

Not from nerves or fear.

From emotion.

Because I honestly didn't know which way any of them would swing.

I just knew I did not lie.

If they moved to shut me down, these people I loved I'd never forgive.

⚡

I opened the door to Ren's place and smelled garlic.

What the hell?

I dumped my purse on an armchair and walked into the kitchen.

Ren was wearing jeans, a loose pale yellow shirt, sleeves rolled up, feet bare, and he was at the stove, a stove that held steaming pots and pans.

"What's going on?" I asked and he turned to me.

"Kiss, Ally," he ordered instead of telling me what was going on.

I walked to him, noting, "I thought we were going out."

He again didn't respond until I got close, put a hand to his abs and rolled up on my toes to touch my mouth to his.

When I rolled back but stayed close, he answered, "You didn't wanna miss your show. I'm makin' stuffed shells."

Jeez.

I couldn't take it.

Just when I thought my man couldn't get any better, he did.

"We'll go out tomorrow night," he muttered.

I focused on him and saw his eyes were probing.

That was when, again, he got even better.

He did this by saying in his sweet voice, "The meet didn't go well."

He read me.

"Not really."

"You wanna talk about it?"

"Nothing to say. They don't want me in the business. That's not a surprise. Now they have a decision to make because I already made mine."

He nodded, read me again and did what I needed.

He let it go.

"You want me to turn on the sauna?" he asked.

That sounded awesome, but if I was in there, I wanted to be in there with him. Not up there alone and him downstairs cooking.

"No, baby," I murmured. "But thanks."

"Then sit your ass on the counter. I'll get you a glass of wine and you can keep me company while I put the shells together."

That sounded better so I complied and Ren got me a glass of wine.

I sipped.

Ren worked.

When he was nearly done, I got off the counter and got on cleaning the pots, pans and utensils so later clean up would be a snap.

I heard the oven door close then I felt arms wrap around me from behind at the same time I felt Ren's hard heat at my back and his mouth at my ear.

"They'll come around," he whispered there.

I closed my eyes, opened them and rinsed a pot.

I put it in the drainer, saying, "I hope so."

He gave me a squeeze. "I know so."

I turned off the faucet and twisted my neck to look at him. "How do you know?"

"Because they love you."

I pressed my lips together and my eyes got hot again.

Then he again gave me what I needed. He bent, kissed my neck and lifted to catch my eyes.

"We'll eat in front of the TV. I'll go turn it on."

I nodded.

He grinned and gave me a squeeze.

He went to turn on the TV, came back and refilled our wine glasses.

I put the last pot in the drainer and followed my man to the TV to veg out and await stuffed shells.

"Jesus," Ren muttered, and I tore my eyes off *Castle* to lift my head from where it was resting on his chest seeing as we were both stretched out on the couch, Ren on his back, me tucked to his side between him and the couch.

"What?"

"Jesus," he repeated, eyes glued to the TV.

He was making me miss it!

"*What?*" I snapped.

He lifted a hand that held the remote and paused the show.

Then he turned his head to me. "Do you watch this show because of that woman?"

I felt my brows draw together. "What woman?"

"The brunette who's the spittin' image of you."

What was he talking about?

"Do you mean Stana Katic?" I asked.

"I don't know her name. The tall knockout brunette."

Jeez. Did he think I looked like Stana Katic, otherwise known as the most beautiful woman on American television today?

"You think I look like Kate Beckett?" I asked.

"Who's Kate Beckett?" he asked back.

"Stana Katic. She plays Detective Kate Beckett, Castle's partner on the show. Or, more accurately, Castle's her partner," I informed him.

"Then no. If she's the gorgeous, bossy, badass homicide detective I just watched for the last five minutes, I don't think you look like her. I think she's the spittin' image of you."

Wow.

Cool!

"Seriously?" I asked.

"Babe," he muttered, his eyes wandering back to the TV where Beckett was paused having a conversation with Castle, "fuck me, definitely seriously."

This.

Was.

Awesome.

I didn't share I felt that, nor did I tell him that wasn't the reason I watched *Castle* (though it was part of it; Kate Beckett was the freaking *bomb*).

I just said the truth. "I never noticed."

He looked back at me. "How could you not notice?"

I probably didn't notice because I was paying more attention to Nathan Fillion.

Since this was the reason, the answer I gave Ren was a shrug.

Ren's arm around me curled me closer, his head turned back to the TV and he hit play.

I turned my eyes to the TV and studied Kate Beckett.

She did kinda look like me.

Totally cool.

I relaxed into Ren and tangled my legs with his.

It was then it hit me we'd never done this, something totally normal like relaxing in front of a TV.

It also hit me it felt nice.

And last, it hit me that after a busy day that didn't end great, this, just this, was exactly what I needed. A belly full of Ren's cooking. A wine glass that, unless I wanted it to be, never was empty. A couch. A TV. A good show.

But most of all.

Ren.

Chapter 23

Impossible

The next morning, post-coffee rush at Fortnum's, the bell over the door rang.

I had a lot to do, and unfortunately part of that was keeping liquid until my insurance check came in. My credit card balance was getting high and my bank account balance was never high. Thus I needed my take from the tip jar.

I twisted from doing dishes at the sink, looked and saw Mr. Kumar and his mother-in-law, Mrs. Salim, enter the store.

They were regulars. They were also (kind of) part of our posse.

Mr. Kumar owned a corner store on Tex's block and he'd been dragged into two Rock Chick Rides, Indy's and Ava's. He was a good guy who, against the odds, kept his little store open. I helped by shopping there occasionally, even though it was out of my way.

I didn't know much about Mrs. Salim except that every time I saw her, I feared she'd keel over and quit breathing, she looked that old. And this wasn't being mean. Seriously, she looked *that old*. Just saying, the woman's wrinkles had wrinkles.

I also knew she liked to read.

As usual, Mrs. Salim shuffled to the books.

Mr. Kumar came to the coffee counter and, weirdly, had his eyes on me.

He stopped and looked at Tex. "Did you speak with her?"

I turned from the sink, grabbing a towel to wipe my hands.

"Talk with me about what?" I asked.

"No," Tex answered Mr. Kumar "I talked to Hank."

"But the police aren't doing anything!" Mr. Kumar suddenly cried, and the skin on the back of my neck prickled.

I moved to the espresso counter, jamming in close to Tex. "Talk to me about what?'

"Hank says they're lookin' into it," Tex told me.

"Looking into what?" I asked.

"And I'm keepin' an eye out," Tex went on, still not answering me.

"Keeping an eye on *what?*" I snapped.

"The rash of burglaries on our street," Mr. Kumar finally answered me.

"You've had a rash of burglaries?" Indy asked, coming up to the counter, hands full of empties.

"Yes," Mr. Kumar answered.

"I'm keepin' an eye out," Tex stated.

Giving big eyes to Tex, Mr. Kumar then turned to me. "Tex looks out for the neighborhood, but he's not finding anything. I talked with some of my customers and we got a... what's it called?"

I didn't know what he was talking about so I couldn't tell him what it was called.

Luckily, he found the word and stated, "*Kitty.* To pay you." He dug in his pants pocket, pulled out a card and turned it to me. "We're hiring a Rock Chick."

I looked at the card, a card I'd asked Brody to make for me way back in the day when Indy and I were searching for Rosie.

Mr. Kumar had kept his.

Righteous.

What was not righteous was, as much as I wanted the business, I had to make coffee, continue my stripper education and robberies happened at night, the same time as stripping did. And last, there was only one of me. Brody was strung out finding out about the books and he never worked in the field, unless that work required him to be in a surveillance van. Darius worked for Lee and was on the stripper case with me.

I couldn't take the case.

And that sucked.

"I'm sorry Mr. Kumar," I said. "I have another case I have to work at night and I can't be two places at once."

His face fell. "But we've had nine cars on our streets broken into," he told me. "Stereos stolen. Glove boxes rifled through. Windows smashed. All this in less than two weeks. People are worried."

Crap.

"I'm keepin' my eye on it," Tex repeated, sounding more than his usual grumpy.

"Tweakers," I muttered, and Mr. Kumar looked at me.

"I'm sorry?"

"Tweakers," I repeated. "People who need to steal car stereos and fence them to buy drugs."

Mr. Kumar nodded.

"No one would hit one neighborhood repeatedly in that time unless they were stupid or desperate, and tweakers are both," I told him.

Mr. Kumar nodded again.

It was then it occurred to me that no one would hit Tex's street because he *did* keep an eye out. He did this by sitting on his porch randomly, but often, with a shotgun across his lap and night vision goggles on his head. The presence of a sleeping cat also in his lap was not unheard of.

This was a weird thing to do, but this was also Tex we were talking about. And except for when Rock Chick business leaked into their 'hood (because Ava lived with Luke now, but she still owned the pad she used to live in there; not to mention Indy's business brought us there, repeatedly), crime was nil. Probably because Tex lived there and sat outside in night vision goggles with a shotgun.

Shotguns were definitely deterrents. Wild men wearing night vision goggles having shotguns were much stronger deterrents.

This meant the culprits likely knew this, kept an eye on Tex and when he went off duty, they did the deeds.

In other words, locals.

I looked up at Tex. "You got a house in the 'hood that's home to a bunch of meth heads?"

"Only about every other one," he replied.

Fuck.

Door to door action.

Hector.

Hector said if I had a case he could work with me, he was there.

It would have to be pre—or post—stripping (likely post, which would make it a long night), but we could hit the houses, gain entry cops couldn't by being badasses (or Hector could be one; I'd pretend to be one), hope they didn't immediately fence the property they stole and therefore call it into Eddie or Hank so they could get a search warrant and roll in.

"I'll take the case," I said to Mr. Kumar.

He grinned.

"I said, I got an eye out!" Tex boomed, and I looked up at him.

"You're getting married tomorrow," I reminded him.

"Yeah, and it's no big deal. A piece of paper. Nance already lives with me and we're not takin' a honeymoon for a coupla weeks 'cause she's got some cruise she wants to take and they were all booked up for the week we wanted so we had to wait. So I can *keep an eye out*."

He said a lot of words, but I was stuck on one thing.

Tex was going on a cruise?

Tex was going to be confined on a cruise ship with hundreds of other passengers?

Tex was going to be lumbering around the decks in his jeans and flannels with his wild-ass beard and hair, frightening unsuspecting vacationers... on a *cruise?*

I burst out laughing.

"What's funny?" Tex asked.

"You," I choked out, "On a cruise." I looked to Indy and saw her shoulders shaking.

"What's funny about that?" Tex demanded to know.

"You," I choked out again. "*On a cruise.*"

"I know," Jet said from behind me, having returned from one of her seven hundred daily pregnancy-related bathroom breaks. "I laughed for fifteen minutes when Mom told me."

"Tex on a cruise!" I cried.

"Shut it, woman," Tex ordered.

I kept laughing.

"It's not that funny," Tex boomed.

It totally was.

I looked to Jet. "You make your mom promise to take pictures. *Lots of them.*"

Tex growled.

I looked back at him and kept laughing.

His eyes narrowed and he declared, "You're on this case, I'm workin' with you."

I swallowed laughter, wiped a tear of hilarity from my eye and caught his.

"Fine. You make a list of houses we need to hit. I'll call Hector, who said he'd work a case with me. I'll get a night when we can hit them before you go on your," I swallowed again then forced out, "*Cruise.* Then we go out and hit them. We find stolen property, we call it into the cops. Yeah?"

"Yeah," Tex grunted.

"Can I get a coffee?" A man standing behind Mr. Kumar asked.

"Are you blind?" Tex asked back.

"Sorry?" the man queried.

Tex threw out a beefy mitt. "Don't you see we're havin' a meetin'?"

The man looked around. He also looked confused.

He looked back at Tex. "I thought you made coffee."

"We do. We also fight crime. Don't you read the papers?" Tex asked, and I heard Jet giggle.

I was right with her.

"Um... yes, but I didn't know you did it when you were making coffee," the man replied.

"Crime don't happen *when you want it to,*" Tex returned. "You gotta be prepared. You gotta plan. And that's why we're havin' a *meetin'.* Now shut it and wait until we're done."

The man gave big eyes to Jet and I. He also appeared indecisive, like he didn't know whether to wait as Tex ordered, or take his life in his hands that Tex might not like it and flee.

Obviously not a regular.

"We'll be right with you," Indy assured him as she moved to walk around the counter.

"We're done meeting anyway," I announced then looked between Tex and Mr. Kumar. "The plan's in place. I'll give you both a heads up when we put it in action."

"Thank you, Ally," Mr. Kumar said. "The neighbors will be very happy to hear this news."

"You're welcome, Mr. Kumar," I replied.

"What'll it be?" Tex boomed to the customer.

But he wasn't looking at Tex. He was watching, with some alarm, as the apparent walking corpse of Mrs. Salim shuffled to Mr. Kumar carrying a pile of seven books in her arms.

All hardbacks.

I fought the urge to leap over the espresso counter to relieve her of her burden just as Mr. Kumar took the books from her and led her to the book counter.

My eyes went there to see Jane standing behind it, and I began to look away when I looked right back.

One of the pink *Rock Chick* books was sitting on the counter and she had her fingers to it; not leafing, lightly brushing. As Mr. Kumar and Mrs. Salim approached, she jolted, like she didn't expect customers (ever) then gave them a small smile.

This wasn't unusual, Jane being startled. She lived in her own world most of the time. And anyway, selling a book didn't happen frequently so seven of them would surprise anybody.

But I wasn't thinking about that.

I was thinking about how she was touching that pink book.

Jane loved books. She was an avid reader. And as a book lover who worked in a bookstore her whole life, she treated them with reverence.

That wasn't what I saw.

Her touch on that pink book was reverent, for sure.

It was also loving.

Hmm.

Before I could move that thought to fruition, Indy interrupted it.

"I got broody Lee last night," she whispered to me as she dumped her empties by the sink.

I tore my mind from Jane and looked at Indy. "What?"

"Broody Lee," Indy answered. "Schedule goes, I get broody Lee at least once a week. A tough case is happening, maybe three or four times. Rock Chick stuff is going down, he veers from broody to annoyed to resigned. Last night, I started with broody Lee because of the meeting and super broody Lee because I told him he needed to quit giving you shit and start giving you support."

Oh crap.

"Indy, I love it that you did that, but you don't have to do it," I told her. "In fact, please don't do it again. I don't want to be the cause of trouble between you and my brother. Let this be between Lee and Hank and me."

"I also told Eddie he needed to sort Lee out," Jet put in. "And Hank. He said he'd have a chat with them."

I stared.

"Really?" Indy asked.

Jet nodded. "Yeah. He says he's seen the tape and he's also seen veteran officers go into a situation like that and not be able to keep their cool when things go south the way Ally did."

Whoa.

Wow.

Righteous!

"Seriously?" I asked.

"You were the shit," Tex boomed, flicking the latch on the coffee grinder to fill the portafilter and doing it so hard the entire grinder shook. "It was fuckin' frustratin'. Whole thing took, like, two seconds, and I only got one punch in on the motherfucker. Then he was down. *Splat!*"

Indy looked at Tex, then at the customer, then at Tex. "Can you *please* watch your mouth in front of customers?" she asked him.

"No," he answered her, then packed the coffee grounds down before shoving the filter up into the machine so the thing lifted off the counter an inch.

"Okay, then can you *please* not abuse my seven thousand dollar espresso machine?" Indy asked.

"No," Tex answered then went on. "Been doin' this years, woman." He flipped a switch and patted the top of the machine (hard). "This bitch is built to last."

Indy glared at him then rearranged her face and looked at the customer. "I apologize for my barista."

"Once you get your coffee," a blonde who'd just approached the counter, a regular I knew by the name of Annie, stated knowingly, "it'll totally be worth it. Trust me. He abuses me all the time, and I don't care as long as I get my coffee."

"I don't even know you," Tex boomed at her.

"I come in every day at eight fifteen," she shot back, and she was not wrong. She did.

"I'm supposed to remember that?" Tex asked.

"Yes," Annie returned. "Because, for years, *I've come in every day at eight fifteen.*"

"I'm sorry, Annie," Indy said.

"Just as long as the crazy guy never loses his touch with the coffee, again, I don't care," she replied then ordered. "Half and half mocha latte with a half a shot of almond syrup."

"I remember *that*," Tex muttered.

"Farewell Rock Chicks and Tex," Mr. Kumar called from the door,

We all looked there and returned his wave (except Tex, who looked but didn't wave). We also all braced when Mrs. Salim lifted a bony hand and waved, undoubtedly every one of us prepared to grab the broom should one (or more) of her digits break off because the blood stopped circulating there fifty years ago.

They moved out.

We all relaxed.

"That woman creeps me out," Annie remarked, looking back after looking over her shoulder. "I don't mean to be mean, but all the zombie movies lately..." she shivered. "Flashback."

"She's a good mother and a good grandmother who keeps her culture alive for her family when they've moved far away from home in order to make a decent living," Tex stated and Annie's eyes shot to him. "So yeah, she looks like the walking dead. She's alive enough for her family."

"I meant no offense," Annie muttered.

"Then don't say people that I know creep you out," Tex shot back.

"Tex, you're always saying shit about people," I pointed out the truth, and he scowled at me. "And, incidentally, *to* people," I went on with more of the truth.

"He's nervous about getting married tomorrow," Jet guessed.

"Oh my God! You're getting married?" Annie cried. "How exciting!"

"Fuck," Tex groused.

"Can I have my coffee?" the other customer asked.

I moved in to finish the guy's coffee as Tex said to Annie, "You want your coffee, shut your trap."

Annie grinned at him.

I handed the male customer his coffee.

He moved away, taking a sip, and stopped dead.

No one reacted to this. This was because a lot of newbies did this.

But what a lot of newbies didn't do was what he did next.

He turned back and looked at Tex.

"I'm gonna say, you scare me. But I'm also gonna say, this lady's right." He tipped his head to Annie and lifted his white paper cup with its cardboard holder. "This coffee is unbelievable. And last I'm gonna say, good luck tomorrow and congratulations. I've been married for fifteen years and every day I wake up next to my wife and feel lucky. I wish for you that you feel the same."

Everyone stared at him except Tex.

He boomed, "What's your name?"

"Barry."

"When you come back, I'll remember you."

Then Tex turned his attention to making Annie's coffee.

I pressed my lips together and looked at Indy, Jet and Annie who were all pressing their lips together and doing the same thing.

This was because Tex just paid Barry the highest compliment he could give a customer.

And we all knew why.

Because Tex already felt that lucky.

It was just that tomorrow, he was making it official.

⌁

"Enjoy the rest of your evening."

It was post-Fortnum's, post-stripper class and pre-going out with Vance that night (an appointment that started very late, and one that Ren knew about but luckily had no comment).

I was in a sexy, clingy, back and cleavage-baring, halter-neck LBD and stilettos. Ren was in a suit. And we were on our first official date.

We not only had plenty of time to enjoy it, we had time to get home and have sex before I had to go out and meet Vance.

And it had been perfect.

The whole night.

Perfection.

We were on the sun terrace at Plato's, an upscale steak and seafood joint on the second floor of a building on Sixteenth Street Mall. We had a table tucked in the corner of the terrace by the railing and behind a big plant that I was certain by the greeting the hostess gave Ren that included her using a "Mr. Zano" in a familiar way, Ren had arranged for us.

It was private and romantic, but still, the lights and hustle and bustle of Sixteenth Street mall made the air seem alive and our view was amazing.

And it was awesome to sit there in the warm May air with Ren looking hot, and knowing the way his eyes were hot on me, he thought I looked the same.

We were finished and the waitress had just slid the leather thingie with his credit card on the table, which meant we were close to the highly anticipated sex portion of the evening.

We'd eaten steak and lobster, shared a slice of rich dark chocolate cheesecake, and drank champagne. The whole time we sat kitty corner to each other.

Close.

This allowed Ren to touch my thigh, my hip, and me to wind my calf around his. It also meant we could lean into each other, Ren holding my hand high, our elbows on the table, my knuckles close to his lips, me having his full attention.

We were living together, committed to each other and our future, and this was our first official date.

That was weird.

But that didn't mean it wasn't the best date I ever had.

Bar none.

Then again, maybe it was because we were living together and committed to each other that made it that way.

Mostly, though, I figured it was because Ren was hot, sweet and so totally into me.

And I was in love.

Ren let my hand go to deal with the bill, but the minute he was finished tucking his wallet into his suit jacket that was slung on the back of his chair, he grabbed my hand again and, both our elbows to the table, he leaned in and put it to his lips.

His eyes came to mine.

"Ready to go home?"

I was. *So* ready.

I was also looking forward to doing the ride along with Vance. Still, I was hoping it wouldn't last long so I could come home, wake up Ren, and continue the sex portion of the date.

I didn't say this, though.

Instead I noted, "You didn't get to Twenty Questions for Ally."

Ren grinned. He rubbed my knuckles against his full lower lip, his eyes warmed and my happy place convulsed.

328

"I decided against twenty questions, baby. Findin' I'm likin' the surprises you give me."

And I liked that.

I leaned closer. "Tonight was a great night, Ren. The best." My voice dipped quiet. "Thank you, baby."

His eyes got even warmer when he replied, "You're welcome, honey."

That was when I got even closer and whispered, "And last night was exactly what I needed. Thank you for that, too."

"Anytime, Ally," he whispered back.

"Ally?"

This came from behind us and we both turned our heads, Ren not letting go of my hand, and I saw Zach Gilligan standing there.

Shit.

Zach looked disbelieving.

He also looked angry.

Shit.

I hadn't seen him since that night at Club. I *had* seen Helen, and I knew she was now with another guy, this one nice, cool and, big bonus, not a cokehead.

"Jesus, Ally," he clipped, moving into our serene romantic secluded spot in a way that made my back go straight, Ren's hand tighten in mine and the air around us turn heavy. Zach ignored all this and leaned deep into me. "You know, that was five hundred dollars-worth of product you made me drop in the john."

Before I could say anything, Ren ordered, "Step back."

Zach completely ignored Ren and kept his angry attention on me. "And Helen kicked me out. I was *this close*," he held a thumb and forefinger half an inch apart, about double that away from my face, and I felt the air turn stifling, "from asking her to marry me."

Again, before I could retort, and I had some doozies, Ren got there.

"Get your hand outta my woman's face," he growled.

Zach, apparently not feeling or not understanding the vibe in the air or the tone of Ren's voice, turned his head to him.

"Fuck off," he snarled at Ren. "Got something to say to this bitch."

That was when it happened. And it happened so quickly, if I had blinked, I would have missed it.

And what happened was that Ren let my hand go and his shot up and out. He cupped the back of Zach's head and slammed him face first, fast and hard enough to make a sickening thud, into our table.

His fingers gripping Zach by the hair, he pulled him back. Zach blinking and his nose bleeding, Ren brought him to within an inch of his face.

"That's a start," Ren whispered scarily, "Do you get me?"

"Yeah man, yeah," Zach replied quickly.

"You see her again, you don't know her. You get that?"

"Yeah, yeah, definitely," Zach said.

"Get the fuck outta here," Ren rumbled and let him go, but did this by jerking his hair back so Zach's neck bent unnaturally and he went flying.

He righted himself and didn't look back, but lifted his hand to his nose and scurried.

I stared after him until he disappeared then forced my eyes back to Ren, who I noted did all that without leaving his seat.

Without leaving his seat.

Holy.

Crap!

"You ready?" he asked, his voice rough, which meant he was still angry. Therefore I quickly nodded.

Ren got up and pulled my seat back for me to do the same, which I did. He grabbed his suit jacket and jerked his head toward the building which was silent pissed-off Italian American badass for *Get moving.*

I grabbed my bag off the table and got moving.

Ren shrugged on his jacket as we went, but caught my hand tight when he was done.

I noticed that most of the other diners were dining. Only a few were looking up, and only because we were moving and caught their attention. Other than that, it seemed everyone missed the action.

Thank God for that plant.

Ren kept hold of me until he opened my door and angled me into his Jag. He got in, started her purring, pulled out and headed home. Even though the air still weighed heavily making it hard to breathe, he drove like he normally drove which was casually, a little fast, but in total control.

I sat next to him while he did it, wondering how to handle this situation. I wasn't certain silence was best. I also wasn't certain, since clearly my "business" had interrupted our fabulous evening, if he was mad at Zach, or me, or both, and if both, which one more.

What I was certain of, and I did not care even a little bit what this said about me, was that what Ren did was all kinds of freaking *hot*.

So I also sat next to Ren fighting squirming because I was all kinds of turned on.

With all this on my mind, alas, we made it home in heavy silence without me saying a word, which I decided was good. Whatever we said would be in his house and everyone knew it was better to have it out in a house, not a car. A car was too confining and if tempers flared, that was bad if the one with the temper flaring was driving.

And as you know, Ren's temper could totally flare.

Ren was at my door before I fully folded out of the car. He helped me the rest of the way, threw my door to, and guided me up to his house, beeping the locks on his car. He let my hand go when he opened his front door but put his to the small of my back to guide me in.

I went in and dropped my bag on the couch. I turned on a light on an end table and turned to face Ren to see he was tossing his jacket to a chair.

"Honey—" I started.

He lifted a hand to me.

Shit.

The Hand from Ren.

I didn't like it, but I thought it prudent to shut my mouth.

He dropped his hand and spoke.

"In making the decision to take you as you take me, it was not lost on me that my concerns about you doin' what you're doing were valid. There are going to be times, like tonight, that your work will leak into our life. Therefore it was not lost on me that I'd have to deal with that. I dealt with it. It's over. If it's something we need to discuss, I'll trust you to explain that to me. But that asshole was not a threat, just a nuisance who, from the little he said, jacked up his own life but blames you. What I'm sayin' is, he does not deserve our time to discuss it."

This was all good.

Really good.

Still.

"Are you angry with me?" I asked quietly.

Kristen Ashley

"No, I'm angry that we had a great night, that jackass tainted it and I got fuckin' blood on my sleeve."

I pressed my lips together, but I did this in order not to laugh.

I unpressed them to say, "I'll get the Shout out."

"Good idea," he muttered irately.

"Can I say something?" I asked and his eyes grew intent on me.

"Any time, any place, anything we're talkin' about, you can say whatever the fuck you want, Ally."

Loved my man.

Loved him.

"That was hot," I declared and watched his body lock.

"What?"

"No. That's not right," I said. "That wasn't hot. That was *smokin'* hot, and I don't care if that makes me a freak. It was hot. You were hot. Now *I'm* hot. So hot, I may have an orgasm, standing here remembering it."

To that, instantly he ordered, "Take off your dress, Ally."

Oh crap.

Totally about to have an orgasm.

It was then I noticed the air in the room had changed.

It was still heavy.

But now it was warm.

"Now," he demanded.

Without further delay, I crossed my arms in front of me, curled my fingers into my skirt, and pulled my dress up and over my head.

I dropped it to the floor beside me so I was standing in front of him in nothing but lacy black panties and stiletto heels.

"Now come here, and baby, if you give me shit about comin' to me, when I get to you, I'm turnin' you over my knee."

This was a conundrum.

But a spanking might delay getting him inside me and at that moment, that would not do.

So I went to him.

Once there, he crushed me in his arms, his mouth slammed down on mine and his tongue thrust into my mouth.

I whimpered into his, put my hands to his shoulders and held on.

332

His hands went to my ass, lifted up sliding down the backs of my thighs until my legs wrapped around his hips then they went back to my ass and he started walking.

He took me down to my back on the couch with him on me.

When his lips slid to my neck, I turned my head and begged in his ear, "Need you now, baby."

He lifted his head, looked down at me and my legs clamped around his hips at the heat in his eyes even as he slid one hand from my ass and it plunged right into my panties.

I gasped.

Nice.

"You take it missionary, Ally."

"Okay," I breathed.

"'Cause I'm gonna fuck you hard, baby."

Oh God.

Yes.

"Okay," I repeated breathily.

His mouth came to mine and his eyes didn't leave me when he murmured, "Panties, honey."

I let him go with only one leg, shoving down my panties on that side, cocking a knee and sliding them over and down off my foot, so he had the access he needed in the least time with the least effort I could take to give it to him.

His hand was working between us and seconds later, the tip of his tongue slid over my lips as he slid slowly inside me.

My eyelids dropped, my lips parted and all was right in the world.

He watched and I knew he entered me slowly so he could.

Because once he was in and I gave him the show he wanted, nothing went slow.

It was hard, fast, rough and amazing.

I came within minutes. I did it hard and I did it crying out his name before I sank my teeth in his shoulder.

Ren took a lot longer, but it was clear from his noises and the brutal beauty of his kisses that he enjoyed it so I gave him everything he needed with my hands, my mouth and my happy place to take him there.

Finally, he got there.

He had his mouth on my neck working me, and I had my hands under his shirt roaming his back, my mind memorizing our evening. All of it. Especially this part, his weight on me, him filling me, the scent of him, the feel of him.

Everything.

So it took a beat before I realized his body was shaking.

"Ren?" I called.

He lifted his head and I saw his smile.

He was laughing.

"What's funny?" I asked.

"Jesus," was his nonsensical answer.

As good as it felt feeling his big strong body move on me (and in me, it must be said), I didn't get it.

"What's funny?" I repeated.

"Only you," he replied.

"Only me?"

"Only you would get off on me slammin' some asshole's face into a table."

I stiffened.

His hand immediately came up to cup my jaw, his body stopped shaking and his smile died clean away.

"Take me as I am," he whispered, and I noticed his voice had *that tone,* his face had *that look,* and I melted beneath him.

"Yeah," I whispered back.

"Love you, Ally."

I grinned. "Love you more, baby."

He didn't grin.

He said, "Impossible."

I frowned.

"If you make me cry, no sex for a week," I declared, but my voice was husky.

"Then I better not make you cry," he murmured, lips twitching.

"Damn straight," I mumbled.

That was when he grinned.

Then his lips came to mine and he ordered, "Go clean up. That went fast. I wanna eat you and fuck you again before you go learn how to bypass security systems."

My entire body trembled.

"'Kay," I agreed immediately.

He touched his mouth to mine, slowly slid out while watching, and said, "Meet you in bed."

He so would.

He rolled off. I rolled the other way, got to my feet and let my panties drop down my leg. I stepped out of them and sashayed, wearing nothing but a pair of stiletto sandals, to and up the stairs.

I hit the bathroom and did as ordered.

Then I met my man in bed.

≈

"Tonight, you watched. Next time we go, you watch again. The time after, you're up."

This was Vance.

We were standing by the driver's side door of my Mustang in Lee's parking garage in the dead of night, and he was being bossy.

He had also taught me sick good things that night, so I decided not to give a shit that he was being bossy.

"Right," I agreed.

He reached into his back pocket, pulled out a small black leather pouch with a zip around three sides and handed it to me.

"Those're yours. Picks. You buy locks at a hardware store and practice. When you're up, I'll be timin' you. You got thirty seconds."

I looked up at him and nodded but said, "I didn't bring anything to give you."

He gave me his shit-eating grin.

I decided to get serious.

"Appreciate you doing this, Vance."

"The grip you got on that guy's junk, no hesitation, bringin' him down to his knees. Fuck. His face," Vance replied. "Half the team's terrified of you. Bobby's having nightmares. I had no choice. Jules and I want more kids. Don't wanna piss you off."

It was clear he didn't feel like being serious so I lifted a hand and socked him in the arm.

He lifted a hand and caught me at the back of the head.

Then he shocked the shit out of me by pulling me in and kissing my forehead before letting me go and murmuring, "You did good tonight."

"Do you kiss Mace's forehead when he does well?" I asked and his eyes got intent.

"Learn now, you're a woman. This is a man's job, not because more women don't have the stones to do it, but because they think they need to have stones in order to do it. The way of the world, men can do shit you can't. What you gotta remember is, you can do shit that men can't. You play to that. You use it. I am not gonna treat you like one of the guys 'cause you're not one of the guys. That doesn't mean I won't treat you with respect. And what you learn now is, even if you get treated differently, there's no difference. Yeah?"

This was very profound. And wise. And I'd never thought of it like that.

But I liked it.

"Yeah," I agreed.

"Now I gotta get home to Jules and Max," he muttered.

"Right," I replied. "Give Max a cuddle for me."

"Will do," he said, moving toward his Harley.

"Vance?" I called and he turned back. "Really. Thanks for tonight. I appreciate it."

"You're a Nightingale," he replied then finished enigmatically, "Anything."

He roared off on his Harley and I was in my car following him when it hit me what his "anything" meant.

He was an ex-con, recovering alcoholic. And Lee had taken him on, trained him, and offered him a different life. A better life. And when he won Jules then they had Max, he got the best life there could be.

And he appreciated it.

I parked outside Ren's, the jazzed feeling I had expiring and fatigue setting in. So I wasted no time getting in and quietly changing into a nightie, washing my face and brushing my teeth.

I slid into bed next to Ren, turned into his heat by curling into his back and snaking an arm around his waist.

He grabbed my hand, slid it up his chest and held it there.

"How'd it go?" he mumbled sleepily.

I pressed closer.

"It was righteous."

His hand gave mine a squeeze. "Good."
He was right.
He fell back to sleep.
Not long after, I followed him.

Chapter 24

Completely Happy

I moved into the middle aisle of bookshelves and did it stealthily.

If I found my target, I didn't want to be disturbed.

It was the next day, late morning at Fortnum's. The store would be closing in an hour so we could all get ready to go to Tex and Nancy's wedding. But Jet, Indy and I were taking off in thirty minutes to hit the mall to buy dresses (and probably shoes).

So I didn't have a lot of time.

I found her in the way back room, beyond the middle room with its table filled with crates, crates that were filled with vinyl.

She was shelving books in Women's Studies.

Tall, extremely thin, dark hair that was graying and she left it at that.

Jane.

"Hey," I called and she jumped.

Then she turned to me. "Hey, Ally."

I got close and asked, "You going to Tex's thing?"

"Yes," she answered.

"Going to Blanca's after?" I asked.

"For a little while."

This meant she'd show her face, leave a present and get the hell out of there.

Let's just say Jane wasn't social.

"You write those *Rock Chick* books?" I went on conversationally, and her eyes went huge.

She took a step back.

Fuck. My gut feeling was right.

She did.

Holy crap.

I followed her. She took another step back and we kept going, but as we did it occurred to me she would think I was on the attack. So I reached out, grabbed her hand and held it just as her shoulder hit a shelf.

"It's okay," I whispered.

"It's... okay?" she asked incredulously.

I nodded. "I'm not mad."

"You're... not?"

I shook my head. "I'm not. But, if I'm gonna have your back, I gotta know why you wrote them and why you didn't tell anyone you did."

"You're going to have my back?"

This was going way too slowly. I had to speed things up.

I squeezed her hand. "Yeah, Jane. I'm gonna have your back. But you gotta talk to me. We don't have a lot of time and we don't wanna get caught talking."

"No one ever comes back here," she spoke mostly the truth.

"Duke does, and he's here and avoiding me, so that's a possibility." I squeezed her hand again. "Chickie, spill."

She stared at me.

Then she licked her lips and said softly, "You probably know, since I was a little girl, all I ever wanted to do was write."

When she stopped speaking, I nodded encouragingly and kept hold of her hand.

"Romances," she went on.

"Okay," I said.

"I've written a lot of books, Ally," she told me.

"I know, honey," I replied.

"All romances," she stated.

"Okay."

"Well, mostly romances, some mysteries."

"Right," I said with waning patience, while struggling with not showing my patience was waning.

Her eyes drifted beyond me and she whispered, "And those romances are the best kind ever."

I knew what she was seeing in her mind's eye and I knew she wasn't wrong about that.

She looked back at me. "Real," she said quietly.

"Yeah," I replied.

"But they're more. They're about love of all kinds. They're about family. Family of all kinds."

She wasn't wrong about that, either.

I felt a tickle in my throat and repeated, "Yeah."

"It's extraordinary. So I had to share it, Ally." This time her hand squeezed mine and she leaned toward me. "I *had to.*"

"I feel you," I whispered.

"But, I did it and the first one is out there and it felt good to do it. To finish one. Then the other. And the next. And let it out there. But putting it out there, something happened."

"What happened, babe?" I asked.

"People... readers... they say it makes them laugh." She paused. "Out loud."

I still hadn't read it, but we were a pretty wild bunch. I could see that.

I nodded.

"It's a gift," she said, her voice funny, deep with emotion. "Watching you all get close, witnessing all that happened making you closer, feeling that love. But it was another gift, maybe even a bigger one, *precious,* knowing that sharing it makes people I don't know laugh. It makes them happy. Some of them write to me. They tell me bad things are happening in their lives. But they read my book and it takes them away. It makes them smile. Laugh. Even if for moments, or better yet hours, they can forget the bad, be with us here at Fortnum's, and laugh." She tipped her head to the side. "That's beautiful. So how can it be wrong?"

"It isn't wrong," I told her.

"Lee's angry," she replied.

He was.

Crap.

"Is that why you didn't tell anyone you were going to do it? Because you had a feeling they would be angry?"

She nodded.

Jeez. Jane.

I shared space with her nearly every day, I meant something to her, she meant something to me, but I had no idea her well ran this deep.

"The newspapers?" I pressed.

"That was me," she said quietly. "When stuff was going down with Stella, they called here. I said no comment. Then I sent letters anonymously. The reporter who reported it doesn't even know it's me."

Another mystery solved.

"These readers that write to you. Can that be traced?" I asked and she shook her head.

"They go to somebody else and they send them to me. But I've been assured it's untraceable."

"Brody's pretty good, Jane."

She pressed her lips together.

I studied her. She was worried.

Then I said, "Leave it to me."

Her brows drew together. "What are you going to do?"

"Nothing, until I have to. Then I'll take care of it."

It was her turn to stare at me before she asked, "Why are you helping me?"

I smiled and gave her hand another squeeze before I lifted it up between us and got closer.

"Because, no matter how old we get, we always need to believe in fairytales."

It was then, Jane smiled back.

Mostly, I knew, because she agreed with me.

⧓

"Oh my God, Herb!"

"What?"

"My God!"

"Woman! What?"

"You might wanna leave some for the other guests."

I took a handful of cashews (Indy's addition to the party and part of what Herb was gobbling up) and popped a few into my mouth, watching Roxie's Mom and Dad (and Tex's sister and brother-in-law), Herb and Trish—in town from Indiana for the big event—fight in Blanca's backyard.

Don't be alarmed. I'd been around them more than once. This was what they did.

Blanca was Eddie and Hector's Mom. I'd known her ages, and when she did something, she went all out.

Tonight, even though this was "just family" (for Rock Chicks though, this meant a huge shindig), Blanca didn't let the team down.

There were bright colored paper lanterns strung in zigzags in the air from house to fence posts across the backyard. There were lit lumieres lining the fence all around. There was low music playing, all love songs, in English and Spanish. There were tables groaning with food, and in the middle were large, bright bouquets of flowers (the flowers, Sadie's contribution). Blanca had even set up a bar where her eldest son, Carlos, teamed up with Willie Moses, were making people drinks.

Jet had made caramel layer squares (three batches). As I mentioned, Indy had brought the cashews. Ren and I brought a mixed box full of bottles of liquor and a couple cases of beer. Roxie, Stella and Sadie had spent the morning helping Blanca and her daughters Rosa, Gloria and Elena in setting up and cooking.

Tex, wearing another suit (and for once, seemingly content in it), and Nancy, wearing a pretty mint green dress with a fancy thing that was kind of a hat but way smaller so it was mostly a decorated headband (and it had a cool-ass feather) got hitched earlier by the Justice of the Peace. They did this while Indy, Duke and I stood by Tex, and Trixie, Ada (Nancy's old neighbor, and by "old" I mean that in two ways) and Blanca stood up with Nancy. Jet and Lottie, by the way, Nancy's daughters, walked at her sides guiding her to Tex.

The deed done, it was time to party.

My favorite time.

And now Herb and Trish were, as ever, going at it.

Herb looked at the table where he had been stuffing his mouth (a table covered in food) to another table five feet away that was also covered in food then across the yard to yet another table which was—you guessed it—covered in food.

Then he looked to his wife. "It's not like Blanca's gonna run out."

"You don't eat from *the bowl,* Herb," Trish shot back. "You get a plate and you *never* double dip."

"First, I don't need a plate when I can stand here eatin'," Herb replied. "And second, I don't got cooties. Who cares if I double dip?"

Gross.

"I do," Trish retorted, and I bit back my verbal agreement.

He glared at her.

Then he declared, "I need a beer."

"You've already had five," Trish informed him.

"Do we got limits?" he asked.

"You can't get drunk at Tex's wedding like you did at Roxie's," she returned.

"Why the hell not?" he asked.

"Because it's rude," she answered

"It's a party!" he pointed out loudly.

Surprisingly, Trish had no reply to that. Then again, Herb was absolutely right.

Herb stormed off.

Trish turned to me. "Roxie told me you've found yourself a man."

"I have, Mrs. Logan," I confirmed.

"Run," she stated then huffed away.

When she did, Jules moved in, noting, "The requisite Herb and Trish scene."

I grinned at her. "I'm kinda bummed it happened so soon and didn't last very long."

She grinned back at me then reached for some cashews.

As she did, a thought occurred to me and I went with it.

"Hey, Jules, can I talk to you about something?"

She popped the cashews in her mouth, chewed, swallowed and answered, "Sure."

"I'm worried about Darius," I told her.

When I said that, her eyes scanned the crowd and mine did, too. What I took in was the fact that we were only an hour into the party portion of the festivities, but both Darius and Jane, who attended the nuptials and showed at Blanca's, were gone.

I also saw Ren smiling down at a talking Roxie who was standing next to an also-smiling-down-at Roxie Hank. My brother (as usual) had his wife tucked close to his side.

Warmth (or more warmth; since I took my spot next to Duke to stand up with Tex, I was pretty suffused with warmth) spread through me.

"He's bailed," Jules noted, and I tore my eyes off my man and looked at her.

"Yeah. He always bails," I said. "The question is, *why?* He's safe here. The people here care about him. He cares about the people here. So why does he accept our acceptance but stay on the fringe?"

Jules didn't even consider this question before she spoke.

"Vance told me about him," she said softly. "He said his father was murdered because of something his brother-in-law was into. He had nothing to do with it. It was a warning."

"I know," I told her, and I did. I knew all of Darius's fucked up sad story.

"Vance also said that this Leon guy, Shirleen's dead husband, offered Darius a chance at retribution, along with providing for his family, if he got involved in Leon's business," Jules went on.

"I know that, too," I replied. "And he was young and made a stupid decision and got caught up in that. But now he's not in that anymore, Jules, and hasn't been for a while. But he acts like..." I shook my head. "I don't know. Like he doesn't belong when he does. He always has. When given the chance, and I'll admit, he didn't give us many—but he stayed close to Lee and Eddie—but when we had the chance, we always acted like he belonged. Shirleen slid right in. I don't know why Darius won't let himself do that. And that's just it. He won't *let himself*."

A gravelly voice came from our sides, answering my question. "He hasn't atoned."

Surprised, I looked up at Duke. And I was not only surprised at what he said, but that he was anywhere near me.

"Can I steal Ally?" he asked Jules.

Oh shit.

"Sure," Jules answered, eyeing us both.

Duke curved his fingers around my bicep.

I looked at Jules and asked, "Can you just keep a professional eye on Darius? I'm trying to figure out a way to get in there and maybe you can help."

"No problem," she said on a smile. "Happy to."

Duke let me get that in then led me away—*far* away from the happy, laughing, talking, boisterous crowd to its very edge by the fence gate.

When he stopped us, he took his hand from my arm.

I took a deep breath and looked up at him.

"Duke—"

"Dolores and I had a son," he announced, and I snapped my mouth shut.

I didn't know that.

No clue.

Oh fuck.

I didn't like how this was starting.

"He was on his bike, ridin' around in the street in front of our house one afternoon, and he was hit by drunk driver."

Oh *fuck*.

That I didn't only not like, I fucking hated it.

"He was eight," Duke went on.

Oh my God.

"Duke," I whispered.

"Dolores, she had a time of it throughout the pregnancy, and she was in labor for seventy-eight hours. Finally, both her and my boy in distress, they took him. But I almost lost them both."

Oh my God.

"So obviously," he continued. "I wasn't big on gettin' her knocked up again. Dolores wanted more. I wouldn't hear of it." He stared at me hard. "In the end, he was all we had."

"I didn't know," I said quietly.

"No one does. Except Ellen. That's why we dropped out. Left Cali. Came home. And probably Lee knows, since he checks out everything. But he also keeps his mouth shut when he needs to."

I nodded.

"It was afternoon, Ally," he told me.

"What?" I asked.

"My Joshua got all his bones broke, his insides mashed, his head caved in by some guy who spent his day gettin' soused and got behind the wheel of a car *in the afternoon*. What kid can't be safe ridin' around on the streets in front of his house in the fuckin' afternoon?"

I shook my head because I didn't have the answer to that. "It doesn't make sense."

He nodded. "It sure the fuck doesn't."

I said nothing.

Duke did. "It wasn't too late. We could try again. But it broke us, both of us. Nearly lost Dolores. She couldn't bear any memory of him, even me. But we got past it, left the life we shared with our boy, and decided not to try again. But it left a hole, Ally. A hole that I didn't think could be filled, losin' my kid, not havin' another one. I bloody gaping hole."

"I get that," I whispered.

"And it was filled when you and Indy came into my life."

My stomach shifted back like I'd been punched just as my heart squeezed.

"You two, so fuckin' nuts, hangin' with Ellen at the store, always gettin' into trouble. Fell in love with you both the minute I laid eyes on you."

My eyes burning, my voice croaky, I said, "Duke."

"So you, out there on your own, doin' dangerous shit, not talkin' to your family about it, your friends, *me*..." He shook his head. "Pissed me off."

Now I understood. God, I understood.

"I'm so sorry," I said gently.

"I was worried about you."

Wanting to touch him, unsure if I should but regardless, paralyzed with the pain of hearing everything he said, I just stood there and repeated, "I'm so sorry."

"But then word got out about what happened at Lincoln's. Tex told me everything. He wouldn't have told you, but he was proud of you, girl. Nearly crowin' about it. Said you knew exactly what you were doin'. Said, top to toe, through and through, you're a Nightingale."

My throat closed.

Freaking *loved* Tex.

"It was then," he carried on, "I realized that there would come a time in Joshua's life, a time me and Dolores didn't get to, when we'd have to let go. We'd have to let him be his own man. Live his own life. And it was then I realized I'd been an ass because I was pissed at you, but I had to let you do the same thing."

"Right," I replied, my voice still husky.

"So I gotta do that and stand by you. Not be pissed. You left that message, it took me a while and Dolores reamed my ass, but here I am, suckin' it up to apologize for bein' pissed-off instead of givin' you the freedom to fly."

I said nothing again. Just swallowed (hard) and nodded.

"Now, sayin' that, you be careful and you come to me whenever you need me."

"Okay, Duke," I forced out through a tight throat.

"Whenever you need me, Ally."

I nodded.

He stared at me.

I let him then whispered, "Love you, Duke."

"Same," he grunted.

That made me smile. It trembled but I did it.

"Now, Darius," he stated then cleared his throat, and I knew we were moving on and I was freaking grateful for it.

"Yeah?" I prompted.

"Scored dark marks in his own soul, darlin'."

"I know, Duke, but—"

He shook his head and I shut up.

"I been watchin'. That boy isn't on the path to redemption. What he's doin' is bidin' his time and givin' himself that time to be with the people who mean somethin' to him. Doin' it knowin' that's as good as he's gonna get, 'cause what he's facin' is damnation and he can't do a thing about it."

My back went straight. "That isn't true."

"You're right. It isn't. That doesn't mean that man doesn't believe it down to his bones."

Shit.

"Your challenge," he got closer to me, "*our* challenge, is to convince him differently."

"How do we do that?" I asked.

"Two choices. We do what we're doin' and hope he wakes up, looks around and understands he's not thinkin' right. Or we snap him out of it."

"I'm for the snapping him out of it option," I mumbled.

"Me too," Duke replied.

"Okay, how do we do that?" I asked.

"Hell if I know," he answered.

Great.

"I just know in dealin' with you women, there's always the time, the right time when you can do somethin' that'll get through the walls, seed, bud and grow, and that's when you plant the wisdom. So we just gotta wait for the right time to plant that seed."

I nodded because this was sage. He was right and I'd watched him do it time and again with the Rock Chicks so I also knew it worked.

It sucked. I was losing patience with this and didn't want to have to exercise more.

But he was right.

"Thanks, Duke."

He jerked up his chin before he looked across the yard and muttered, "Best get back to Dolores."

"Okay."

He looked back at me. "You're a good kid, Ally."

I smiled at him but warned, "Thanks. But if you make me want to cry again, I'm kicking you in the shin."

He shook his head, mouth twitching, and sauntered away.

I was about to hightail my ass to the bar and order a tequila shooter from Willie when I was suddenly set upon by Roam and Sniff.

I looked at the two teenagers.

Roam and Sniff had been runaways that Jules talked into her shelter. She then grew close to them. So close, Roam took a bullet for her in an attempt to save her life.

After that, Shirleen took them under her wing and they'd been living with her since. And when I said "took them under her wing," I meant she treated them like they were her own. In other words, she mothered them as only Shirleen would do. With sassy tough love.

But the operative word in that was *love.*

Roam was a tall African American kid who'd always been good-looking. So it wasn't a surprise that as the months passed, he got a might taller, bulked out, the boy started leaking out of his features and they were becoming all man, and he was hitting downright handsome.

What was a surprise was that Sniff, always small, skinny with a face riddled with acne, bloomed late. With Shirleen feeding him and getting him to a dermatologist, he was no longer skinny and his face had cleared up. But he'd hit a growth spurt and shot up five inches. Not only that, his features were also maturing and doing it well. *Very* well. So a kid that was always clever and funny now was giving his best bud a run for his money in the looks department.

Seriously.

They still hung with Jules often, but they got their male influence by hanging with Vance as well as the Hot Bunch. They spent a lot of time at Nightingale Investigations, worked the surveillance room, did ride alongs and worked out with the guys.

They loved it, totally got off on it in a way that it was not hard to predict their future careers, and this would be proved irrevocably with what would happen next.

"Got a minute, Ally?" Roam asked as both boy-men affected a huddle with me.

"Yep," I answered, examining them closely.

Total badasses-in-training. Their faces gave nothing away.

"We heard you're workin' the Smithie gig," Sniff stated.

Oh man.

I tensed and repeated, "Yep."

"The guys were talkin' at the offices," Sniff went on. "Overheard them sayin' you're workin' the bouncer angle."

I wasn't working anything just yet. But I didn't tell them that. I just nodded.

"So we're lookin' at the girls," Roam declared.

I fought rolling my eyes. They were both seventeen, nearly eighteen. So I was not shocked that they'd take this stripper job opportunity to "look at" a bunch of strippers.

"Boys—" I started.

"Just listen, Ally, yeah?" Sniff coaxed.

I studied him a beat and nodded.

"We still got school so we can't do much, but Sniff took some, I took others, and after school we followed them," Roam told me.

I didn't know if this was good or bad. I just knew they'd been around the Hot Bunch not a little but a lot, so they probably weren't doing stupid shit.

I also wanted to know what they saw.

So I prompted, "And?"

"And, I saw one hand over an envelope to your bouncer guy," Roam stated. "Had binoculars, saw the guy look through the envelope. Lots of bills. Ones, fives, tens."

"Tip money," I said quietly.

"Can't get in the club so don't know her take, but my guess, yeah," Roam replied.

Why would a dancer be giving this guy her tip money?

"He's got somethin' on 'em," Sniff answered my question and I focused on him. "Don't know what and Roam only saw that one hand over her cash, but that's what we reckon."

"You see these women do anything else?" I asked. "Anything that he might be making them do? Anything that he might be holding over them?"

350

I got two negative shakes.

Crap.

"You want us to stay on 'em?" Sniff asked.

"Only if Shirleen knows you're doing it and she's cool with that," I answered.

They looked at each other then they looked at me.

Sniff grinned.

Roam looked focused.

But I knew from their reactions that Shirleen would say it was okay. Then again, she was raising badasses who she would prefer used their badassness for good rather than evil, so she wouldn't say no.

I lifted my hand and waved it out in a "move along" gesture. "Go forth, get permission, keep your eyes on these girls and report in to me frequently. If you don't already have it, get my number from Shirleen."

This got me nods.

"And keep Darius in the loop," I added.

More nods.

"Thanks, guys," I finished.

Another grin from Sniff. A chin jerk from Roam.

Jeez.

Roam chin jerking.

Save me.

They took off.

I hit the bar.

I'd just downed my tequila shooter when an arm wrapped around my belly from behind, a pair of lips touched my neck and my man's voice sounded in my ear, "Havin' fun?"

I turned in the curve of his arm, looked up at him and nodded. "Yeah. You?"

"Mm-hmm," he mumbled and his eyes slid down to my chest. "Best part is watchin' you in this dress."

It was a wedding, but still, I went clingy, baring and sexy.

It was my way.

This time though, not black. Lavender

"I aim to please," I told him.

"You do well," he replied.

I smiled.

He bent in and touched his lips to mine.

"*Herb!*" we heard snapped (loudly) from across the yard.

Good news.

Trish felt the need for round two.

Leaning into Ren, I turned my attention to the Midwestern contingent of our posse just as Tex boomed, "Jesus Jones, woman, leave him be!"

"Ugh! Why am I surprised? You men stick together!" Trish shouted back.

"My people are Italian, loud and fuckin' crazy," Ren whispered to me. "And still, your people beat mine by a mile."

I looked up at him. "I know. Aren't we lucky?"

Ren shook his head.

Then he smiled.

Since most people had plastic cups, three hours later when Blanca wanted everyone's attention, she held up a filled margarita pitcher and tapped it with a long thin spoon.

As the crowd quieted and turned her way, she announced, "Lee has something to say."

Standing in the curve of Ren's arm, having just been shooting the shit with Stella, Mace and Shirleen, we all turned our attention to Lee, who was holding a bottle of beer in one hand, Indy close to his side in the curve of his other arm.

Incidentally, Indy had a can of Fresca.

Lee didn't delay.

"Two years ago, I met Tex while he was assisting my now pregnant wife with a B&E."

There were giggles and chuckles and out-and-out laughter, but Lee kept going.

"Not long after that, he saved her life."

Everyone quit laughing.

"Since then, a load of shit has gone down. As it did, we always knew two things. One, we'd wouldn't be able to guess what mayhem would happen next.

Two, Tex would be there." Lee pinned Tex with his eyes and stated, "We knew Tex would always be there."

Oh shit. My eyes were getting hot again.

Lee kept going.

"I've learned in the last two years that when life gets rough, and even when it doesn't, the best thing a man can have is a good woman at his side."

I looked to Indy to see she was pressing her lips together.

Just like me.

"So if there was anything I wished for you, Tex," Lee continued. "The kind of man you are, the kind who deserves it, I wished that for you. So we'll just say I'm fuckin' pleased you found her and tied her to your side today." He lifted his bottle. "May you have many years with her right there. To Tex and Nancy!"

Everyone looked to Tex, who was holding Nancy close, and she was leaning into him doing the same, smiling the knockout smile she gave her daughter with tears wetting her cheeks. We all lifted our drinks and many (including me, but not Ren) shouted, "To Tex and Nancy!"

Once we'd thrown some back, we found Lee wasn't done and he was still looking Tex and Nancy's way.

"Now, Luke and Ava couldn't be here, but they wanted to give you something to celebrate. And Ava told me the best thing they could give you was something you'd appreciate. Something loud and possibly obnoxious, but definitely spectacular. So here's your gift from Luke and Ava, gone for now but here in spirit." He then turned and shouted toward the back fence beyond which was an alley, "*Go!*"

He barely said the word before we heard a shrieking whiz.

And over Blanca's festive backyard, with a loud boom, a huge firework exploded.

There were oo's and ah's.

Then came another.

And another.

And another.

Then more, *tons* more, the night sky lit up with beauty, and jeez, Luke and Ava spared no expense.

It was amazing.

As it kept going though, I tore my eyes from the display and looked Tex and Nancy's way.

The big man still held his wife close and Nancy still leaned heavily into him, but their heads were tipped back, colors lighting their face.

And warmth so sweet it was difficult to process stole through me.

This was because Tex was smiling.

And completely happy.

Chapter 25

Tush

"Well?"

That was me, the afternoon after Tex and Nancy's wedding, standing on Daisy's stripper stage at her house, wearing a robe Daisy just threw over my shoulders that I'd pushed my arms through, tying the belt tight.

Daisy had suggested, and I agreed, that before I stepped onstage that night that I do my thing in front of a live audience so that I wouldn't be breaking that particular seal in front of, well... a live audience.

This meant that sitting around Daisy's stage in chairs she got Marcus's boys to drag in were Indy, Jet, Roxie, Stella, Sadie, Daisy, Shirleen, Annette, Tod, Buddy, Lottie, Nancy, Ada, Smithie and one of Smithie's three women (yes, *three*; don't ask, just know it works) LaTeesha.

"Jumpin' Jehosphats!" Annette shouted. "I wanna be a stripper again!"

"That. Was. *Awesome*," Indy breathed.

"Blooming heck, I don't even know what to say. That was *aces*," Sadie put in.

"Child, you do the sisterhood proud," Shirleen told me.

"I might add a striptease to my stage show," Stella announced.

"I think I turned ungay for about two minutes," Buddy murmured.

After all these compliments, Daisy gushed, "Momma's so proud," on a sideways hug.

But I knew the girls (and gay guy) would give me props.

So I only had eyes for Smithie.

"Smithie?" I called as he stared up at me, face blank. "What did you think?"

"Please," he whispered and I blinked because I'd never heard Smithie whisper. "Dance for me full-time."

Righteous!

He liked it.

"Will it work?" I asked and he stood.

"Bitch, it not only works, I'm givin' you the stage for your own fuckin' song," he declared.

Oh shit.

Dancing with a bunch of other dancers who might take attention off me was one thing.

Dancing like Lottie danced as the headliner, having the stage all to myself and all eyes on me, was a-fucking-nother.

"Uh…" I mumbled.

"Excellent idea!" LaTeesha proclaimed on a big white smile and a clap.

"You totally have to do that!" Lottie cried.

"That would be sofa-king *phat,* sister!" Annette exclaimed.

Tod was giving me a sideways look, reading me, I knew, when he turned to me full-on and decreed, "You do know, if you're only dancing for a song, you can spend the rest of your time keeping your eye on things, talking to the other girls, getting the job done and…" he paused, *"only dancing for a song."*

"Three songs," Smithie announced and looked at Lottie. "She's lead in for you on all your sets."

"Works for me," Lottie replied to Smithie and turned to grin at me.

Shit.

"Decided!" Smithie yelled and pointed to me. "Three songs. You pick. Get me the music. I'll get it to the DJ. You start tonight. Lottie's first set is at nine. You go on at eight fifty-five. Be fuckin' ready."

My heart started beating. Hard.

Smithie turned to LaTeesha and pulled her out of her chair, murmuring, "Come on, baby. Gotta get you to work."

After LaTeesha sent us a finger wave, they were gone.

I jumped off the stage, taking my life into my hands because I was wearing platform stripper shoes, and the gang gathered around.

"I sure do wish I was fifty years younger and I could strip," Ada fortunately noted, and this was fortunately because her doing it cut through my nerves and made me smile.

"I'm sorry I'm going to miss your debut, honey," Nancy said to me then smiled her gorgeous smile, "But I gotta get home to my hubby. A hubby, incidentally, who has stated he has your back with anything you want to do, but is not about to watch you strip."

Tex not being there worked for me.

I moved my smile to her then everyone moved as we heard Daisy order, "Make way! Make way!"

They made way and I saw Daisy coming through carrying a big red box with a huge black satin bow.

She plopped it on the stage, turned to me and declared, "We all got together to get you these."

"Let's hope this case doesn't go long or she'll need more." I heard Tod whisper. "Then again, maybe not. They were fun to shop for."

But I was looking at the box because I loved presents and I wasn't particular about what was inside.

I reached out and yanked on the end of the bow. It came undone and slithered away. I flipped the top open, dug through the tissue and caught my breath as I unearthed all that was inside.

Laying the last bit out, I breathed a reverent, *"Righteous."*

"They're perfect, aren't they?" Indy asked.

They were. Beyond perfect, whatever that was.

"I'd use some of those for my stage show, too. If I didn't think Kai would lose his freaking mind, that is," Stella whispered.

Sadie giggled.

I touched one of the pieces.

"You'll do great," Daisy said softly to me.

I looked at her, let my breath out, then turned to the group. I lifted both hands, fingers extended in devil's horns, and shouted, "Rock on!"

Everyone gave me a devil's horn, "Rock on!" back.

Even Ada.

<hr>

Lottie and I sat in the dressing room at Smithie's.

The back of my neck was prickling and bad.

This was not because I was there, in one of the three new outfits the girls gave me, ready to strip (very soon). Nor was it because I knew the gang was all outside and some of them had not yet seen my performance (though, it should be noted, none of the men were there; not one, including Ren, thank God). It also wasn't because Smithie and Lottie had introduced me to all the girls, the bouncers, the waitresses and bartenders, because they were all cool.

No. This was because something bad was going down.

Not a little badass'll-fix-it kind of bad.

357

Something big.

If I were to say the girls were subdued, what I would mean was, they were *subdued.* They smiled, they were nice, but they did their jobs, took care in their whispered conversations, and fear permeated the air.

And none of this had anything to do in any visible way with bad guy bouncer, Dan Steiner.

I'd met him and I got it immediately. Friendly, eye contact, lots of smiles and an impressive-seemingly-genuine, "Don't worry. The guys got your back. You feel trouble, just give us a heads up."

Smooth. No red flags. No warning signs. He didn't even give me a once-over.

Totally professional, even as my gut and the look he could not hide behind his friendly smile told me: totally bogus.

"I'm not liking this," I whispered to Lottie.

"Told you," she whispered back. "It's bad."

"How long has it been going on?" I asked.

"Steiner started about three months ago and this shit started, I don't know, maybe a month after that."

"Slow or fast?" I asked.

"What?" she asked back.

"He go girl for girl or did he take them all at once?"

She thought about it and said, "Slow. Girl for girl, I guess."

"You see any money change hands back here or anywhere?" I went on.

She shook her head.

I looked across the dressing room at Meena, one of the strippers who was on break and re-oiling. She wasn't avoiding us, but although she smiled and waved when she walked in, she hadn't approached for any small talk.

"He's not targeted you because of your cop and Nightingale connection," I deduced.

"Yeah," she replied.

"And he's also keeping the girls clear of you because of the same thing," I said.

"You think?" she asked. I looked from Meena to her and nodded. "That makes sense," she concluded.

"Which means whatever they have on their minds, whatever talk they do, they do it when you're not around so you don't overhear them."

"Yeah, probably," she agreed.

"So with my last name, I'm fucked. And with the fear these girls have *and* my last name, no way we're gonna get one to wear a wire."

"Mm-hmm," she mumbled.

Crap.

This meant we had two choices.

Since the girls were never going to talk to me, my being undercover was a bust. We'd have to abort, find another woman to go undercover and possibly alert Steiner to our activities because of it. Worse, this would cause an unacceptable delay and make these women live in fear for even longer.

Or I had to make the girls talk to me.

Which meant I had to find a way to make the girls trust me.

And the only way I could do that was become one of their own.

As if on cue, there was a knock on the door and when Meena called out, "Decent!" Lenny, one of Smithie's bouncers, stuck his head in.

"Five minutes, Ally," he said to me and his head disappeared.

Shit, shit, *fuck.*

Lottie reached out and squeezed my knee. "You're gonna be great."

"Mm-hmm," I mumbled, straightening from my chair.

Lottie grabbed my robe and we headed out.

"Knock 'em dead," Meena encouraged, smiling at me as we passed her.

"I'm just hoping not to puke on any of them," I told her honestly, and her smile got bigger.

"We all felt that way the first time," she informed me. "And we all got over it. You'll be fine."

Right.

We headed out and Lottie led me backstage. Through a small part in the curtain I could see the dancers gyrating and I felt bile slide up my throat.

Lottie got close. "Breathe deep," she advised.

I breathed deep.

The bile went away. The nerves didn't.

"Two minutes, fifteen seconds, and it's over," she told me.

That was right. Two minutes, fifteen seconds then I was off the stage.

Though, my second song was longer.

Shit!

The place went dark and I felt the girls run by us, coming off stage.

Shit, shit, *fuck!*

That was when I heard Smithie's voice coming loud, saying into a microphone, "You're all in for a fuckin' treat tonight! We're debuting a new act. So put your eyes to the stage, put your hands together and welcome *the Rock Chick!*"

More darkness.

Lottie gave me a shove through the curtain and I walked through the dark, passing Smithie who muttered, *"Fuck,"* into the microphone as he tripped over the cord on the way out.

By rote, I went to my mark, in my head saying over and over again, *two minutes, fifteen seconds, two minutes, fifteen seconds.*

Then out loud, I whispered, "You can do this Ally."

But I knew it didn't matter. I could pep talk myself for another year.

I wasn't going to be able to do it.

That's when the guitars blared, the scratchy-fast *"Yea,"* hit, the lights came up, blinding me, and it happened.

It was like someone flipped a switch.

And the switch they flipped was rock 'n' roll.

Specifically, ZZ Top's "Tush."

I just started to move, everything Lottie and Daisy taught me flowing through my veins.

And then some.

I strutted. I squatted. I wiggled. I crouched low with one leg straight out to my side, slapped the stage and tossed my hair back as I pushed my breasts forward. I slithered. I undulated. I swung my black leather, *short*-shorts covered ass out and I did it wide.

Then I tore off the black tee that was cut off under my breasts and was held together at my shoulders by safety pins and tossed it aside, exposing a black bra with black and silver sequins.

Right after that, I ran on my black leather studded stripper platforms toward a pole, launched myself high, caught it, swung around, legs parted, and I felt a hush roll over the crowd.

I curled in, flipping my legs up high, well over my head and torso, straddling the pole, legs still wide, sliding down until I got near the bottom.

Once there, I put one hand down, then the other, swung out one leg, then the other until I was in a backbend. I pushed up off my hands to come to standing.

Immediately, I went into a squat, came up, swung my ass again while my fingers undid the heavy silver buckle of my studded black belt and I slid my shorts over my ass, hips, down my legs. I kicked them free and I was in black and silver sequined leather undies cut high in the back so they showed some cheek.

It was then I felt—actually *felt*—the crowd come to their feet.

In my platforms and sequined undies, I ran from pole to pole. Catching one, flipping over, wrapping my legs around it, letting go with my hands and arching my neck and back as I slid down, using only my legs until my hands hit stage.

A modified cartwheel then a run and grasp of the next pole, twisting around and around it at a dizzying pace, one leg curled around the pole, one leg held straight out.

Back to the next one where I caught it high and swung all the way out from my hands, toes pointed, legs spread wide and ended it curling in and doing a flip off the pole to land on my feet, ass near to the ground, knees bent high, legs spread and I slapped the stage with my hand between my legs.

I pulled out of that deep squat and strutted back up the stage with super-long strides, one foot in front of the other like the most kickass model in the history of models after she bitch-slapped all the other models before she hit the runway.

Too soon, way too soon, I heard the song winding down and right when the final guitar riff hit, I reached behind my back with one hand as I reached up my front with the other. I flicked the clasp at my back and yanked the bra away just as the guitars faded.

The lights went dark.

I ran offstage and Lottie was there to throw my robe around my shoulders. I shoved my arms through and pulled it closed.

That was when I heard it.

Nothing.

Silence.

Shit.

What the fuck?

On that thought, it happened.

A wave of sound so strong, no fucking joke, it nearly knocked both of us over.

The kind of sound I'd only heard at a rock concert.

Clapping, shouting, hooting, hollering, catcalling, feet stamping, hands slapping tables and finally a chant of, "*Rock Chick! Rock Chick! Rock Chick!*"

My wide eyes went to a smiling-huge Lottie just as she framed my face with both her hands, got close, and whispered, "Welcome to the sisterhood, baby."

She touched her lips to mine just as we heard Smithie shout over the wild-ass, out-of-control ovation, "Knew you motherfuckers would like that! Now, get a load of Lottie Mac!"

Lottie dashed onto the stage.

Smithie came off.

And before I knew it, I was in his arms, held there tight.

"Knew that was hard. It's always hard. But you did that for me and my girls. And you did me proud. Thank you, darlin'," he whispered in my ear.

Before I could even blink, definitely before I could begin to process his heartfelt words, he was gone.

I watched the place where he disappeared for two beats before I walked into the hall and down it to the dancers-only bathroom. Buzzing so big I felt like I was vibrating, adrenaline sluicing through my system, I entered and thankfully found it empty.

I walked to the sink and stared at my face in the mirror made up in full-on slut, my hair curled and teased out *to there.*

I did this for a long time.

Then I whispered, "Fuck yeah. I'm a goddamned, fuckin' *rock chick.*"

I just caught my own huge-ass smile before I turned from the mirror and sashayed out of the bathroom in order to keep doing my job.

⚡

Being quiet because it was dark, late and I saw by the moonlight lighting the room that he was asleep in bed, I entered Ren's and my bedroom.

I bent to my shoes to take them off, just as a light came on and lit the room.

I straightened and looked to the bed to see Ren pushing up to lounge against the headboard, hair tousled (hot) but not looking sleepy (weird).

"Hey," I whispered like he was still asleep. "Sorry I woke you."

He said nothing. He just looked at me.

This was strange and a little scary. He knew what I was doing that night and he'd been cool about it. He said nothing. He asked nothing. He didn't even give me any looks where his jaw was clenched or his lips were tight.

Now, the deed was done and he knew it'd been done.

So maybe he was no longer feeling like ignoring it or letting it go. Maybe he was feeling like reacting to it. Maybe in a not so good way. Maybe in an Italian American hotheaded macho alpha way.

Before I could ask, he twisted, stretched out an arm and grabbed something from his nightstand. He only had it in his hand for a second when he started to lounge back. But before he got into position, I froze, a chill running over my skin.

This was because "Tush" started playing from the Bose dock on his nightstand.

Fuck.

"Someone told you," I guessed.

He shook his head.

ZZ Top rocked on as I stared at him.

Then, my throat closing on the words, I asked, "You were there?"

"Absolutely," he answered. "You think I'd miss that?"

Oh shit.

Oh fuck.

Shit!

"I thought——" I started.

"Baby, you take your clothes off right now, you do it to this song, for me. My guess, those four posts'll hold. If you break the bed, I don't give a fuck."

I just stared.

"You want me to start the song again?" he offered.

What was happening?

"I——" I began.

"Christ, you were so fuckin' hot up there, I'm still hard."

Oh my *God!*

He kept going.

"I'm gettin' that my woman puts her mind to something, everyone better watch their ass. Because whatever she's got a mind to do, she's gonna kick *its* ass."

Relief flooded through me, along with something else. Maybe a lot of something else's. His words singing straight to my soul, I dashed to Ren's side of the bed and launched myself, landing on Ren.

His arms closed around me instantly and he rolled us so I was on my back and he was on me.

He lifted his head and looked into my eyes.

"Don't remember you dancin' horizontally, honey," he noted.

"That kind of dancing is just for you."

I just caught his sexy, gorgeous smile before I closed my eyes because he kissed me.

After that, we had a whole load of horizontal fun through "Tush," "Sharp Dressed Man," "Gimme All Your Lovin'," "Legs" and then some.

And Ren only paused the fun to grab the remote and turn the music up.

Chapter 26

Not a Towel Throwing Type of Girl

My ass on Ren's counter, Ren leaning against the counter kitty corner from me, I looked up from my plate and saw my man's eyes on me.

They were probing.

"What?" I asked.

"You good?" he asked back.

"Yeah," I answered, confused. "Why wouldn't I be?"

"You got in last night at three. I kept you up a fuckuva lot later. It's not even seven, but you look fine and you got hardly any sleep."

"You didn't either," I reminded him.

"Yeah," he agreed. "And I'm draggin'."

He didn't look like he was dragging. He looked like Ren. Confident, even just standing there eating. And hot (of course).

"How do you do it?" he asked.

I shrugged and turned my attention to my eggs. "Live the rock star life, babe. Have for a while." I forked up some eggs, chewed, swallowed, looked at him and grinned. "Sleep is overrated."

He grinned back and took his plate to the sink. After I ate my final strawberry, he took mine and it joined his.

Then he got in position between my legs, arms around me, so I wrapped mine around him.

"What's up for your day?" he queried.

"Go make coffee. Go over office furniture catalogues with Daisy. Try to make inroads with finding out what's bugging Darius. Strip. Hit some tweaker houses with Hector and Tex to see if we can crack the case of the Highland burglaries. Come home to my man." I tipped my head to the side. "You?"

"Power play day," he stated strangely then asked, "Find out what's bugging Darius?"

"Yeah. Something's up with him. He's got issues. I'm gonna sort them out," I told him. "But what's power play day?"

"Vito and I got into it yesterday."

I felt my head jerk right before I fired questions at him. "What? Why? When? Why didn't you tell me?"

"You had your stripping debut last night. I figured you had shit on your mind so I'm tellin' you now," he replied.

"Okay," I gave that to him because it was sweet. "Then what? And why?"

He sighed and got closer to me.

"He's pushin' for a decision, that decision namely bein' me changin' my mind. He knows what's goin' down with you and me and he's scramblin' to get me further in the fold before what I got with you turns me irrevocably. His problem is that he isn't realizin' that that turn has already been made. We had words. Dom's tryin' to keep things smooth and I'll give it to him, he's tryin', and I respect that. But Vito doesn't respect Dom much and is makin' that clearer and clearer by the day. Dom isn't liking that. He's towed the line for some time and Vito's not cuttin' him any slack. It's a faulty play. But Dom now has a family, and Sissy and him are lookin' at tryin' to grow that family so I'm gettin' the sense Dom's rethinking things, same as me. Way Vito's acting, he's turnin' Dom, too."

Wow.

Interesting.

"So what does power play mean?" I asked.

He started to run his hand up and down my back and I worried this was soothingly, telling me to brace, but I would find with what he said next it was just affectionately, something I liked a whole lot better.

"I was gonna just walk away. Still not happy about him showin' up at your parents, and that was part Vito, part him makin' a statement to me about who's the boss of this family. With that and him pushin', if he doesn't back off and let that happen, I'll make this hard on him and everybody."

"How?"

"Because I'm clean. Not squeaky, but I'm clean," he explained. "And because of that, should something happen to him or Dom, they needed the legitimate holdings to be clean with the understanding that someone would take care of families. What that means is, we got an LLC but it's not a partnership.

I'm the only name on it. So the cops or Feds couldn't seize our assets if someone went down."

Wow again.

That was freaking smart. Then again, so was my man.

Ren kept going.

"This also means my name is on everything. Everything we own as well as the office lease. We got no board to answer to. The only thing tying me to Vito's authority is respect. He plays the wrong game, instead of lettin' all that go and walkin' away, I take it all with me. Or, in this case, kick his ass out."

Holy crap.

He was carrying all the chips!

I smiled huge. "Zano, that's awesome."

"He doesn't think I'll do it. He keeps pissin' me off, I will. This is what I'm gonna tell him today."

If Vito didn't think Ren would do it, he was a fool, and that surprised me. Hell, Zach had barely got the chance to get in my face before Ren sorted that situation. My guess was that it was partially Vito, maybe a little of it in his genes, that made Ren not a man you messed with. Therefore, Vito should know better.

"I'm guessing this will be unpleasant," I noted.

"Something's gotta give," Ren replied. "We've been back and forth for a while. I keep thinkin' he'll get his head outta his ass. It feels like he's stallin'." He smiled at me and dipped his face to mine. "But the rest of my life is where I want it." His arms gave me a squeeze indicating (righteously) he was talking about me. "That's the last piece to slot in. I'm impatient to get this shit done."

I repositioned to circle his neck with my arms and offered, "You need to talk or anything, you know how to find me."

"Yeah," he said softy then pulled back an inch and announced, "Goin' with you tonight to do that thing in the Highlands."

I blinked. "What?"

"Goin' with you tonight to do that thing with you in the Highlands," he mostly repeated.

"Zano—"

His face got close again. "Baby, not gettin' in your business. But after last night, wanna watch you do your thing."

That feeling stole through me again because he didn't sound like he was doing this to horn his way in to find a way to protect me, or alternately, find a reason to talk me out of doing it.

He sounded like he was genuinely interested in what I did.

And it had to be said, I was good at what I did, and after his reaction last night, where he gave me absolutely no shit in a situation where any alpha badass would lose his mind, but instead he got off on it, it seemed Ren was coming around.

Spectacularly.

"Right, then you're going with us tonight," I agreed.

He grinned, moved in and kissed me. It was sweet, but short (unfortunately).

He lifted his head and stated, "Find time between one thing and another to have dinner with your man."

Bossy.

But since this was something I wanted too, I nodded.

He gave me a brush on the lips and moved away, saying, "Don't worry about the dishes. I'll rinse 'em then deal with 'em when I get home. We both gotta get goin'."

Another order that I could accept so I nodded again and jumped off the counter.

Ren ran water over the dishes as I prepared travel mugs of coffee for us. We walked out together, Ren locking up after us.

His Jag was at the front of the house (it always was and the street was busy, meaning he might have parking voodoo, too). Mine was across the street and down some (which, without parking voodoo, was a better than average spot for me).

Being Ren, he walked me to my car. Another brush on the lips before he stood with his hand on the door while I folded in.

"Later, babe," I said, my hand on the handle to pull the door closed, but he nor his hand moved. I looked up to him to see him looking down the street. "Zano?" I called.

"You know that guy?" he asked.

I twisted in my seat and looked out the side of my car. I saw nothing but a car driving away.

"What guy?" I asked back and looked up at him.

He was still gazing down the street then he looked down at me. "He got in his car and took off as you were gettin' in yours. You get a look at him at all?"

"No," I answered. "Who was he?"

"Seen him at your apartment building," Ren said, and I felt the skin on the back of my neck prickle. "I'd come over. He'd hear me knock and look out. Four doors down from you."

So that was why Ren was always staring down the hall.

I tried to think who lived four doors down from me and realized I didn't know. I'd known a number of people in my building but who was behind that door wasn't one of them.

"Just thought he was nosy," Ren said and I refocused on him. "But that shit isn't right."

It wasn't.

"I'll call my landlord and see if he'll give me details on who lives there," I told Ren.

"Do that today," Ren bossed me.

I fought an eye roll and murmured, "I'm on it."

He leaned in, gave me another brush on the lips, pulled away and said quietly, "Later, honey."

"Later," I replied.

He slammed the door. I belted up, started her up and took off.

I did this looking in my rearview, watching Ren in his suit sauntering to his car.

And enjoying the view.

⋈

"Ralphie says no," Sadie told us.

It was late morning at Fortnum's and we were sitting in the seating area at the front of the store. Daisy was in with her furniture catalogues. Sadie was in to get coffees for her and Ralphie to take back to her gallery. But Sadie had been corralled into trolling the catalogues (of which all of them, and there were five, had dozens of plastic sticky tabs jutting out the sides).

She'd been sending photos of the furniture Daisy had narrowed it down to (with the word "narrowed" used loosely) to Ralphie.

And Ralphie had so far nixed all the photos.

"What's wrong with that set?" Daisy asked. "It's black. It's class. And it fits in our budget."

"I don't know," Sadie replied. "He just said no."

"That's the seventeenth no," Daisy returned irritably.

"I know. I'm maxing out the memory on my phone," Sadie shared.

Daisy stared at her phone then looked to Sadie. "You got a top of the line phone. How can seventeen photos max it out?"

"Because my guy is Hector Chavez. He's the most handsome man I've ever seen. And we have a dog. Hector plays with Gretl and I take pictures of them. Loads of them." She leaned in. "*Loads.*"

If Ren and I had a dog and his hot guy badass was out playing with her, I'd do the same thing.

That meant we *so* needed a dog.

But in the meantime, I would live vicariously.

So I demanded, "Chickie, let me see."

Sadie shot a smile at me and leaned toward me while hitting her screen with her thumb, but it pinged as she did.

"Photo text from Ralphie," she murmured, hit her screen again then turned her phone to Daisy and me. It had a picture of black office furniture on it that looked like it was a photo of a photo on a computer screen.

"That's it!" Daisy cried.

I studied the photo. It looked like most of the seventeen other choices Ralphie poo-pooed.

Daisy snapped at Sadie with her fingers. "Tell him to order a catalogue from wherever that is."

"Daisy, you know they probably have all the photos on the website. We just need the web address and we won't have to wait on a catalogue," I told her.

"If we don't have a catalogue, we can't put these sticky-tabby things on them," she told me, pointing a long lethal nail at the tagged catalogues.

"That's very true," I replied. "But if you like that, Ralphie likes it, it fits in the budget, you could also order it, say, *today,* and have the freaking *furniture* on its way so you're closer to sitting your ass behind a desk, rather than waiting for catalogues you can put sticky-tabby things in and delay your ass being behind an actual desk."

"Good point," she mumbled and looked at Sadie, "Tell him to send the web address."

Sadie bent to her phone.

The bell over the door rang.

I looked to it to see Eddie coming in. His eyes were aimed to the espresso counter, and I knew he saw Jet when I saw his dimpled smile.

Then his eyes came to me and his smile fled. He lifted his hand and crooked a finger at me before he turned it toward the bookshelves and pointed there.

There was a time when Eddie Chavez crooking his finger at me would make my happy place spasm. Alas, your brother's best friend was off-limits. Not to mention he had a thing for Indy before he lost his heart to Jet. So I had no shot.

Now, him crooking his finger at me and ordering me to the shelves in nonverbal badass I found annoying.

Still, he was championing my cause with Lee and Hank so I figured the least I could do was haul my ass to the shelves.

"Be back," I muttered to the girls and hauled my ass to the shelves.

I didn't know how deep into the bookshelves we needed to be for whatever Eddie had to say so I hedged my bets and stopped at the vinyl in the middle.

It appeared this was satisfactory because Eddie did no more pointing nor did he give me a chin lift or head jerk.

He stopped close to me.

"Bomb guys and police are done goin' through what's left of your apartment. They've released what they could find of your belongings that survived the blast. Hank wasn't around so they gave it to me. It's not much, two boxes, but I'll drop it by Zano's place."

We had to be in the shelves for this?

I didn't ask that.

I said, "Thanks, Eddie."

I then wondered what survived the blast, and hoped it was my *Firefly* series DVD.

"Heard you're gettin' up in Darius's shit," he stated, and I focused on him to see his eyes were intent.

I was wrong. *This* was why we were in the shelves.

"Yes, Eddie, I am. And don't give me any lip about it, all right? You guys need to give each other macho badass space? Fine. But I'm not a macho badass. I'm a girlie badass. And I'm getting into his space."

Eddie made no reply. He just held up his hand, two fingers extended, and between them was a small piece of folded paper.

I took it, unfolded it and saw an address written on it.

"Anyone asks, you didn't get that from me," Eddie said firmly.

I looked up at him. "What is it?"

"You go there, you'll know," he replied mysteriously.

"Eddie, just tell me what it is," I demanded.

"Like I said, *chica,* you go there, you'll know."

"Why the mystery?" I asked.

"Because I worked my ass off for fuckin' years to keep Darius in my life. He's *mi hermano.* What we got, our history, he means a fuckuva lot to me. And if he knows I gave you that, he's a memory to me. I give you more, honest to God, no tellin' what he'd do. So you take that. You go there. You'll know why I gave it to you."

He leaned into me and his voice dropped low.

"But I'm trustin' you, Ally. You go cautious with what you do with what you find out. You fuck this up, we got problems. Hear me?"

Holy crap!

What was at this address?

"You didn't answer me," Eddie prompted.

"Right, big badass cop, I'm standing right here so I heard you. And just to say, I'm tight with Darius too. We also have history. So you saying that shit to me means you don't understand that what I'm trying to do is get him right. *Not* fuck him up further and definitely not drive him away."

Eddie held my eyes then leaned back, lips twitching as he murmured, "Jeez, you've always had balls, Ally."

"No, I don't. I'm a girl. What I've always been is a Rock Chick," I retorted.

"Whatever, same thing" he muttered. "We're done. Gonna go see my wife."

Then without a good-bye (or even a chin lift), he was gone.

I looked down at the slip of paper in my hand.

Then I rearranged my afternoon.

I sat in my car, eyes on the house at the address Eddie gave to me.

It was a new build in Stapleton. Not big. Not small. Well-kept, but then again, in this 'hood, the HOA Nazis wouldn't let it be anything else.

It was late afternoon and I'd sorted what I needed to sort for my night's activities. I'd also called my ex-landlord and got voicemail, but asked for a return call. I also left a voicemail to Brody because I didn't think it was fair to let him keep obsessing about the *Rock Chick* books when the mystery was solved.

I just didn't know exactly what to say to him to get him to stop or if I was going to let that cat out of the bag. And if I did, how to do it at the same time managing damage control.

Coming to no conclusions about any of that, and since nothing was happening on my stakeout and I was curious (okay, worried), I called Ren.

He answered with, "Hey, baby."

"Hey back at cha," I replied. "How's your day?"

"If that's non-invasive Ally Speak for how did things go with Vito, it went shit."

Oh man.

"What happened?" I asked.

"He said if I try to pull our assets from under him, it means war."

Holy shit!

"Oh my God, Ren," I whispered.

"Babe, Vito... he's got a bark *and* he's got a bite. With me, he won't bite. Me and Dom are the only sons he has and there's no mistaking I'm a favorite. That said, it gets down to it, he's also the only father I've had, and he knows that means something to me. He's savin' face. It's bluster. He'll think on this, give me shit, then he'll back off and one of two things will happen. The Zanos will go legit, or we'll go our separate ways. Either way, I'll be the fuck out."

"Well, I hope you go legit because I like it that your offices are across from mine."

This was true.

It also meant I would have many opportunities to get creative and fuck up Dawn's day.

Repeatedly.

I heard Ren's soft laughter in my ear before he said, "Gotta say, honey, since I signed that lease, I've been thinking the same thing."

"We could carpool to work," I suggested and got more soft laughter.

Really.

Totally.

This together *togetherness* was super easy.

The door to the house I was watching opened and my back went straight.

The garages were in the back but I couldn't stakeout back there without being seen. Therefore, I knew, unless I could find a vantage point to the garage not in my car, I would be lucky if I saw anything since coming and going activity would all happen at the back.

I was tenacious and this had to do with Darius, so I tried it anyway.

But now I was seeing something.

And I couldn't fucking believe my eyes.

A very handsome African American boy-man, maybe sixteen, was walking out of the house. He was tall, his hair cut close to his head, very well-muscled, and he had a basketball held loosely under his arm.

But it wasn't just him that had my attention.

Coming out behind him but stopping on the front step was Malia Clark. She was wearing attractive business-style clothes, but her feet were bare like she'd kicked off her heels when she got home. Her thick, black, straightened hair was long and had soft curls at the ends but the front was tucked behind her ear in a casual sexy way that worked great with her oval face and big eyes.

She was smiling at the boy as he walked away and they were talking to each other. I knew this since her mouth was moving and he kept looking over his shoulder.

Malia Clark had been Darius's girlfriend in high school. I hadn't seen her since his father's funeral.

She backed into the house and closed the door.

My eyes went to the boy and my heart thumped.

"Holy fucking shit," I whispered, completely forgetting I was on the phone with Ren.

"What?" he asked.

"Holy fucking *shit*," I repeated, staring at the kid.

"Ally, *what? Are you okay?*" Ren clipped in my ear.

"Zano," I said quietly because I was too shocked to get my voice to go louder. "Right now, I'm staring at Darius Tucker's teenage son."

Silence.

Then, "Wherever you are, get the fuck out of there, Ally. Now."

An order. A firm one.

And a surprising one.

I tore my eyes away from Darius's son, stared at the steering wheel and focused all my attention on the phone.

"Why?" I asked.

"Just do it."

"Why, Ren?" I pushed.

"I got shit to do. Can't get away. Come to the office."

"*Why, Ren?*" I snapped.

"Baby, I'm askin' you, just do it."

I lifted my head and looked down the street. Well down it, Darius's son was now jogging and dribbling the ball.

Fuck.

Shit.

Fuck.

"I'll come to your office," I told Ren.

"See you soon, honey."

"Later," I replied, disconnected and started up my car

I gave one more look to the fast disappearing boy-man and one last look at the front door to Malia Clark's house.

Then I drove to Ren's office.

⚞⚟

"Hey, Ally," Dawn greeted me with such sugar-sweet fakeness, my teeth hurt.

"Hey, Dawn," I replied, otherwise ignoring her.

Instead, I was taking in the fact that Ren's offices were sah-*weet*. Lots of dark wood. Lots of glass art. Just like Ren, total class.

I kept walking toward the inner hall when Dawn called, "Ren likes guests to be announced."

"Don't worry. He knows I'm coming," I told her as I disappeared in the hall.

I turned into the opened door to my right and the minute I entered Ren's office I saw him coming my way, nearly at the door.

"Thought I heard you," he murmured, making it to me.

"I'm here," I noted the obvious.

He leaned in to give me a distracted touch on the lips then moved beyond me to close the door.

Oh man.

Here we go.

I took that moment to look around his office to see it was more of the same from outside. The difference being that his desk was a mess.

My man worked. That was obvious.

I liked that.

What was better was that Indy had told me that Lee allowed Dawn to come into his office and keep his desk tidy.

Clearly, Ren did not allow the same thing.

This almost made me smile, but I didn't do it when I felt Ren's hand at my back and I looked up to see he looked distracted but serious.

He led us around his desk, then, with a hand in my belly, he gently pushed me so I sat on the papers on the top. He sat in his chair, turned it my way and looked up at me.

"What I'm gonna tell you, Ally, you do not *ever* repeat."

That was not a good start.

"Zano, you're freaking me out," I whispered.

"Good. Then you'll take me seriously."

Oh my God.

I braced, and it was good thing.

A very good thing.

"In my world, everybody knows everything they can know. You know it so you know how others operate. That way you can make educated guesses at their plays. You also know it so you know what's important." He paused and his eyes grew even more intense. "And what lines not to cross."

"Oh God." I was still whispering.

This wasn't getting any better.

He went on.

"Seven years ago, Shirleen and Tucker had a falling out with one of their crew. A smartass, he had more confidence than brains. He also had a big mouth. When they got shot of him, he had big words to say pretty much everywhere about how he was gonna make them pay and take over their business. Fortunately, he didn't share widely about *exactly* how he was gonna do that, and what

I mean by that was his chosen tool at how to exact vengeance. Unfortunately for him, he was the kind of man who would carry through with his plans.

He stopped talking. I nodded, and he kept going.

"Tucker never did their wet work."

My stomach roiled at these words used in conjunction with Darius. But I fought back any response, including keeping my expression blank.

"He'd order it, as would Shirleen, but neither of them would do it. Both of them could be cold-blooded. They had to be to get where they were and stay there. They did other things to inspire loyalty. But to make a point with this guy, Tucker stepped in."

"Zano." It came out as a soft plea.

"Liam Edward Clark is off-limits, baby."

I closed my eyes.

Liam Edward.

Lee and Eddie.

Oh my God.

Ren kept talking and I opened my eyes.

"This guy was gonna make his play usin' this kid. How, I don't know. But he also had a point to make, so I could guess. Tucker made sure he didn't do that. And he made sure *how* he did it that no one would get that same idea. And no one has. Not again. Although it is not known widely what Malia and Liam mean to Tucker, it's known by those who do know, no matter if Shirleen and Tucker are no longer in the game, you do not get near this kid. You do not get near his mother."

"So, Darius takes care of them," I guessed.

He nodded. "Yeah. They have his protection. Other than that, he gives them money and they don't know where it comes from. The reason they don't is because every month, Lee Nightingale and Eddie Chavez take turns bringing her an envelope, sayin' that shit is from them. But it isn't. It's from Tucker. As for Tucker, he has nothing to do with them."

My back went straight. "What? Why?"

"That, I don't know. What I do know is that for everybody, including you, they don't exist."

"That's ridiculous," I snapped.

"It's what it is. You do not get near them, Ally."

"But the reason I would—"

He cut me off to ask sharply, "You care about your friend?"

I clamped my mouth shut and nodded.

"Then they do not exist. You do not tell Indy. You do not share with the Rock Chicks. Fuck, don't even tell Tex or Duke."

"I don't understand this," I admitted, because I fucking well didn't.

"Then ask yourself why Dominic Vincetti was entirely okay with being an asshole who dipped his wick into everything that moved and did whatever Vito told him to do until he discovered someone had hit his wife. Then he and Sissy had a kid. Now he's lookin' for ways to get out. Being in love does shit to you, Ally. I know that as a goddamn fact. I'm not one but I can guess, being a father does shit, too. And it did it to Tucker."

"I'd understand that if Darius was part of their lives," I returned.

"The kid's sixteen," Ren told me.

"And?" I prompted.

"Count back the years, baby," he said gently.

I did.

But Ren did the math for me. "She was pregnant at the funeral, Ally."

"So?"

"What do you know about Malia Clark?" he asked instead of answering.

"I know she was a cheerleader. I know she was gorgeous and still is. I know she went with Indy and me and a bunch of our friends to a Prince concert that Indy got front row seats to. And I know that Malia almost passed out with glee when The Purple One did a twirl, his sweat flew off and it hit Malia. I also know before Darius's dad was murdered, he and Malia were tight. And now I know she was knocked up at his dad's funeral, which was why she dropped out of sight her senior year and I haven't seen her since."

"And what was Darius doin' his senior year?"

I didn't answer that. This was because, instead of being on the football field as he had been the three years previously, he was under the bleachers, dealing dope for his uncle.

Ren let my silence be my response and went on.

"Well, I know she was a court reporter who studied at night to become a paralegal, which is what she now does. I also know that Liam Clark has already signed a pre-commitment to a college. This has part to do with the way he can run a ball on a football field. But mostly it has to do with the fact that he's hitting his junior year in high school next year, he's already taking almost a complete schedule of AP classes and the college he's committed to is Harvard."

Whoa.

"No shit?" I breathed.

"Darius Tucker is no fool. He's also fuckin' sharp. Malia Clark isn't one either, and she's a hard worker. And the kid they made didn't fall far from the tree."

This was cutting me deep already.

Knowing all this, it was killing me.

I leaned into Ren and said, "Then he's gotta know his kid. He's got to show him where he got some of how awesome he is. He's got——"

"Do you honestly believe Tucker thinks he gave *anything* good to that boy?" Ren asked.

I sat back and snapped, "Well, he did."

"You know that, baby, and so do I. But Tucker doesn't."

"Zano——"

"How would you feel, you're set to go to Harvard, your life laid out beautifully, and your ex-drug dealer dad shows up and fucks with your head?" he asked.

"I don't know. Probably about the same way Darius, who had much the same scholarship to Yale for exactly the same reasons, his life laid out beautifully, felt when his dad was murdered," I shot back. "Difference is, his dad was dead and couldn't show him the way to get rid of his anger in a healthy way. Darius is not dead."

"Do you think he has the tools to give that to his son?"

"What I think is, neither of them will know if they don't try."

"Ally——"

But it was safe to say I'd had enough.

"This is fucked up bullshit," I hissed.

"Baby——"

I jumped off the desk and stated (loudly), "If he'd let us *in,* he'd know we'd have his back. His kid doesn't need to know any of that shit. And we'd be there to prove how great Darius is. Anyone knows the people around you that give their hearts to you shows to the world the person you are. He's got tons of friends who love him, which means he's not only making Liam live without his father, he's making all of us live without Liam. And, Ren, that is not on."

Ren stood and put his hands to either side of my neck, dipping his face close to mine.

"You need to tread cautiously with this, and by that I mean leave it alone," he advised.

"Why? Do you think Darius would whack me?" I snapped sarcastically.

"No. What I think is that you love him and you'll have difficulty living without him in your life. And more, you'll have difficulty explaining to Shirleen, your brother and Chavez why Darius got shot of the lot of you because you stuck your nose in."

Fuck!

He was right.

And I suspected Darius would do that. This was why Lee and Eddie hadn't already stepped in. Maybe they'd tried and got their hands burned. So they learned.

"Goddamn it," I bit out.

He knew I was stymied and that was why he pulled slightly away and some of his intensity left him. But, in an effort to make me feel better, he stroked my throat with his thumb which, even frustrated as all get out, kind of worked.

Then he asked, "How'd you learn this shit?"

"An anonymous source, namely Eddie Chavez. And if you share that with anybody, I'm telling Smithie to ban you from entry so you can't watch me strip again."

His lips quirked, but his eyes went reflective.

So I asked, "What?"

"Surprised Chavez shared that with you."

"He's as stymied as I am. Probably wants to do something about it, can't, so he's heard I'm all over Darius's ass and, obviously, is willing to throw me under the bus."

"Hmm," Ren mumbled.

"Hmm, what?" I asked.

"Hmm, if I tell you what that means, you'll get ideas so I'll keep the what of my hmm to myself."

I narrowed my eyes. "Do you honestly think that's gonna work?"

He studied me. Then he slid his hands from my neck so he could wrap his arms around me loosely.

I returned the favor and waited (but not patiently).

When he didn't say anything, I said a warning, "Zano."

He pulled me closer and asked bizarrely, "Have you heard the song *Hold on Loosely?*"

Had he temporarily lost his sanity?

I was a Rock Chick.

Of course I'd heard it.

"Hello?" I called unnecessarily. "I'm Ally Nightingale."

He took my meaning therefore stated, "So you know the words."

I rolled my eyes, rolled them back and said shortly, "Yes. Now can we get back—?"

"I heard that song this morning on the way to work and realized that's how I gotta deal with you."

I snapped my mouth shut.

Then I stopped being peeved.

Because he was *so* right.

And that was sweet.

"So I'm gonna tell you what that hmm means. But first, I'm gonna say that what Tucker's givin' you is all he thinks he has to give. I'm sensing that isn't enough for you. And before you do shit, you need to ask yourself if what he has to give is enough, because what you have to lose with him is everything. You also have to understand that what's at stake for you is at stake for everybody in your posse. You have to make that decision for everybody. All or nothing, or accept him as he comes. And that's a huge decision to make, baby."

"I get you," I said softly.

He studied me a moment, obviously took in that I processed what he said, then he again spoke.

"My hmm meant that Chavez would not share shit with you if he didn't trust you to use it wisely. He has faith in you to handle this situation. He's not throwing you under the bus. You're his partner in a tag team and he just tagged you in. But he's expecting you to enter the ring and kick ass. Not let the team down. Now you gotta decide if you go through those ropes, honey, or throw in the towel."

"I'm not a towel throwing type of girl, Ren," I shared honestly, and his arms got tighter.

"I know. Still. Think about it."

I nodded.

"Good," he murmured. Then louder, "I got to clear some shit, it'll take me about half an hour. You good to wait? Then we'll go out to dinner."

"I'm good to wait," I told him.

"That waiting would be in here with me. Not out in reception, givin' Dawn shit, knowin' she can't retaliate."

Well, there went my plans for the next half hour.

"I wouldn't do that," I totally lied.

"You so fuckin' would." He knew I was lying.

I rolled my eyes, but it was all for show.

Ren knew this because on the downward roll, he was kissing me.

After kissing me, he got to work.

I inspected his office.

But I did it thinking on how I could get Darius back with his family.

Without the one he already had losing him.

Chapter 27

Runs Deep

I stood in a dark corner of Smithie's, surveying the scene.

I'd had a call that evening from Roam, reporting in. And what he'd reported was that he saw a waitress do a handoff to Steiner. Alarmingly, Roam then reported that he'd followed Steiner.

Fortunately, Steiner hadn't noted the tail. Also fortunately, Roam followed Steiner directly to another meeting, and this wasn't another girl. It was Steiner dropping off the take to a man Roam described as big, bulky, light brown hair, and "a white dude that'll fuck you up rather than look at you," (Roam's words).

After I told him to punt this information to Darius, not follow Steiner again, *definitely* not follow the other dude and not to use the f-word, I added surveillance onto my night at Smithie's.

It was a good move because, in moments, I clocked him.

A man of that description was sitting at a table somewhat back from the stage. Steiner, who worked the room, gave him a wide berth, saying to anyone who knew what they were looking for that he was doing all he could so no one would associate the two.

As I stood there, back to the wall, I watched the man sitting at his table like he owned the joint, not Smithie. The waitress at his section served him, but she was jittery. She wasn't having a bad night. She served her other tables more comfortably. That meant she knew him or understood his threat.

And Roam's description was apt. Completely. This guy would fuck someone up rather than look at them.

I kept my eye on him, and Steiner, with plenty of time to do it. I'd already danced my first song so I had time until the next one. And this, essentially surveillance, was one of the few things I could do patiently.

Therefore I also saw him leave his seat once for a private lap dance with JoJo.

She came out of the room where they did the private dances looking freaked.

He came out looking the same as normal, strolling back to his table that the waitress had shooed three customers from and resuming his seat like he was king of all he surveyed.

And he was.

I just didn't get why.

My cell in my hand vibrated. So its light wouldn't illuminate my face and bring attention to me, I moved from my spot to the dancers' hall and down to the end.

I had a text from Darius. It said *Outside.*

By the way, this was badass for *Meet me outside, please.*

Coming, I texted back then moved out the backdoor the bouncers used to take the dancers to their cars.

Darius was right there with a brick in his hand. He grabbed my hand, pulled me out, bent and put the brick on the ground by the jamb so the door didn't close.

"It locks and I don't want you goin' back inside through the front," he murmured as he again grabbed my hand and pulled me away from the door.

"What's up?" I asked when we stopped.

"The motherfucker Roam clocked?" Darius asked back.

"Yeah," I answered.

"Name's Cyrus Gibbons. Got his own strip club in Lincoln closed down 'cause he forced his girls to do lap dances that went the extra mile. Did six months."

Shit.

Not.

Good.

"Don't know his connection with Steiner," Darius went on. "Do know he moved from Nebraska to Colorado about four months ago, which was when he got out. Not sure, though, if his PO received his change of address form."

"PO" was "Probation Officer" and they tended to frown on ex-cons going over state lines.

I didn't mention that to Darius since he already knew.

I noted, "Which is about a month before Steiner got the job here."

"Which gave him plenty of time to assess the talent and decide on his mark," Darius added. "Had a sit down with Brody. Lee already tore him off the book thing to do other jobs. Told him shit here was bad and he needed to find time to get on Steiner and Gibbons. He'll have something tomorrow."

"We need to know who else is involved," I said. "But, just saying, the guy's in the bar, lording over it like his name's on the deed."

"Copy that, also saw him go in," Darius replied then told me, "Dude's packin'."

I stared at him a beat before asking, "He's carrying concealed at a strip joint?"

Darius nodded.

"Fuck," I whispered, then stated, "His waitress is scared shitless of him. And he got a lap dance from JoJo and she came out looking freaked."

"Steiner makes the pickups, Gibbons provides the threat," he deduced.

"But what's the threat?" I asked. "Any of those girls knows they say one word to Smithie, he'll sort this whole thing."

Darius shook his head. "No clue. We need to be all over those guys. Told Shirleen I want Roam and Sniff off this shit. Bobby and I are gonna look into it."

"Good," I murmured. "Tell him to keep track of his hours and we'll sort something through Daisy with Smithie."

"Got it," Darius replied and his eyes grew intent. I was doing my all not to react to what I'd learned about him that day and keep my mouth shut about it until I could figure out what I was going to do when he said, "Guy's got a weapon, you be smart in there."

I nodded. "Always."

"I'm eyes out here. Don't like you in there without backup, but if one of the boys shows, they'll wonder why they're there when their boss's sister is strippin'."

"Ren's coming later," I told him and grinned. "And then there's me."

Darius looked relieved, but I would find it was not about the me taking care of me part. "This guy's even a little clued into the players in Denver, he'll have heard of Zano. If he knows you're his woman, he'll be smart."

Shit.

"That might mean he knows about me," I remarked.

"He's gotta be pretty clued in to the game here to know you, Ally. You do good, and one of the ways you do good is you keep your head down. Your jobs have got around, but to players like Lee, not guys like him."

"My apartment just exploded, Darius," I reminded him. "That kind of thing gets a lot of attention. And my brother is a cop, the other one a PI."

"Hold your cover and ride it, Ally. Bobby's on board, Brody doin' his gig, it'll be done soon."

That I could believe.

I nodded. "Gotta get back in there. Tell Bobby thanks from me."

"Will do," he murmured, moving to the door.

After he grabbed the brick and was holding it open for me, I looked him in the eyes. "Thank you too, honey."

"Jeez, got yourself a man, you're gettin' soft."

My back went straight. "Am not."

"Gushy."

"I'm just expressing gratitude," I pointed out.

"Expressed. Now get your ass in there so no one wonders where the fuck you are," he returned.

"Bossy badass," I muttered, moving through the door.

"Ally?" he called and I turned back. "You're bein' a soft, gushy chick. But you're also welcome."

I watched him grin huge.

Then I watched the door close.

And then I thought about how Liam Edward Clark was missing out.

Huge.

I shook off this thought and went to the dancers' dressing room. I bided my time, shooting the shit with Lottie until the opportunity came about five minutes before I went on again. I gave Lottie a look, she took off mumbling about needing the bathroom and I moved to JoJo, who'd come in for a break and stripper makeup refresh (a hefty undertaking, trust me).

I moved to her, and without a lot of time before I was due onstage, I had to get my message across and fast.

So I stood behind her and looked in her eyes in the mirror. "Hey."

"Hey, Ally," she replied on a smile that wasn't quite real. But she tried, I could see. "You're killing. After that big thing last night, the girls and me watched your next dance. You rock."

"Thanks, babe," I replied.

"You gotta show me how to do that pole flip," she said.

"How's tomorrow before shift change?" I asked.

"Works for me," she went back to her blusher. "Tips went wild after you and Lottie left the stage." Another smile to me, this one making the back of my neck prickle because it was melancholy. Possibly because she just handed her tips to Gibbons, or knew she'd be handing them to Steiner. "Thanks for that."

"No probs," I replied.

She again turned her attention to her blusher.

"JoJo?" I called. Her eyes came to mine in the mirror, her brows went up and my voice dropped low. "No matter what it is, you put your faith in the right person, they can move in and work it out. You with me?"

She was with me. She'd frozen and looked utterly freaked.

"Just take that in," I whispered. "You don't have to do anything. Just take it in. Yeah?"

She nodded slowly.

I smiled at her and moved away, hoping she'd more than take it in.

Then I moved into the hall because it was time to strip.

⋈

The rendezvous point for our late, *late* night activities was Tex's house.

After finishing my last set, Ren followed me home so we could drop his Jag. We were taking my car, because in Tex's 'hood where tweakers were abundant, Jags were like shining beacons calling all to commit mayhem.

When he came to my 'stang, he opened my door and leaned in. It was then I saw the look in his eyes, which meant I was hoping this business would be done, and quick, so we could get back home and fuck each other's brains out.

In other words, one could just say that Ren liked to watch me take my clothes off while dancing. He might prefer it if I was a private dancer, but he still liked getting it as it came.

However, once positioned in my door, he proceeded to boss me with, "Get out, babe. I'm drivin'."

My reply was, "It's my car, Ren."

Which got me a, "Yeah. I know. And I'm drivin' it."

Thus commenced a Rock Chick/Macho Badass exchange of words that got mildly heated and lasted ten minutes before Ren leaned further in, undid my seatbelt, hauled me to my feet, shoved me against the car and laid a hot and heavy one on me.

While I was recovering, he pushed me aside, folded behind the wheel and didn't delay in adjusting the seat.

I allowed myself five seconds to fume. Then, as I couldn't execute the same maneuver, I stomped to my side and angled in.

But once in, I declared immediately, "That lost you head for a week."

"Bullshit, baby. I get you breathy and tell you I want your mouth, you'll suck my cock deep so fast I won't be able to blink."

His words made me want to go down on him right there.

I didn't give indication of that.

I buckled in saying, "We'll see."

"Yeah, this is done, we will."

That sounded like a promise.

Hmm.

Ren drove to Tex's. I grabbed my little pepper spray and stun gun out of the glove compartment before I got out. Shoving my stun gun in the back waistband of my jeans and my pepper spray in my front pocket, I stormed the rest of my pique off by stomping up to the door, Ren following me.

Tex opened it before we got there and ordered, "Keep it quiet inside. Nance's sleepin'."

She would be. It was three thirty in the morning.

We would also know to do this since Tex now had an official ball and chain and if she wasn't flitting around serving coffee, we'd know to keep it down.

I understood why he gave us this warning when I walked in and noticed several things right off the bat.

One, Tex seemed to have twice as many cats as usual, and since he had about fifteen of them the last time I was there, this was a lot.

Two, Hector was there, as expected.

Three, Mace was there, as was *not* expected.

And four, The Kevster *and* fucking *Rosie* were there, as was *insane*.

"What the...!" I started on a shout. Tex cut his eyes to me and I brought it down about ten notches, "Hell?"

Rosie, looking like Rosie—that was to say a less kempt Kurt Cobain (except, obviously, alive)—jumped up from Tex's couch and said (on a whisper), "The Kevster went to get some stuff from Kumar, Kumar told him what

388

was goin' down tonight. He told me and I came to help. It's my way of sayin' sorry."

I glared at Kevin then I transferred my glare to Tex. "Why didn't you kick them out?" I demanded to know.

"Did I *not* mention Nancy's sleepin'?" he asked back on a low boom.

Crap.

I moved my glare to Rosie. "Daily deliveries of flowers for a year, replacement of my *Firefly* DVDs, and twenty-five rock 'n' roll t-shirts say I'm sorry, Rosie. You showing up prior to a mission does *not*." I looked back at The Kevster. "And you know better."

"Dudette," he replied then said no more.

Then again, often for The Kevster, that was all he had to say.

I stared at The Kevster, who had a ginger cat in his lap he was stroking, a tuxedo kitty snoozing at his side, and a tiger cat on the floor by his leg, batting at the ragged hem of his jeans, and I sucked in breath.

"Two potheads and bring your boyfriend to work day. This isn't startin' great," Mace noted, and I looked at him.

"And what are *you* doing here?" I asked.

"Not convinced about you. Here to get convinced," he stated then uncrossed an arm that was crossed on his chest and swung it out before finishing, "Though, gotta say, this shit isn't convincing me."

It was nice he was considering backing my play. It was better he was there to help.

He was still annoying me.

"I've been here a minute and Ren can take care of himself, which I suspect you know. So keep your pants on, I'll deal with shit and we'll move out," I returned.

"Right," he replied, still obviously unconvinced.

I didn't have time to chat with Mace. I had tweaker robbers to locate, a fight with my man to finish, then I wanted sex. Though, I could combine the last two. Angry sex worked for Ren and me, seeing as we mostly existed on that for a year.

I turned back to Rosie and The Kevster and ordered, "Go home."

Rosie felt like being obstinate, unfortunately.

389

"No. We're gonna help. A tweaker will open a door to one of us way faster than they'd open one to one of you." He, too, threw out an arm to indicate the crew. "We can go in, get the lay of the land, give the high sign."

I stared at him and saw what I didn't want to see.

That was to say, it was clear Rosie brought some of his primo pot from New Mexico for personal use.

He was lit. Which meant he'd fired up very recently.

"And bad shit goes down, you're high, you think you can handle it?" I asked. Then went on, "And seriously, smoking a doobie at Tex's? What's the matter with you?"

"We smoked it in the car before we came in," Kevin offered.

"Brilliant," I snapped.

"Ally——" Rosie cut in, but I moved and did it quick.

Getting in his space and face, I stated, "You are not helping. All you're doing is wasting time and pissing me off. Go home. Now."

"But——"

"*Now*," I bit out.

"I feel bad," he said.

Seriously?

"You should," I shot back. "I lost everything because you're an idiot. But pissing me off isn't the way to make it up to me. Now, we're done. Go." Since I was done too, I turned from him to look at Tex and asked, "You got a list of houses?"

He was smiling big at me and he answered, "Yup."

"How many?" I asked.

"Seven," he answered.

Jeez.

Tex and Nancy needed to consider moving.

"Right, we split up. Hector and Tex on one team, Mace, Ren and me on another," I decided. "Mace, did Hector brief you?" I asked. On his jerk of the chin (meaning *affirmative,* by the way), I nodded and looked to Tex. "Tex, you take three houses, give the addresses for the other four to Ren."

Tex moved.

Mace asked, "You got walkies?"

No. But I was going to tell Daisy the next day to fit that line item in our budget.

"Negative," I answered Mace.

"Then how we gonna talk to each other?" he returned.

"Uh... cells?" I asked sarcastically because it was not lost on me I was in test phase for Mace and that pissed me off (more). "Just to say, the squawk of walkies won't help us be stealthy so put your phone on vibrate and we'll be fine."

That must have been acceptable because Mace moved on.

"You got a plan for approach?"

"My plan is, Hector and Tex can do whatever they want. You two," I pointed between Ren and Mace, "are gonna stay out of sight while I approach the door. I'm less of a threat, but I can assess one. I give you the sign, you move in."

"What's the sign?' Mace pushed.

"I was thinking a rain dance on the front lawn. That work for you?" I replied snottily.

"Woman, we gotta know what we're lookin' for," Mace growled.

"And you got enough experience, you pay enough attention, you'll know it when you see it. I have to be free to operate without fitting in some bullshit move that isn't gonna look right and might alert them I have backup. So just pay attention, yeah?"

Mace stared at me a beat then he looked to Hector.

Hector was grinning.

Whatever.

"We ready to roll?" I asked, looking through the crew and noting that Ren was also grinning, but his eyes were again burning so I didn't look too long because I needed to think about what I was doing, not my happy place getting happy.

"You armed?" Mace asked.

I pulled out the stun gun but said, "No. You are. Don't let me get dead."

"You're goin' in unarmed?" Mace pressed.

Jeez!

"The objective is to call the cops in," I informed him. "We reach our objective, cops show, I'm a trainee investigator gathering hours. I've got a gun and a permit but I'm not licensed to carry concealed, and seeing as I know a few of them, I know cops frown on gung ho idiots who carry weapons. That's why I have Hector and, since you're here, *you.*"

Then I turned toward the door, but saw that Rosie and The Kevster were still there and both of them were looking at me.

"You haven't left," I noted.

"You totally *are* badass," Rosie breathed.

"It's nearly four in the morning, I've spent the last eight hours in a strip club and I want to have sex with my boyfriend before I pass out. So the longer this takes, the more I'll want to *kick* someone's ass. You stay five more seconds, that someone will be you," I returned.

They must have taken me seriously because I got two wide-eyed stoner looks and they moved.

"Rosie?" I called when he was almost through the door. He turned back to me. "You drop my name again, I'll hunt you down and cut off everything that protrudes from your body. You get me?"

Wider eyes and he nodded.

He got me.

"Advice," I continued. "Find another job as a barista and spread your joy that way. You keep growing, you being you, you'll be dead in five years. I'm seriously pissed at you, but I don't want you dead. Stop being a moron and make that happen."

He nodded again though this was less sure.

God.

Rosie.

"Now go," I ordered.

He went.

My man got close to my back and his mouth came to my ear where he said quietly, "Hurry this shit up, baby, 'cause what you got last night after I watched you slide down a pole upside down while straddling it is gonna be nothin' to what I give you tonight watchin' you be badass."

I turned and glared up at him. "Don't turn me on while I'm working, Zano."

His lips quirked.

"Jesus," Mace muttered.

"Enough out of you," I demanded, pointing at Mace. I swung my eyes through the crew and finished, "Now let's go."

And with that, we went.

We pulled up to the last house on our list, Mace driving one of Lee's black company Explorers, me in the passenger seat, Ren behind me.

I stared at the house, sheets covering the windows, weak light coming from nearly every window in the house. There were people moving behind the sheets, and not a few.

Den o' Tweakers having a late night party.

Shit.

"This is it," I whispered.

"Fuck yeah, it is," Mace agreed.

I turned to him, leaning forward and pulling out my phone. "I'm calling Hector. We don't go in until they're here. You're lead. You go to the front, Ren the back. I'm on you. You got an extra gun for Ren?"

"Glove compartment," Mace grunted.

I hit go on Hector, put my phone to my ear and opened the glove compartment to get the gun for Ren. I undid my seatbelt and leaned around the seat to hand it to him. I heard gun noises as Ren got familiar with it, and it didn't surprise me he was familiar with guns.

I didn't let my mind go there, and couldn't as I engaged with Hector. I told him where we were and to get to us. I also told him their positions. He confirmed and I disconnected, shoving the phone back in my jeans pocket.

"Hector and Tex will take the sides." I looked around the seat to Ren. "Shit goes down, baby, you disappear," I ordered gently.

I saw his mouth get tight and the muscle jump in his jaw. This was silent badass for *Want you to disappear instead of me,* and I belatedly rethought Ren's ride along.

It should be noted, though, that I loved him like crazy, but I loved him more when he kept his mouth shut and just jerked up his chin.

"The feel of that house, this operation just became mine," Mace declared, and I looked at him. "You steer clear unless you get *my* signal, yeah?"

"Gotcha," I replied immediately, and he did a slow blink.

He thought I'd argue.

He'd learn.

And what he'd learn was that I was a badass. But not a stupid one.

"Stun gun at the ready, Ally," Mace kept ordering.

I nodded.

We saw the headlights of a Yukon coming our way, the lights going out before it parked.

Hector's ride.

"Move out," Mace muttered and we moved.

Ren disappeared quickly. I saw Hector waste no time crossing the yard and vanishing around the side of the house. Tex was lumbering, but his position was closer. He also wasted no time and took it.

I turned on my stun gun as Mace walked right up to the front door.

I stood, back to the house at the side of the door.

He looked at me and gave me a head jerk which I had to interpret on the fly.

I made an educated guess, turned my head the other way, leaned forward and looked into the window at my side.

Mace knocked loud.

All the shadows behind the sheets dropped.

I looked back at Mace and shook my head.

Without delay, he lifted a long leg and put a boot to the door, shouting, "Bond enforcement!"

Interesting.

We had no warrants for anyone inside, but that didn't mean someone inside didn't have a warrant on them. So that was a good call. And smart.

I stopped noting that for future reference because the rest happened fast.

Mace went in.

There were noises, thuds, shouts, running feet.

Someone came out the front. I put my foot out, tripped them and they went flying, landing on their front on the cement walk. I moved in quickly, stunned them and they went lax. I grabbed a wrist and started to haul them off the walk so they wouldn't be trampled if anyone else tried to escape out front. As I did this, I saw Hector running in the front door.

That was when I heard Mace's whistle.

I took that as his sign.

I got in, Tex coming in behind me, and it appeared Mace had had all the fun, what with the bodies littering the floor and some tweakers cowering in a corner.

But Ren was having fun, too. Across the room, he had hands on a guy—arm and back of the neck. He slammed him face first into the wall, let him go and the guy dropped straight to his back, o-u-t, *out*.

My man.

Totally hot.

After allowing myself a quiver in my happy place, I took in the space. There was a lot of mess, some not so great furniture, and three car stereos sitting on a filthy, battered coffee table.

That night's take.

And last, little baggies of meth crystals and drug paraphernalia everywhere.

No weapons.

I looked at Mace. "You hogged all the fun."

Mace got close and talked low. "We need a reason to be here. You and Tex talk to each one. Get names. Call Brody and have him run them for warrants. Warrant or not, after you talk to Brody, call the cops. They get here, I'll deal."

I nodded and turned to Tex to see he'd gone back out and was now dragging in the one I dropped outside. He was doing it by the dude's hand so the head and the rest of the tweaker bumped and cracked against everything even as he was coming out of the stun. He was probably also tweaking, so that didn't help.

"Tex, a little care," I told him.

"Got shit for brains already, don't matter I stir it up," Tex replied.

Since I didn't need a lawsuit on any of my cases, I scratched a chat with Tex about his sidekick do's and don'ts to happen at a later date and got busy, taking Tex with me.

When I was done, I gave a nod to Mace who was standing sentry at the entrance, while Hector stood sentry at the door that led to the back of the house.

Mace was studying me, looking broody.

Even after Stella gave him good loving and his family back, Mace could be broody. Usually it was hot. Unfortunately, now it served to hide whether he felt I passed or failed.

Whatever. He didn't sit on the Licensing Board. I failed the Mace Test, I'd live.

I turned to Ren who was providing badass presence at Tex and my backs.

"You good?" I asked.

He was looking beyond me at the wired, strung out, unkempt tweakers, and I didn't have to know him as well as I did to know he didn't like what he was seeing.

He then looked at me.

"You sure this is the company you wanna keep?" he asked.

"No. What I'm sure of is that tomorrow and the next day and the next, some person in this 'hood is not gonna walk out to their car, see their stereo stolen and feel violated," I replied.

He studied me several beats, grinned and murmured, "Good answer."

"So you're feeling me," I noted.

"Not yet," he replied.

I rolled my eyes.

When I rolled them back I noted his grin got bigger.

It was then, I heard sirens.

⚜

Oh God.

I was close.

I threw my head back and breathed, "*Ren*."

My man, on his knees behind me, pulled out.

On my hands and knees in the bed, I looked at him over my shoulder and whispered, "No, baby."

"On your back. Knees up. Spread," he ordered, his voice thick.

Okay, I could do that.

So I did it.

He covered me and not a second later slammed into me.

My back arched and I wound my arms around him.

"Every guy watchin' you move onstage at Smithie's wants his dick right here," he growled, thrusting fast, hard, deep and I focused on him (barely).

He got off on that.

Like, seriously.

Suddenly, I did too.

He drove in, then ground in, his mouth coming to mine. "But this is all mine."

It so totally was.

"Yes," I panted.

Inexplicably (and tragically), he pulled out again and moved down my body. His hand went between my legs, his finger working me, his mouth went to my breast and he sucked my nipple deep.

That was all good, *way* good.

But I needed him inside.

"Honey, please," I begged.

He rolled my nipple with his tongue, his finger rolled between my legs and my back left the bed.

He blew on my nipple then whispered, "My woman kicks ass at everything."

Oh *God*.

He moved his beautiful torture to my other nipple and after the tongue roll and blowing, I breathed, "*Ren.*"

His mouth came back to mine, but his hand continued to work between my legs when he encouraged, "That's it."

I slid my fingers in his hair. "Need you."

"You'll get me. Gonna bury myself inside you when I make you burn."

I was already burning.

"Need you," I repeated.

His hand between my legs moved so his fingers thrust inside and his thumb hit the spot.

That wasn't what I wanted, but I'd work with it. And I did, my hips moving desperately with his hand.

"Fuckin' fuck me, so goddamned hot."

"Ren."

"Ride that, Ally."

I rode it. Hell yeah, I rode it.

"*Ren,*" I cried, and it hit me.

The instant it did, his fingers disappeared and he drove inside me, swinging my calves in at his back. I closed my legs around him and dug in my heels, my hands fisting in his hair, my lips parted, my back in an arc, my hips moving to accommodate his.

It burned through me and Ren kept thrusting powerfully, my body jerking. I moved my hands from his hair down his back to grab hold of his ass, lifting my head and breathing into his neck as he slammed into me.

"Love this, baby," I whispered into his skin.

He grunted into mine.

"Love *you*, Ren."

His thrusts became savage.

I nipped his earlobe and moaned, "You feel so damned good, honey."

He powered deep, then bucked once, twice, again, again and again as he groaned into my neck. I took his weight for long moments, holding him tight to me, breathing him in, before he rolled us.

But once to his back with me on top, he pushed me up so I was up and straddling him, Ren staying on his back and still buried deep.

One hand curled around my hip, he lifted the other one and put it between my breasts. With me watching him, his eyes watching his hand, he moved it down to below my breast where he cupped me, lifting my breast, his thumb gliding gently over my rock-hard nipple.

His touch at that sensitive spot scored through me. My hips jerked and I sank my teeth into my lower lip. His eyes moved to my face and he did the nipple glide again.

And got the same reaction.

His eyes sated but still burning, his hand moved down my ribs to my belly, then down between my legs where his fingers separated, surrounding our connection.

He kept his hand there but his eyes moved everywhere.

"Ren," I whispered.

"Quiet. Sit still," he ordered softly. "Wanna look at you connected to me."

God.

He was turning me on again.

His hand slid from between us and moved over my skin, everywhere, belly, ribs, sides, breasts, nipples, chest.

I studied the hot, content look on his face as he watched it go and fought squirming.

"Knew you felt deep," he muttered, his gaze on his hand trailing down my midriff. Then it came to mine. "Had no fuckin' clue how deep you ran."

"What?" I whispered.

"Everything you do, what you eat, what you drink, how you live, how you love, how you work, all of it runs deep. You give it everything. It means everything to you." His hand suddenly caught mine that was resting on my thigh and he gave it a squeeze. "Come here, baby."

I bent to him and his hand went to the small of my back, sliding up my spine and into my hair.

"Teach that to our kids, will you?"

He liked what he saw that night. He got why I do what I do.

And he trusted me.

God.

Beautiful.

I closed my eyes and buried my face in his neck.

He turned his head so his mouth was at my ear. "Will you do that for me, Ally?"

"Yes, Ren."

His hand gave mine another squeeze. "Thank you for lettin' me come tonight."

God.

Seriously!

Could he get better?

"Thanks for wanting to come."

"And thanks for makin' me come just now."

I started laughing, lifted my head and said through it, "My pleasure."

He grinned. "Noticed that."

"Mm-hmm," I mumbled, still chuckling.

He slid his hand through my hair and turned his head to look at the clock. After turning back to me, he said, "Thank fuck tomorrow's Saturday."

I got closer, "Sleeping in."

"Yeah," he replied.

I brushed my mouth against his, slid him out of me and rolled out of bed. I took care of business and pulled on a nightie, but not panties, before I slid back into bed beside him.

Ren positioned us spooning.

"Maximum contact, you doing that, not me," I pointed out.

"Last night you burrowed into me," he noted.

This was true.

I said no more.

I felt Ren's soft laughter all around me.

I wiggled into it.

"'Night, baby," he whispered.

"'Night, Ren."

He kissed my neck.

I closed my eyes, and within seconds was asleep.

Chapter 28
Key to Her Dreams

Hank

The next morning, Hank Nightingale moved up the bricked front walk to Lee and Indy's duplex.

He hit the bell, and a minute later Lee opened the door.

Hank lifted his chin to his brother as Lee moved out of the way. He entered hearing retching.

He stopped in the living room, but looked to the ceiling and back to Lee. "Morning sickness?"

"No, seein' as it lasts until the afternoon." Lee looked up the stairs, murmuring, "She can't keep anything down."

Hank studied his brother and could see it plain. Lee was worried.

"Women have been doin' this awhile, man," he said softly and Lee looked at him.

"Know that. Doesn't mean I gotta like it."

Hank nodded. He wouldn't like it either.

Lee jerked his head toward the kitchen. "Get yourself some coffee. I'm just gonna run upstairs to check on her."

Not waiting for a reply, Lee jogged up the stairs.

Hank moved to the kitchen.

He had a coffee mug in hand and was leaning against the counter when Lee reappeared saying, "She's lyin' down. She says hi. But this time of day it comes often and fast so she wants to be close to the bathroom.

Hank nodded again. Lee got his mug, reloaded, rested his hips against the counter and gave his eyes to his brother.

"We're supposed to go to viewings later. Thinkin' that's out," Lee remarked.

"You're movin'?" Hank asked.

"Keepin' the place. It's Grandma Ellen's. Indy wants it kept in the family. We'll rent it but we need more space."

They absolutely did. Two bedrooms, Indy and all her crazy (not to mention clothes) and a kid?

They needed more space.

"Keep that on the quiet," Lee warned. "She hasn't told Tod and Stevie yet. Stevie'll take it in stride. Tod's gonna have a shit fit, not havin' Indy or the contents of her closet close. Indy's already freaking at the thought of moving away from them, not to mention not having Chowleena around frequently. So it's likely I'll need to get her a dog, too, to fill the void of Chowleena." Lee drank some coffee then finished, "Though it won't be a fuckin' Chow dog."

Hank again nodded, his mind expelling the idea of his brother owning a Chow, at the same time making a note not to be anywhere near when Indy broke the news to Tod that she and Lee were breaking up the family.

He took a sip of his coffee, then said, "You called me for a meet, man, but I got somethin' to go over with you first."

"Yeah?" Lee asked.

"Before I left, got a call from Mace."

Hank watched Lee take a sip from his mug, his actions casual, his eyes intent. When he was done, he stated, "Got one too."

"He went out last night with Ally," Hank told him something he already knew.

This time, Lee nodded, but other than that, he didn't give anything away.

"He said she didn't do well, she did *well*. She made all the right moves. Confident, not cocky. Tough when she needed to be. When the situation became uncertain, she stood down without a fight and took orders. He said she has the feel. And he said Hector thinks she's the shit."

"Hector's a wild man, and she's not his sister," Lee pointed out.

"Lee," Hank said low, "they grew up together. She isn't, but she is."

Lee took a breath in through his nose. This meant he saw Hank's point.

Hank laid it out. "I'm gonna give her space. I'm also gonna ask you to train her."

"Hank—"

"She wants this," Hank said quietly. "And it'd make me sleep a fuckuva lot easier knowin' you gave her the skills she needs."

Lee's jaw clenched.

Hank continued. "And she's good at it. You've seen the tape. Ice cold at Lincoln's. Like she'd been doin' that shit for years."

"Easy for her to do that when she knows she's got firepower at her back," Lee countered.

"Yeah. You're right. But Darius told both of us, since he laid it down for her months ago, she never made a move without him bein' in the know and him bein' at her back if she needed him. She's not gung ho and proving a point. She's moving forward smart and doing it making all the right moves."

Indistinct noises of more retching floated into the room. Hank lost Lee's attention when his brother turned his head and looked at the door.

"You wanna go to her?" he asked, then offered, "I'll wait."

Lee looked back at his brother. "She gets pissed, I get too much in her space."

That was Indy. Like Ally, two peas in a pod. They needed everybody, but were damned if they'd let it show.

Hank took a sip of coffee, thinking he looked forward to making babies with Roxie. He looked forward to having a family.

He did not, however, look forward to this shit.

He gave his brother a second then declared, "I'm gonna have a conversation with Ally. You do what you need to do, but what I'll ask you to do is think about it. You could teach her things she needs to know. You could also help her get licensed so she can make a better go of this."

"She's not findin' trouble gettin' cases," Lee noted. "She doesn't even have an office and she's had two fall in her lap."

"Could that be because she's already established a reputation for getting the job done?" Hank suggested.

Lee said nothing.

"Just think about it, yeah?" Hank prompted.

Lee gave him a nod.

Hank took a sip of his coffee before asking, "Now, why'd you want me over here?"

"My phone's been busy this morning. Mace. Hector. Tex. Even fuckin' Kumar," Lee told him.

"Yeah?" Hank said.

"And also Brody," Lee went on.

"And?"

"Jane wrote that *Rock Chick* book," Lee announced.

Hank went still before he whispered, "What?"

Lee shook his head but said, "Yeah. Jane. Middle of the night last night, Brody found a trail from the person who gets reader mail to Jane."

"Fuck," Hank bit out.

"Yeah," Lee agreed.

"What now?" Hank asked.

"That's why I asked you here," Lee answered. "I don't know. No tellin' what Indy's gonna do. She thinks of Jane like family. I don't know if she'll lose her mind or defend her. Bein' Indy, though, my guess is she'd defend her. But right now, her sick all the time, she doesn't need this shit. She's also told me about Jane. That woman loves books, always wanted to become a writer. She's written fuckin' dozens of them that went nowhere. Now she's livin' her dream."

"Off our lives," Hank pointed out.

"That's the rub," Lee stated. "'Cause what does it hurt when what it does is give one of our own the key to her dreams?"

Hank stared at his brother. "Are you shitting me?"

"Tod and Stevie have been over here cackling about that book least a dozen times since Indy and Ally found it. Fuck, Tod's highlighted parts that he reads out loud to us. And I gotta admit, that shit is funny. Wasn't then. My woman in my bed, wearin' my ring, pregnant with my baby, it is now."

"I'm not sure I'll get there," Hank replied.

"You asked me just last night, I would have said the same thing. Then when Brody told me it was Jane, Indy pukin' in the bathroom, us having viewings to get a bigger place to prepare for our family, I didn't have it in me to get pissed. Jane's got nothin' in her life except that store and us." He paused. "And now her books."

Hank thought about Jane. Quiet. Always working. Most of the time there, but always on the cusp. He'd known her since he was a kid and she'd always been the same. It wasn't that she kept herself removed. Hank reckoned it had more to do with the fact she didn't quite know how to get involved.

And Roxie had read the book. Hank had heard her laughing through the whole fucking thing. She knew Hank was pissed about it and didn't say anything to him, but he also knew, if she found out it was Jane, she wouldn't give a single shit.

"My thought is," Lee carried on and Hank focused on him. "I tell the men. They tell their women. I'm not gonna say shit about how they react, seein' as they can react however the fuck they want. I'll wait 'til Indy's in a good spot and tell her, and same goes for her. Jane did what she did, the chips will fall as they fall."

"Not thinkin' any of the women will have an issue with it," Hank noted.

"Seems the case," Lee agreed.

"But even one of those guys loses it and gets in Jane's face, how's that gonna go down?" Hank asked.

The look on Lee's face said precisely how it was going to go down. Jane barely had the courage to live her life. One of the men got in her shit about those books, she could break. Which could mean she'd leave the store. Which would mean Indy would lose her.

Which would not be good.

Just like her grandmother, Indy regarded everyone who walked in that store on a regular basis like blood family. Grandma Ellen had looked after Jane. Indy did in her way, too.

She'd lose her mind if one of the men lost it with Jane.

"My guess," Lee started, "is that those men will also think about how that'd go down. And if they do confront her, they'll have a mind to that."

That, fortunately, was true.

"They also have a right to know," Lee continued.

Hank nodded and sipped more coffee.

"You gonna tell Roxie?" Lee asked.

Hank's brows went up. "The Rock Chicks knowin' something she doesn't know? And then her knowin' I knew and didn't tell her?" Hank shook his head. "She'd have a fuckin' conniption. She rode my ass half our honeymoon about Ally and Zano."

Lee grinned, but Hank didn't find it funny. Ally making a scene with Zano at their wedding reception, clueing the Rock Chicks in to something the men already knew, was not taken kindly by his then-brand new wife.

Luckily, he was able to be creative in getting her to shut up about it.

"Darius says Zano is lookin' into those books, too. You have a sit down with Ally, will you give her that heads up?" Lee asked.

"Yeah," Hank answered. "And since I'm out, that's up next."

He took his last sip of coffee, rinsed the mug and put in the dishwasher.

Lee walked with him to the door.

At the door, Hank brought up their earlier conversation. "You'll think about Ally?"

"Said I would," Lee replied.

"She's got what it takes, Lee," Hank pointed out.

"She's also got no fear," Lee returned. "Never has. And sometimes that's not a good thing."

"You get scared before you do a job or do you just know you can get it done?" Hank asked.

Lee again said nothing.

"You're measuring her by another yardstick, brother," Hank noted quietly. "Careful of doing that. It's not only not fair, she'll cotton on and the results of that will not be pretty. But, I'll point out, you're holdin' the key to her dreams. Our sister is the kind of girl who'll bust the door down anyway. And she's doin' that. But it'd make it easier, you just hand her that key."

For long moments, Hank withstood his brother's intense stare before Lee lifted his chin.

Again, point taken.

There was no more he could do, so Hank opened the door.

"You leaving, Hank?" he heard Indy call from upstairs.

"Yeah, Indy. Got shit to do," Hank called back.

"Sorry I couldn't come down," she yelled.

"Understandable. Another time," Hank yelled back.

"Later," she kept at it.

"Later," Hank replied.

When he was done, he caught Lee smiling.

His smile died when they both heard more retching.

"Seven months, man, and you're a dad," Hank pointed out.

That did it.

And what it did was get him another smile.

***

Ally

"Babe."

I snuggled into the pillows.

"Ally."

I batted around my head like an annoying gnat was there.

The hand warm on my back slid to my hip and gave me a squeeze. "Baby, wake up. It's nearly noon."

My eyes fluttered open. I turned my head and saw Ren sitting on the side of the bed wearing jeans and a tee and looming over me.

His eyebrows went up and his tone was teasing when he asked, "Sleep is overrated?"

"Whatever," I muttered, looking away and snuggling back into the pillows.

I heard his chuckle before, "Honey, your phone is buzzing with texts and Hank called. He's on his way over."

Shit.

I rolled from my side to my back and asked, "Why is Hank on his way over?"

"He didn't say. He called me when he couldn't get you and just said he was comin' over."

Interesting.

"And Eddie brought your stuff," Ren went on.

Interesting.

Time to check for *Firefly* DVDs.

Also time to haul my ass out of bed.

I threw the covers back, leaned into him, touched my mouth to his then jumped out of bed and headed to the bathroom.

I was brushing my teeth when Ren walked in and slid a mug of coffee beside the sink. He looked into my eyes in the mirror, his smiling, before I watched him dip his head and kiss my shoulder.

Nice.

Then he left me to it.

I was in running clothes by the time I made it downstairs. I also had my phone in my hand and saw that I had texts from various Rock Chicks (Roxie asking me if I wanted to go shopping; Jules telling me her Uncle Nick was going to look after Max, Vance was on the path of some dude who skipped bond, so she asked if I wanted to go to a movie; and Daisy asking if I wanted to come over and do home facials).

I also had a text from my ex-landlord.

Ren came out of the kitchen when I stopped by the boxes on the floor in his living room and I looked up at him.

"Do you know Snookie Rivers?" I asked him.

"Who?" he asked back, coming to a stop by me.

"Snookie Rivers. I asked my landlord who lives in that apartment where you saw a dude looking out and he said his name is Snookie Rivers."

Ren shook his head. "Never heard of him."

I looked back at the phone, murmuring, "Me either."

"Sounds like a drag name," he commented.

I grinned and looked at my man.

My man looked down the length of me.

When I got his eyes back, they were burning. "You goin' for a run?"

"After I talk to Hank."

"Right," he muttered, his mind, I could tell, on happy things.

My mind was on those same things when I dropped to my knees and started rooting through the boxes.

Ren crouched beside me.

"Anything good?" he asked.

No. There wasn't anything good. Kitchen utensils. A lamp base without the shade. A picture frame, slightly scorched. But the picture was of the Rock Chicks at one of Stella's gigs, standing with her and her band, The Blue Moon Gypsies, on the stage. All of us were doing devil's horns (even the band, except her saxophonist, Hugo; he was checking out Ava's ass). Every Rock Chick had one of those pictures so I could get another copy. Still, nice to have it.

And, in box two, although it needed soot cleaned off it, my Lelo Lily vibrator.

Righteous!

"What's that?" Ren asked, and I looked at him to see him studying it.

"Pure goodness," I answered.

"What?"

I tested it by hitting the on button.

It vibrated.

Perfect working condition (once the soot was cleaned off).

Ren's eyes came to me and they were again burning.

A knock came at the door.

Ren stood from his crouch and headed to the door. I dropped my Lelo back in the box and straightened to see Ren letting Hank in.

"Yo," I called to my brother.

"Ally," Hank replied.

Ren looked between me and Hank, came to me and slid a hand along the back of my waist, leaning in.

"Goin' to the store, you need anything?" he asked.

He was giving us time for whatever this was.

My man.

So cool.

"No, but do you want to wait and I'll go with you?" I asked back.

"No. I want to have it done and be back when you get in from your run."

I wanted that, too.

Big time.

"All right," I said.

He gave me a touch on the lips and turned to Hank. "Hank."

A chin lift, then, "Ren."

Ren looked in my eyes again with a small smile before he sauntered out the front door.

"You want coffee?" I asked my brother.

"Hit Fortnum's before hitting here. I'm juiced up," he answered.

"And you didn't bring me one?" I asked.

"Sorry, Ally. Didn't think about it. Gotta have a word with you about a coupla things, then I gotta get back to Roxie."

Hmm.

I was curious, so I decided not to give him shit about dissing me on the coffee.

I moved to a couch and sat with my leg tucked under me. I dipped my head to the other side and Hank moved there, settling in.

"What's up?" I asked.

"We got a lock on who wrote that book," he answered.

Oh shit.

"Honey, it's Jane," he finished.

I took in a breath and admitted, "I know."

He did a slow blink. "You know?"

"I figured it out a few days ago. I've been trying to decide what to do with it."

"You figured it out," he stated.

"Uh... yeah," I confirmed.

My brother stared at me.

Then he shook his head while looking away with a small smile playing at his lips.

That was weird so I called, "Hank?"

He looked back at me. "Mace phoned this morning."

Here we go.

I was going to find out if I passed the Mace Test.

"And?" I prompted.

"And he said you were great last night, Ally."

I passed.

So I smiled.

"I've asked Lee to train you," Hank continued.

I stopped smiling and stared.

Then I asked, "What?"

"You need experience with a skilled investigator. The best in town is Lee. You need a license so you can charge enough to take care of you. He can help you get that. So I've asked him to train you."

Oh my God!

I had Hank's vote!

"And?" I said again.

"He's thinking on it."

Crap.

"Which means no," I stated.

"It doesn't mean no. It just doesn't mean yes."

Mm-hmm.

Whatever.

"I'm gonna tell him you figured it out about Jane," Hank said. "And I'm gonna tell him you sat on that in order to figure out what to do, rather than reacted and fucked shit up. Even Lee didn't know what to do. And you caught on before Brody. And as for me, through anything, I'll have your back."

I was beginning to get pissed-off.

Not about Hank having my back, I loved that. It felt great. He was an awesome brother and that was just one of the many ways he proved it.

I was pissed-off about Lee.

"I don't actually have to have his blessing, Hank. This would be indicated by the fact I'm already taking cases."

"He can teach you a lot," Hank noted.

"So can Darius, who already has, Vance, who also already has, Hector, Bobby, Ike and Mace," I returned.

"That's correct," he conceded.

"So you don't have to convince him. You don't have to do anything." I reached out, grabbed his hand, gave it a squeeze and let it go. "And having your support is all I need from you." My voice dropped quiet when I finished, "It means everything, honey."

Suddenly, he reached out and caught me at the back of my neck. Pulling me forward, he leaned into me and rested our foreheads together. And his voice was quiet when he spoke too.

"My little sister, livin' with a guy and bein' a badass."

Uh-oh.

My eyes were getting hot.

I lifted my hand to wrap my fingers around his forearm. "Hank—"

"You'll never be a big brother, honey, so you'll never understand how this feels. Lettin' go. Givin' care of the girl you love and looked after a long fuckin' time to another guy. Seein' her make her way in a world like that."

Oh God.

He was killing me.

So.

Loved.

My big brother!

"Honey—"

"It sucks. I'm happy, but that doesn't mean it doesn't feel like I've lost something."

Oh *God*.

"Please—"

"Give him time," he whispered.

He meant Lee.

And now I got it.

I was his little sister and Lee wasn't ready to let that go.

I pressed my lips together before I nodded, our foreheads rolling. Hank lifted a bit away but didn't let go of me, mostly because I squeezed his arm.

"I get you," I said softly. "But I hope you never let go."

"Good to have your permission, 'cause I see in him that you're it for him. He's all about you. His world has become you. And he can have that." His fingers tightened around my neck. "Still, in the way I can, I'm gonna keep hold."

Hank saw in Ren that his world had become me.

I liked that.

I wondered if Ren's sisters saw the same in me.

And my brother was going to keep hold.

Righteous.

"Good," I replied.

"Now I'm gonna go before you go girl on me and burst out crying."

I jerked back and declared, "That's not gonna happen."

That wasn't a lie. It was true.

Still, I was close.

My big brother smiled at me.

Then he let me go and got up, muttering, "Shit to do."

I had shit to do too. I had to run and get sweaty and come home and get laid by my man.

I did not share this.

I walked Hank to the door.

He opened it. I followed and stopped in the jamb.

It was then I remembered to ask, "What did you and Lee decide about Jane?"

He turned and answered, "He's gonna tell the men. He's gonna tell Indy. I'm gonna tell Roxie. And we're gonna keep our eye on shit but let the chips fall."

Time to scratch a conversation with Jane on my list, and I decided to give her a heads up before I ran.

The good news was, neither Hank nor Lee had gone ballistic. That might make Jane fret less.

Still, I'd have to keep an eye on things, too.

Hank leaned into me and I thought he was going to kiss my cheek.

He didn't.

He put his lips to my ear and said, "He hurts you, I'll fuck him up."

Loved my big brother.

"That won't happen," I replied.

He pulled away, saying, "It better not."

I rolled my eyes, and when I rolled them back, I saw him smiling.

I stuck my tongue out at him.

He smiled bigger.

Then he was gone.

⌁

I rushed offstage at Smithie's after my final dance, keen to get the hell out of there and get home to bed.

And Ren.

It was another bust of a night at Smithie's. Even though I'd approached a couple of the girls and had a chat with Tanya, one of the waitresses, there was no thawing of the informational freeze-out.

I'd also had a chat with Smithie about what he knew about Gibbons. I wasn't telling him our progress on the case because I didn't want him to lose it and screw the pooch if what Steiner and Gibbons were doing went deeper.

But Smithie paid attention in his club. So he knew exactly who I was talking about.

And his response was, "He's an asshole. Shit vibe. But good customer. He drinks. Tips the girls good. Gets a lap dance every night. Don't love every one of my regulars. But I don't bitch when they buy drinks and take care of the girls."

Gibbons would tip the girls "good" since he'd see a return of that money, and not in the normal way.

"Why you ask?" Smithie finished.

"Just keeping my eye on things and he gives me the heebie-jeebies," I told him.

"Yeah," he replied. "Asshole written all over him. Then again, that's every other guy who walks through my fuckin' door."

He was right. But not *that* brand of asshole.

I left it at that.

Then I went about my business, hoping that Bobby and Darius would turn up something or one of the girls would suck up the courage to give me a lead.

And soon.

But now the night was over and the workday was done for me. The girls had half an hour of dancing before they were finished, but there was no reason for me to stay. Therefore, if I did, it might be noticed and wondered about.

So I headed to the dressing room as the girls headed toward the stage to take over once Lottie was done.

"Have fun," I said on a big smile.

"Mm-hmm," JoJo replied on a forced one.

"Have a good night, Ally," Meena said as she passed me.

She also grabbed my hand.

I thought that was weird.

Until I felt her pressing something in my palm.

I closed my fingers around what felt like a piece of paper and a jolt of energy surged through me making it hard to keep my voice modulated when I called, "See you tomorrow night."

"Later, babe," JoJo called back.

Meena turned back and waved.

But her face said it all.

Fear.

Shit.

I rushed to the dressing room, got dressed, grabbed my stuff and hauled ass. My palms were itching, but I didn't want anyone to see me reading the note.

So I waited until I was sitting at a stoplight before I yanked the paper out of my pocket, unfolded it and read it.

We pay, or they do it. We talk, and they do it.

They have more guys. Eyes all the time.

We don't pay or we talk, they're gonna hurt Smithie.

I stared at the paper.

Then I whispered, "Fuck."

⟨⟩

I sat cross-legged on the bed in my jeans and tee (but I'd flipped off my flip-flops).

Ren was up against the headboard, sheet to his waist, chest on view.

For once, I didn't appreciate the view. My mind was on other things.

He was studying the note which, incidentally, was what my mind was on.

In other words, I was obsessing over it.

Ren had elected not to go to Smithie's that night and instead stay in and get some shuteye.

But I'd woken him up after I flipped off my flip-flops and turned on a light.

Then I'd shown him the note.

He looked from it to me. "You want me to put Lucky and Santo on this?"

This surprised me.

"Would Lucky and Santo be helpful?"

"One of many things those two have goin' for them is everyone underestimates them." He held my eyes. "Heads up to you, don't underestimate them."

I nodded.

That was good to know, and as Curious Rock Chick, also a relief to have that intel.

"So you want me to put them on this?" he pressed.

I leaned toward him and put my hand to his chest. "No, baby. But thanks for the offer."

"Ally—" he started, his voice cautious, and I knew where he was going.

This was bigger than me. Even bigger than me and Darius.

This needed team play.

So I cut him off in order that he wouldn't worry. "I have to talk to Lee."

Ren let out a breath.

I took one in and said, "I had this feeling when it started. It wasn't bad. It was *bad*. Darius on it, bringing in Bobby and Brody, I felt better." I tipped my head to the note. "That? Smithie needs the big guns."

To that, Ren weirdly asked, "Do you know what's amazing?"

"Well… no," I answered, bemused at this turn of conversation.

"That you give a shit enough about what you do, and about Smithie, to be big enough to set pride aside to do the job right."

He.

Was.

So.

Awesome.

"You're just saying that so I'll kiss you," I replied.

"No. I'm sayin' it 'cause it's true. Though, I'm also sayin' it so you'll kiss me. But mostly I'm sayin' it so you'll fuck me."

My happy place spasmed, but my eyebrows drew together.

"I was dancing all night and you want me to do all the work?"

"Babe, you dance for eight, ten minutes tops. That hardly puts you out of commission."

"I also had a run today," I reminded him.

He grinned. "Yeah, I remember."

That grin—another happy place spasm.

"So I'm thinking my man needs to put in a little effort," I kept going.

"I did that after your run."

This was true. And it was more than a little. This was because, before I got back from my run, Ren had cleaned my Lelo.

"Okay, a little *more* effort," I amended.

"Are you sayin' you're good with missionary?" he asked.

"Missionary is growing on me," I shared.

Ren grinned a grin I felt in my nipples *and* my happy place.

Then he set the note on his nightstand and lunged toward me, taking me to my back on the bed with him on top.

His lips to my lips, his eyes looking into mine, he suggested, "Let's see if I can take it to number one."

I was all for that.

Totally.

And I shared this by lifting my head and kissing him.

Hard, wet and wild.

Ren kissed me back the same way.

Chapter 29
Top of That List

My eyes fluttered open as I woke.

Ren's arms gave me a squeeze.

"Babe, you awake?"

I grinned to myself and rolled from Ren spooning me to me snuggling front to front with my man.

He wrapped a hand around my jaw, tipped my head back and moved in, giving me a soft, sweet morning kiss.

Oh yeah. This together *togetherness* rocked.

And did in a way that would last forever.

So that rocked a helluva lot more.

He disengaged and said in his sweet voice, "Mornin', baby."

"Mornin'," I replied, snuggling deeper into his warm, hard body. Then I declared, "I have to apologize."

He did a slow blink and asked, "For what?"

"For going back on the promise I made myself last Sunday that I'd make you breakfast in bed every Sunday morning until the day my arthritic hands couldn't crack open an egg." I watched his face get soft(er) and thus hot(ter) and kept talking. "But I have to talk with Lee, and I have to get to Fortnum's to check in." I snuggled even closer and finished on a whisper, "But you pick a day this week, I'll make up for it."

"You don't have to make up for it, Ally," he replied.

"Yes, I do."

"Babe, you don't."

"Babe, you liked it," I stated. "And I liked that you liked it. And I like doing things for you that you like. So give that to me and think on a day when you'll take my rain check."

It was him that pulled me closer when he said, "All right, honey."

I kept snuggled close as I moved on to the hard part. "There's something else I need to tell you when you're in a sweet, waking up Sunday morning mood."

His eyes came alert and his lips muttered, "Oh shit."

Oh yeah, oh shit.

"Okay, there hasn't been a good time to tell you this because there is no good time to tell you this, but also things have been kinda busy, so I'm picking now because you need to know," I explained.

"Just tell me, Ally," Ren demanded.

"I know who wrote that book. She's a member of the Fortnum's family. Her name is Jane," I said quickly.

"Fuck," he growled, "Seriously?"

"I don't know if you've met her but——"

"Does your brother know?" he cut me off to ask.

"Which one?" I asked back.

"Either one, Ally," he clipped, impatient.

"Um... well, yeah. Both of them do."

"And what're they doin' about this shit?"

"Nothing."

Ren stared at me a beat before he asked, "Nothing?"

"She's a member of the family, honey," I said quietly.

"Who's tradin' on the private lives of that family," Ren returned.

"Who's weaving fairytales," I countered and slid up so we were eye to eye. "She's wanted this her whole life."

"I don't give a fuck."

"It's beautiful, Ren. All of it. Why shouldn't the world know?"

His head jerked against the pillow and he clamped his mouth shut.

"I'm not mad," I told him. "None of the girls are mad. Neither Hank nor Lee freaked about it. And I want you to try to dig deep in you to find that to give to Jane because I care about her. And I believe in what she's doing." I shot him a smile. "Everyone should know how righteous we are."

"Does it matter to you that I don't want everyone to know how righteous I am?" he asked.

"Yes," I answered. "And if you dig deep and find that you can't get there, you tell me. I'll do what I can. In the meantime, I think we both need to read Indy and Lee's book so we know exactly what we're dealing with."

He drew in a breath before he murmured, "That I can do." My lips started turning up again, but his arms gave me a squeeze. "I don't wanna do it, babe.

That kind of book is not my thing and there are things about your brother and his woman I do not want to know…" He paused. "Like everything."

I again had to fight my lips turning up as he carried on.

"But I should know how bad it is before I make a decision."

"Or how good it is." I gave him an alternate option.

"Whatever," he mumbled.

I let loose my grin.

Ren caught it. The irritation leaked out of his eyes and he sighed.

Loved my man.

"I need to call, Lee, baby," I reminded him.

"Right," he replied and rolled to his back, taking me with him. He let me go to reach to my jeans on the floor where he pulled out my phone, settled back in bed and handed it to me.

"Thanks," I muttered and went about engaging Lee.

After two rings, my brother answered with an, "Ally."

"Yo, bro," I replied. "Do you have some time for me this morning? It's important."

"Need to talk to you, too," he stated.

Interesting.

My curiosity peaked, I asked, "About what?"

"About Indy," he answered. "Last few days, morning sickness hit. It's not good. It's gonna be tough for her to be at the store. I know you're workin' a case, but with Indy in this state and Jet gettin' to the point where she shouldn't be on her feet for hours, she needs you. Indy feels shit she can't take Jet's back, but when she's pukin' half the time, she can't do it. She won't ask, but I will. She needs you."

"Of course," I said instantly. "I'm going to the store anyway. But need to talk to you."

"About what?" he asked my question.

"Face to face, bro."

"Shit," he muttered.

"It's not bad." I thought on that statement and changed my tune. "Well, it's not good. Actually it *is* bad, but I'm hoping it can be fixed."

A pause before he asked, "You want me to come to you or you to me?'

"You're close to the store, and I'm going there anyway so I'll come to you."

"Text me when you're on your way and I'll meet you at the store."

"Copy that."

"Later, Ally."

"Right back at 'cha, Lee."

We disconnected and I looked to Ren. "Indy got hit by morning sickness, so I'm gonna be needed more at the store."

"I take it that means there's no time for a quickie," Ren remarked.

Alas, that was what it meant.

I frowned at him in disappointment.

He grinned at me, curled up and gave me a light kiss.

When he was done, he whispered, "Go get 'em, baby."

I bent my neck, kissed his throat, gave him a smile then jumped out of bed in order to do what I did.

That was go and get 'em.

⤝⤞

Lee studied the note from Meena.

We were at Fortnum's standing way at the back in the religion section. We were there because we needed optimum Fortnum's privacy and this was the best there was. The religion section, right or wrong, didn't see a lot of action.

Lee looked from the note to me.

"This is not good," he stated.

"I know," I replied.

"Ally—"

I leaned into him. "I need your help."

He stared at me.

I kept talking. "It's bad there, Lee. The vibe is total shit. The girls are scared out of their minds. Roam has seen Steiner take money from dancers *and* waitresses. I haven't seen anyone else in the club who was giving me the willies, but my guess is that when Meena said there were eyes all around, she didn't just mean Steiner and his partner. Something has to be done about that, and *soon*. Smithie's in danger and, bottom line, this is bigger than me."

Lee just kept staring at me.

So I kept talking.

"If you don't want to take the case, then I need some of your guys. I need more of Brody's time. I'll pay them and—"

Lee cut me off. "It's not about the case."

"Then why are you hesitating?" I asked. "This is Smithie."

He stared at me another beat and right before I lost my patience, he stated, "We'll get into the why later. Right now, I'm gonna make some calls and get some boys in the field, focus Brody. I'll call you when we got something and we'll have a meeting. Yeah?"

We'd have a meeting?

We?

Me, my brother, *and his team?*

I didn't ask. I didn't do cartwheels. I didn't grab him and do a girlie hug. I just nodded and said, "Yeah."

"Roam and Sniff off this thing?" he asked.

"Darius called them down when Gibbons entered the picture," I answered.

"Good," he muttered, looked at the note again and back at me. "Got shit to do. Keep your phone on you."

I nodded.

He gave me nothing; not a look, not a smile, not a thing, and he was gone.

I wandered out of the books, got to the front and saw Daisy with her Juicy Couture covered ass in a couch with a laptop on her lap surrounded by Jet, Roxie, Stella and Sadie (not in Juicy Couture, and Stella's awesome rock tee was making me nostalgic for my collection that was destroyed by an explosion).

Time to hit some concerts. Then again, it was always time to hit some concerts.

Daisy looked up and spied me.

"Sugar, get over here!" she called excitedly. "Roxie's put some website ideas together and brought them in."

"They're all the bomb," Stella said as I moved that way, curious to see and also feeling that feeling I was getting to know and oh-so-definitely loved flowing through me.

"I don't know how you're gonna pick," Jet told me.

Sadie moved to an armchair so I could squish between Daisy and Stella.

"Here's one," Daisy stated then clicked. "And the next." Another click. "And the third," she said. "Aren't they *amazing?*"

They were.

Every one.

Totally.

Kristen Ashley

I looked across Daisy to Roxie. "They're righteous."

Roxie grinned. "I'm pretty pleased with them." Her eyes moved to the screen. "Though, you need a name. It's hard for Ava and me to come up with looks and color schemes if you don't have a company title."

"Rock Chick Investigations," I announced and felt all eyes on me. "Colors, hot pink and black."

"*Aces,*" Sadie breathed.

I looked at her and grinned. "I know, right?"

"That's perfect," Jet said.

"Hot pink and black, like the book," Roxie pointed out.

I moved my eyes to her and nodded.

As if on cue, Tex boomed from behind the espresso counter, "Loopy Loo! B.A.! You feel like workin' or you gonna hen peck all day?" He looked to Duke who was beside him. "And where's Jane? Indy's at home hurlin'. Loopy Loo's in the bathroom all the time. We need fuckin' help."

He stopped booming long enough to point at me before he started up again.

"You! B.A.! You got a man in your bed now, you get pregnant, I'm quittin'."

The customer waiting at the end of the counter for her coffee turned to me and immediately begged, "Please don't get pregnant. My life sucks. All I have to look forward to every day is this crazy guy's coffee. If he quits, what will I do?"

"I'm not getting pregnant," I assured her and she looked visibly relieved. I then turned my attention to Tex. "And you've only got two customers. You and Duke can handle it."

"I got two customers, but I'm low on mugs. You want me to fill 'em, you wash 'em. I don't wash. I fill. That's the deal," Tex shot back (loudly). "So get to clearin' and cleanin'."

This was true.

Still, I was doing something.

I was also curious.

"What's with the B.A. shit?" I asked.

"Bad," Tex pointed at me, "*Ass.*"

Holy crap!

I loved that!

I was Fortnum's own Mr. T, except white, female and without the Mohawk.

422

Righteous!

"You know," Jet put in. "Because Indy's not here doesn't make you the boss. If anyone's the boss, it's Duke."

Tex turned to Duke and declared (again loudly), "I don't wash."

"Man, been workin' beside you two years. I know you don't wash. I don't care that you don't wash. What I do care about is you shoutin' at me when I'm two feet away. And don't shout at the girls either. They'll get to the empties." Duke shook his head. "Jesus. You just got married a few days ago. You'd think connin' a good woman into takin' your name would get you to cool it."

"You got married?" the customer Duke was handing coffee asked Tex and didn't wait for an answer before she said, "Congratulations."

"Shut it," Tex boomed.

"Tex!" Jet snapped.

"What?" he snapped back.

Jet gave up on Tex and looked at the customer. "I'm sorry."

"He's told me to shut it three times this week," the woman replied then took a sip of coffee, lifted her paper cup and let that say what she needed it to say (and it said it) before she wandered out of the store.

Tex piped down and I turned my attention to Sadie when she asked, "Where *is* Jane anyway?"

There were some looks and no one said anything so I waded in. "Do you all know?"

"About the book?" Jet asked and I nodded.

"Yep," Stella said.

"Mm-hmm," Roxie mumbled.

"Hector told me this morning," Sadie added.

"Marcus told me last night. Shocked the shit outta me at first, then I got it," Daisy said.

I tested the waters. "Are any of you angry?"

"Hell no," Stella answered right away. "My record company is beside themselves. They say those books are gonna sell a shit ton of records. Mace is still pissed though. First he was pissed because the books existed. Now he's pissed because he can't say anything. Then again, Mace has a short fuse and he gets pissed a lot."

This was true, but the sultry grin on her face said, at least for her, this wasn't a bad thing.

"I know," Jet put in. "Anyone but Jane, those guys would lose their minds. Jane, though, she wouldn't hurt a fly. So what do you do?"

"Hector doesn't care," Sadie added. "Then again, he was more worried about me." Her eyes wandered the room and she continued quietly as they did, "But this place, it's where dreams come true." She looked to us. "So why shouldn't Jane's come true, too?"

"You got that right, sister," I replied and Sadie smiled.

The bell over the door went and a couple of customers walked in.

Tex took this as his prompt to shout, "Hello! Empties?"

Jet jumped up.

I reached in, commandeered the laptop touchpad, clicked and looked to Roxie. "Can we work with that one?"

She smiled. "Absolutely."

I smiled back, got up and got to work.

In order not to set Tex off, I bided my time and corralled Duke when Tex had plenty of clean mugs to fill, Jet was not in the bathroom and we were in a rare lull.

I approached Duke behind the book counter.

"Two shakes?" I asked.

"Got as many shakes as you need, darlin'," he answered.

I grinned, got close and put my back to the room. "Don't wanna take you out of this space and make anyone curious by going into the books but I need your wisdom. I also need your promise you won't share anything I say until we decide it needs to be shared."

"Won't say a word, Ally."

I nodded and got a little closer. Then, as quietly as I could, as fast as I could but as thorough as I could, I shared the situation with Darius, Malia and Liam Edward Clark.

When I stopped talking, his eyes were wide and his lips formed the gravelly words, "Fuckin' hell."

"I know," I agreed.

"Fuckin' hell," he repeated.

"I know, Duke," I replied. "Now what do we do?"

For some reason, he turned his head and looked to the front door. What he did not do was look back at me.

"Duke?" I called.

That was when he looked back at me to say, "It's worse than I thought."

"Mm-hmm," I mumbled.

"I need time with this," he told me.

I got that, so I nodded.

"Fuckin' hell," Duke repeated.

"Duke—"

He interrupted me. "Would sell my soul to have Joshua back. He's got a boy in this town he don't see?"

Uh-oh.

I got closer. "Duke—"

"No, Ally," he shook his head, "not angry. Just thinkin'. And I need time to think more."

"Okay, I feel you," I said. "But can I ask you don't take too much of it? We're already way out of the zone where a successful reunion would be anything but difficult for them. We don't need to be so out of that zone it's an impossibility."

His gaze grew intense. "No way I'm gonna fuck around thinkin' on this, Ally. There are many things in life that are precious. Your child is the top of that list."

I pressed my lips together and nodded.

Duke started to walk away, but before he could pass me, I reached out, grabbed his hand and squeezed.

I let him go just as quickly as I grabbed him and he kept going.

I got back to work, but I found the time to hit the shelves again to make a call to Jane to let her know at least the girls were cool so she could come out of hiding. But I got her voicemail so I left a message.

As I was walking out, while I was shoving my phone back in my pocket, it binged.

I looked at it and saw a text from Lee. I didn't need to open it as it was short and the entirety of it fit on the notification.

Team meeting. Office. Two hours.

He had something.

Already.

God, my brother was *good.*

Team meeting.

That feeling stole through me again.

Therefore, I was grinning when I went about yet again collecting empties.

Chapter 30

For Me

Ren

Ren Zano hiked the strap of his workout bag more firmly on his shoulder as he walked from the gym to his Jag while pulling out his ringing phone.

The display said *Santo Calling.*

He engaged and put it to his ear. "Santo."

"Boss, you need to get here."

Ren stopped at the door to his car and looked at his boots, his gut twisting.

This was because he gave Santo a job that morning. And that job was getting into Snookie Rivers's apartment to have a look around.

"What?" Ren asked.

"You need to see," Santo replied.

Ren clenched his teeth and beeped his locks.

Pulling open the door and folding in, he asked, "Is he out for a while?"

"Lucky's on him. He makes to come home, Lucky'll give me the heads up."

"Be there in ten," Ren stated.

He disconnected and turned on the ignition.

When he hit Ally's old apartment complex, he saw construction had already begun on her blasted out unit. There was some structural damage; not much, mostly the windows blown out and fire damage, but they weren't wasting any time fixing it.

He parked, got out, kept his phone in his hand and jogged to the building, in and up the stairs.

He tapped a knuckle on Rivers's door and it was immediately opened by Santo.

Ren didn't like the look on his face.

"Show me," he ordered.

Santo got out of the way. Ren entered the apartment, moved aside and let Santo lead the way. Santo moved down the hall to one of the bedrooms but stopped at the door and turned to Ren.

"Boss, this is fucked up," he warned.

Ren looked him in the eyes then moved beyond him and into the room.

Once in, he stopped dead.

Three beats later, he whispered, "Fuckin' fuck me."

"You want Lucky to nab him?" Santo asked.

Ren's eyes moved around the room, his gut no longer twisting. It was tied in painful knots and it felt like something heavy was pressing on his chest.

This was because, all around the room, the walls were littered with pictures of Ally. Entering her apartment. Leaving her apartment. Walking down the hall. In the parking lot walking to her Mustang. Getting in or out of it.

And more.

Ally in Fortnum's. Ally at Stella's gigs. Ally bartending at Brother's. Ally at the mall with one or more of the Rock Chicks.

And Ally entering and exiting *his* house. Some from months ago. Some from days ago.

The whole room was covered in Ally.

Every inch.

There were so many pictures, they were several layers deep.

"Boss? Lucky?" Santo prompted and Ren cut his eyes to the man.

"Yes, I fuckin' want Lucky to nab him," he growled. "And call Dom. Now." He threw out a hand. "And take pictures of this shit. Detailed."

After he issued his orders, he spent no more time in that space.

He walked right out.

His gut still tied up tight.

His chest now burning.

꘎꘎꘎

Ally

I walked into the down room at Nightingale Investigations to see the gang all there.

Every one of them.

This included Lee, Eddie, Hank, Vance, Mace, Hector, Darius, Matt, Bobby, Monty, Ike, Jack, Brody and even Luke, who just got back from his honeymoon with Ava that morning.

Jimmy Marker was also there.

This meant things were not as bad as I thought.

They were worse.

I didn't call my welcome back, glad-you-survived-all-that-unadulterated-nookie to Luke.

I just cut my eyes through the men, got a bunch of chin lifts (seriously?), moved to a weight bench and sat my ass on it.

Lee watched me do it and turned to the team.

"Brief," he began, his voice terse, indicating things weren't worse, they were *worse.* "You all know the case Ally's on and you all know about the payments, the players already uncovered and the note Meena gave to Ally last night."

No one nodded. They all just kept their eyes on Lee.

After looking around, I followed suit.

"Brody found the trail," Lee went on. "Cyrus Gibbons's cellmate in Nebraska has links to Steiner and the crew here. This morning, Darius tailed Steiner and Bobby tailed Gibbons to a crew meet. There are five of them. Darius was able to get into position without bein' seen to listen in. Their gig is, they got a man on each of Smithie's women, and therefore his kids."

Oh my God.

I closed my eyes.

"Gibbons is on Smithie," Lee continued and I opened my eyes. "The girls don't pay, givin' their tip takes, they put the hurt on *all* of Smithie's family. They talk, they put the hurt on *all* of them. They don't give Gibbons what he wants during his private dances, he puts the hurt on Smithie."

Seeing as my head was suddenly about to explode at Lee's words, I had to let some of the pressure out.

Therefore, I couldn't stop myself from hissing, "You're shitting me."

Lee looked at me. "Ally——"

"He's raping them at Smithies?" I snapped.

"Forced blowjobs, same thing," Lee answered, his voice tight.

I surged from my seat, shouting, "You've got to be *shitting me!*"

"Ally, cool it," Hank said quietly.

429

"*You* cool it. You haven't spent your nights working alongside a bunch of girls who're being violated!" I shot back.

"This isn't going on for another day, Ally," Lee stated. "We're takin' them down tonight, all those fuckers. And you got your part in that. I get you're pissed. I get why. We're all pissed. But we got a job to do. You need to shift that anger to focus, 'cause you're a go tonight."

I was *a go?*

What the hell did that mean?

"What?" I asked.

"We have to take them down simultaneously so they don't have the opportunity to talk, see or hear the others were taken out and do something about it, namely put one of Smithie's women or kids in danger. At the club tonight, Steiner will be Darius's. Gibbons, yours."

"I'm on Gibbons," Darius stated and I knew why. He was the greater danger.

Lee looked to him.

"They're steerin' clear of Lottie because of her connection with Eddie and likely the rest of us. This means they know the connection, so he'll know you. You enter when Ally's dancin' and Gibbons has eyes on her. Steiner will either have eyes on her or the crowd. You go for Steiner. Ally makes Gibbons part of the act and she goes for him." Lee looked at me. "It sucks and it makes me wanna vomit sayin' this, but you dance for him. You do it smart. You'll have backup, Ally. Luke and Mace are on you. But you gotta disarm him and not get shot doin' it."

Holy shit!

Lee looked like he'd eaten something rotten when he asked, "Can you keep him occupied to do that?"

I stared at him. I looked to Hank to see a muscle jerk in his cheek. I looked through the men.

They all had eyes on me.

I looked back at Lee and sat my ass down again, saying, "Absolutely."

Lee nodded.

"While he's eyes to you, Darius takes Steiner out, Mace and Luke will get into position," he went on. "You just have to get your hand on his gun. Shoulder holster. His left side. Once you got it, you get the fuck outta the way. Mace and Luke will move in."

I nodded.

His voice dropped lower when he said, "You got the feel, Ally. You demonstrated that at Lincoln's. If it hits you it's goin' bad, he looks like he's goin' for his gun, you get the fuck out. Mace and Luke will roll in. But I want his ass jacked by a dancer. I want him disarmed and unmanned by a woman and I want that to have an audience. You with me?"

Oh, fuck yeah.

I was with him.

When I nodded that time, I was grinning.

Lee studied me. Then he turned to the boys.

"Vance, Bobby, you're team one. Hector and Matt, team two. Jack and Monty, team three. Brody will give you the details you need. Jimmy, Hank and Eddie will sweep up."

Lee's eyes were looking at the men he was addressing then he came back to me.

"After you take yours down, we're closin' Smithie's and you work the girls. You get them to trust you. You get them to trust us. You get them to trust the cops. And you get them to make statements and press charges."

"Copy that," I replied.

Lee studied me again before he looked back to his men. "You have your assignments. This happens during Ally's first dance. Eight fifty-five. Track your men. Find them. Report in. And the time comes, take them out."

More chin lifts.

Jeez.

The gang broke up just as Darius's phone rang.

But I looked to Lee. "Need a second. In private. Eddie, too."

My eyes went to Eddie to see him watching me intently.

"Ally, got shit to do," Lee said, sounding distracted.

"A second, Lee," I replied quietly.

It was my quiet that got him to give me a look. He transferred his gaze to Eddie and then he nodded to me

I avoided all eyes as he moved out of the room and I followed him, Eddie following me.

Lee took us to his office, but stood at the door until Eddie and I made it through. Then he closed the door and turned his back to it, not moving further into the room.

Right. His position reiterated he was giving me only a second, he had shit to do.

So did I, so I cut to it.

I took a deep breath and reminded him. "You know I'm worried about Darius."

"I do," Lee confirmed. "But is now the time for you to get up in our shit about it?"

"I know about Malia and Liam."

I watched Lee's entire body get tight, and I didn't normally get scared but that sure as fuck scared me.

"Zano tell you?" he fired at me, his words like bullets.

"No," I answered, shaking my head for emphasis. "I found out like I find out a lot of shit. I know a lot of people. I ask a lot of questions." I looked to Eddie. "I did it on the down low so there's nothing for you two to worry about."

"You're wrong," Lee returned, and I looked back to him.

"I know this is privileged information and the person who told me was not real big on me knowing it. But I got the information and I'm gonna do something about it."

Lee leaned toward me, his eyes narrowing. "You're not gonna do shit."

"I am," I whispered. "There's a boy growing up without his father."

Lee leaned back. "That's Darius's choice."

"It's the wrong one," I retorted.

"That's not your call," Lee clipped.

"Yes, it is. Yes, it absolutely is," I shot back, lifted a hand and shook my head. "Don't worry, bro. You don't want to be involved with whatever I decide to do, don't be. That's *your* call. Though I'll assure you, I will not make a production of this. And I won't drag the Rock Chicks into it. What I'm gonna do is take a big risk and point out some important facts to a man I love and have loved since I was a kid. He cuts me out, so be it. But there's the slight chance he'll listen to me, maybe not now, maybe eventually, but then he'll find a way back to his family. And that's important enough, not just for Darius but for Malia and especially Liam, I'm willing to take that risk."

Lee glared at me.

I looked to Eddie and the instant I did, he said, "Don't fuck this up."

"I can't guarantee that," I told him honestly. "What I can do is do my best to make certain this is about me and Darius and it doesn't leak to the rest of the posse. And I'll do that."

But Lee was now glaring at Eddie, and after I finished speaking, he bit out, "You cannot be cool with this."

"I'm not. Then again, *hermano,* I haven't been cool with this shit for seventeen fuckin' years," Eddie replied.

Lee again closed his mouth.

He wasn't cool with it either.

I took in a breath and held it.

Lee looked back to me. "I'm not involved."

This was disappointing. It was also unsurprising. There was never a time when there wasn't a Lee, Eddie and Darius. Even when Lee and Eddie were fighting (which happened often) and when Darius was on the wrong side of the law and Eddie was a cop.

They had a bond. They were brothers.

And if you love your brother, you had his back and backed his plays.

So I nodded.

Lee's body partially relaxed when he informed me, "You don't know this but he takes care of them."

"I do know that. It isn't about money and protection, though," I replied. "It's something bigger and you know it."

"He does what he can do," Lee stated and I totally dug it that he was defending his best friend.

But he needed to *wake up.*

"Your baby is growing in my best friend's belly," I reminded him and his head jerked. "And God forbid something happens between you and Indy or to you to change you or take you away from them in any capacity. You think on that. You think on Indy going it alone raising your child. She'd have money, no doubt. But you know that's not even the half of what it takes. And, last, you think on your child growing up without knowing all the righteousness that is you. That would be a tragedy. So you think on that, Lee. Then you come back to me and tell me I'm doing the wrong thing. I still won't believe you and I'll still do what I intend to do. But I'll be even more disappointed in you." I looked to Eddie and finished, "The both of you."

I thought that was a good parting line so I made it one, moved forward, shoved past Lee and walked out the door.

⚜

"Babe, it's going to be cool."

That was me, sitting with Ren at his dining room table, watching him not eating the seafood linguini he'd made us and instead sipping wine, staring at the table and brooding.

I'd told him everything. About what was happening at Smithie's and about the wheels I set in motion in regards to Darius.

I did not expect him to lay a hot and heavy celebratory kiss on me after he shouted, "All right! My woman is going to be in the line of fire tonight!"

So I was giving him his space, but I still wanted to assure him I was going to be all right.

I mean, Mace and Luke had my back. That was nothing to sneeze at.

At my words, he turned his head to me, sipped more wine and when he was done, he stated, "I'm gonna be there tonight."

I fought back a sigh but nodded.

I expected that. It was intrusive and maybe wrong. But my man had a protective streak, and until he was entirely down with what I was doing, I needed to give him some leeway.

He went back to brooding.

I reached out and touched his thigh. "Honey, I'm gonna be okay."

He looked at me and declared, "Santo got into Snookie Rivers's apartment today. He has a room dedicated to pictures of you. He's a stalker, and not the tame harmless variety. The sick and twisted variety. Lucky was on him and he must have made him, because when Lucky went to get the drop on him, he got the drop on Lucky and got away."

I shot back in my seat.

Holy shit!

"There's an unknown weirdo out there taking pictures of me?" I asked.

"Yeah. Everywhere. All you. At work. At home. Both of 'em. Your apartment and here. Just you. Hundreds, maybe thousands of them."

Hundreds was bad.

But *thousands?*

"I... what..." I stammered, then pulled myself out of my shock and got it together. "What the hell?"

"I don't know. My mind doesn't work like that. What I do know is while I've been thinkin' on this and whether or not to tell you, I didn't think on whether or not to give Darius the heads up. So I did. And you might be pissed, but he's at your back often so he needs to keep an eye out. I left it up to him, and now you, if you share with your brothers. But my vote, you do, and someone, I don't give a fuck who, closes that guy down."

This grossed me out, but still.

"I'm not sure it's illegal to take pictures of someone, Ren."

"The way he's doin' it?" he asked, but didn't want an answer mostly because he already had one. "Fuck yeah it is. You need a restraining order. Which won't do jack. So that means he gets a message. And I'd like it to be me that gives it to him. But if Darius, one of your brothers or one of his men get there before me, I won't argue."

This did not make me feel warm and fuzzy.

"It was that bad?" I asked quietly.

"Thousands of pictures, Ally," he answered, not quietly.

Whoa.

He wasn't being broody about my job that night.

He was being broody because I had a sicko taking photos of me.

"Do we have a picture of him so I know who I'm looking for and they will, too?" I asked.

"Darius says he's got Brody on that. DMV. Whatever. Brody will find somethin' and he'll give it to me."

I nodded.

"You watch your back. You also drive to work tonight with me."

Oh man.

"Ren—"

"Do not fight this, Ally," he cut me off. "It'll get ugly, I assure you, baby, and you won't win. I got a man fixated on my woman and you gotta let me do what I have to do. You with me?"

I thought on it, but not long enough for the Italian Hothead to wake up and decide he needed to make his point.

Then I said, "I'm with you, honey."

He took in a deep breath and let it go.

Relief.

"Though, I'll say, I miss our fighting," I continued.

His chin jerked back and his brows went up before he asked, "Have you lost your mind?"

"No. Without fights there's no angry sex."

That got him

His lips quirked. He put down his wineglass and picked up his fork as he asked, "Am I fallin' down on that part of the job, babe?"

"I will point out, we haven't had sex today," I shared, also digging back into my linguini.

I was lifting a load to my mouth when I felt his eyes on me. So I gave him mine.

"The day isn't done," he replied.

I grinned.

Then I quit grinning so I could shove delicious linguini and shrimp into my mouth.

⚜

"I get him, you get off stage. You get the girls in the dressing room and keep them there. You keep the dressing room door closed and locked. Lenny's gonna be outside. You keep your phone in your hand and you hear something you don't like, you call 911. And you keep the girls calm."

I was giving the instructions Lee gave to me by text to Lottie.

I was about to go on. And Lottie was going on with me.

Double the viewing entertainment, double the distraction from what would be going on in the club.

I'd briefed her and Lottie knew what was happening.

All of it.

And she was all in.

I got closer and said quietly, "This ends for them tonight. But our jobs aren't done tonight."

She nodded.

"He get them all?" I asked something I didn't want to know but, alas, needed to know.

She nodded again but said, "He's partial to JoJo. Sometimes he has a taste for Meena. But he's tried them all."

I lifted my hands to the sides of her head and pulled her to me so our foreheads were touching. "We'll see to them."

She nodded but said, "Smithie's gonna unravel."

Smithie knew nothing about this. This was because Smithie would first commit murder.

Then he'd unravel.

"We'll see to him, too," I promised.

She nodded again.

"You do that onstage, I'll give you both fifty bucks as a bonus and I'll name my next fuckin' kid after you," Smithie said as he approached.

Lottie and I broke apart and looked his way.

"We're already dancing a double," I reminded him.

"Yeah. I know. This is why you're in my fuckin' will," Smithie replied as the music silenced and the girls ran off the stage.

I drew in a deep breath and grabbed Lottie's hand.

Smithie went onstage and walked across it to get the microphone.

"Remember," I said, staring through the crack in the curtain. "When I get him, you get the girls."

"I remember," Lottie replied on a hand squeeze. "And if, when you get his gun, you accidentally squeeze off a round, I'm your witness that it was accidentally."

Great minds think alike.

"So put your hands together, motherfuckers!" Smithie was concluding his introduction. "'Cause the Rock Chick and Lottie Mac are teamin' up, and it's gonna blow your *motherfucking minds!*"

It certainly would.

In a lot of ways.

The club went black, Smithie stumbled off and Lottie and I dashed on.

In the dark, the opening riffs of Nickelback's "Something in Your Mouth" hit the space. The rest of the band kicked in, the bright lights hit the stage and Lottie and I hit each other.

It was an ingenious plan. No man in that room would look anywhere but at Lottie and I as we double teamed. Squatting down and sliding up each other's bodies. Smacking each other's asses. Circling a pole low while the other went high. Flicking each other's hair. Kicking a leg over the other who was in a squat. Both of us swinging our asses out to the audience in tandem.

And frequently, we sucked on our thumbs.

And each other's.

If this wasn't part of a mission, I would have giggled my ass off through the whole thing. It was a blast. Absolutely. And the light in Lottie's eyes told me she felt the same.

We were both down to sequined bras and panties and platform stripper shoes when we broke off. Lottie caught attention by catching the pole high, swinging out, rolling off and hitting her hands and knees, crawling on the stage with back arched, ass high, lips parted, hair in her face.

She was the total shit.

I jumped off the stage and it was during one of the rapid-fire rap parts of the song so I could make some moves on a couple men on my way to my target.

And as the song broke down, I did a lot of gyrating, hair whipping, slow walking, dipping my ass into laps only to pull away before flesh hit flesh, and shimmying.

I found my way in front of Gibbons just as the song kicked it up again.

I looked into his eyes.

He was looking at my breasts.

Fuck yeah.

It didn't matter my last name was Nightingale. It didn't matter that I might be a threat.

I had tits.

And that meant I had him, the asshole.

I leaned down, putting my hands to his knees and whipping my head around. I turned around and gave him a personal, long drawn out ass sway when Chad Kroeger did the kickass drawn out "everyone."

I flipped around and mounted his lap.

His hands immediately went to my hips.

I barely controlled a lip curl at his touch and I moved on him. I put my hands on his shoulders, pulsing my hips under his hands, whipping my hair in his face, catching his eyes to see his at my crotch.

Yeah.

I had him.

So I took him.

Reaching in his jacket, I went right for his gun.

His fingers on my hips bit in and his eyes shot from my crotch to my face.

I felt for the snap, flipped it and yanked his gun out just as I jumped off his lap, his hands sliding clean free since I was oiled up (and good).

I got three feet back and pointed the gun in his face.

The music stopped and the lights went up. There was some clapping, but everyone around Gibbons and me had seen the dance change and were shuffling away, seeing as there was a stripper with a gun.

Gibbons stared into my eyes, and I knew he was about to go for me right when he was out of his chair and being slammed face first into the floor by Mace.

Luke came to me and took the gun out of my hand.

"I need to find a way to erase the last three minutes," he muttered, sounding aggrieved.

"Why?" I asked.

"I just watched my boy's sister strip. There's laws against that," he replied, not taking his eyes off Mace who was cuffing a non-struggling Gibbons, but I had a feeling what Luke was doing was studiously avoiding seeing me in sequined undies and stripper shoes.

"No there's not," I said to Luke and he finally looked at me.

"Babe, there are. Trust me," he stated.

At his tone, I trusted him. Then again, he was a guy. What did I know what rules guys lived by?

Luke moved in to help Mace jerk Gibbons to his feet. They didn't go cautiously and his head snapped around, and not a little.

A lot.

I fought a smirk.

"What's goin' on? What the fuck is goin' on?" Smithie shouted, elbowing his way in.

"Don't know how I took him down, seein' as I've gone blind," Mace stated, ignoring Smithie.

"I hear you, man," Luke agreed.

"What *the fuck* is goin' on?" Smithie yelled.

That was when Lee appeared.

My brother. He didn't let me know, but he was also taking my back.

Kristen Ashley

I was feeling slightly gushy and very jazzed when Lee said, "Cruiser's out-side. Haul him out. Smithie, you come with me."

"You gonna tell me what he fuck is goin' on?" Smithie asked.

"Yes," Lee answered.

Smithie glared at him. Then he glared at me.

I tipped my head to the side and gave him a scrunchy face.

Lee either didn't see Smithie's glare or didn't care. His eyes went beyond Smithie and he ordered, "Clear this place out."

I looked that way just in time to see Lenny saying, "Gotcha."

Lenny moved out and I looked at Gibbons.

He didn't look upset.

He looked smug.

"Uh... just so you know, asshole dickhead of huge proportions," I called. His eyes came to me, and I noted when they did, "Good you know your name. Your crew?" I asked and shook my head. "Right now, they're taking rides in cruisers, too."

Gibbons stopped looking smug.

"Funny, thinking with your dick brought you to this pass, seeing as you *are* a dick," I noted.

"Smithie," Lee cut into my fun. "Your office."

On a lingering glare at all of us, Smithie moved toward his office.

Lee moved, too.

He moved into Gibbons space and he got nose to nose with the asshole (or kind of; Lee was three inches taller).

"After your stay at the penitentiary, you get out, you get the fuck out of town," he ordered. "Denver's mine, and I don't like your kind here. Now you think on that. You ask around. Name's Lee Nightingale, but I suspect you know that. And I suspect you know to get your ass out of my town. You don't and we meet again, there won't be a cruiser."

"Fuck you," Gibbons spat.

"Good," Lee whispered, getting closer. "I hope you're not smart, because I'm lookin' forward to meetin' you again."

Gibbons held Lee's eyes.

Lee didn't give him the honor of a staredown.

He sauntered away.

"*We'll* meet again, bitch," Gibbons promised me, and my eyes went to his.

I clasped my hands together in front of me and cried in a shrill girlie voice, "Oh goodie! I didn't get to use my balls-in-a-vice move tonight and I was *so* wanting to."

Mace jerked Gibbons around and started marching him to the door.

Luke grinned at me before he followed.

I watched for a beat then looked through the thinning crowd the bouncers were showing to the door to see Ren standing at the edge, arms crossed on his chest, eyes on me, face carefully blank but eyes burning.

"I still have some work to do, honey," I told him. "Can you wait for me?"

He shook his head, but his lips quirked and he answered, "Yeah, babe."

I smiled at him.

Then I hightailed my sequin-pantied ass to the dressing room.

<hr />

Led by Eddie and Jimmy Marker, detectives and uniforms were in the dressing room taking statements from strippers, waitresses and the female bartender.

After I'd changed into tee, boots and jeans, I'd talked all the girls into making statements. I would like to have been able to tell my brother my efforts at this were heroic. But once they all learned that Smithie and his family were no longer in jeopardy, they jumped at the chance.

I was leaning against the wall with my arms crossed on my chest beside the door as I watched Jimmy with a hand light on JoJo's arm moving toward my station. JoJo was looking at the floor. I was looking at Jimmy.

"Me and Mizz Christensen need to chat in private," he murmured as they passed me.

I nodded. I knew what that meant. She had not so fun things to say. And Jimmy, a good man (the best), was going to take her someplace comfortable to say them.

Jimmy kept moving, but he did it with eyes on me.

I tipped my head to the side.

He jerked up his chin.

Then he winked.

I smiled.

He disappeared.

I jumped when not a second later, Luke's head and shoulders were where Jimmy had just been and he growled, "Ally. You're needed."

What?

I didn't get the chance to verbalize that question. Luke disappeared.

I shoved away from the wall and followed him.

I heard it when I got into the main area of club. Someone was tearing something apart.

And the noise was coming from the direction of Smithie's office.

That was when I started running.

I passed Luke and hit the stairs to Smithie's office which was up high, where he had a window out to keep his eyes on the club. I ran up the steps and ran by Ren, Mace and Lee who were standing inside, close to the door, all alert but giving space.

When I hit the office, I saw I was right. The office was a disaster. Completely torn apart.

And Darius was there, close to Smithie, hand out, mouth murmuring, "Calm down, brother."

Smithie picked up something from his desk and threw it across the room. It slammed into the wood paneling, the paneling buckling all around, and it stayed lodged there.

Then he turned on Darius and shouted, "You been workin' this case with Ally for days and you didn't shut that shit down?"

"We didn't know how bad it was until today," Darius replied. "Now sit down, you need a deep breath and a drink."

"I don't need a fuckin' drink!" Smithie yelled. "I need to fuck somebody up."

I got close to Lee, got on my toes and whispered, "Call LaTeesha."

He turned his eyes down to me. "Ally—"

"Do it, bro."

I held his eyes. He nodded, peeled off from Ren and Mace and disappeared out the door.

I approached Darius and Smithie.

"Stay back, Ally," Darius ordered.

"Smithie," I called, ignoring Darius, but Smithie's eyes were already on me. "Calm down a sec. The cops are gonna need to talk to you. Then you can continue destroying your office."

He threw out his hands. "What am I gonna tell 'em? That I didn't know dick?"

"They'll have some questions, honey. Just tell them what you know," I replied.

He leaned into me threateningly, and I saw Darius get close and felt the men at my back move forward.

"I can tell them what I know fuckin' *now.* I know that motherfucker—in my own fuckin' *house*—extorted fucking *blowjobs* from *my* girls." He thumped his chest on the word "my."

"Smithie—"

"Took their money."

"Smithie, please, listen for a—"

"And they gave all that shit up, for *me.*" Another whack to his chest.

"I know, but—"

"*For me!*" he roared in a way that the entire room stilled.

He stood there, staring at me, breathing heavily, and I knew it was going to happen before it happened.

So I ordered quickly, "Everybody out."

Then it happened.

His arms went to cover his face and head and his legs went out from under him.

I rushed to him, looking at Darius and mouthing, "Out."

Darius nodded and moved.

I got down on my knees by Smithie and pulled his big quaking body in my arms.

"For me," he whispered, his voice breaking.

"They love you," I whispered back.

"For me," he repeated.

I said nothing. Just held him in my arms.

This lasted a long time before, not looking at me, still curled into himself in my arms, he started to ask, "How do I—?"

"I don't know," I interrupted. "I just know you will." I pulled him closer. "I'll help."

He dropped his arms and turned his head to look at me. My breath caught and my heart squeezed at the ravaged look on his face, his bloodshot eyes, the wet on his cheeks.

Kristen Ashley

"They did that shit for me," he said, and it sounded like he was pleading. Like I could take his words and make them and the fact that all this happened go away.

"They love you," I repeated and lifted my hands to his cheeks, moving my face closer. "And that, Smithie, is a beautiful thing. You take care of them. They took care of you. It was awful how they had to do it. But every single one of them did it. That's how much they love you."

He shook his head, taking my hands with it. "I can't fix this," he told me.

"Everything can be fixed," I returned.

"Not this," he whispered.

"Daisy? Ava? Sadie?" I gave him examples of women who lived on, valiantly and magnificently, after being violated. I shook my head before I lifted up, kissed his forehead then looked back into his eyes. "Everything can be fixed. *Everything.*"

He held my eyes.

Then he nodded.

"Baby." We heard, and I let Smithie go in order to turn around.

I saw LaTeesha rushing in.

I got out of her way, and as she helped Smithie off the floor, I gave them their privacy.

Mace was at the top of the stairs.

When I looked at him, for once, he wasn't looking broody. His eyes were warm and his face was soft.

It was a good look for him. Then again, for Mace, they all were.

"Good job," he murmured.

"Thanks," I murmured back and turned to the steps.

I was halfway down when he called quietly, "No, Ally."

I turned back and looked up at him.

"All of it," he said. He pointed at the office. "In there." He pointed toward the club. "And out there."

Fuck, but that felt great.

I didn't say that.

I nodded and repeated, "Thanks, Mace."

He nodded back.

I went back to descending the stairs.

At the bottom were Darius, Lee and Ren.

I looked at Lee. "Am I done?"

"Yeah, Ally," Lee answered softly.

444

His eyes were warm and his face was soft, too.

I gave him a chin lift. He gave Ren a look.

I didn't try to decipher that look. I just turned to my man and he didn't make me say a word.

He just grabbed my hand and led me out the door.

———※———

We were in bed.

I had my face in Ren's neck, my legs tangled with his.

He had an arm wrapped around me and he'd pulled up my nightie. He was drawing lazy patterns on the skin above my ass. The fingers of his other hand were laced with mine and he was holding them over his heart.

He hadn't made a move on me. I didn't make one on him. We just both got ready for bed silently and then he drew me into him and held me close.

I suspected he did this because he knew it would happen.

And it did.

Dragging his hand with mine up to my face, I pressed them against my lips as the sob ripped its path up my throat and out and my body bucked violently.

Ren let my hand go and turned into me, both his arms closing around me and holding tight.

I cried into his throat and I did it a long time.

When my sobbing started to die out, Ren pulled me even closer, giving me a squeeze and whispering, "Love you, baby."

That was it. No coddling. No offers to talk it out. No pressure. Nothing. He let me be at the same time he gave me exactly what I needed.

"Love you too, Ren," I whispered back.

And I did.

More and more every day.

And right there in that bed with Ren was the reason.

Precisely.

Because when I had to be a badass all day and cases got tough and I came home, or when life just sucked, or when life was awesome and going along fine, I knew this was what Ren Zano would give me.

Always.

Exactly what I needed.

Chapter 31

On My Team

Late morning the next day, I stood in my newly painted, newly carpeted office space—more accurately, in *my* soon-to-be office—and I looked out the window at the view.

Downtown. Mostly other tall buildings. But around the corner of the one across the street, I could see the mountains.

Righteous view.

Slowly, I turned my head and took it all in. In my office, there was a box containing a brand new computer. There were two more, one in Daisy's space, one in the extra office. There was also a printer box, scanner box and a fax machine box as well as boxes holding routers and other IT shit in Daisy's space.

There was a copy machine in the conference room.

And *The Majestic* was already on the wall. Ralphie and Buddy had come in and hung it that weekend.

The furniture was on order and would be delivered on Wednesday.

Brody was showing on Wednesday night to set up the network.

In other words, Daisy had been busy.

And Ava had phoned that day and said she'd emailed five different logos to look at. It had been hard to choose, but I'd picked one that was classy and professional and had more blacks and grays than the hot pink, just so it wouldn't be too girlie.

Further, Mr. Kumar had stopped by Fortnum's that morning to give me the "kitty" he'd collected from his neighbors. It wasn't a lot, but since Tex, Hector nor Mace would accept payment, it worked.

This meant I'd closed and been paid for my first case.

And I was standing in my offices that would be furnished and operational by Thursday.

It had happened.

Me. Ally Nightingale was in the business.

I smiled.

The door opened and Lee appeared.

My smile died and I drew in breath.

Indy had come into Fortnum's forty-five minutes ago, saying she was over the worst of it and was going to give work a try. Five minutes after that, Lee had called asking to meet me at my offices.

I wasn't apprehensive. I knew I'd passed the Lee Tests, all of them. He wouldn't have involved me, given me a choice (and dangerous) assignment or a soft look before I left last night if I hadn't.

I just didn't know what he was going to do with that.

I didn't move from my place at the window as he walked in, eyes on me, and stopped in the doorway.

He leaned against the jamb.

"Nice space," he remarked, even though he barely looked at it.

"Yep," I replied because it sure the fuck was.

Then he announced, "Luke fell last night."

Hunh?

I felt my brows draw together. "Luke fell?"

"If he was even on the fence," he went on.

"Lee, you've lost me," I told him.

His eyes grew intent when he said, "Thinks you're the shit, Ally."

That was when I got it.

Luke was backing my play.

This meant I had them all, except Monty. And Jack and Matt hadn't weighed in yet.

Okay, I had a majority.

That feeling hit me again, the fucking good one.

But I just nodded and said, "That's great."

"It was the right decision to come to me with that note," Lee stated.

I didn't reply because I already knew that.

Lee kept going.

"I gotta say, that shocked the shit outta me. But in a good way."

"You've seen I'm good at what I do," I reminded him. "And you know to be good at it, you gotta be smart."

"You got that goin' for you."

I drew in a breath at the compliment.

Lee again spoke.

And when he did, he rocked my world.

"I want you on my team so I can teach you and sign off on your hours."

Oh my God!

This time I sucked in a breath.

Then it hit me.

I looked around the space and back to him. "Lee, I—"

He cut me off. "Contract, Ally. You take your own cases. Once I assess your skillset, you contract with me when I need your skills or when I need a woman. One of my boys works your cases with you so they can validate your hours for the Licensing Board and to expand your abilities. I'll back Shirleen's play and punt cases to you that you'll excel at. But it would be a mistake for us to work together on a day to day basis. The men and I work well together, but that's because we have years workin' together. We used to butt heads and frequently. Now, we know each other's boundaries. You and me, we'll likely butt heads unless we give it time to get used to each other. I'd like to avoid that."

I could not believe this.

I was loving it, but I couldn't believe it

"I would too," I agreed instead of doing a war whoop of joy.

"So no day to day. But contract will work."

"Yeah," I replied quietly.

"You were excellent last night, honey," he stated, just as quietly.

My eyes started burning.

"I'll talk to Dad," he continued. "Mom's already on board. She knows she didn't raise a weak woman and she knows you're all Nightingale."

Oh shit. It was coming.

I looked to my feet.

"Ally," he called.

I deep-breathed and looked to Lee.

"There are a million other things I'd want for you. It took me a while and Hank to lay it out, but the thing I should want most is what you want. So now I'm tellin' you, like yesterday with that note, don't ever doubt it, anytime you need me, I'm there."

He always was.

Always.

"I love you," I whispered.

"I know," he replied.

I clenched my teeth to fight crying.

Lee wasn't done rocking my world.

"After you left yesterday afternoon, Eddie got in my face."

Oh man.

"We had words," he carried on. "But I heard him and I heard you. Now I'm askin' you to back off Darius."

Oh no.

Hell no.

He wasn't buttering me up with flattery, acceptance and promises to work with the Hot Bunch Dream Team and then socking this shit to me.

I turned fully to him. "Lee. No way."

He lifted a hand and dropped it, shaking his head. "Eddie and I are gonna talk to Malia. See if she's down for a possible approach from Darius. We'll make sure she knows it's only possible. But if she's not, and gives indication she never will be, Eddie and me do not want this brought up to him. He'll fight it, but he also might hope. If there's no hope, I don't want to set him up to feel that pain."

That made sense.

"Okay, I'll give you and Eddie time," I agreed and jotted a call to Duke to give him a status report on my list of things to do that day.

"We make a miracle happen and talk Darius around, we pull in Jules. She knows the way to go about this shit and she can ease this for all three of them."

That was such a brilliant idea I wished I'd thought of it myself.

"Right," I said.

"And until all that's in motion, Indy, Mom, Dad, Tom, Shirleen, no one knows about this. Darius is not gonna take kindly to us gettin' in his shit. He needs fallback positions. If he picks someone in our crew, you out of his picture, it'll be Indy or Shirleen."

I nodded.

"You down with that?" he asked.

"Absolutely."

That was when Lee nodded.

"This is the right thing to do," I told him.

"It always has been," he told me.

He was right about that, and suddenly I realized this had been weighing on him, and Eddie, and it had been doing it heavily.

For seventeen years.

Which sucked.

He looked away and I saw his jaw tighten before he looked back at me.

"Eddie and me, both of us, when he got into that shit, we almost lost him, Ally. I was in the Army when he got dug in deep with Leon so I wasn't around to get involved. Eddie was and did. Hank was and did. When I was around, I did. But there was no turning back for him, he was that angry. His mind fucked, he made misguided decisions, not cluein' into the fact that the man who was usin' him was the man who deserved his anger. If he can hold anger that deep and extreme that it blinds him to the right path, you need to be prepared for what will come of this."

"I am," I assured him.

Lee studied me a moment and it felt like he was assessing the validity of my statement.

I would find he wasn't when he admitted, "I'm not."

"That right there," I declared instantly. "That loyalty to Darius, loyalty that would make *you,* the strongest most fearless man I know, shy away from doing what's right in order not to lose your friend, that's what Liam needs to know is in his father."

I muscle jumped in his jaw before he jerked up his chin.

Badass for *You're right.*

I fought my smile.

Time to move on, though not to more pleasant things.

"I have a stalker," I announced.

Immediately Lee straightened away from the jamb.

"What the fuck?" he whispered scarily.

"Not an old client or anyone affected by my work. An old neighbor. Don't know him. Never met him. He was just around. And he takes pictures of me."

"Are you shittin' me?" he asked.

I wished I was.

I shook my head and said, "Ren clocked him and looked into it. Found the pictures at his pad. He's not happy. As in Grade A, bona fide *pissed.* He's protective of me and has made it clear he's leading this charge, but he wants you invol—"

I stopped talking because Lee turned on his boot and stalked to the door.

Well, I guessed Ren was going to have an unexpected guest.

451

And that meant Dawn was going to come face to face with the man she'd wanted for her own (though she'd had no shot) who chewed her ass out and fired her.

I really wanted to go watch that, but with the way Lee moved, I figured I already missed it.

It then hit me that Dawn likely didn't know that Lee knocked Indy up.

And she would *hate* hearing that news.

I also scratched it on my to-do list to inform her of that and with Lee's meeting done (and entirely satisfactorily, in a *big* way), I had another item on my agenda while at that location.

Actually two. The first one, not so easy. The second one, talking Ren into having sex on his desk; probably not hard.

So I had Torture Dawn Time.

Since I wanted to get to the second one, as well as ruin Dawn's day, I hauled my ass across the office so I could see to the first one.

I hit the hall, moved across it and entered Ren's office.

Dawn looked a little freaked, which made me smile and greet enthusiastically, "Hi, Dawn."

She stopped looking freaked and glared at me for a nanosecond before her mask slipped into place.

"Hey, Ally," she replied, sugar-sweet.

I stopped at her desk. "Did you see Lee?"

Her nostrils flared but she answered, still in her sweet voice, "Yes. He's in with Ren."

"Cool," I stated. "Did he tell you the good news?"

"No," she forced out, the sweet faltering.

"Indy's expecting. How awesome is that?" I asked.

"Brilliant news." She was now sounding strangled.

"So, let me see," I said, lifting my hand and counting it off. "Jules had Max, but I figure they're due to start trying again." I leaned toward her and smiled huge. "Not that they aren't trying—just that they aren't *trying,* if you get what I mean."

She stared at me, lips thin.

She got what I meant.

I added another finger. "Jet's due in a few months. Indy's knocked up. Ava and Luke got married a little over a week ago, and the way they go at it, who knows when she's gonna have a baby on board. Mace and Stella aren't married yet, but she's a rock 'n' roll goddess. They could decide to start before they're legal." I dropped my hands. "All this happy, I'm beginning to feel maternal. Maybe I'll talk to Ren about trying. Do you think it's too soon for us?" I queried chattily.

"I wouldn't know," she replied coldly, sweet gone, pure Dawn all I could hear and see.

"No," I shook my head, inwardly giggling my ass off. "I want him all to myself for a while." I leaned into her again and dropped my voice, "Seeing as there's *so much* to enjoy. You with me?"

Her head made a weird jerk that I decided to take as *Yes*.

"Anyway," I started to move away. "Thanks for the chat."

I hit the hall and Dawn said nothing.

I *so* could not *wait* to invite the girls over for Dawn Torture Sessions. My office was perfectly located for hitting Dawn with Rock Chick verbal drive-bys.

On this thought, I *really* hoped my next meeting would go well, and I'd already *really* been hoping it would.

There were a number of doors off the hall, the Zano offices way bigger than mine, and I had to guess which one was his.

But I knew he was in because I saw his Caddy in the parking garage.

I made my choice, tapped on a closed door, heard an impatient, "What?" and found I chose right.

I opened the door and stuck my head in. "Hey, Mr. Zano. Got a second?"

He'd looked up from his desk looking ornery when I'd opened the door, but the minute he saw me his face was wreathed in smiles.

"Ally," he called, getting up and throwing his arms out. "A pleasant surprise. Of course I have a second for you."

I entered, closed the door and turned back only to have Vito on me, hands firm on my biceps. I made a mental note that the old guy could move when he pulled me in, kissed one cheek, then the next, then pushed me back and jiggled me.

"And you don't call me Mr. Zano. Uncle Vito!" he declared.

"Right," I murmured.

He let me go with one hand and pulled me deeper in the office with the other. "Now, *why* do I have this pleasure?"

"I was just across the hall checking out the progress on my offices and thought I'd pop by."

Lie.

It was totally planned.

I then stopped lying. "Ren's busy so I needed to wait and I didn't want to wait in reception. Dawn..." I trailed off as we stopped by one of the chairs in front of his desk and I gave him a look.

"Ah, Dawn," he mumbled, indicating a chair with his hand so I sat. He moved around the desk and continued talking. "Not hard to look at." He sat behind his desk and leveled his eyes on me. "But sometimes something pretty on the outside can hide..." he paused and stated extremely diplomatically, "*interesting* things on the inside."

He had that right.

And he had Dawn's number.

Then again, no one would mistake Vito Zano for dumb.

"I hope you don't mind me interrupting you," I said, and he again threw out a hand.

"Not at all. I've been wantin' to hear how your meetin' went with Father Paolo."

Hmm.

"I haven't spoken with him yet Mist... uh, Uncle Vito."

He ticked a finger back and forth at me. "Don't delay, *cara*. Catholic classes last a year."

They did?

A whole year?

Yikes!

"I've been kinda busy," I told him.

He nodded and watched me closely. "The business at Smithie's." He shook his head. "I heard. Very disturbing."

He had that right, too.

"It's done now. Time to heal," I shared.

"I would say that last part would be the part you and your Rock Chicks would be involved in. Not the..." another meaningful pause, "other."

He knew I was stripping.

"You do what you have to do to get the job done," I informed him

His eyes narrowed and he leaned toward me, but I got there before him and leaned toward him, putting my hand on his desk.

"Don't, Uncle Vito. With respect, I've worked this out with Ren and my family. I understand and appreciate your concern, but they've come around, and although that's important to me, bottom line, it's my job, my choice. And, no offense, truth be told, what you need to focus on is not me or what's happening with Ren and me or Catholic classes. It's doing everything in your power not to lose your son."

I heard his swift intake of breath and caught the flash of pain in his eyes he couldn't quite keep hidden before his expression turned scary.

But I was a Nightingale. This didn't affect me.

So I kept going.

"You're hurting him with this. He's torn between loyalty to you, loyalty to his mother and where he's at in his soul. You're the only father he's ever known. Are you really okay with attempting to bend him to your will? Even understanding his will was forged through your own blood, so you know that won't ever happen? Thus forcing him to make decisions that will hurt people he loves?"

"This is not your business, Ally," he clipped, eyes cold.

"Ren is absolutely my business, Uncle Vito," I returned.

We went into staredown.

I didn't back down.

He didn't either.

This meant our tense silence lasted a long time.

Surprisingly, Vito broke it.

"I'll not discuss this with you," he stated.

"I'm okay with that," I replied. "Just as long as I know you heard me."

He scowled at me and said nothing.

He heard me.

"I'm gonna see if Ren's free," I said.

"You do that."

Meeting done, and by the look on his face, I didn't make a friend.

God.

Vito.

Stubborn.

I nodded and got up.

But once up, I looked down at him and fired my parting shot.

"I love him. He's my world. So obviously I want him to be happy. This dissension is making him unhappy. I also want to work across the hall from him so we can carpool. He wants that, too. And I know you want him to be happy. There is no way the man who looked after Ren and his family, the man who gave a father to a fatherless son, the man who stepped up for Ava and Sadie, would hurt someone he cared about. Not that deeply. And it would be disappointing to me, devastating to the man I love, to learn that's not true."

On that, I took off.

But I'd seen his head jerk and I hoped I got in there.

I closed the door behind me and headed to Ren's office, wanting Lee to be gone. Not because I didn't love my big bro, but because I didn't want to delay in breaking in Ren's desk.

I didn't stop at Ren's door because I heard a voice in reception. It was Dom's, and he sounded angry.

I was Ally. Always curious. So I moved stealthily toward the mouth of the hall, but stopped when I could hear and not be seen.

"...IT guys and they found that shit," Dom bit out.

"I—" Dawn started.

"Fuck no," Dom cut her off. "That's your written warning. From now on, company email only. Not that bullshit you been writing to your girls. That's fucked."

I grinned.

Ren had had Dom check her emails.

And I'd been right. She was catting with her girls on company time.

Now she was getting a written warning.

This was *so totally* a happy day.

"And, just sayin'," Dom continued. "That fucked up shit you been tellin' your girls about what's gonna go down between you and me, get that shit outta your head. I'm married. I got a wife I love and a kid I also love. I'm not gonna do jack to fuck with that. Not with you. Not with anybody. And, babe, just sayin', take a good look at my wife the next time she comes in. I know you think your shit don't stink, but you don't hold a candle to her."

Suddenly I decided I liked Dom.

Unfortunately done tearing Dawn a new one, he stalked into the hall and scowled at me.

"That was righteous," I whispered when he got close.

"That bitch is a bitch," he replied, not in a whisper.

I couldn't argue that.

Dom continued stalking down the hall.

For (hopefully) future reference of the lay of the land at Zano Holdings, I made note of which office he went into.

Then I went to Ren's, knocked and entered when he called, "Yeah?"

"Hey," I greeted, closing the door behind me, noting Lee wasn't there, so no delays to nookie.

"Hey," he replied, getting up and making to move around the desk.

"You don't have to get up, babe," I told him, moving to him.

We met up. He lifted a hand to cup my jaw and tip my head back before he bent to give me a quick kiss.

When he lifted his head he said, "Yeah, I do."

Stand up kissing with Ren. Only second best to lying down kissing with Ren.

So I agreed, "Yeah, you do."

He slid his arms around me. "How's the office?"

"Operational come Thursday."

He gave me a squeeze and murmured, "Good, baby."

"I told Lee about Snookie Rivers," I informed him.

"Yeah. I got that."

I bet he did.

"Any news on that?" I asked.

"Not yet," he answered. "But I suspect there soon will be. Both Santo and Lucky are on it. I was just about to go in and talk with Vito and Dom so they'd know Santo and Lucky have a priority mission and are unavailable. Lee and I agreed to tracking you. He's having a device put on your car, he wants one in your bag and he's going to get Brody to track your phone."

My man *so* loved me.

So did my brother.

"I'm cool with that," I told him then asked, "Anything I can do?"

"Although Lee'll be keepin' an eye on you, I still want you to let someone know where you are, or alternately where you're gonna be, and when you expect to get there and do that at all times."

I could do that.

So I replied, "Copy that."

He shook his head but his lips quirked.

"Okay, so, I have to get to Smithie and check in. But first, I have to have sex with my man on his desk. Can we do that pronto so I can get a move on?"

It wasn't a flowery statement or a seductive one, but on the word "sex", his eyes heated and his body moved, backing to his desk and taking me with him. This I took as him agreeing to my plan.

And he did. He just had additions.

"First, you go down on me in my chair. Then I fuck you on the desk."

Total happy place spasm so big it sent quivers down my inner thighs.

"You get that, then I get you returning the favor with me on your desk," I bartered.

Ren was an easy sell.

I knew this when his mouth came to mine, his eyes burning, and he replied, "Done."

Then his arms closed tight and he kissed me.

In the end, I really couldn't tell you which phase of sex on (and around) Ren's desk was the highlight.

So I figured we had to do it again, and soon, just so I could make sure.

Really hoped Vito would cave so my man could be close to me.

Seriously.

And not just so we could carpool.

Chapter 32

Salvation

One week later...

I drove my Mustang into underground parking at my office.

It was nearly noon and I was still working mornings at Fortnum's because Indy was still in the throes of morning sickness, and according to her doctors, would be for a while.

Although this was gross, she now had so much practice hurling, a quick, "Hang on," dash to the bathroom, return, "I'm back" happened frequently.

My BFF.

Nothing fazed her.

All was settling in Rock Chick/Hot Bunch Land, which also meant in Ren and Ally Land.

For me, it was mornings at Fortnum's, work my cases, evenings with Ren.

For Ren, it was work enduring a Vito freeze-out and thus working to wrap things up in order to leave, then evenings with me where I tried to make him feel better.

He hid it, but it was wearing on him.

I'd done what I could do with Vito.

The rest was up to Ren to decide.

That was, of course, if I didn't lose it, charge into Vito's office and rip him a new one. Though, I suspected that wouldn't help.

And I had cases. Two of them. One, Shirleen (and thus Lee) had punted me. One was from a friend who had a friend who needed help.

Surprisingly, when I shared that I didn't accept gift cards or discounts as payment anymore; she said she'd talk to her friend and share this info. Then her friend came in and chatted with Daisy. After that, she hired me.

Both cases were domestics and I was working them with Matt. From experience, neither case would last long. That said, it was interesting having a partner.

Interesting in a good way.

Matt was kind of the Unknown Hot Bunch Guy. I'd spent time around him. Partied with him. Shot the shit with him. I knew his girlfriend, Daphne. I knew he was hot in a boy next door kind of way. But other than that, not much.

Now I knew he was good at his job.

Oh, and since we were working the job together and this necessitated communicating, I also now knew that he'd bought Daphne a ring. I further knew that the day of the Big Ask was this coming Saturday.

"And if you tell even a single Rock Chick, Ally, I'll shoot you," he'd warned me with a not-very boy next door look on his face.

So Matt could be badass.

Good to know.

I'd zipped my lips. He'd shaken his head. But I didn't tell a single Rock Chick.

I was one of the girls.

But now I was also one of the guys.

How totally fucking righteous was that?

The one pall hanging over everything was the fact that neither Lee and his boys, nor Ren unleashing Lucky and Santo, had meant success in finding Snookie Rivers.

I tried to tell myself that he'd realized he'd been made and he'd found someone else to stalk. When I did this I didn't believe myself, nor did I like the idea of him stalking someone else. So this concerned me and I was keen to have that situation done.

But Brody had a lock on my phone. I had devices in my car and purse, and they tracked me in the surveillance room at Nightingale Investigations all the time. Not to mention, I frequently saw Lucky or Santo hanging close.

So I was covered.

I still wished someone would find the sicko.

As I made my way to the elevator, I texted Ren with, *In the building.*

In the elevator on the way to our floor, my phone binged with, *All right, honey.*

I grinned, not caring that I had to check in (and frequently), with Ren. If it made him breathe easy, I'd do it. If I could do anything to make him breathe easy, I'd do it (mostly).

I exited the elevator, walked down the hall, opened the door to my offices and was confronted with World War III.

Namely, Daisy and Shirleen going at it.

"You're makin' me look bad!" Shirleen shouted, hands on hips, leaning across Daisy's desk toward Daisy.

"So do the filin', and not the kind you do to your nails!" Daisy shouted back, also with hands on hips doing the leaning thing.

Uh-oh.

I moved in, making sure the door swung closed, hoping that would drown out the noise.

"Ladies——" I began.

Daisy looked at me. "Just so you know, sugar, I got an appointment for fills, I do it on my lunch hour."

"Suck up," Shirleen snapped.

"I'm not suckin' up!" Daisy snapped back.

Shirleen leaned back. "At least Shirleen don't suck up."

Daisy slammed a hand on the desk, her long nails (white with green glitter tips) clicking, and she screamed, *"I'm not suckin' up!"*

Hmm.

That would filter into the hall.

Definitely.

Time to end this.

"Yo!" I shouted, and they both swung their eyes to me.

Okay. So. I didn't get scared.

Shirleen and Daisy pissed with their eyes to me?

I had to admit. I felt it.

"Daisy isn't a suck up. She doesn't have to suck up. We're a team," I told Shirleen.

"See," Daisy said snottily.

"Just like," I put in quickly when Shirleen opened her mouth, "you're a member of Lee's team. You have your way of doing things over there." I threw out an arm. "We have our way of doing things here." I pointed to the floor.

"You're workin' with the boys," Shirleen said to me. "They'll see Daisy in action and get ideas."

Was she high?

I wasn't certain that Lee's boys even knew Daisy worked for me. And if they did, it was in passing and they didn't give a shit.

"Does Lee care if you file?" I asked.

"The word 'file' isn't even in Lee's vocabulary," Shirleen answered.

This, I figured, was true.

"Do the boys pay any attention to administration at all over at Lee's?" I kept at it.

"*Hell* no," Shirleen replied.

I swung an arm out again. "Then why would they here?"

Her head cocked to the side.

"I see your point," she muttered.

Jeez.

"Okay. So are we done with this ridiculous fight?" I asked.

"I am," Daisy declared, sitting her ass, encased in a skintight green skirt, down in her office chair. This afforded us a view only of a white blouse that was unbuttoned *way* beyond professional levels that had the added attraction of being nearly see-through, so we saw the miles of lace that was her bra. Not to mention a head of hair that needed its own area code.

Shirleen narrowed her eyes on Daisy, and I cautiously got closer to the desk.

"What's really on your mind?" I asked Shirleen and she looked at me.

"Shit's boring," she decreed.

Oh man.

Tex in black woman form.

I didn't know which was worse, but at that moment, with Shirleen close and in a pissy mood, she was.

"Everyone's hooked up, you were the last, and you were boring," she complained. "Sure, you stripped. And it was hot. La-di-da. But now, no more apartments exploding. No one's left to get kidnapped. Nothin'. The boys, they take care of business. I answer the phone. I send invoices. I run payroll. Then I go home and watch TV. I didn't sign up for that shit."

"So you came over and picked a fight with Daisy?" I asked.

"What the hell else am I gonna do?" Shirleen asked back then leaned in. "*File?*"

My answer to that would be yes.

If I was insane enough to verbalize it.

I wasn't, so instead I studied her and got closer.

My voice also dipped lower when I pressed, "Okay, Shirleen, now tell us what's *really* on your mind."

She pulled in a breath, looked at Daisy, looked at me then declared, "Sniff's got a girlfriend."

Oh shit.

"They're tight. He's never home," she went on.

Crap.

"I never see him," she kept going. "And when he's home, he's on the phone..." she paused, "*with her.*"

Hmm.

Momma wasn't liking her cubs shifting away from the den.

Shirleen wasn't done, and she saved the scariest for last.

"And we gotta have *the talk,* and not only do I not wanna have *the talk,* I don't know *how* to have *the talk.*"

I was thinking, with Roam and Sniff (mostly Roam, but it also could be with Sniff) it was a little late for *the talk* as in, *the sex talk.* Both had been serial daters for a while, with Roam going for the world record.

I didn't share that either.

But Daisy (as always) was in the mood to share.

She flicked a wrist and advised, "Just buy him a pack of condoms and put it on his pillow."

"Say what?" Shirleen asked, eyes huge.

"That says it all," Daisy answered.

"What it says is I'm down with him havin' sex, which I am *not,*" Shirleen fired back.

"He's a boy. He's seventeen. It's gonna happen, if it already hasn't, sugar," Daisy pointed out.

"He's *my* boy and it's *not* gonna happen until he gets what it means," Shirleen retorted and finished, "And it has *not* already happened."

Hmm.

Maternal denial.

I moved to switch subjects by asking, "What does it mean?"

She swung her gaze to me, and I successfully stopped myself from taking a step back.

"You don't know?"

"I know what it means to me. I just don't know what you want Sniff to know what it means," I replied.

"You do the business with Zano. What's that mean?" she returned.

"I said I knew what it meant *to me*," I repeated, trying for patience. "I want to know what you want to share with Sniff."

"That he should find a girl that means something to him so it will mean what it means when you do the deed with Zano. Or Indy with Lee. Mace with Stella—"

Daisy interrupted Shirleen with, "We get it."

Shirleen looked at her. "You with Marcus."

"Oh darlin'," Daisy waved a hand, palm out, "to get to a Marcus, he's gotta get in the saddle before he finds The One. And do it a *lot*. Comprende?"

"And maybe along the way get some silly white girl knocked up?" Shirleen shook her head. "No fuckin' way."

Daisy leaned toward Shirleen and put her hand to the desk, reiterating with strained patience, "That's why you *buy* him a *pack* of *condoms* and put them on his goddamned *pillow*."

"Uh... just saying," I butted in, and both of them looked to me. "You don't want to do the talk. You don't know how to do the talk. But you know about eight guys you can call on who are tight with Sniff and found a woman where sex means what you want it to mean to Sniff who can talk to him."

Shirleen's eyebrows nearly hit the edge of her enormous afro. "Lordy, are you sayin' you think one of the Hot Bunch should give my boy the sex talk?"

"That's what I'm saying," I confirmed.

"Are you crazy?" she asked.

"No," I answered.

"Well, just sayin' right back at cha, all 'a those boys have been in the saddle so often before they got their Rock Chick, it's a wonder none of them are bow-legged," Shirleen remarked.

"Doin' the business doesn't require the man to have his legs open," Daisy muttered, and Shirleen swung her glare to her.

"It's been a while for Shirleen, but I remember that part," she snapped.

Seemed it was time we hooked Shirleen up.

"Personally, I think we should ask one of the Hot Bunch," Daisy stated, her hand reaching to the phone on her desk. "And tape it. *That* I would love to see."

Holy shit!

I would, too.

Totally.

"Call Mace," I ordered, immediately losing interest in our earlier subject. "That would be *awesome*."

Daisy nodded, her hair nodding with her, and she started jabbing buttons on the phone with the tip of a nail.

"Daisy girl, put that phone down," Shirleen demanded.

Daisy held the receiver aside and lifted her eyes to me. "I'm changin' my mind. Luke."

I shook my head and grinned. "Hector. Totally Hector."

Shirleen's hand darted out, pulled the receiver out of Daisy's and slammed it in its base while Daisy's head snapped back and she yelled, "Hey!"

"Fuck it," Shirleen muttered, stomping to the door. "I'll do it."

"Shirleen," I called.

She turned, hand to the handle, and bit out, "What?"

"Hank," I said softly. "And while he's at it, get him to talk to Roam, too."

Her face got soft.

She got me.

Hank would be perfect for *the talk,* and we both knew it.

"Hank," she said.

"And, just so you know, any other issues with the Hot Bunch, your Hot-Bunch-in-the-making at home or anything, you wanna come over and gab. Do it. But bring coffee instead of attitude next time," I said.

She rolled her eyes, turned and was gone.

I turned to Daisy. "Right. Crisis over. Anything I need to know?"

She nodded. "Roxie's got the beta version of the website good to go, so you need to look at it. And Ava sent the finals for the letterhead and business cards that you need to approve so we can go to print. I sent all that shit to you, it's in your email."

"Cool," I replied.

"And Smithie called. He wants me to have a sit down with JoJo this afternoon, so I'm takin' off to do that. And tomorrow they're puttin' our plaque on the wall in the hall."

Tomorrow they were putting our plaque on the wall in the hall.

I smiled at her.

She smiled at me.

Then I hauled my ass to my office and booted up my machine.

I was clicking through the website Roxie designed for me when Daisy called from my door, "I'm gettin' a sandwich, darlin'. Want me to get you one?"

I shook my head. "I'm not here long. I've gotta go meet Matt and go over our strategy for tonight. I'll pick something up on the way."

"Gotcha," she murmured and turned on a wave and a, "Later."

I watched the door close on her.

Then I thought about my plaque in the hall and meeting Matt later.

This brought me to thinking about Hank and Lee.

This sent my hand to my phone.

I called Shirleen.

"Girl, I just got done rappin' with you," was her greeting.

"You know," I told her, getting to the point of what was really upsetting her, "they're gonna grow up and when they do, they're gonna leave."

She said nothing, but I felt the vibes, and they were not good. Not angry, just unhappy. So I kept speaking.

"But what you need to know and never forget is that the love and stability you've given them since you've had them is the most precious thing they've had in their lives. And they'll never forget that either. So they're gonna grow up and they're gonna live their lives. And because you gave them that, you are not ever gonna lose them." I took in a breath and used Duke's words. "But now, you need to give them freedom to fly."

She again said nothing and I waited.

Then she said something.

"You're right, child."

"I know, Shirleen."

"Still, gonna kick his ass if he knocks up some skinny white girl."

I laughed and said, "I'll help."

"Good to know," she murmured. "Later."

Disconnect.

I put my phone on the desk and my eyes to the computer. I had them there approximately three seconds before the door to the suite opened.

Ren was sauntering in. Trousers. Dress shirt.

Delicious.

"Hey," I called, getting out of my chair and moving around the desk.

His lips were quirking when he said, "You know, you don't have to get up, babe."

I made it to him, got on my toes, put a hand to his abs and touched my lips to his before I replied, "Yeah, I do."

He shook his head, lips still quirking, and he asked, "Got a sec?'

"Sure," I answered.

He jerked his head to my desk as it hit me we hadn't broken that in yet, and I made a mental note to schedule that for the near future.

I moved to sit in my chair. He moved close and leaned against my desk, arms crossed on his chest, chin dipped, eyes on me.

"Vito and I just had it out," he declared.

Shit.

Ren kept going.

"It was ugly and I'm done. I resigned."

Fuck!

Ren wasn't done.

"I got shit to tie up and Marcus isn't quite ready. Vito's got a month of me around to make the transition. Then I figure you and me can spend a couple of weeks on a beach. That'll give Marcus time so when we come back I can get down to that."

Nice.

Me. Ren. And a couple of weeks on a beach.

One could not say I liked why he had time for a vacation. But I was not going to argue with it.

Therefore, I agreed, "Okay."

"Can you arrange it so you're not workin' anything and you can get away?" he asked.

"Absolutely," I answered.

"Good," he muttered, but the look on his face said that nothing was good.

I reached out a hand and slid my finger down his thigh. "You okay?"

"Always had hope," he told me.

People always did when shit was going down with families.

"He still has a month," I reminded him.

Ren shook his head. "No. I've committed to Marcus. It's done."

I got out of my chair and got close. He uncrossed his arms and wound them around me, pulling me off my feet so I as leaning into him. I returned the favor and settled in, curling my arms around him.

"He's stubborn. His loss," I said gently.

"Still sucks."

It totally did. Ren excommunicated by Vito and us not able to carpool.

Not that we rode to work together much.

But still.

I pressed closer and gave him a squeeze. "Well, the good news is, you'll have another desk we can break in."

His eyes warmed and he grinned at me.

I pressed even closer and whispered, "I'm sorry, baby."

"Me too," he whispered back on his own squeeze.

"How about we go out tonight? Maybe to Brother's. Relive our first date with food this time. And, of course, sex on the stairs at home," I suggested.

His eyes seriously warmed and he replied, "Works for me."

I grinned. "Cool."

He bent in and gave me a quick kiss before pulling away and saying, "Gotta get back."

"Yeah. I gotta go grab some lunch and meet Matt. Since we're in separate cars, I'll meet you back at the house. Say five thirty?"

"Yeah, honey."

He leaned in and gave the top of my hair a kiss before he moved me back and disengaged.

"Later, Ally," he called as I watched his broad shoulders in his dress shirt as he walked away.

"Later, honey," I replied.

He gave me a look over his shoulder and a low wave before the door closed on him.

I gave some thought that made my happy place tingle as to how I was going to take away Ren's bad day that night. Then I turned my attention to my computer.

I sent Roxie some changes, sent approvals of the proofs to Ava and shut down my computer.

I grabbed my phone, shoved it in my back pocket, and tagged my purse. I took off, locking up, and thinking about where I'd hit in order to get lunch.

I took the elevator down to the parking garage, texting Ren as I went, *On my way to lunch and Matt.*

I knew I wouldn't get his return text until I drove out because the signal was lost under the building. I also knew I'd get it when I drove out because he always returned my texts.

I had my keys out and was close to my car when I felt it.

I wasn't alone.

I braced and turned to see Darius baring down on me.

He did not look happy.

Oh man.

"Hey," I greeted.

"Fuck hey, Ally and," he lifted a finger and jabbed it at my face when he got close and stopped, "*fuck you.*"

What the hell?

"Darius, why're you—?"

He cut me off, his handsome face twisted with fury. "I know it was you."

Uh-oh.

"Me what?" I asked hesitantly.

But I had a feeling I knew what.

"I know it was you. Ally, always up in everybody's shit, tellin' me you'd be up in mine. So it was fuckin' *you,*" he jabbed his finger in my face again, "that set Lee and Eddie on Malia."

They'd had the talk.

They hadn't told me, but Darius sure found out.

Fuck.

"Darius—"

He got in my face and I snapped my mouth shut.

"You stupid, nosy, fuckin' *bitch.*"

My back snapped straight, but Darius wasn't quite finished.

"We're done," he clipped. "You and me. And 'cause of you, me and Lee and Eddie. We're done. It's all done. It's..."

He kept blasting me with angry words, but I felt another presence. My eyes went around him and they got huge.

Fuck!

"*Darius!*" I shouted, grabbing his hand.

But it was too late.

Snookie Rivers, or at least the man in the DMV picture Brody got, was there and he was ready.

As Darius turned, Rivers slammed a tire iron in the side of Darius's head. I saw the blood start to flow even as he went down.

No.

No.

No, no, no, no, no.

I screamed, reaching into my purse for my pepper spray as Rivers turned to me.

I started backing up quickly, still screaming.

He was on me before I had the pepper spray out, but I got my hand on it and pulled it out as he shoved me into the side of my car. He swiftly lifted a hand, and I felt a sharp stab in my neck just as I got the pepper spray out and up between us. I blasted him in the face and he reeled away, choking.

I wanted to go to Darius but to get him help, I needed to get away and find somebody.

So I ran.

The problem was I got five steps in, and on the sixth, my leg weirdly gave out under me. I hit the deck on my hands and knees, still shouting, but weaker now, as a strange lethargy invaded my limbs.

I kept crawling, fell to my stomach and started dragging myself before my cheek planted into the cement and everything went black

I heard the gunshots.

One.

Then two.

It took effort but I forced my eyes open.

I managed this, but I couldn't get my wits about me. My head was fuzzy and I couldn't focus on anything.

I struggled to get it together and sensed movement.

It was then I struggled to focus and saw something looming over me.

"Shot him in both legs." I heard. "He wakes up, he can watch, but he can't move." Then the voice went on musingly, "If he doesn't bleed out first."

I had no idea what whoever that was was talking about, and I didn't have it in me to put it together.

470

I did have it in me to feel that whatever I was laying on moved and the thing looming got closer.

So I could focus.

Rivers.

It all came back to me.

Fuck!

His fingers came to my face. "Now it's just you and me, Ally. Just you and me. Finally."

Fuck, shit, *fuck*.

I realized I was drugged, but that didn't mean I didn't try to scoot away as he bent over me.

I didn't succeed and I felt his mouth wet on my neck, shifting up to my ear.

My stomach roiled.

"When we're done, I'll get rid of him. Your man. The black one. Then I'll find the other one, the Italian, and get rid of him, too. And then it'll *really* be just you and me," he whispered in my ear.

He'd seen me with Ren *and* Darius.

He'd so totally been watching me.

Sick.

"Get away from me," I pushed out between my lips.

His mouth moved from my ear and his face came close to mine. "Never, Ally. *Never*."

It took a lot out of me, but I focused on his eyes.

They were burning with a light that scared even me.

Not a little.

A lot.

I was terrified.

God, I had to get my shit together.

Pronto.

I took stock.

I was on a bed. And I could feel my phone still at my ass.

This was good. I didn't know where my purse was, but Brody had a lock on my phone. I had no idea how much time had elapsed since Rivers took me, but when I didn't meet Matt or even before, when I didn't text Ren that I was with Matt, they'd mobilize.

I needed to buy time

"Is Darius here?" I asked.

He tipped his head to the side and his eyes moved over my face. Then he moved into me, curled his arms around me and lifted me up so my torso was pressed to his and my chin was to his shoulder.

I squinted then swallowed, my head swimming, my heart clutching, my eyes seeing Darius prone on the floor about ten feet away. He was bleeding from two gunshot wounds to his thighs and a wicked gash on his head.

God.

Please.

God.

Please.

Let Darius be okay and let Ren have mobilized Lee.

My mind went off that thought when Rivers's hands went into my tee and pulled it up. Unable to do anything else, my body not at my command, my arms went up and it was gone.

This was not getting better.

He laid me gently and sickeningly lovingly in the bed, still bent to me.

"I've been waiting for this for a long time," he told me, his hand moving on the skin of my side, stroking me.

I tried to lift a hand. I got it up, weakly, and rested it on his forearm.

I took this as good.

"We need to talk," I told him.

"I like this," he replied and I was hoping that was an affirmative on our talking. Though, what he wanted to talk about when he spoke again, I didn't like all that much. "I didn't expect him to be here, but I like it. He had so much of your time. You smiled at him. You laughed with him. You teased him. So now, if he wakes up, he gets to watch *me* with you."

I lifted my other hand and tried to push it against his chest, but I didn't have enough in me to do anything but rest it there.

"Snookie, please," I said softly. "I feel funny."

His hand slid over ribs and toward my breast, his lips curling in a creepy smile. "You know my name."

"Yeah. Now, please—"

"I like that you know my name," he told me.

Gack!

"Snookie—"

He leaned in closer.

"I'll make you feel good, Ally," he promised.

Oh God.

Shit!

"Just five minutes. Please. Just five—"

His mouth came to mine and he brushed it there, back and forth, and again, and again before he replied, "No, Ally. I've been waiting too—"

He stopped speaking and my body jerked in surprise as two hands cuffed together came between us. They yanked back at Rivers's throat and Rivers was gone.

I struggled to sit up and saw Rivers on top of Darius, his back to Darius's front. Darius's cuffed hands were pulling back hard on Rivers's neck, and by the sick sounds he was making, it was clear Darius was choking him.

I rolled to my side. It seemed to take years while Rivers gurgled and he and Darius grappled on the floor as I went for my phone. I fumbled with yanking it out of my back pocket, cursing to myself and keeping my eyes to the men on the floor.

Then Rivers took one hand from pulling at Darius's cuffed wrists at his neck and it went to his belt.

My eyes went to his belt.

He had a knife there.

"Darius," I whispered, swallowed, and went for it again, trying for louder, "Darius! He has a knife!"

Darius rolled Rivers but Rivers was fighting for his life. He wasn't wasting time.

And thus he didn't waste time yanking out a huge-ass hunting knife, twisting it around, and sinking it into the flesh of Darius's side.

And yanking up viciously.

Darius grunted, but by some miracle he did not let go of his hold on Rivers's neck.

Shock and terror pulsing through me, along with adrenaline (thankfully), I shrieked, "No!" and moved to grasp the edge of the bed.

I pulled myself off and pushed up on my hands and knees, scooting toward them, my hands slipping on Darius's blood flooding the floor.

"Fuck!" I shouted, making it to them as they rolled this way and that. Rivers's face was now blue, his legs kicking in panic and agitation. Darius was grunting, the noises full of exertion and pain. I got my hands on the knife still in Darius's side in order to use it on Rivers and get him off Darius, but they slipped free over the warm blood. "No," I whispered, going for it again just as sunlight hit the scene.

I looked up to see Ren charging in, Lee and Hank behind him, Eddie and Luke following.

Thank God.

Thank you, God.

Thank you, God.

"Ambulance!" I shouted. "Darius. Shot and stabbed."

Ren hauled Rivers off Darius and dragged him away.

I didn't look to see what Ren was doing, although I distractedly heard a fist thudding into flesh then flesh thudding into a wall (or the floor).

Instead, moving urgently, I slid on the blood to get closer to Darius who was on his back and not moving.

Lethargic, panting, my heart beating so hard it was painful, I didn't need the knife to sink it into Rivers and help Darius, so I left it where it was but pressed a hand to his wound. I lifted my other hand to his chest and got in his face.

"There're here. There're here. You're gonna be okay," I told him.

Darius stared at me and I could hear Luke saying, "Gunshot wounds. Stab wounds. Head wound. It's bad. We need a medic immediately."

I felt hands on me and heard Lee speaking.

"Ally, let me get to him."

I reached out and grabbed Darius's hand. With effort pulling it to his chest and pressing in, I got even closer.

"You're gonna be okay. The ambulance is coming."

He kept staring at me.

I pushed in at his chest with our hands. "Talk to me."

"You're gonna be okay," he repeated my words quietly.

For some reason, hearing his voice sent relief sweeping through me.

"Yeah. Yeah," I nodded. "I'm gonna be okay."

"They're here," he said, his voice weak.

Shit. Shit. *Fuck.*

"Yeah. They're here."

"So you're gonna be okay."

The hands on me grew urgent. "Ally, honey, let me in there."

I ignored Lee and said to Darius, "Yeah."

"'Cause they're here," Darius said to me.

I pressed harder to his wound as his blood flowed over my hand.

"No." I shook my head. "Because *you* saved me."

He held my eyes and lifted a hand to my face. "Yeah."

I pressed my cheek into his hand and held his other one tight.

It was then, he closed his eyes and his lips curved in a smile I *did not like*.

"Finally," he whispered. "Salvation."

Then his hand fell away, landing at his side.

Lifeless.

After that, I threw my head back and screamed.

Chapter 33

Pain in My Ass

The drug having worn off, my faculties back to mostly functioning, I sat in the hospital waiting room with the rest of the crew, Ren holding me close to his side with one arm, my hand held to his chest in his.

I had my head on his shoulder.

By the way, the hospital waiting room part of the Rock Chick Ride?

Not my favorite.

Ever.

And this one particularly.

They'd had a look at me when they brought me in. I was fine, still drugged, but I lost it when they tried to clean Darius's blood off me.

I struggled, spat, clawed and no one could calm me. Not Ren, who tried first. Not Hank, who got in there with Ren. Not Indy, who Lee pulled Ren and Hank away so she could get in because he thought she would do it.

She couldn't.

The person who did it was my mom.

And she did this by putting her hand on the nurse's arm and saying, "She needs it. Let her keep it. We'll see to her when the time is right for Ally."

The nurse didn't like it, but she moved away.

I stopped fighting.

So I still had his blood on me, there, in the waiting room.

Because Mom was right. I needed it. I needed some part of him with me.

I knew this sounded weird.

But I didn't give a fuck.

Ren, being Ren, said nothing about the blood even though now it was on him.

And we were waiting.

All of us.

Indy and Lee. Eddie and Jet. Hank and Roxie. Jules and Vance. Ava and Luke. Stella and Mace. Hector and Sadie. Tex and Nancy. Marcus and Daisy. Roam and Sniff. Mom and Dad. Indy's dad, Tom, and his girlfriend, Lana (incidentally, Lana was Mace's Mom; so yeah, we were incestuous—whatever, it worked). Tod and Stevie. Buddy and Ralphie. Smithie and LaTeesha. Annette and Jason. Jules's uncle Nick and her friend May. Jimmy Marker. Brody, Monty, Matt, Ike, Jack and Bobby. Blanca, Rosa, Carlos, Elena and Gloria. Dom and Sissy. Vito and Angela. Willie Moses. Brian Bond. Darius's Mom, Dorothea. Duke's wife Dolores. And even Stella's band, Floyd, Buzz, Pong, Hugo and Leo showed up.

A motley crew of cops and crooks, bounty hunters and baristas, PIs and rock stars, hot guys and Rock Chicks.

Darius's people.

Darius's family.

And last, Shirleen was sitting beside me.

Close.

There was some shifting and my eyes flew to the door, hoping it was a doctor with good news. But I saw Jane walk in.

She'd been around, not much, and her usual quiet. I knew a couple of the Rock Chicks and Hot Bunch spoke with her. Since she didn't return my calls or give me time when I approached her, and since (for once), I didn't press, I didn't know what they said or how she reacted.

All I knew right then was that she came straight to me, her eyes never leaving mine.

She stopped in front of us. Ren's hold tightened, and I looked up to her.

"Nothing ever *really* bad happens in a fairytale, Ally," she whispered, her eyes, locked on me, bright with tears.

And hope.

"I hope you're right, chickie," I whispered back.

"Me, too," she said. Her eyes slid to Ren, then to Shirleen, who she gave a small smile before she moved away.

Ren's hand gave mine a squeeze.

I gave his one back, let him go and shifted.

But not away. Only so I could reach out and find Shirleen's hand.

When I did, hers closed tight.

I looked to Lee, who Indy was holding, her cheek to his chest, his chin to the top of her head, his eyes to the door, his jaw hard. My BFF, though, had her eyes on me.

She smiled.

It was fake, but I smiled back.

Then I looked to Eddie, who had Jet in what Jet called the Eddie's Woman Hold. That was his arm wrapped around her neck, holding her tucked deep into his side.

His eyes were also on the door.

Jet's cheek was to his shoulder and her eyes were on her husband's profile.

I then looked again to the door when there was movement there. I pulled in breath and it caught when I saw who was walking through.

Not the doctor.

Duke.

And Duke was not alone.

Following him were Malia and Liam Clark.

Holy shit!

I sat up straight.

"What the fuck?" I heard Lee growl.

But my eyes were pinned to Malia, who was looking around, but doing it looking freaked way the fuck out, and Liam, sticking close to his mom, looking around and doing it looking cautious but confused.

Eddie broke from Jet, Lee from Indy. They headed her way and I moved.

"Ally," Ren called, but I ignored him.

No one was going to stop me.

Fucking no one.

Lee caught me with a hand in my belly before I got to them, warning, "Not the time, Ally."

But I ignored him, too.

Eyes to Malia, I moved them to Liam and lifted up my hand, covered in dried blood.

"That's your father's," I announced, and Malia moved close to Liam as Liam's eyes got huge and they riveted to my hand.

I heard a gasp and I suspected it was Dorothea's.

Interesting.

Apparently Dorothea didn't know about her grandson.

I didn't have time to ponder that for a variety of reasons.

One of which was Eddie, biting out from close, "Don't Ally."

"Lay down the truth, darlin'." Duke's gravelly voice encouraged, and my eyes went to him. He nodded. "Now's the time."

Kristen Ashley

"It's not the fuckin' time," Lee ground out, his hand going away from my belly so he could turn to Duke.

Before they could get into it, I kept at it.

I looked to Liam. "A bad guy was touching me. Your father had already been shot in both legs and slammed in the head with a tire iron but he still got him off me. He barely got a hand on me and your father dragged himself to me and pulled him off. I was drugged. I couldn't defend myself or help him. But he kept him off me even when that asshole stabbed him. He kept him off me until help came. Blood pouring out of him and he kept him *off me.*"

"Ally—" Malia whispered, her voice pained, but I kept my eyes glued to Liam.

"Look around you," I ordered. "All these people, *this,*" I jerked my bloody hand in the air, "*that's* your father." I looked to Malia. "I don't know what went down with Eddie and Lee. What I know is, if Darius makes it through this, he's gonna stay away. From you. From his son." I swung an arm out behind me. "From everybody."

I took a step toward her. Liam put an arm around her waist and pulled her back just as Lee put an arm around mine and stopped me.

Time to wrap up.

So I whispered my plea, "Don't let him, *please.*"

"Zano, a little help," Lee said about two seconds before Lee released me and immediately two arms clamped around me. One at the chest. One at my belly.

Ren's lips at my ear, he said in his sweet voice, "All right, baby, that's out. Now come sit with me."

I drew in a breath.

It failed to calm me.

But I'd laid it out. That was all I could do. I had nothing left in me.

"Don't let him," I repeated to Malia.

Before I could turn back to my seat, Malia moved forward and caught my hands.

Even them being bloody.

"I talked with Liam this morning and he wants to meet his dad," she whispered.

Oh.

Well.

480

Shit.

Apparently my dramatic speech was unnecessary.

Whatever.

"Well, uh... that's good," I muttered.

Her head tipped to the side and a ghost of a genuine smile played at her mouth even as her hands squeezed mine. "I see you haven't changed."

"Nope," I agreed, and my gaze went to Liam. "Though I'm not usually this crazy."

Liam looked like he didn't believe me.

"Yes, she is," Eddie said.

I glared at Eddie.

Ren pulled me away, but I got a squeeze back to Malia before I let her go.

He took my hand and I walked stiffly back to our seats with my man.

Once I sat, I gave Duke a look.

He gave me a chin lift.

Jeez.

Even Duke did the chin lift.

Well, again, whatever.

I gave him one back and watched his face get soft.

Shirleen caught my hand.

I looked at her profile.

She didn't look at me.

But I saw the tear slide down her cheek.

And I saw her lips trembling.

So I held my man's hand and I held my friend's hand.

But it was Shirleen's shoulder I laid my head on.

And she rested hers on mine.

⚞⚟

Half an hour later...

For the fiftieth time (maybe an exaggeration), I caught Vito looking at Ren. And for the fiftieth time (okay, so maybe the twenty-seventh), I saw Ren avoiding his uncle's eyes.

So I turned to my man.

I found his ear with my lips. "Go to him."

He shook his head and I pulled back slightly to look at him.

"Now's not the time," he told me.

"Now's the perfect time," I contradicted.

He dipped close. "Ally, baby, that's done."

"Part of it's done. But the family part will never be done."

Ren's jaw got hard.

"Go to him," I encouraged.

"Honey—"

I lifted a hand to his cheek. "You have a window of opportunity. It's fucked up *why* you have it, but you have it. He feels this, what's happening right now. He wants to come to you but he's too stubborn. So you have to take this opportunity and go to him."

"Babe—"

Urgently, I whispered, "Life's too short."

His beautiful eyes moved over my face. Then he nodded, leaned in for a quick kiss and straightened out of his seat.

I watched him walk to his uncle. Angela's face lit up with hope and Dom led Sissy closer.

Five minutes later, Vito pulled Ren in for a back pounding hug.

I looked away, and as I did I caught Hank's eyes.

He smiled at me.

My brother had a beautiful smile.

I smiled back.

It was small, but this time it wasn't fake.

⚜

An hour later...

After Lavonne and Bear, friends of Jet's and Nancy's, showed with five pizzas that only Roam and Sniff touched (and also Tex, Dom and Smithie)...

After Sniff's girlfriend showed (and she was cute and way into him as he was way into her), she got close to her boyfriend, stuck there and made me nearly smile (nearly) when I caught Shirleen staring at them. She caught me staring at her and she rolled her eyes...

After four of Roam's girlfriends showed (yes, *four*), that he somehow corralled and got them out of there so if there was a drama, it didn't happen close...

After there was a slightly elevated conversation between Stella, Hugo and Pong when they evidently learned I'd been stripping and were aggrieved Stella hadn't shared that intel with them...

After all that, a man in scrubs and a white lab coat walked through the door.

"It's been explained to me that you're all here for Darius Tucker," he announced. "Is there immediate family?"

"Me," Dorothea chimed in, but her voice sounded croaky. So she cleared her throat as she walked his way, for once not longingly staring at Liam Clark, who for some reason she didn't approach. Then again, Malia and Liam steered clear of her, too. Her throat cleared, she repeated more strongly, "Me. I'm his mother."

Shirleen got up and moved in behind her sister.

And Ren's hold on me got tighter when Malia, who was standing to the side with Liam, Indy, Lee, Jet and Eddie, broke free and edged near.

I held my breath.

"He made it through surgery," the doctor told Dorothea, and I let out my breath. It caught again when he went on, "However, there was a great loss of blood and quite a bit of damage, including head trauma. He's in critical care."

I clenched my teeth when the doctor lifted a hand and curled it on Dorothea's shoulder.

That was not a good sign.

His voice dropped quiet (another not good sign) when he went on.

"I'm sorry, Mrs. Tucker. Although he survived surgery, we still have concerns. He's not conscious, but it would be good if you didn't delay visiting him."

Definitely not a good sign.

I heard sobs (probably one of them Roxie; she cried all the time) and felt the vibe—already low—plummet, as everything leaked out at me and I collapsed into Ren's side.

Dorothea nodded, her chin lifting to hold it together, her body stiff.

"Can I... can we...?" Malia started, her hand going out behind her toward Liam. She took two steps forward, her eyes on Dorothea. "Can Liam and I visit with him?"

Without delay, Dorothea raised her hand toward Malia.

Malia walked to her, took it and turned back to Liam. "Baby?"

Eyes never leaving his mother, probably knowing all eyes were on him, without hesitation, Liam moved to her.

A good kid.

Darius's kid.

We all watched them follow the doctor.

For some reason I didn't get and I didn't try to process, I searched the room until I found Jane.

She was already looking at me.

She smiled and shook her head.

Even after this, she still believed in fairytales.

I wanted to believe.

Boy, did I want to believe.

But I had to admit, I was losing faith.

"Baby."

My eyes fluttered.

"Ally, honey, wake up."

I lifted my head from what, I noted from looking around, was Hank's thigh. It had been some time, I'd finally cleaned Darius's blood from my hands and I was curled up on the chairs of the hospital waiting room with Hank providing my pillow. Ren was crouched in front of me.

I shook sleep away, got up on a hand and focused on my man. "What?"

"Darius is awake, honey. And he's asking for you."

No longer even slightly sleepy, I surged to my feet.

Lee and Eddie were standing at the door. Lee stretched a hand to me. I hustled to him and took it. Quickly, both of them flanking me, me holding my brother's hand, we moved into the hall and stopped at the elevator.

"Is there a change in his condition?" I asked, looking up at Lee.

He looked down at me. "No, honey. He's just awake."

"Isn't that good?" I asked.

"No clue, Ally," Lee answered, his hand tightening in mine.

I looked to Eddie.

He smiled at me, but I knew it was totally fake.

I knew this because there was no dimple.

The elevator doors opened and no one spoke as we rode up to the critical care unit. We were expelled into the hall and Lee guided me to where Dorothea, Shirleen, Malia and Liam were huddled with Indy and Jet.

Before I could say a word or take in the vibe, a nurse appeared and asked me, "Are you Ally?"

I nodded.

"Follow me," she said.

She seemed to be in a hurry. I didn't like that. Still, I followed her and did it quickly.

She instructed me to wash my hands. Impatiently, I did. Then she gave me a gown. More impatiently, I pulled it on.

Then she led me to Darius in his hospital bed.

His eyes were closed like he was sleeping. But other than that and all the tubes and shit sticking out of him, and of course the bandage wrapped around his head—not to mention, Darius didn't wear hospital gowns (as in, *ever*, and I loved him but it was not a good look, on *anybody*)—he looked like just Darius.

I got close to his bed, bent down and grabbed his hand.

"Darius?" I called softly. "It's Ally. I'm here."

His eyes opened and he focused on me.

I forced a smile, but as much as I fought it, I felt it trembling.

"How you doin', bro?" I asked.

It was then he spoke.

And he did it to rasp:

"Jesus, Ally. You're a pain in my ass."

⚡

Lee

Standing in the hall with Indy, Eddie, Jet and Darius's family, Lee Nightingale's body jerked and his head twisted around when he heard his sister burst out laughing.

Epilogue
Righteous

<hr>

Six years later...

"She's faking it," I mumbled, doing so with my mouth barely moving.

"Shut it, Ally." I heard Sniff's voice coming from the bud in my ear.

"Totally faking it," I kept at him, succeeding in not smiling, but doing this since I had lots of practice.

We were discussing Sniff's love life. And teasing him about it.

Totally lots of practice.

Suffice it to say, Roam nor Sniff had found their Rock Chick equivalents. But they'd been practicing for the time they made that discovery.

Copiously.

"Sniff's convinced he gives good lovin'," Roam put in.

"That's 'cause I do," Sniff's deep pissed-off voice clipped. "No complaints so far."

"And *that's* because they're faking," I said.

"Cut the chatter on the line," Luke butted in, ending our fun.

I pressed my lips together in a further (successful) effort to fight my smile and did a scan of the club. I was in an LBD, strappy sandals and had big hair.

In other words, I was a honey trap who would, eventually, withhold the honey.

The skin at the back of my neck prickled when I saw him.

"Got eyes on him. He just entered," I muttered, the microphone in my cleavage picking up my voice.

"Copy," Lee came through. "Positions?"

"Check," Roam said.

"Check," Sniff said.

"Affirmative," Luke said.

"Roger that," Lee said. "Brody, got eyes?"

"Do I ever *not* have eyes?" Brody asked, offended.

"Appropriate responses are check, affirmative or negative," Lee growled.

Years of this, my brother still found Brody annoying.

I, on the other hand, found him hilarious.

"Whatevs," Brody replied. "Affirmative."

"Roger that. Ally, you're a go," Lee told me.

"Copy. Out," I told him.

Lifting a hand and pulling out the ear bud, I dropped it in my purse, clamped it shut and slid off the barstool, eyes on my target.

Fun and games done.

Time to get to work.

⚡

I opened the front door to Ren's and my house, entering and seeing the space dark except for the flickering light of the TV.

My husband.

Since I was kidnapped, he waited up for me.

Always.

I closed and locked the door, walked in, was assaulted by our brown and white Boxer, Payton, and stopped.

This was because I needed to give my dog some loving. It was also because it was way late and my man was flat out on his back on a couch, head turned, eyes to me and our two year old daughter was dead asleep, curled up on his chest.

"You do know she has a bedtime," I noted quietly.

"What Katie and I do during father daughter nights is up to us, baby," Ren replied, just as quietly.

I rolled my eyes on a, "Whatever," and moved their way.

I bent low, touching my lips to his then putting my hands to my girl. Lifting and turning her, I held her to my chest and she snuggled deep.

Even asleep, she knew Momma was home.

Loved my girl.

Totally.

I looked down at Ren. "Putting her down."

He looked up at me, and even with the flickering light I could see his eyes were warm and sweet. They got that way frequently, but they got the way they were right now when he was looking at his wife with his daughter.

And I loved my man.

Totally.

"Right," he replied.

I moved to the stairs, Payton following me, seeing as he doted on his sweet Katie.

Halfway up, the flickering light went out.

I put her down. She shifted around a second and I stood by her with a hand on her back until she settled. But I didn't leave her until I'd touched her ear, her dark hair and the soft fuzz of her cheek.

Only then did I leave, Payton settling with a groan in her room. He'd start there. He'd come to Ren and me later.

I entered Ren's and my room, closing the door halfway behind me, and saw him walking out of the bathroom in chocolate brown pajama bottoms.

Delicious.

"She wake?" he asked.

"Not really," I answered, moving to the bed and sitting on it.

I leaned down to unstrap my sandals.

"Unh-unh."

That came from Ren.

My happy place spasmed as I bent my head back to look at him.

"What?"

"Fuckin' you with those on," he told me and continued, "You can lose the dress, though."

Eyes never leaving him, I stood up and lifted one of my hands to the side zip.

Slowly, I pulled it down.

Ren's eyes watched as his mouth asked about my night's activities, "You get your man?"

"Yep," I answered.

Zip down, I tugged up my dress and it was gone.

Strapless lacy black bra, high cut lacy black panties, and heels.

Ren's eyes didn't leave my body when his mouth noted, "You're gonna do that twice tonight, baby."

Righteous.

I grinned at my husband.

My husband lunged at me.

※※

"*Ren,*" I breathed.

I was on my back in our bed, Ren over me, my legs spread, knees high. He had my hands held in his at the sides of my head, pressed into the pillow, our fingers laced, but he'd angled up so he could watch as he thrust into me.

But when I spoke his name, his eyes came to mine.

"Wrap your legs around me," he ordered.

I complied.

He kept being the kind of bossy I didn't mind (at all). "Move with me, baby."

My hips complied.

"Fuck yeah," he growled, going faster and doing it deep. "That's it."

It definitely was.

"Dig in, Ally."

I dug the heels of my sandals in, gaining purchase to tip my hips.

He rammed in deeper.

"*Baby,*" I panted.

His head dropped so he could watch again and he groaned, "Fuckin' beautiful."

Oh yeah.

It totally was.

But I was close.

My hands clenched in his. "Ren."

He drove in faster, harder.

"*Ren,*" I whispered, and suddenly I had his weight, his mouth, his tongue and that did it.

I came. Thighs squeezing, heels digging in, fingers clasping, moaning against his tongue, *hard.*

It took a while, but when it left me, he rolled so I was straddling him and lifted up, taking us from missionary to lotus.

My number one.

Righteous.

One of his hands went between my legs as his other one gripped my hip encouragingly. "Ride me, honey."

I didn't need to be asked twice. My arms sliding around his shoulders, I rode him and did it fast, taking him deep, my lips to his, eyes locked, breath mixing.

His thumb pressed in and circled.

I whimpered.

"You're goin' again," he demanded.

I hoped so.

"Okay," I breathed, moving faster.

"Fuck," he muttered, his hand sliding up my hip, side, in over my ribs to cup my breast, his thumb dragging over my rock-hard nipple. "Get there, Ally."

Too late.

I was there.

My head flew back, but Ren drove a hand into my hair and tipped it forward.

I gasped. I bucked. I gave him a show he liked and I knew it when his arm wound around me and ground me down. He shoved my face in his neck and I took his groan in mine.

My whole body shivered.

Sweet, God, my man, so sweet, after he came down, his lips and tongue worked my neck as his hands slid lightly over my skin. His mouth ended at the guitar pendant dangling at the base of my throat and I felt his tongue sweep it inside. I knew he sucked it deeper when I felt the gentle tug at the chain around my neck.

Another whole body shiver.

While he did this and after I felt him release the pendant, I returned the favor with lips and tongue and hands (without the pendant part, of course) and we did this for a while.

Finally, I lifted my head, put my hands to either side of his neck and announced, "If it's a boy, he and I get mother son time."

Ren went still.

"And we're naming him Darius."

Ren stared up at me.

"He, or she, depending, will be here in seven and a half months, give or take a few days."

Ren didn't move nor speak.

"I'll be clearing certain cases. I'll tell Daisy she needs to refer out now inappropriate ones. And I'll talk to Lee about agreed limitations. But after Katie, they know the drill."

Ren kept staring at me.

By the way, I wasn't alarmed at his reaction. When I told him I was carrying Katie, he behaved the same way.

He liked the news he was going to be a daddy (even part two), and liked it so much it made him speechless.

"I like to think it happened during that time on the stairs. But according to the doctors, I think it's that time in the sauna." My eyes wandered away. "Or on the landing." I tipped my head to the side. "Or the dining room table."

"Baby, look at me."

I looked at my husband.

"You're the best thing that ever happened to me."

Oh my God.

I stopped breathing.

He wasn't done.

"And you keep getting better."

God.

Seriously?

I.

Loved.

My.

Man.

I loved him for many reasons. One of them was because he said shit like that to me all the time.

And I never got used to Ren Zano taking my breath away.

I dipped my head so my lips were to his and only then did I grin and whisper, "You happy?"

Ren didn't whisper back. "Fuck yeah, I'm happy."

That was when I smiled, and right before I kissed him, I said softly, "Righteous."

⚜

The next morning, Ren walked into the bedroom just as a tater tot went flying past him.

Katie was in a "feed Payton" mood, which occurred daily, three times and was, I suspected, why Payton doted on Katie.

I lounged next to my daughter in our bed, phone to my ear, lips curled up as I watched my husband watch the potato treat fly and land on the floor in the landing.

He then ignored it, and Payton chasing after it, and continued into the room with two fresh mugs of coffee.

I bit back laughter as Indy asked, "So can you pick it up?"

"Yes," I answered.

"The cake's kinda important," she told me.

"Uh... duh," I told her.

"You forget things," she informed me.

My back snapped straight.

"I totally don't forget things," I informed her.

"Lee's birthday that year," she said.

"Uh... I was kinda in the middle of pushin' out my kid two days before Lee's birthday *that year*," I reminded her. "I think Lee gets I had my mind on other things."

She was not deterred. "The balloons you were supposed to pick up for that thing for Sam."

"I didn't forget. I just didn't do it because Vance told me not to. He said at the thing for Max, Jules had so many balloons, he was running into them for days and stepping on them for days after."

"Ally, *you're a Rock Chick*," Indy snapped. "You don't do what the Hot Bunch says."

"Indy, *I work with Vance*. I was around when he was balloon cranky. You do not wanna be around when he's got a newborn, two hellions, otherwise known as male species toddlers, and balloons all over his house. Trust me."

"You're always picking the Hot Bunch over the Rock Chicks," she complained.

"That's because they keep me from getting shot at," I retorted.

I felt eyes and looked to Ren who was now lounging on his side across the bottom of our bed, keeping an eye on Katie feeding Payton. I caught his expression and made an, *I'm lying to make a point* face with a shake of my head even though I wasn't and, instead, was silently lying to Ren.

He sighed and turned to Katie.

He knew I was lying.

Kristen Ashley

I returned my attention to Indy when she murmured. "Crap, Tod and Stevie are here. They're early and I haven't done my hair."

They were early because Tod and Stevie completely doted on Indy and Lee's kids, Callum and Suki (never fear, that was just my niece's nickname, used so we wouldn't have confusion; my big bro and BFF named their daughter after me, which... was... *righteous*).

And Indy shouldn't be surprised. Tod and Stevie took every opportunity to "pop by" or "come early" and usually ended up essentially kidnapping the kids until Indy had to call and beg them to bring them back (or Lee had to call and threaten them; Lee's tactic worked better).

Unfazed, they kept doing it.

"Like they'll care," I replied. "Anyway, ask Tod to do your hair. He'd love that."

"He's already claimed Suki," she said swiftly. "And I want the kids here today, and Tod's got that look in his eye that says ice cream, mall, extreme spoiling and me with two children who don't understand why everything he or she points at isn't at their command."

This was true. I'd witnessed it. Repeatedly.

"There are worse things," I pointed out.

This got silence before a soft, "Yeah, there are."

I grinned and said, "Cake."

"Don't forget," she repeated.

"Cake and catfight if you keep saying that," I returned.

"Whatever," she muttered then, "Later."

"Later, chickie," I replied and we disconnected.

"So I take it we're picking up the cake," Ren asked, and I looked to him.

"Yeah," I answered.

Katie threw another tater tot. Ren looked to his girl and poked her gently in her rounded belly.

"*You're* supposed to eat them, baby," he told her.

She giggled.

She also threw another one.

That was when I giggled.

Ren just smiled.

Then he leaned in and kissed his daughter.

After that, he leaned further and kissed me.

494

It was Sunday breakfast in bed at the Zano house.

Yeah.

You guessed it.

Righteous.

"Yo!"

That was Lee.

We were in the kitchen at Indy and his house: Lee, Indy, Tex, Nancy, Jet (with her latest son, Cesar, or son number three, attached to her hip), Eddie, Ada and me.

The Kevster and Leo, Stella's bassist, were wandering through, heading toward the back door.

Lee was scowling at Leo and Kevin.

"What?" The Kevster asked.

"Keep it in your pocket or give it to me," Lee ordered.

"What?" The Kevster repeated, trying to look innocent.

And failing.

"You say 'what' one more time, I'll pat you down, confiscate it and it'll be in the garbage disposal," Lee warned.

Kevin gave up the ghost and cried, "But it's a party!"

"You don't smoke that shit at my house," Lee informed him.

"We weren't gonna," The Kevster replied. "We were gonna smoke it in your backyard."

I could swear I heard Lee growl.

"Kevin, just abstain, all right?" Indy waded in.

The Kevster looked at Indy then looked at Leo. "You're famous, right?" he asked.

"Yup," Leo answered, and he was.

The Blue Moon Gypsies had hit the big time. Totally. Red carpets. Their frequent brawls splashed all over the tabloids. Pong even had a sex tape that was still circulating the internet.

Totally rock 'n' roll.

"So, do you have, like, a limo or something?" Kevin asked.

"We ride around in Escalades," Leo shared. "That doesn't say rock 'n' roll. But they're roomy."

"Do you have one here?" Kevin asked.

"Yup," Leo answered.

"Let's go," The Kevster said, and they switched directions but got only a couple of steps in before Ada was there.

"Are you two young men going to smoke a doobie?" she asked.

Leo just stared at her.

The Kevster tipped his head to the side and hedged, "Maybe."

"I've never smoked marijuana," she informed them excitedly, her meaning clear to everybody. Including Kevin and Leo, who were unclear about most everything.

"Jesus. Someone shoot me," Lee muttered.

"Live large, mama," Leo said to Ada, an invitation coupled with an arm going out, leading the way.

Ada sent a happy grin to Nancy and shuffled out, followed by one famous and one infamous pothead.

I shared a smile with Indy and Jet before I looked to Tex because he was booming.

"I was wrong," he stated. "Shit never gets boring. It just gets more and more freaky."

He was not wrong.

"And just now, that old woman gettin' stoned with the stoner to end all stoners and a rock star, just plain crazy," he went on.

He was not wrong about that, either.

And Tex, being all kinds of crazy calling something crazy, said a lot.

But we were used to crazy.

And, none of us, not a single one (okay, maybe the Hot Bunch were exempted), would have it any other way.

"You have chocolate crumbs in your beard, honey," Nancy told him, lifting a hand and brushing away crumbs and Tex (yes, *Tex*) let her. "And what's that?" she asked. "Caramel?"

"Loopy Loo's brownies," he shared.

"Tex, you're not supposed to eat anything until the special guests arrive," Indy snapped.

His brows shot up. "Woman, you think I'm gonna wait for a brownie?"

"Yes," Indy answered.

"Well, you're wrong," Tex stated the obvious.

My mom walked in, Katie on her hip, her eyes going to Lee. "Sweetheart, do you know where Luke or Ava are? Ralphie's got Maisie and he says she needs changing, but we can't find either of them or their diaper bag."

Lee looked to his boots.

That meant that likely somewhere in Indy and Lee's five bedroom house, Luke was giving Ava the business.

I gave wide eyes to Jet. She gave them back to me.

Indy advised, "Talk to Sadie or Jules. They may have spares."

"Right," Mom muttered and moved out.

Shirleen walked in right after Mom disappeared.

"Got the call," she lifted up her phone, her eyes happy and dancing, "they're close."

Then she disappeared.

Indy handed a bowl of cashews to me and asked, "Can you put that on the table?"

"Sure thing," I muttered as Indy started dashing around the kitchen.

I moved to the door and heard as I walked through it, "Liam Nightingale! Get back here and grab those bowls of chips."

Ha-ha.

Lee got it from Indy.

Yeah, so I was a thirty-eight year old pregnant woman with a husband and a daughter.

I was still a Rock Chick.

And a little sister.

Some things never change.

That meant I was grinning as I entered the great room.

I put the cashews on the table covered in food and was immediately attacked by my niece, Leah, three years old. Roxie and Hank's first.

I bent, lifted her up, tossed her in the air and then pulled her close to me.

"Hey, beautiful," I whispered as her eyes, Hank's eyes, *my* eyes, looked back at me.

"Heyannieally," she replied, all in one word, and it sounded like a song.

"You having fun?" I asked.

She nodded.

"You being nice to your brother and cousins?" I asked and her eyes wandered.

This meant no.

Total Rock Chick in the making, even at three.

Roxie loved it. She thought it was a hoot.

Hank was screwed. And he knew it.

But he secretly loved it, too. I knew that.

Then again, he just adored his little girl.

May, a close friend we met during Jules's Rock Chick Ride, sidled up to me with Harry, Jules and Vance's youngest at her hip.

"Are we allowed to eat yet?" she asked out of the side of her mouth.

"They're almost here," I answered out of the side of mine. "But if you're about to expire, a few cashews probably won't be missed."

She didn't reply. She went for some cashews, took a handful, then disappeared in the crowd.

I was going to go back to the kitchen to help Indy but Daisy, snuggling a sleepy Tallulah, Stella and Mace's first (and only, so far), caught me.

By the way, Stella and Mace did get married on a beach in Hawaii. As Tod called it, she also wore a white crochet bikini, a sarong, a lei and a band of flowers around her forehead (Mace wore jeans and a white shirt). She looked awesome. Mace looked hot. The entire wedding was the bomb, even if, at the reception, there was a helicopter circling.

Furthering the coolness of their nuptials, it was in *Us* magazine.

Ren and I, if you're curious, had the Pope's blessing (I hoped) because I'd converted.

But I still got my red and black wedding. Tod did it up sah-*weet*. It was *awesome*.

I also got a three week honeymoon that started in Vegas and ended in the Bahamas.

Everything I ever wanted.

Especially the husband.

"You wanted to talk, sugar?" she asked, reaching for some cashews and not bothering to do it stealthily.

"A little later, they're almost here," I told her.

She looked up at me. "Is everything good?"

I smiled at her. "Yeah, totally."

She screwed up her face and studied me for two seconds before her eyes went wide, her face got bright and she opened her mouth.

She figured it out.

I moved fast and covered her mouth with my hand. Not to be left out, Leah leaned over and covered my hand on Daisy's mouth. Tallulah, thinking it was a game, did the same, but she did it slapping and giggling.

"Don't say anything," I whispered. "Indy doesn't know."

A drowned-out tinkly bell giggle escaped the three hands (two of them tiny, but still) and Daisy, eyes now dancing, nodded.

I took away my hand, taking the girls' with me.

"After the big thing, we'll share Ren and my big thing, but quietly," I told her.

Daisy, through more tinkling giggles, nodded.

I tipped my head, studied her and guessed, "You can't talk because if you open your mouth, you'll shriek. Right?"

She nodded again.

I shook my head, but did it grinning and bumping into her with my shoulder.

Tallulah put her hand over Daisy's mouth again.

Daisy gave it a raspberry.

I spied a runaway toddler, followed by another one, both females. These two were followed by a lumbering black man nearly bent double.

He caught up, scooped both up with arms at their bellies, and straightened Smithie with Suki in one arm, Lola, Sadie and Hector's firstborn, in the other.

The girls were giggling and squirming.

Smithie was scowling.

"Jesus. You bitches breed like rabbits," he bitched then totally gave it all away by bending in while lifting up Lola and shoving his face in her neck.

She squealed in glee as Smithie turned and strolled away.

"Smithie," Jet murmured as she passed us, putting something on the food table and finishing, "Total softie."

That was the damned truth.

My eyes slid through the crowd and I saw Amalea now had Katie. This was because Mom was chasing after Callum.

Jeez.

We did.

We bred like rabbits.

I kept looking through the throng and stopped when I saw Ren, Dom and Sissy standing with Vito and Angela.

We'll just say that after I was kidnapped and we nearly lost Darius, I was right. Vito had had a wakeup call. His "excommunication" of Ren lasted about eight hours. Then it was back to family.

I knew he wouldn't be able to keep it up.

And I loved being right.

Especially this time.

This wasn't to say that Ren went back to him. He'd made a commitment to Marcus. He'd followed through with his resignation and we had our two weeks at the beach where we did nothing but drink rum and fuck on the beach under the stars (and elsewhere). When we came back, Ren went into partnership with Marcus.

Dom went with him.

Vito decided to retire early, turning over the reins of the Zano criminal empire to Santo and Lucky.

Word on the street, they were doing well which was both good news (because I liked them) and bad news (because they were running a criminal empire).

This meant Dawn lost her job (the first order of business for Santo and Lucky was canning her; and luckily they let me watch, it was *awesome*). I'd done a check on her just because I was nosy. I found out she was living in Alabama. Still single. Still a receptionist.

But doing it far, far away.

Which worked for me.

It also meant Marcus and Ren took over the Zano Holdings offices.

So, when we could, my man and I carpooled.

"Their car's coming up to the curb," Stella's throaty voice could be heard calling from the front of the house.

Everyone moved that way.

Once in positions, we waited.

The door opened and Darius walked through, holding to his hip a gorgeous little girl with cute little pompom pigtails sticking out at the top sides of her head.

He was followed by Dorothea.

And Dorothea was followed by Malia.

Coming up the rear was Liam.

"Now!" Shirleen shouted and we all started doing what she'd been brow-beating us to practice for the last week.

We sang *Ten Thousand Men of Harvard.*

And we did it poorly.

Luckily, Tex got into it and his booming baritone drowned the rest of us out.

But it didn't seem to matter.

Because through it, Liam stood there grinning.

Then again, what else did you do when you were serenaded by family at your college graduation party?

It.

Was.

Righteous.

⚜

By the way, Darius lived in LA now. He worked at Mace's security agency.

At Mace's request, I flew out to do jobs with them occasionally, and if you thought the Hot Bunch was hot...

Just saying...

Seriously.

⚜

Malia lived in LA with Darius.

Don't ask, it's a huge-ass story.

But, as you can tell, it had a happy ending.

⚜

Liam lived in Cambridge, Massachusetts.

That was, until very recently.

⚜

An hour later, I was standing having some alone time with Gracie, Luke and Ava's first little girl. I was holding her close to my front. She was fascinated with my guitar pendant and I could see this was fascinating. I'd worn it every day for years and I was still fascinated with it.

But right then, I was fascinated with her little girl fascination.

I felt a presence get close and looked to the side to see Darius moving in there.

"Yo," I greeted.

He grinned. "Ally."

I looked across the room at Liam standing with Dorothea and Shirleen. He and his grandmother were grinning at Shirleen. She was saying something she really meant because her head was shaking and her afro was swaying.

I looked back to Darius to see his eyes on the same thing.

"Thanks for bringing him here so we could celebrate with him," I said.

His gaze came to me. "Not a problem."

I grinned at him. "So, am I still a pain in your ass?"

He grinned back and answered, "Yes."

I frowned. "How can I still be a pain in your ass? You live hundreds of miles away."

"Your brand of pain in the assedness extends great lengths. It might even span dimensions."

I rolled my eyes, and on the roll back to Darius, declared, "'Assedness' is not a word, Darius."

"Badasses can make up words, Ally."

This was true. They could do whatever the hell they wanted.

Darius reached in and confiscated Gracie from me. I wanted to protest, but when she smiled up at him, put her hand to his cheek and I watched him turn his head to kiss her palm, I decided against it.

I looked back across the room when I heard Liam and Dorothea laugh, Liam now holding his grandma close to his side with his arm around her shoulders.

Then I felt warmth sweep through me when I felt Darius kiss the side of my hair.

In my ear, he whispered, "Love you, Ally."

That?

Sheer beauty.

I turned my head, caught his eyes, mine were hot, and replied, "I know."

⌖

Ren and I were on one of Indy and Lee's couches. Katie was crawling on her daddy and doing it with Gus, Sadie and Hector's youngest.

Alex and Dante, Jet and Eddie's eldest and middle boys, were sitting next to me, eating cake and ice cream. Or smushing it all over their faces and getting it all over their tees.

But they were little kids. That shit happened.

So, whatever.

I was supposed to be watching Alex and Dante.

What I was doing was scanning the room.

A motley crew of cops and crooks, bounty hunters and baristas, PIs and rock stars, hot guys and Rock Chicks.

My people.

My family.

All together, safe and happy.

I turned to look at my man just in time to see him yank his little girl tight to his chest and set her squealing as he tickled her.

My man.

My girl.

My family.

Katie pretended to try to get away and Ren pretended to let her, going after Gus, probably to tickle him too, when he felt my eyes on him and he looked at me.

"What," he asked.

"We did it," I told him.

His head tipped to the side and his eyes grew intent, probably because he was reading the look on my face.

And reading the look on my face, his voice went sweet when he asked quietly, "We did what?"

"That night, after we found out Indy was carrying Callum and we made a pact to work on being that happy for the rest of our lives?" I reminded him.

He got me.

I knew this when his face got *the look*.

"We did it," I whispered.

He didn't answer.

He pulled Katie and Gus close so he didn't lose them when he leaned into me.

His kiss wasn't long, but it did include a touch of tongues so it *was* righteous.

Then again, they all were.

"Can I steal her?"

Ren and I broke apart and looked up to see Indy standing there, eyes to Ren.

"Sure," he replied.

I studied my BFF.

Then I turned to Alex and Dante and said, "Hey, buddies. Do me a favor and scooch closer to Uncle Ren while you eat, yeah?"

They looked up at me, both with big black eyes, chocolate crumbles and vanilla cream all over their faces, and nodded.

I turned to my husband, leaned in and touched lips, then I did the same on my daughter's wet mouth.

When I was done, she shoved her face in her daddy's neck and giggled. This was because her daddy was tickling her again.

As for me, I just smiled at her daddy.

Then I followed Indy through the room to the stairs.

She led us to her bedroom. In it were Jet, Roxie, Jules, Ava, Stella, Sadie, Daisy and Shirleen.

Oh man.

"What's going on?" I asked.

"Don't know," Ava answered.

"Oh God, please tell me no one's pregnant. I can't keep the birthdays straight already," Roxie moaned.

Daisy gave me a look.

I ignored it.

Indy went into her walk-in closet saying, "Be right back."

"Does anybody know what's happening?" Sadie asked.

"Not me," Stella answered.

All eyes came to me.

I shrugged.

All eyes grew dubious.

I threw up my hands. "Seriously," I snapped. "I don't know."

Luckily, at this juncture, Indy came out of the bathroom carrying a bubble envelope.

"I hope that isn't a secret mission we all have to go on because I'm kind of liking this kidnapping-free, stun-gun-free, car-explosion-free lifestyle," Jules said. "And for a while now, we've had a good roll going."

"That's because you don't live in LA," Stella muttered.

We all looked to Stella and nodded.

We got her.

Suffice it to say, Mace's men in LA had much the same taste in women as the men in Denver.

But in LA, you could get up to *all kinds* of crazy.

"Um... just to say, I kinda miss stun gunning," Jet admitted

That was when we all looked to *her* and nodded.

We got her.

Though, I didn't share that I'd stun-gunned someone just last week.

"It's not a mission," Indy told Jules and handed the envelope to me, her eyes coming to mine. "It's from Jane." She looked through the girls. "She wanted us all together and she wanted Ally to open it."

I had a feeling I knew what was coming.

Because after pink and through green, lilac, blue, peach, salmon and ice blue, Jane had asked us to do the same thing.

I didn't know why Jane didn't participate in the festivities, but I did know that was her way.

With all eyes again on me, I slit open the envelope and slid out what was inside.

It was a berry colored book with a film strip and a white title.

Rock Chick.

Up the side in black, there was a strip that said *Revolution.*

It was my turn.

Righteous.

One thing I knew.

That book was going to be interesting.

And another thing I knew.

An Italian hothead was not going to be very happy.

Kristen Ashley

I wasn't worried. He'd get over it.

Because by then, he was used to it.

But mostly because he'd do it like all the men did it.

In his case: for me.

(And he didn't fool me. I'd seen him grinning when he was reading the other ones.)

I scanned the cover and saw on the bottom, stuck to the side, was a sticky note. On it was an arrow pointing to the name, "Kristen Ashley" that said under it, *New York Times Bestselling Author.*

And next to that was written:

See?

Told you.

Fairytales come true.

I couldn't help it and didn't try.

I burst into tears.

At the same time I burst out laughing.

Then I flipped the book around for all to see.

That meant all the Rock Chicks gathered around me did the exact same thing.

Through my laughter and tears I lifted my hand straight up in the air, index finger and pinkie extended in devil's horns.

The Rock Chicks did the same as me.

And because we were Rock Chicks, at the same time, we shouted two words.

We did it loud.

And we did it proud.

"Rock on!"

Except Shirleen.

She shook her head, looked around and muttered, "White women."

Which of course meant we quit crying.

But we kept laughing.

Stay tuned.
We're gonna follow Mace and Stella to Los Angeles.
'Cause you can get up to all kinds of crazy there.

506